Cruise

Also by Peter Baker

TO WIN A PRIZE ON SUNDAY

CRUISE

Peter Baker

G. P. Putnam's Sons
New York

Cruise

Turn-round

"THE company had no right making the appointment as it did." Captain Corlett packed his pipe more tightly and studied the reactions of the younger man as he let the hurricane flame dance across the crackling tobacco.

David Welch stared at the blue smoke eddying from the Master's desk. "How did the company make the appointment, sir?"

Captain Corlett knew he was being needled, and resented it. "I should have thought you'd have been well aware of how the appointment was made, Mister."

"As I understand it, your last Chief Officer had to be relieved because of ill health. The poor devil's got some cancer or other, hasn't he? And the company in its wisdom decided that I was right for the job, sir."

"I've been to sea with Ben Wilson for more than twenty years. He was an old Navy man. Too young to have his own command, too experienced to be wasted as some damn fool motor-car salesman when the cutback came at the end of hostilities. But that was a generation ago. You're too young to remember the days when Britain really ruled the waves."

"I'm forty-two."

Captain Corlett was a big-boned man with a face crimped by the weather, small blue eyes, and a head of silvery gray stubble. He sucked noisily on his pipe and tried hard to like the younger man who was to be his new Chief. After all, it was not Welch's fault that illness had forced Ben's replacement; but if only the man would project himself better, say something to assure him that the company's decision had indeed been wise. Instead right from the start this first meeting had been a disaster. He had taken an instant dislike to the man's bent and shaped peaked cap. He looked more like a bus conductor than a ship's

7]

officer, and the Chief Officer at that. And his hair: fair, almost ginger, waved and dovetailed to lap over the stiff white collar, the pampered, perfumed hair of a West End pouf. And his reluctance to talk: not about trivialities, for he had immediately tried to start a babble about the indisputable merits of the new Jag and about the new baccara room at the Mizzen Club, but to talk about himself, his past career, the stuff he was made of, why he of all the possible choices merited posting as Chief Officer of the S.S. *Queen Dee*.

"And in another few years you'll be master of your own ship, is that the idea?"

Welch said disarmingly, "If that's what the company wants, yes."

"I doubt it'll be the *Queen Dee* for a while. You know Captain Arkwright, of course?"

"Very well. He's another Mizzen man. He's been with the company a long time. Much longer than I have. His promotion's well deserved."

"He's been with the company exactly five years." There was no mistaking the bitterness in the old man's voice. "It would appear that all the company wants these days is the right college background and the right profile with which to charm the passengers. Apart from that, they can be as wet as a scrubber and still jump rank over the heads of men with service records as long as your arm."

The Chief Officer shifted uncomfortably in his chair. He had expected the first meeting to be difficult, but not as difficult as this. "It must be very hard at your age, sir, particularly this being your last voyage, to see other people taking over. I understood that the Marine Superintendent had consulted you where I was concerned."

"I had a letter from him two days ago telling me you were the right man for the job. But I prefer to know my officers, mister, not to have them wished upon me like so many plumber's mates."

"Yes, sir. I see how you feel."

Outside, the April showers, carried by a near gale-force wind, were beating relentlessly on the officers' promenade deck. Occasionally a net of fresh vegetables would dangle momentarily beyond the starboard window, followed by a distant barking of husky voices as the final provisions came aboard. Inside, the cabin was warm and oppressively quiet.

Captain Corlett said, "I understand you've spent the last few months working at the head office."

"As you know, sir, the company's refitting the *Ardmore*. They thought I could be of some advisory use. Equipmentwise."

"And before that?" He was determined to make another attempt to pry something out from his Chief's past, damn it, for he had a right to know more than he did about the man in whom the company was demanding he share their trust. Even if it was only his sleeping habits.

"I've been around. No little woman back home to worry about, you see. Even did a stint once as technical adviser for some crappy film. That was the easiest thousand I ever earned, showing some actor fellows how to belay a few ropes and remember there's a little red port left in the bottle."

"And you didn't regard that as a waste of time for someone with a master's ticket?"

The Chief Officer crossed his legs and swung a highly polished black shoe irritatingly under the older man's nose. "I assume the company has confidence in me because of my all-round experience. I hope, sir, you will share that confidence. I assure you I will have no hesitation in carrying out everything according to your orders."

For a moment the Master wanted to fan their mutual dislike into a fiery row, to insist that the company respect his seniority among the captains of their fleet and allow him to select his own replacement for Ben. But he decided against it. In three weeks it would all be over. He'd be brewing tea for Sarah, letting the grandchildren on Susan's side of the family handle the retirement gold watch, and starting to fret about how far the pension would go in an age when prices rose more quickly than a floodtide.

"Very well, Chief, I won't detain you any longer. I'm sure you have a number of personal things to attend to before your first watch. Just remember I want this to be a happy ship, a trim ship . . . and a safe ship."

"Yes, sir."

The Chief Officer paused to replace his cap at an insolent

angle and then he was gone, leaving the Master to drag
his thoughts back to the paper work in front of him. He was
still scratching his signature across government forms and company indents when Daisy shuffled into the cabin. George
"Daisy" Bell was a skeleton of a man in a white monkey jacket,
eyes sunk in deeply recessed sockets above an indelibly blue
chin. He had been captain's tiger almost as long as the captain
had been master of the *Queen Dee,* way back when she was
known as the *Delhi,* way back longer than either of them
could remember at all clearly, or cared to try.

"Permission to replenish the bar, sir."

A hand, white and delicate in contrast to the toughened face
above it, waved impatiently from the desk. "Yes, yes, George.
But hurry it up. Couldn't you have attended to it earlier?"

"I'm sorry, sir."

By the slightest inflection of his voice, Daisy let it be known
he thought the criticism unfair. And Captain Corlett scratched
away, irritated with himself for having vented his temper on
the person who least deserved it. He had himself given the
man permission to go ashore to do some shopping, some of it
for him. The papers formed a protective wall. Ever since he'd
made it known that he was accepting retirement at the end
of this voyage instead of the next, he had been anticipating the
moment his steward would make the inevitable approach,
touch his long-ago receded forelock, and ask "Beggin' your
pardon, sir, but would you know what the company intends to
do about me when you're gone?" He didn't know, simply because he hadn't asked. Companies were not sentimental and
neither was he: but now suddenly he realized it was a responsibility he had no right to try to avoid. For when all was said and
done, he'd spent more hours with Daisy Bell than he had with
his wife.

"Attention all members of the ship's company. At three this
afternoon the ship's company will muster on the Promenade
Deck for inspection by the Master and officials of the Board of
Trade." The loudspeaker announcement from the bridge
echoed into the day cabin with a metallic ring. ". . . and
muster cards must be shown at the inspection. When your name
is called, answer with the number of your lifeboat and Yes or
No as to whether or not you hold a lifeboat certificate."

The Chief Purser's gentle tapping was barely audible above the noise, but Daisy sensed it, ushered him in, pushed a chair under him, and produced the decanter of dry sherry he knew both men would drink—the Chief Purser because he prided himself on having the palate of a connoisseur, the Master because he never touched the hard stuff until the sun was well over the yardarm.

"Well, Mr. Craddock, have you solved your problem yet?"

"More or less, thank you, Captain. We've got the twenty men we needed for the galley, so no one will starve. Doctor's examining the last of them now."

Leslie Craddock was a fussy little man in his early fifties, heavy framed glasses seated on a grog blossom of a nose that was his one permanent problem. It diminished his authority with his staff, and was the object of countless jokes from the more insensitive among the passengers.

"Crews get more difficult to keep together every year," the Master said. "I can remember the time when we had deck boys who went right through the lot, OS, EDH, AB, and never thought of changing ship, least of all swallowing the anchor. Take Sam Climpson, for example. I remember when he had a mop of black hair and a couple of buck teeth. Now he's as gray as Father Time and wears dentures like the rest of us. But with the rest: here today, gone tomorrow. The pride in belonging to one particular ship's no longer there. They make a pile on a couple of trips and they're ashore till it's gone. After that, any old rust bucket will do to make another pile so long as she's not going to cold waters or doesn't fail to measure up to their idea of home comforts. Huh, home comforts!"

The Chief Purser poured sherry and fussed with his folder of papers while the Master stood looking down at the loading into the forward hold, drawing heavily on his pipe and contemplating the seemingly endless years of home comforts ahead.

"Here's to another successful voyage, sir." He raised his glass but failed to catch the old man's attention. It had been a little like this on the last trip, the attention wandering, the less frequent appearances in the public rooms, an almost masochistic pleasure in the isolation of command. But now the rot seemed to have set in with a vengeance. He only hoped the old man would perk up once they got under way. It was not good for business if he was going to be in this mood every evening for dinner. First-class passengers expected their captain to be either a Romeo in black and gold or an Old Sea Dog: and this one was neither, he was just a very ordinary man facing up to retirement in a very ordinary way. "Captain, sir. To the voyage!"

The big man turned on his heels, his face suddenly alive and buoyant. "I'll drink to that, Mr. Craddock. Now. Tell me the worst about my passengers."

"It's a full ship. Not a berth to spare in tourist class and only three three-bedded cabins on A Deck unoccupied in first class. And Fairbairn telephoned this morning to say it's almost certain two of those will be taken today. Chairman of Bessinghams and his family. Missed St. Moritz in February. Finds he has the next two weeks clear. Wife. Sister-in-law. And Mrs. Bessingham senior."

"Any faces I want to see?"

"The Paxtons. This will be their sixth year. And there's a Colonel Jamieson. Fairbairn says he wants to be remembered to you. Did the India passage in the old days. We thought it might be prudent to place him and his lady at your table. Old customers, you know."

"Jamieson . . . Jamieson. The name's coming back to me, but damned if I can recall the face. Hope it's not the old soak who came to blows with the Sheik of Ataba. Keep him waiting for a table placing until I get my bearings. Who else is there?"

"I'm afraid we have Miss Peebles again."

"I positively refuse to have that woman at my table. It's bad enough being expected to read her dreadful novels without having to listen to language that would make a stoker blush. Try to convince her that her professional reputation won't suffer if she dines with the Chief Officer. They'll probably mix like oil and water, but that'll be Mr. Welch's problem and not mine."

"Her books have a phenomenal sale."

"So does toilet paper."

The Chief Purser laughed at the Master's little joke and said, "There's an American family. Name of Brewer. Husband's a dental surgeon. There's just the son. They're the only aliens traveling First and I thought perhaps. . ."

"If I must. Far be it from me to be responsible for ending the special relationship."

"Which leaves Sir Gerald and Lady Pratley to complete the table. With your permission, sir, I'll make up the other officers' tables as seems advisable when all the passengers are aboard."

"Yes, do that, Mr. Craddock. By the way, is Sir Gerald boarding tonight as he originally threatened?"

"They're driving down from the manor in the morning."

"Thank God for that. At least I'll have one quiet evening to myself."

"Yes, sir." The Chief Purser emptied his glass and prepared to depart. "But the change of plan isn't going to be very popular with Mr. Welch."

"With my Chief Officer? He doesn't know Sir Gerald, does he?"

"Very well, apparently, sir. He's had a champagne party laid on for them this evening in the Orchard Room. And he's had Lady Fiona's sitting room decked with enough flowers to start a shop."

"The devil he has!"

"Perhaps I shouldn't be telling you this, sir, but he's sent word to the Quartermaster on gangway duty that he wants to be notified the moment Sir Gerald and Lady Fiona come aboard."

He would have asked the Chief Purser more, but Mallory, the company's PRO, had announced his arrival with a party of North of England travel agents who were waiting for a conducted tour of the bridge. The Master carefully knocked out his pipe, paused momentarily to adjust his tie, and strode briskly the few paces from his day cabin to the bridge to beam the company's message of reliability and goodwill to the waiting salesmen. But the whole time he was putting on his act his mind was trying to fathom what it was that Sir Gerald and Lady Pratley had in common with his Chief Officer, so much in common that it needed to be celebrated with champagne.

B AND E LINES "COME TO THE SUN" CRUISES

DREAM of your ideal holiday. Think of long, lazy days of sunshine, magnificent food, extravagant surroundings, exotic sights, convivial company. All these, plus the inimitable thrill of a sea voyage, are part of your cruise through the sun-drenched Mediterranean, cradle of legends and history, in the magnificent, fully stabilized and air-conditioned *Queen Dee*.

Nothing quite equals the wonderful atmosphere on a *Queen Dee* cruise. Elegant restaurants, spacious lounges, friendly bars, luxurious cabins with shower or bath and private toilet. The *Queen Dee* has every facility. You're cosseted and pampered by the ever attentive but unobtrusive services of the ship's staff.

Cruising into sunshine on the *Queen Dee* you play out your holiday at your own pace. You unwind, you relax, you bask away the time in the bronzing rays of the sun and the soothing Mediterranean breezes. Or you can swim in the ship's pool, dance, read, see a new movie, listen to music, or play your favorite deck game. And punctuating your days of contentment come visits to some of the world's most romantic places—the Côte d'Azur, Naples, Athens, Rhodes, and the Near East.

This year B and E Lines' cruise ship *Queen Dee* will call at more than thirty-five ports, so you have an astonishing range of cruising to choose from. A B and E cruise is the best value that any holiday can offer. Fares start from as little as £105 first class and £62 tourist for a short cruise. If your idea of comfort and security is a big British ship, then you will feel fine with B and E Lines. Ask your travel agent about *Queen Dee* cruises today. Or write for a fully illustrated brochure to Dept. ST, B and E Lines Ltd., Luddard Street, London, E.C.3.

10:15 Boat Train

PAMELA WESTCOTT was traveling first class for the first time in her life. She had new luggage, a new hat, and the expectancy of a new life. At thirty-eight one did not think of losing a husband. Particularly under the wheels of a taxi, even if statistics might prove that more people die on the road than from accidents in the home, in the air, or at sea. But that was precisely how Arnold had gone. Under the wheels of a taxi, aged forty-one, just crossing the road by Woolworth's to buy an evening paper, fourteen months ago. It had been mercifully instantaneous. Mercifully for her: for she knew she was weak, with a built-in dread of illness, and couldn't have borne to see him suffer, day in and day out, until the end. They'd married young. His father ran the best bakery in Westborough and her father was a fruiterer in Marine Parade. Arnold kept making jokes about plucking her cherry, and when he finally did, in a drab South Kensington hotel during a lightning London jag, they both realized that with a little help they had something that might last. Arnold helped it last by supplementing a somewhat patchy wartime education by attending night school four times a week. And she helped by trying not to be like the other girls, expecting only a good time, wanting only to have money and attention lavished upon them. It all seemed an age ago. Two other people learning to live together. And one of them now dead.

"Hey, snap out of it, Dearest. You were daydreaming again. Shall I put this on the rack, or will you want it before we reach Southampton?"

"Let me hold it on my lap. I may want to freshen up a bit before we get there." She took the pink and white cosmetic box from the youngster's hand and wriggled it between the arm rest and her thigh. But the moment she had done so she realized it was not the correct thing to do in a first-class compartment, and wished she'd let him put it on the rack as he'd suggested. "You're sure the big cases are all right?"

"Now stop worrying. Didn't we agree I'd organize you? I saw them into the luggage van with my own eyes."

There was a flurry of steam between coach and platform. Shouting heads were thrust from windows and the train slowly pulled out of Waterloo to bury itself in the cheerless drizzle of the South London suburbs. Everyone had seemed to have a well-wisher except him, and Dearest.

"Excuse me, madam, but would you object if I smoke one of these?" The old boy in the corridor corner, with the tweed suit, cravat, and poached-egg eyes, hesitated on the brink of a cigar wallet.

Mrs. Westcott was embarrassed by such courtesy. "Please, do. I'd have chosen a non-smoker if it annoyed me."

The old eyes sparkled as a steady hand and wet lips began rolling and licking a Corona-Corona for the flame. "Not every lady is prepared to accept cigar smoke, madam. For years Alice wouldn't let me light up anywhere in the house except my study. But now she allows it anywhere. Well, almost anywhere. Not in the bedroom, and not in the dining-room before meals. Times change."

Alice, a ghostly gray woman in purple, sat straight as a broomstick, gazing steadily through the window at the swishing rows of Victorian houses, with their tin baths, toy tricycles, and scrubby patches of vegetation scattered in endless monotony about their backyards. A forest of television aerials clung to charred chimney stacks, and glimpsed quickly through uncurtained scullery windows were washing machines, refrigerators, spin dryers and gleaming new cookers. Alice said to no one in particular, "The poor are so rich these days."

"As we shall doubtless be seeing a lot of each other during the next three weeks, introductions will not be amiss," the old boy said. "The name's Jamieson. Colonel Ian Jamieson. Third King's Own Light Dragoons. Lifetime in India. Wasted, of course. All wasted. Put the pinks in Whitehall and they can't give away the Empire fast enough. Nothing wrong in being proud of being British, what? And this is my wife, Alice. Married the old girl in 'twenty-one, on leave after the first of the

Amritsar uprisings. Only a young pup of a subaltern then, of course."

"I'm Pamela Westcott. And this is my son, Richard."

The Colonel's head stuck from an over-large collar like an ancient tortoise as he turned to get a better view of the fair-haired youngster, whose legs had outgrown his gray flannel trousers by a good inch, and whose herringbone jacket was beginning to fray at the left cuff. "And how old are you, lad?"

"Nearly eighteen, sir."

"And what college are you at?"

The boy hesitated. "I'm not anywhere at the moment, sir."

Mrs. Westcott said anxiously, "We sent him to Tor Beeches."

"Tor Beeches, eh. Sound enough. Not military, of course, but sound enough. What have they taught you to be, lad?"

"I haven't made up my mind yet, sir."

"Perhaps your father will decide that for you." The Colonel fixed his poached-egg eyes on Mrs. Westcott. "Would Mr. Westcott be in trade, or the professions?"

It was a direct question Alice always liked hearing her husband ask. It made things plain right from the start, particularly if it was to be a long journey. She began preening herself for the reply.

"I'm afraid he's not in either." Mrs. Westcott was suddenly aware that her voice sounded shrill and a little nasal and hoped the Colonel and his lady hadn't noticed. "I'm afraid he died. A little over a year ago."

Alice said, "How tragic. Just at the age a boy so needs a father."

Richard watched the green, rain-soaked fields flash by the window, and thought about why he needed a father. The fact was that most of his life he had only known his mother and his housemaster. When he was a little kid, his mother and father had doted upon him and everyone seemed to be agreed he was a beautiful child. It was, perhaps, a beautiful family. He remembered people saying what a lovely couple mother and father were, how their life was a never-ending honeymoon, the perfect pair; but how else life could be, he didn't know, then or now. By the time he was twelve his grandfather on his father's side had died and Dad had taken over the bakery, expanding it like an octopus, working long hours building a complex chain of blue and white delivery vans until the Westcott Loaf was the staple diet for a third of the homes within a forty-mile radius of the steam-hissing ovens. It was necessary, he'd heard them say, if he was to be given a decent education. Looking back, he realized that getting him into Tor Beeches had not been easy. A boy from the local elementary school in Westborough with a baker for a father and a greengrocer's daughter for a mother was not a prime candidate for a public school like Tor Beeches, which required something more than money and very high test marks of its applicants. But it had happened. Dad had found the right strings to pull through the Westborough Chamber of Commerce and both his parents took him themselves to the noble Cumberland seat of learning, gray among the sullen hills like a prison, and there could never have been a happier, lovelier couple. After that, he'd only seen them between terms and had written them once a week, every Sunday before tea. It had almost seemed that the moment they left him to the care of Tor Beeches, the pressures of living eased for them. The bakery had become a desirable property for a South London combine and his father had kept a commendably cool head in the short but heated takeover battle that followed. The Westcott Loaf would disappear, only to reappear in three months with a Dough Boy wrapper, untouched by hand, and perhaps better untouched by mouth. There had been an equally short but heated domestic battle over the ethics of surrendering a family business based on crusty bread of infinite variety to an entrepreneur of steamed rubber purveyed to the advertising-prone in "the Happy Dough Boy pack." But, as was well known, they were a lovely family, and the row that flared quickly died, extinguished in the flames of money to burn. Dad had joined the board with special responsibility for Dough Boy's southern area marketing, and Dearest spent a dizzy month buying a mews cottage in Marylebone and furnishing it at Harrod's. Such changes in family affluence seldom went unnoticed at Tor Beeches and the just reward was thrust upon young Richard in the form of a prefectship in little more than two terms. Even Old Hickson began to think that giving him a perfect English accent mattered and eagerly coerced him into private tutorials. Then one year when he went home for the Easter holiday, home wasn't there any more. The previous Christmas his father had been more relaxed than he had ever known him. He'd given him a gold wristwatch, a cheap gold wristwatch, but one with a small spaceship which appeared to float in space to indicate the seconds. It had made the other boys green with envy. Perhaps that was why he needed a father. They'd talked a lot that Christmas and he got to know him for the first time in his life, rather like knowing one of the other boys, like Jackson, who was building a dinghy with his dad to sail off Weymouth. He'd gone back to school and then, what seemed like only a couple of days later, he was home again to watch his father's smashed body being dumped in the ground.

"I've never been on a ship before," Mrs. Westcott was telling the Colonel. "Of course, Europe's not completely strange to me. Arnold took me for a winter vacation in Austria the first year Richard went to his school. So that I wouldn't feel too lonely."

"You've never ridden to hounds?" the Colonel asked.

"No. Well, you see, we never had the opportunity."

"Damned fine sport. Good for the liver."

"Somehow when you're shopping in Marylebone High Street it's not the kind of sport one naturally thinks about," she said.

Alice said, "Quite poor people are riding to hounds these days. Ian, you know the Wymans. Seven Pines. He's an accountant, I'm told. Not even chartered. The East Dideston Hunt wouldn't have allowed it when I was a girl. Very selective they used to be. But all the wrong people have money these days, don't you agree, Mrs. Westcott?"

Mrs. Westcott felt herself blushing and heard herself saying bravely, "I suppose it's what one does with one's money that matters."

"If it buys a boy a good school, a good horse and a good club, then it's been well spent." Colonel Jamieson flicked a large piece of cigar ash onto the British Rail carpet, caught the eye of a passing buffet-car attendant, and ordered coffee for everyone who chose to join him.

Mrs. Westcott sipped the coffee and was relieved that the old boy had not suggested anything stronger, not that she refused alcohol, it had been a great comfort to her during the months

immediately following Arnold's death. Better than the pills
which she still carried with her, bitter blue comforters to which
she clung as a baby to its plastic teat, only she had no loving
mother to force the parting when comforting was no longer
necessary or to be desired. The thing that surprised her most
about herself was that she hadn't taken to excessive drinking.
She had always thought of herself as the alcoholic type, given
the money or the excuse. She drank, but only with friends, and
in the evening. And the Jamiesons were hardly friends, although within the first few minutes of their acquaintance they
were asking her the kind of questions and getting the kind of
replies that she had never even exchanged with Arnold's
brother Bruce. Bruce, who looked such a callous man, small
thin lips that seldom smiled, yet who had been so kind to her
after the—

"One meets such nice people, cruising." Alice's voice broke
her meditation.

"Does one?"

"Ian and I usually do the Caribbean each year. But just for a
change we thought we'd try the *Queen Dee*. We used to sail
on her in the old days. To India. She was called the *Delhi* then,
of course."

"I didn't know, did you, Richard?"

Richard said no and returned to his own private world, gazing out of the window. He looked such a beautiful boy, but like
all boys of his age hated his mother telling him so, although
even that would change soon enough when he had his first girlfriend and wanted to start making the best of himself. Soon
now. He'd be wanting to break free, so soon. Perhaps he'd been
sheltered from the outside world too much up there at Tor
Beeches. It would have been more natural for him to join the
rest of the pack of modishly geared teenagers in their coffee
cellars. Dear God, don't let him be attracted by one of those
boyish plastic freaks. Life was going to be dreadful without him
near her. Still, the break would have come before now if it
hadn't been for his father's untimely— It was always the
same, she could think of nothing without it making the full circle back to the wheels of that damned taxi. Always she thought
of Arnold, and death. His death, her own death, Richard's
death. Even out shopping it was the funeral parlors that first

commanded her attention, standing out like decayed teeth in a healthy mouth of supermarkets. There had been that horrible skeleton cigarette box on the joke counter at Selfridges. And Mrs. Parkinson's dead goldfish; she'd gone on about those dead goldfish for hours, about their water, their food, their little diseases, as though it was all Arnold's fault that they had died. Even the newspapers seemed obsessed with death. Yesterday. That psychiatrist writing about a woman's change of life. "Oppressive thoughts about death are in inverse proportion to sexual intercourse." The papers shouldn't print such distasteful things. There was nothing beautiful in her life any more except Richard, and he was so beautiful, in mind and body. He sensed her loneliness and had hardly left her side the last twelve months. But it was not natural, a boy of his age, cutting short a good education, thinking nothing about a career, just hanging around a sad house where life somehow refused to begin again. She'd suggested making the move to a different place. Reigate. It was far enough away not to bring back old memories, yet near enough to friends not to be plunged into a new, perhaps more dreadful isolation. And Richard had suggested the cruise. They could afford it: money, for the first time in her life, was no problem. With insurance, capital invested and a generous payment by Dough Boy Bakeries, even after death duties she was good for at least forty-five thousand. Richard was quite right. The cruise would give them both time to think about the future. And when they were back, their minds decided, kind friends would have moved them into the new house.

Alice smiled sweetly. "Mrs. Westcott, you must be careful of the advances of the unattached young men on board. And the not so young. A lot of things go on on these cruises of which I really don't approve. Do you, Ian?"

"What? What's that, my dear?" The old boy had lost the thread of the conversation as the train rattled and jerked over a junction.

"I said Mrs. Westcott must mind herself. That is, unless she is looking for attention."

Suddenly they were there, the train a tabletop toy against the rearing white cliff of the *Queen Dee*. Stewards were pouring from the first-class entrance like ants, down the canvas-covered gangway, across the few feet of wet, muddy quay, toward the reception shed, gloomy with its cheap-suited passport-thumbing officials. Willing hands grasped bags, and baskets, and cases. Smiling faces proffered umbrellas as protection from the windblown drizzle. Cheerful voices were giving their first assurances of friendly service.

"Look, Dearest. Isn't she fabulous? I had no idea a liner was so big. Gosh, but the chaps at school would like to see this. Bet old Tomlinson would be green with envy. This is the most exciting thing that's ever happened to me. Ever."

But Mrs. Westcott wasn't listening. She couldn't listen. Her mind kept repeating the last words that the Colonel's lady had flung at her. "Looking for attention." Was that how everyone else would sum her up? A widow barely forty, after the season's prize catch. The vast steel hull looked like a floating prison and it frightened her. She saw a steward's red, smiling wet face, and burst into tears. Richard, troubled by an emotion he couldn't understand, took her arm.

"Arnold. Arnold, dear," she whimpered. "Please tell us we're doing the right thing."

"All visitors ashore!"

THE 33,500 tons of the *Queen Dee* were straining at the leash, hawsers fore and aft as thick as a man's wrist, edged seaward by the sou'wester which had moderated to Force 6 overnight. Seven hundred and sixty feet of her, with a cruiser stern and raked bow, sparkling with fresh paint, smelling of a heady mixture of salt and oil—2,158 tons of heavy, 110 tons of diesel. Eight of her decks sat above the water line, and four, crammed with machinery, tanks and stores, plunged deep to her double bottom, itself filled with 4,295 tons of fresh water, water ballast and emergency oil supplies. Her 730 passengers, 210 of them first-class human beings, were already spreading themselves over the six decks allocated to their comfort; and behind the plastic panels, below the thick pile of the Orchard Room, 408 men and 23 women were waiting to serve—83 to command the decks, 33 in the *Queen Dee*'s mechanical guts, and 315 to cook, to scrub, to clean, to polish, to entertain, to carry, to pamper, to kowtow. Tons of meat, pounds of caviar, sides of ham and smoked or poached salmon, cellars full of French wines, glistening kegs of British beer, ampoules of penicillin, 1,000 bathmats, 23 electric typewriters, a ton and a quarter of commercial soap powder, a triple-effect evaporating plant capable of converting 250 tons of sea water per day into fresh water . . . for all of it, all 33,500 tons, the Master was responsible. And for the 1,161 souls on board.

"Isn't this your watch, Second?"

Junior Second Officer Malcolm Rigg, a dark, frail-looking Scottish lad of twenty-nine, the baby among the deck officers, turned to see the Chief Officer standing behind him. "Sir."

"Well, is it, or isn't it?"

"It is, sir."

"And what are you doing here, then?"

It should have been perfectly obvious to Chief Officer David

Welch what Rigg was doing there: what, in fact, all the other deck officers with the exception of Hewson, who claimed to be happily married, were doing there. From a vantage point on the starboard side of the officers' promenade deck there was a good view of the passengers embarking. Although there was a mutual pretense among the officers that the customer was always wrong and was strictly to be left to the mercies of the Chief Purser and his staff, the arrival hour never failed to attract them from whatever duty they were performing, or from no duty at all, to what Chief Officer Ben Wilson always referred to as Father Neptune's Market Place. The appraisal of the cargo was innocent enough, even among the bachelors. They all knew it was a game. Most of the passengers were too old for sex anyway, and as though to make doubly certain of their employees' chastity, the company from time to time drew their attention to the rule: "No officer may entertain anyone who is not a member of the ship's company in his private quarters." Which was fine for Phyllis and Doris, the resident manicurists; but in spite of any suspicions the more sex-starved among the passengers might harbor, the officers of the *Queen Dee* were normally far too busy when she was at sea even to get around to them.

Rigg was about to explain this to the Chief, but decided against it. Instead, he said, "I hand over to Hewson in five minutes, sir."

"Then you should be making up your log."

"Rounds made. All's well. No oil pollution observed. Gangways and moorings tended. All port and company regulations observed. Cloudy with continuous light rain. Sir!"

There was no mistaking the contempt in the voice. The other officers—Tyson, Mathis, Langdon—turned, expecting an explosion. But the explosion was averted by the arrival of a seaman bearing the Quartermaster's compliments and the report that Sir Gerald and Lady Pratley had just come aboard.

Tim Mathis looked after the departing Chief. "What was that all about, Riggie? Rubbed him the wrong way?"

"Hardly exchanged a word since he came aboard. Some difference to old Ben."

"Mark my words, that Jonah's going to see to it that this isn't a chummy ship any more. There's only one way to deal with

bastards like him. Square your own yardarm, boy." Second
Radio Officer Bruce Langdon, having delivered his solemn
warning, returned to his vantage point for checking the arriving
cargo. "Jesus Christ, I swear that cow's wearing a beehive! A
whole damned beehive! What will they try next to have the
suckers running round their honeypots?"

The drive down from Hadsham Manor had left Lady Fiona
in a bad temper. Not because the ice-blue Rolls was too cold, if
anything it was heated to excess; not because Saunders was
driving too slowly, actually he had broken almost every speed
limit on the way; but simply because she had had to be confined in a tiny space with the old coot for the best part of two
hours. Sir Gerald was a small man with a large pink head which
was as hairless as a baby's bottom, splendidly contoured, and
garnished with a liberal scattering of freckles. Below the shining dome, his face curtained down to what had once been a
square jaw, but had receded now with age into nebulous folds
of tightly collared flesh. Yet he was still a trim man, and had
there been hair where the freckles were, could have passed
comfortably for an early fifty. And if her ladyship had her way,
hair there would be; but for Sir Gerald, a toupee was quite out
of the question—who'd ever heard of a sailor with a toupee?

"Do hurry up, Gerry, I'll catch my death of cold out here!
Do you want me to be ill for the whole damned voyage?" Lady
Fiona nagged him from the gangway as he paused to give last-
minute instructions to Saunders about the luggage.

"Coming, my dear." He paused momentarily at the foot of
the gangway, stiffened himself under the astrakhan overcoat,
and ran nimbly for his age between decks with every expectancy that a pipe would announce his arrival. Instead, trying
to keep pace with her ladyship, he stumbled over a tartan traveling case and was prevented from landing face down only by
the restraining hand of a tall American in a virtually colorless
cream suit and a black and green polka-dot bow tie.

"Hey, steady there, friend. You must wait 'til you've got your
sea legs before you try any of the fancy stuff. You're not hurt,
are you? The name's Brewer. Kenneth Harrison Brewer. Dental surgeon. Detroit. I'd introduce Doris—Mrs. Brewer—only
I guess she packed everything except the Kleenex and right

now she's somewhere looking for the drugstore. I'd no idea you Britishers had boats like this. It's like Main Street on skids."

Sir Gerald brushed down his dignity and switched on his party-political charm. "But how very nice to meet you. Pratley's my name. Captain Sir Gerald Pratley. Old R.N. man. Retired now, of course. And this is my wife—"

My wife, who was commanding the undivided attention of three stewards, cut through the *blague*. "Now perhaps you'll wear your glasses as the doctor told you, you old coot. And do come along. I need a bath. I feel a wreck."

They disappeared into a purple-seated elevator, to be borne some fifty feet to the observation deck, leaving Kenneth Harrison Brewer to flutter round the returning Mrs. Brewer. "Doris, why weren't you here? Royalty. I've been introduced to royalty! There's a British lord traveling with us. Isn't that just something?"

The Rose Suite was immediately beneath the bridge with a splendid panoramic for'ard view, and was flanked by the smaller Violet and Delphinium suites. It had pastel-pink walls and elephant-gray carpets. The walls were hung with reproduction Canaletto, the furniture was suffocated with chintz, and in the sitting room there was a mock-Regency fireplace which cunningly disguised the air-conditioning intake.

"Red carnations. Ugh! Have someone take them away. I can't stand red flowers." The steward looked at the four vases of blooms which had given the air a pleasantly heady perfume, shrugged his shoulders, and followed her ladyship into the bedroom to deposit two small cases, the first of a pantechnicon array.

"It's very comfortable. We shall be just like home here. Thank you for everything," Sir Gerald was telling Chief Purser Leslie Craddock, who had scurried from his commanding point for lodgements to make certain the ship's most important passengers were lacking nothing.

"What have you done to your nose?" her ladyship demanded of the startled Chief Purser, who was not accustomed to having his dignity publicly diminished.

"Nothing, your ladyship. I'm afraid it's done something to me," he muttered.

Sir Gerald beamed goodwill. "I can tell you're an old Navy man, Mr. . . . er . . ."

"Craddock, sir. Leslie Craddock. Addison, your steward, will see that you have everything you want." He felt his tension easing. Down in his office on B Deck his two assistants and four clerks would be hard-pressed dealing with demands for larger cabins, harder beds, softer beds, accommodation shared with a friend, accommodation that didn't have to be shared with anyone. The first few hours of every cruise were always the same. It was as though the company's chief booking agent had made one colossal foul-up. But his team knew how to handle people. The tiniest cabin in Tourist shared with a total stranger (of the same sex, of course) could be made to appear the work of an organizing genius who could not bear to think of any one of B and E Line's customers being lonely. There were the few very important passengers, however, Sir Gerald and Lady Pratley among them, whose wishes must be his command. And the Chief Purser was very, very relieved that their wishes were not going to be too commanding.

"What are you saying to the man, Gerry?" her ladyship was shouting from the bedroom as she emptied the contents of one of the cases onto the nearest bed and searched frantically for a missing something-or-other.

"I was telling him everything was fine, my dear."

"Well, you can tell him to remove these revolting bed covers for a start. And find a lamp that doesn't look as though it belongs on the table of some Harrogate tearoom." She rummaged without finding the something-or-other and tipped the whole lot back into the case. "Surely this isn't the best suite they have? It's worse than having to live in a council house."

At £550 for the three weeks—per person—Sir Gerald did not think it was a fair comparison; but Fiona had never been a fair woman. He consoled himself with the thought that because of his business association, the company had generously given them both a free passage. And he had no illusions about the generosity, because the spring cruise was always fully booked, the Rose Suite often two years in advance.

He was running through his mind how he could best load the extras which would have to come out of his own pocket against income tax, when the Chief Officer presented himself. "Good evening, Sir Gerald. Welcome aboard. I hope you are being looked after properly."

"Yes, my boy. Sorry we couldn't make it yesterday evening. Had to go over to Dysons. Last-minute changes in the specifications for the *Megham*'s resistance thermometers and self-balancing electronic recorders."

Lady Pratley came from the bedroom the moment she heard his voice. "David. I've been wondering all week what you'd look like on board. And you look exactly the same as you do on shore. Not a spit different. Isn't that so, Gerry? Put your bum here and give me a cigarette."

The Chief Officer put his bum where he was told and waited for Sir Gerald to offer a light. "I'm sorry you couldn't make it last night. I had a little party laid on. But there'll be plenty of time for celebrations later. I hope you like the flowers?"

"They're lovely, David," she said. "I adore red carnations."

"Damned lucky to make it at all," Sir Gerald elaborated. "Dysons wanted to load me with some new electric-hydraulic steering gear they want looked over. Think it's the greatest innovation since man invented the rudder. I told them that as far as I'm concerned they can leave it sculling till I get back. A fellow's entitled to a holiday twice a year, don't you agree, David boy?"

Her ladyship said, "Stop talking business, you old coot, and go fetch me a jar of cold cream."

"Where do you keep it, my dear?"

"I don't keep it. I haven't any. Why do you think I'm asking you to buy some?"

"Buy? Where?"

She scolded him like a child. "Yes, buy. B-U-Y. With money. It's very simple. Down in the shops near where we came in. Now don't tell me you can't steer your way to the shops, Gerry. You, with all your mumbo-jumbo about electronic this and self-balancing that."

The older man made a token effort to retain his dignity. "We were all sent to serve one another, weren't we, David?" he said.

Both men knew why he was being sent on an errand. When he had gone David turned to her. "Why must you always treat him like that when I'm around?" he asked.

"You flatter yourself. I also treat him like that when you're not around. Does that make you feel any better?"

"No."

She eyed him for a few moments, taking in the cut of his uniform, the glint of gold in his hair. "I think you've been deliberately avoiding me these last few weeks."

"Good Lord, of course not," he said, offering her his best smile. "I've been hard at it, Fiona."

"Hard at what? Refitting the *Ardmore*? Or have you been hard at something else?"

"Now Fiona, you know me. Would I—"

"Yes. At every opportunity." Her hand twitched the cigarette nervously. "And I suppose I'm the same. It's a dreadful, dreadful disease. But it's rather delicious all the same. Come and help me unpack. If I leave it to the maid I won't know where anything is."

She got to her feet and walked briskly toward the bedroom, he protesting that he was only making a courtesy call, that he had duties on the bridge, that it was indiscreet for him to stay too long with her alone, that a Chief Officer's function was a little more complex than helping passengers to unpack.

"Stop boring me, David," she said. "Here. Put these on hangers. God, what a depressing view!"

"It'll change," he said, not bothering to look out at the wind-blown, rain-soaked quay and the straggle of distant ships hidden in the mists of Southampton Waters. "By Tuesday you'll be soaking up the sun in the Mediterranean."

She was already tanned, a cunning, time-consuming combination of sunlamp and cosmetics. The effect made her look somewhat younger than forty, not that Sir Gerald had seemed to notice. But then, the last time he'd paid her a compliment she'd called him an old lecher; and when he held his tongue, she nagged him for his indifference. "You had my virginity. Do you realize that? I've given you the best years of my life. And all you do is to bore me with your silly mumbo-jumbo." But then, after the attack, she felt remorse. It was her Thespian temperament to smolder like a volcano, and then suddenly erupt.

"I hope you're going to be better company than you've been the past few weeks."

"I won't have a lot of free time. Fiona, you must understand—"

"Then you must make time. You can get somebody else to do whatever has to be done, can't you? You've only had the job a couple of minutes and you're already forgetting who got it for you."

He tried to control his flaring temper. "Yes, and I'm the sod who's got to keep it!"

She came close to him, put a hand around the soft hairy nape of his neck and drew his lips to hers. Her other hand was playfully frisking his body through the heavy black uniform, feeling his thighs, the warmth between his legs.

"Yes, you've got to keep it, David," she said.

Under his jacket he was wearing one of the monogrammed shirts he had bought the first weekend in London. D.W. in neat blue embroidery. He was the kind of man who needed monogrammed shirts, unlike her husband, who could present himself anywhere, monogrammed or unmonogrammed, and exert instant authority. Suddenly she didn't feel like exciting him any more and was grateful for the sound of movement in the sitting room.

"Gerry? Is that you?"

Addison appeared in the doorway. By not so much as a flicker of the eye did he recognize the Chief Officer's presence. "Beggin' your pardon, madam. I was just about to remove the flowers."

"Are you mad? I haven't been in my room for five minutes and people are coming and going trying to tear it apart."

"Yes, madam, but—"

"Don't but me, whatever your name is! Unless you want to help with the unpacking, get out!"

Addison quickly decided that to help with the unpacking under the present circumstances would be to court disaster, and got out.

"Fiona, I'm going to be hellishly busy for the next twenty-four hours," the Chief Officer said as soon as the steward had gone. "At least until we're clear of the Channel shipping lanes. But by tomorrow evening things will have eased off. I'll buy you a drink in the Tudor Room or the Americana. Depending whether you feel ancient or modern."

It wasn't a very good joke, and he was afraid she'd rise to it; but she hadn't even noticed it. "Darling David, I only agreed to come on this silly old cruise because you'd be here. You know how lonely I get stuck out there in the country."

"I must say I'm a bit surprised you're here. You've never struck me as a cruise type."

"And just what is the cruise type?"

"Take a look around the bars. Old. Or defenseless."

"Thank you for the compliment," she said, turning toward the rain-streaked windows. "God, will it never stop pissing? Sometimes I feel that if I live in this country another year I'll grow webbed feet."

"I've got a problem, Fiona," he said, taking advantage of her better humor. "I've been using the Mizzen Club quite a bit in recent weeks. Being ashore, meeting people from the *Ardmore,* and all that. Shaken a few dice. Spun the wheel a couple of times. I've got between three and four hundred to wipe off the slate. Three hundred and eighty-two to be precise."

"No, David," she said.

"There's bound to be a row if it's not met. I hoped to have the money cabled ashore before we sail."

Her face hardened perceptibly. "Then it will have to be your money. What's the screw the new job carries with it? Eighteen hundred? Ask for an advance."

"It's impossible. The company won't do it."

"Then you'll have to settle your debts later, won't you?"

He said sullenly, "Yes, I suppose I will."

The first call "All visitors ashore!" was being made as he left the suite. Sir Gerald had not returned from his errand, prob-ably scared that if he returned too soon he'd see something he'd prefer not to see. The money was a bit of a problem. She'd paid his debts before. It wasn't as though she was short of it; the family coffers were a bottomless pit. He had a nasty feel-ing the glamour of the uniform was wearing a bit thin. She'd only have to clap eyes on someone else with the right rank, the right age, the right experience, the right length-breadth-and-frequency-of-performance, and he'd have had his chips. Heigh-ho, that was life! In at the deep end and out at the shallow.

"Where the devil have you been this last hour, Mister Welch? I wanted to discuss the course with you well in advance of de-

parture time." Captain Corlett quickly paced the short distance
from his day cabin to the chartroom.

"I'm sorry, sir. I had some personal business to attend to."

"Then kindly remember in the future to attend to it earlier," the old man grumbled. "I see no reason why your absence
should cause me to neglect certain social duties which the company expects me to perform. I haven't yet made a courtesy call
on Sir Gerald and Lady Pratley."

"They're quite comfortable, sir. I saw to it myself." The
Chief Officer studied the Master's reaction in the reflection
from the barometer glass.

"The devil you did!"

Mrs. Westcott never missed afternoon tea. Shopping,
Women's Voluntary Service meeting, hot or cold, wet or dry,
home or abroad, the day was not complete without the pause.
She wandered down endless veneered corridors of mottled
blue, over miles of red plastic floor, the whole time Richard
nagging her to ask someone where tea was being served. But
there was no one she could ask. Stewards were busy sorting out
piles of luggage. In almost every cabin they passed, good-byes
were being said. Occasionally the gold rings of an officer flashed
by, too busy or too grand to be asked about tea. The whole ship
was coming slowly to life like some primeval monster about to
shake itself from slumber and plunge forward into the great
unknown. Generators were humming. Pumps were pumping.
Distant, distorted, unintelligible voices were barking orders.
The harbor sheds with their long lines of cranes moved ever
so imperceptibly beyond the open ports as the old *Queen*
strained to be away. And above all the sound and movement
was the faint exotic smell of sea and oil.

They found tea being served in the Orchard Room, which
was not down on C Deck as Richard had insisted, but up on the
promenade deck, near the front, on the right.

"Starboard side forward, Dearest. Not 'near the front on
the right'," Richard chided as a steward showed them to a table.

They barely had time to take in the shock effect of the trellis
arches, artificial cherry trees, scarlet and black cane chairs before an American matron and her skyscraper of a husband

descended on them. "Excuse us, but may we join you folks? I guess since we're going to be together for the next three weeks we all ought to start right now getting to know each other."

Mrs. Westcott said Yes, how sensible, and thought What a nerve, only Americans would behave like that.

"Say, your name rings a bell," the big man said to Richard. "Westcott. Richard Westcott. You're the young man who's sharing a cabin on A Deck with our John. John Brewer. A tall, lanky fellow like me."

"There is another chap in with me, sir. But I haven't met him yet." For the present he was more interested in the plate of cream cakes.

"We told him to find us here," Mrs. Brewer said. "He's had a visitor on board all afternoon. A boy he knew in San Francisco who's been working in the Embassy in London. He said he was just going to see him off. He should be here any moment."

"Is Mr. Westcott joining us, Mrs. Westcott?" her husband asked.

Time and again she had visualized such questions, the inevitable explanations, and the cruel void in which they would leave her. And time and again she had told herself that such situations would have to be faced, sooner or later. "No," she said, "I lost my husband. Just over a year ago."

"Oh, you poor dear!" Mrs. Brewer's beaming face became all motherly. "And you're so young, too. No one would ever believe this husky young man was your son."

"I don't know what I'd do without him," Mrs. Westcott said. "He's been such a comfort to me. Helping me pick up the threads again where I dropped them."

"You're so lucky to have him at home still. We haven't had our John for all of three years. Isn't that so, Kenneth? That's why we're vacationing in Europe. So as to see him. He's just crazy about the theater. None of the other professions is good enough for him. Of course, we didn't encourage it. Isn't that so, Kenneth? His father has such a wonderful practice. He has four qualified men working for him and six staff nurses. Isn't that so, Kenneth? But John just didn't want to go into it. Went out and got this scholarship from some trust in San Francisco, or something like that. Anyhow, he has enough to make out in Europe he says for five years. Studying theater every place. Then when the money runs out someone will either offer him a job, or he'll be back on our doorstep. Only it'll be too late for him to go to dental school then. Isn't that so, Kenneth? You kept telling him it would be too late after he was twenty-five, didn't you, dear? Kept telling him. But young people are so headstrong these days. They don't listen to a word you say."

The steward cautiously interrupted the tidal wave of conversation. "Excuse me, ladies and gentlemen. You are all passengers, are you? Last call for all visitors ashore is just being made. We'll be under way in a few minutes."

Captain Corlett was signing the customs manifest when the pilot came onto the bridge. He was expecting Mr. Teal but instead it was Mr. Firth, whom he was more pleased to see because, years ago now, their daughters had been at the same school together.

"And how does the garden grow this weather, eh, Dick?" the Master asked.

Mr. Firth grimaced. "The rose standards I put in last November have been washed out. The lot of them. Money down the drain. But at least the water's done the grass good. Lawn's looking a treat. Trouble is, I don't get enough time to break my back over it."

"I suppose I'll soon have to be developing green fingers myself."

"Of course, I was forgetting. This is your last time out, isn't it?" He was embarrassed, trying to find the right words, while the Master wished he wouldn't try to find any. "Well, Ted, when they finally make you swallow the anchor, you can at least be sure a good man'll be taking over."

"Arkwright?"

"He was being considered for the *Ardmore* after her refit. Seems they think he's the right type for cruising instead of their mail line."

"Just what is the right type? Someone who can cope with Miss Peebles' table manners, or someone who knows this old hulk from stem to stern, inboard and outboard?"

"You were on her for her maiden voyage, weren't you?" He hadn't, after all, found the right words, damn it.

"I was that. Chief under old Flint. Liverpool. Bombay. Calcutta. The S.S. *Delhi* as we knew her then. Nineteen-thirty-six she was launched. And every log has my signature on it, wartime and all, since that day, Dick. You wouldn't remember Flint. Pensioned off soon after we'd licked Jerry. That's when they made me Master. The official notification came through on the very day of my forty-sixth birthday."

"So you'd be younger than Arkwright when you got her?"

Captain Corlett knew the rebuke was intended kindly but he resented it, the more so coming from an old friend. "You're forgetting I was Chief, right here on this bridge, for more than ten years before that."

"Sorry, Ted, no offense meant." He looked at his pocket watch, steely round like a fat oyster, and compared it with the ship's chronometer. "Well, I'm ready when you are."

It was twilight. The wind had dropped during the afternoon with the change of tide. From the vantage point high in the wheelhouse a mass of damp gray city rooftops lay to starboard, and on the port bow were the murky harbor waters, heavy with the twinkle of navigation lights and the glare of other liners at berth or being piloted home. The moment's silence was stabbed by a telegraph ringing the stand-by below.

Chief Officer David Welch gave Mr. Firth his best salute, too best to be true, the Master thought. "Good evening, sir. Force three wind, east-southeast. Barometer twenty-nine point eight six. Falling. Dry temperature sixty-one. All gangways up and ports secured. Bridge gear tested and correct time given to engine room. Sir."

He was overdoing it and the Master was not surprised by Dick Firth's retort. "Let me know if the barometer falls a point before I leave you," he said acidly.

"Very well, sir."

"You must be Ben Wilson's replacement."

"That's right, sir."

"How is Ben?" He turned to the Master. "Have you heard anything yet, Ted?"

Captain Corlett shook his head sadly. "We know it's cancer. Taken him in the bowel. They're making an exploratory operation this week. Must wait for the result to know when he'll be out of drydock. Or if he'll ever be out. Poor devil."

The Chief Officer turned his back on Ben's problems and took up his position for'd. Third Officer Tyson was already at the wheelhouse telephone, in contact with Second aft. Quartermaster Sam Climpson was at the telegraph, a vast silhouette in the whispers of light. Master and pilot took up their positions near the slender brass wheel behind the ancient binnacle of the magnetic compass. On the port side of the wheelhouse was the radar sweep, the engine-room telegraph and the gyro-compass: on the starboard, the automatic pilot, the emergency docking and steering telegraphs, rudder indicator, and the pilot's VHF telephone. And behind, a thousand switches, dials, contacts, telephones: to detect smoke, alarm passengers, test fire sprinklers, close watertight doors, broadcast instructions to the crew, bring stabilizers into action, switch-on switch-off start-stop or merely to wish passengers everywhere a safe and pleasant voyage.

It was nineteen-thirty when the order "Stand to stations" was given. By nineteen-forty-three the tug *Joey Boy* was fast aft and four minutes later, the tug *Big Heart* was fast for'd. Capstans turned, the tugs pulled, hawsers slackened and inch by inch, then foot by foot and yard by yard the 33,500 tons of the *Queen Dee* were dragged away from the berth. It was exactly twenty hours when Third Officer Tyson relayed the order "Let go fore and aft!" Telegraph bells stabbed the quietness. Five minutes later the tugs were gone and clear. "Dead slow ahead." "Dead slow ahead, both, sir." The telegraph rang again. Down in her guts the engines were gently eased to thirty revolutions per minute and the old *Queen* glided forward into the darkness of Southampton Waters. One knot, two knots, six knots. She was under way.

Lat. 48.41N Long. 5.06W

. . . 9:30 All electric watertight doors operated. 10:00 All passengers who embarked at Southampton mustered at their emergency muster stations and instructed in the ship's emergency procedure and the method of wearing a life jacket. Warning given against throwing cigarette ends or matches overboard. 10:30 Commence extending stabilizers. 10:40 Stabilizers extended and working. 11:00 General inspection by Master and Staff. 12:45 Reduced to 82 rpm. 13:18 Ushant light on bearing 008° (T) × 15 miles. Alter course 208° (Gyro) 215° (Std.) Compasses compared. Correct time given to Engine Room. Rounds correct. Moderate WNWly. Swell. Fine and clear.—H.H.

PAMELA WESTCOTT woke with a start. "Arnold, is that you? What was that noise?" But there was no noise, only the silence of an empty chintz-covered bed next to her own in Cabin 26 on the Observation Deck. There was a vibration, a deep pulsing feel, as the *Queen Dee*'s engines thundered nine decks below; and there was movement, almost imperceptible, as the great ship rode the swell of the Western Approaches. But there was no distant traffic, no birds to wake her, no shuffling of the postman's feet, none of the sounds to which she had grown familiar, only a strange, heart-quickening silence. She hadn't thought about the empty bed when they'd told her there was no single cabin available. All she knew was that she didn't want to share with a stranger, and it wouldn't be fair to ask Richard to keep her company, he was too big a boy for that, and besides, she had to get used to his wanting to live his own life. Almost before she was aware of the cost, she had agreed to pay the extra in order to have the double to herself: they'd do it all comfortably under a thousand. Arnold's thousand. He'd worked hard enough for it, unlike some men who just played at business. She only wished she could be sure this was what he'd want her to be doing with it. Back in the Westborough days a thousand pounds would have been regarded as a nice little nest egg, not to be squandered. Her parents looked upon people who went on cruises as the idle rich. There was a grain of truth in all their prejudices. Mum and Dad. They didn't seem to be in her world any more, and hadn't been for ten, almost fifteen years. It was hard to say when the break came: it had come ever so slowly, and it wasn't just the money, Arnold's success, the whirl of London life that had done it. They were so negative in their attitude to Arnold, not envious, just maddeningly disinterested. She had had rows with them, but they absorbed abuse like blotting paper. They were not the kind of people that reacted to things, and in almost no time at all she had lost touch with them. She found them crude and stupid, not because they hadn't had her chances in life, but because all along the line they had turned down opportunities to do more with theirs. Mum didn't have to watch television all day. Dad didn't have to close his mind to other people's lives with such determined insularity. She'd never forget his words at the funeral. "He'd have burned himself out if he hadn't gone that way. I always said he was a one to live beyond his means. He'd have burned himself out keeping up with all that smart life of yours, Pam. You'd have lost him sooner or later, anyhow." Callous, prejudiced, and untrue. Then there had been Fred, her own brother, who at least wasn't ashamed of making his pile as quickly and as easily as possible. He'd had the good sense to get out of Westborough and the smelly, woody little shop in Marine Parade, with the rusty bin of rotting fruit stacked out back next to Mrs. Turton's chicken house. Unmarried, unchaste Fred. That dreadful Christmas three years ago when, from a sense of family guilt, she'd invited him to spend the day with Arnold, Richard and herself. Fred had given her a large box of cheap chocolates and, regardless of Richard, made coarse banter about what a girl had to do when a man gave her a box of chocolates. "All the nice girls know what they have to to do when a bloke gives 'em a box of chocs. They have to take the cellophane off or they can't get at 'em." But it didn't stop there. Richard had come out with a bit of schoolboy scatology about the rabbit that washed its thing at night and couldn't do

a hair with it in the morning, and then Fred had told a most un-
funny revolting joke. And Arnold had shouted . . .

"For God's sake, stop it! Stop it! Stop it! Stop it!"

The tapping on the cabin door broke the chain of self-
inflicted hysteria. It had been worse than it had been for six
months, just when she thought she was snapping out of it, these
dreadful bouts of brooding on the past, exaggerating all the
things she couldn't bear to remember, because they were things
she was powerless to do anything about.

"Is madam ready for breakfast?"

The steward—Hyslop he had said his name was last night
—must have heard her shouting. He was a middle-aged, shape-
less man, scrubbed so clean he looked innocent of all sins
of the flesh. She knew by the way he was looking at her that he
had heard her shouting, that his intrusion was part curiosity,
part responsibility for her well-being, and had nothing to do
with whether she wanted an early breakfast or late.

"What time is it?"

"Quarter to eight, madam."

It *was* early for breakfast, but she wouldn't get any more sleep
now and it wasn't good to lie there, to risk fretting again:
she'd prefer to be up and about, to let the ship charm and
soothe her with its novelty. She said, "Just a simple breakfast,
please. I don't eat much."

He left her to bathe, and when he came back with the tray
she was dressed and standing by the window looking
south across a sullen sea to the distant, shrouded French coastline. "Here you are, madam. And there's a copy of the ship's
newspaper to read. Not that much has happened since we left
Southampton. But it gives you some information about the
compulsory boat drill at ten this morning. I'll be back later to
show you where your life jacket is and how to put it on."

"Life jacket? Nothing's likely to happen, is it?"

"No, madam. There's nothing to worry about. You're as safe
as at home on the *Queen Dee*. But it's better to be safe than
sorry, now isn't it?" Hyslop, she was soon to discover, was full
of such homilies.

The boat drill was a fiasco. It was a cold, cheerless morning
and few passengers wanted to stand about on deck bundled in

regulation canvas and cork. The deck officers did their best to muster the paying customers. Those who refused to be mustered pleaded indisposition, a prior engagement in the comfort of the forward Smoking Room, or the rights of a customer to be always right. Two ladies lost hats overboard, and an elderly gentleman whacked his cranium on the side of the boat that might one day save his life, and was chided by a junior officer for having wandered on the wrong side of the stanchions guarding the damned thing. Third Officer Tyson and Fourth Officer Mathis pranced to and fro checking numbers, names, and forms; and the handsome man with the devilishly bent cap and the three rings on his arm, who appeared to be their chief, was assuring everyone that he personally would see that not a single life was lost in the event of a disaster—not that they were ever to think about such things, because they were there to enjoy themselves, and all the officers would see that they did just that. "Silly cunts!" Miss Peebles was heard to mutter, which was not a mode of expression to be found anywhere in her literary achievements.

It was shortly after ten-thirty that Captain Corlett finally got around to making his courtesy call on Sir Gerald and Lady Pratley. Sir Gerald had just returned to the suite from doing his duty mustering and was taking some papers from a briefcase preparatory to spending the morning doing his homework. He had, he estimated, five weeks' homework with him for the three-weeks voyage. Her ladyship, who had pleaded indisposition, was having an argument with the housekeeper, to whom the news of her ladyship's displeasure with the bed covers had already filtered through.

"Sir Gerald, please forgive me for having delayed this meeting for so long," the Master said.

Sir Gerald switched on the charm. "My dear Captain, no excuses necessary. I'm not altogether unfamiliar with present-day traffic in the Channel. Like Piccadilly in the rush hour, eh?"

The Master had heard it said that the most the old barnacle had ever done during the war was an inspection tour of the Mediterranean before the big blowup, after which he disappeared on a stone frigate somewhere in the wilds of Scotland where weekends were made hell for the local grouse. But he

said, "We're honored to have you aboard, sir." And made it
sound as though he meant it.

"Fiona, my dear, come and meet the Captain," Sir Gerald
called into the bedroom.

She came in wearing a purple house robe edged at the collar
and hemline with a froth of white fur. "They put you in charge
of the whole caboodle? You're as ancient as this old coot. And
they won't let him push anything about bigger than a pen."

Rumor had filtered down from head office that her ladyship
was—well, Mallory had summed her up, with the discretion
of all PRO's, as "a bit of a character," while his assistant had
been much more to the point, "a class AA readership with a class
C mind."

Captain Corlett said, "I have heard it said, Lady Pratley,
that the pen is mightier than the sword. Anyway, my passengers
won't have to put up with me much longer. This is my last voyage."

She didn't apologize, but stood there nervously biting her
lower lip, almost as though she wished she hadn't been inad-
vertently cruel in her morning effort to dazzle. Instead of apolo-
gizing, she redirected her attack. "You couldn't have called at
a better time. Will you please tell this mad woman that the bed
covers have to be changed. They're hideous. And you're not going to tell me you can't find two different covers on a ship with,
how many cabins?"

The Master said there were 287: 103 first class, the rest tourist.
And he was sure the housekeeper would do her best, although
her ladyship should bear in mind that when the *Queen Dee* was
last given a refit, the company had put in standard equipment
and that, he feared, included the bed linen.

She continued the tantrum, partly because it kept the old coot
in his place, partly because she enjoyed shocking new faces. "I'm
plagued by housekeepers. There's Mrs. Bartholomew, who's
supposed to run the manor for us. Most of the time she expects
me to run her. She came to me only last week mumbling something about her daughter down in the village. Said she was the
age when she needed to be told the facts of life, and as I knew
so much about those things, would I tell her. 'Why me?' I
asked. 'I can give you the addresses of a couple of sailors. They
ought to fix her.' "

Sir Gerald said Fiona was not to be taken seriously. The Master displayed his mettle by commenting that many a true word was spoken in jest. And the housekeeper bobbed and curt-sied her way out of the suite, praying she might never again have to cope with her ladyship and the Captain both at the same time.

But her ladyship snatched one of the covers from the freshly made bed and waved it at the departing housekeeper like a cape at a charging bull. "The woman we had before Mrs. Bartholomew was a stupid German. I tell her I don't want to be bothered by anyone on the phone, to say I'm out. And what do you think I hear her telling someone or other? It might have been the vicar for all I knew. 'I'm sorry, sir, but her ladyship is on the streets.' That's what she said. And the girl before that fled in less than a week because this old coot insists on doing his morning exercises with bars and expanders without a stitch on. It would frighten the life out of anyone! It even frightens me, I can tell you."

Sir Gerald smiled his smile of pained apology. "My wife used to be on the stage, you understand. She's the last person to want anyone to take her seriously."

Captain Corlett had no intention of doing any such thing and was beginning to wonder if Sir Gerald was to be taken seriously himself. "I have to make my inspection of the ship at eleven. Usual drill first day out, you know," he said, by way of indicat-ing the courtesy call was over.

"Perhaps we could join you," Sir Gerald said disarmingly. "I'm familiar with most of the company's fleet, but until now the *Queen Dee* seems to have eluded me."

It wasn't exactly the way Captain Corlett had planned to spend his morning, but Sir Gerald was not a person he could easily refuse. Lady Pratley stuck a bronzed and slightly muscu-lar unclad leg through the purple house robe. "I can't come like this or I'll have the whole damned crew foaming at the mouth."

"I don't think Fiona would enjoy the inspection very much, Captain. She tires easily. You remember Spithead, don't you, my dear?"

Captain Corlett said, "We can finish up in the Americana at about noon for a drink. Perhaps Lady Pratley would like to join

us there. It's aft on this deck." He pointed in the approximate
direction in case she didn't understand. "Just down there."

"Don't point," she said petulantly. "Hasn't anyone ever told
you it's rude?"

The general inspection by Master and staff was as cursory as
the boat drill had been ineffectual; but regulations had to
be observed in spirit if not to the letter. The Master knew it was
a lot of damned nonsense. If he were really to inspect every inch
of the *Queen Dee*'s twelve decks, it would take him as many
hours as it did minutes. He was on parade for one good reason:
to convince passengers and ratings alike that he was keeping
a benevolent eye on them.

"You'll be able to tell me how she compares with the
Ardmore, Sir Gerald," he said as they left the bridge and
made for the Boat Deck. "I believe you've been closely concerned
with her refit."

"In my capacity as technical adviser to Fomona. Federation of
Manufacturers of Navigational Aids, you know the setup, of
course. Sir Edgar is this year's chairman. Keeping the B and E
flag flying on the technical side. The *Ardmore*'s going to be a
first-class ship by the time we're through with her. That's right,
isn't it, David?"

Chief Officer Welch, who was leading the procession of officers behind the Master, obediently said, "Yes, sir" and wished
like hell Sir Gerald hadn't chosen to address him by his first
name. There was no point in rubbing old Corlett the wrong
way. He'd be through in less than three weeks and Len Arkwright would be in the saddle. It was *his* arse he'd have to lick,
not this old codger's.

"Your Chief Officer's a good man," Sir Gerald went on.
"Has an academic mind he can apply to practical experience.
He made his mark with Sir Edgar over the *Ardmore* refit. And
that's no small achievement where a company the size of B and
E is concerned. All too easy for a good deck officer to get lost
among the head office paperwork."

Captain Corlett said curtly, "I expect all my officers to be
good men, Sir Gerald," and brooded on the fact that on the few
occasions he had had reason to meet the chairman, he had apparently failed to make a mark himself. But then, he had merely

sailed one of the company's fleet a little over half a million miles without so much as a scratch on her freeboard: his was not the environment of high-level boardroom discussions on whether or not the *Ardmore* would be better with pale pink or pale blue toilets. A replacement for poor old Ben was a matter of urgency, he was well aware of that, and maybe the Marine Superintendent honestly thought Welch to be the best man for the job and not the one most conveniently available. But he could at least have phoned him about it, had a personal word. There would even have been time, just, for him to have traveled up to London for consultation. That five-line letter of instruction was just not good enough, not after a lifetime's service with the company, man and boy. Things had never been the same since they took over the old East Africa Cargo Line. The whole outfit had grown impersonal in the last fifteen years. He'd soon be well off out of it. That damned lawn! He was going to hate most cutting that cursed bit of green for Sarah.

"Good morning, Captain. When are you going to give us some better weather?" The small man with heavy horn-rimmed glasses sat well wrapped in a deck chair brazening the cold damp air with his wife, both sipping the midmorning bouillon.

The Chief Purser moved quickly to the Master's side and whispered a name. Craddock was a genius at remembering faces. And the Master turned on the company's charm. "A couple of days, Mr. Lennard, and we'll have you both basking in the sunshine. Is everyone looking after you properly, Mrs. Lennard?"

The woman went all coy in the face of benevolent authority. "Yes, thank you, Captain. Everything's wonderful. Just wonderful."

Captain Corlett led his entourage briskly down the nearest companionway to the Observation Deck, past the port-side cabins and down another companionway onto the Promenade Deck near the empty, canvas-covered swimming pool. He was about to move on again when his roving eye spotted a cigarette butt near the canvas.

"Fourth. Any explanation for this?" he snapped.

"No, sir." Young Mathis stepped forward to make sure the butt wasn't smoldering.

"Then find one." And with that the Master continued

the inspection, leaving Mathis to demand of the bo'sun what the hell the deck boys were supposed to be doing.

For the next half hour the entourage covered the Tudor Room, the Assembly Room, the Orchard Room, the Writing Room, the Smoking Room, strolled across the recreation deck where a few hardy souls were attempting a game of quoits, took the elevator down to the cinema on B Deck, made a detour through the shops, then back to say good morning to Dr. Hammond in the hospital bay. In the first-class restaurant on C Deck, stewards flitted like a flock of gulls as they laid the tables for lunch. Then through the steamy-steeled kitchens and out aft into the tourist-class restaurant, a clutter of plastic table-tops and marquetry walls. The tourist-class public rooms were crowded with people anticipating the Master's visit like a coronation crowd, for it was possibly the only time during the cruise they would get a close-up look at him. Being looked at was something Sir Gerald most enjoyed. He stood close to Captain Corlett, hands clasped nonchalantly behind the well-worn blazer with its RN crest, and basked. But the public acclaim was short-lived. The Master, appearing to have little time for his less-than-first-class passengers, made a brief sortie through tourist cabins barely above water level on D Deck, past the starch-heavy laundry and into the brightly lit labyrinth of crew's accommodation, humid, athrob with the old *Queen's* pounding engines, smelling unmistakably of Scots and Cypriots, Limeys and Ities, men who worked, relaxed and slept together.

"I take it you've satisfied yourself that the refrigerated stores are in order, Mr. Cunningham?" the Master paused to ask Purser Catering. And without waiting for reply added, "Very well, we'll pay our respects to Mr. Herrington, and then, Sir Gerald, I think a drink."

They entered the engine room from the Orlop Deck. Chief Engineer Robert Herrington, a dour Scot with a high forehead and a toothbrush moustache, resented anyone entering his part of the ship, even the Master. He gave the bridge the power they wanted—how was his concern and his alone. But his suspicions turned to a canny Scottish charm when Captain Corlett introduced Sir Gerald and pointedly mentioned his involvement with the *Ardmore* refit.

"We're powered by a twin-screw high-pressure-geared turbine installation, as perhaps you know, Sir Gerald," Herrington said. "Major considerations in design were fuel efficiency over a large power range, effective use of watch-keeping staff, and ease and speed of overhaul. Normal shaft power of the installation is forty thousand."

They walked over catwalks, down clanging steel companionways, past generators for the ship's electric power, evaporating plant for her fresh water supply, refrigerating plant for the food stores and air-conditioning, pumps for feeding oil, pumps for getting rid of water, switch gear, dials, alarms. It was hot, noisy and grimy down there in the *Queen Dee*'s guts, and the men who worked her had a hotly honest look to their shining white faces, a different breed from the coldly calculating lackeys who scurried silently around the customers, smiling obsequiously at every demand and for every reward.

"Splendid. I see you have an overhead traveler lifting system," Sir Gerald said, looking upward with the reverence of a tourist inspecting Michelangelo's Sistine wonder. "Switch points to port and starboard oil fuel filling stations. What load can you accommodate?"

"Two tons. Those hoists and travelers enable us to shift gear straight to shoreside cranes through the filling stations." Herrington had taken an immediate liking to Sir Gerald. He knew what he was talking about and, above all, he wanted to talk about Herrington's beloved machinery.

"Most impressive. Most impressive," Sir Gerald muttered. "When was all the new gear put in? It certainly wasn't here when the old girl was laid down."

"Most of it in 'fifty-nine when the company turned her over to cruising."

"Tell me, are you using the Mega pump to deal with contaminated bilges?"

"Yes, sir, we are."

"Delivering through a hundred ton-hour Mason electronically controlled oily water separator, I take it. No troubles? You find the separator can cope with any maximum condition in the bilges?"

"A drink, I think." The Master had seen enough of Mr. Herrington and his machinery for one day. The inspection was over.

Richard Westcott and John Brewer had spent the morning together making their own inspection of the *Queen Dee*. Richard was not the kind of boy who made friends easily, even among the boys at Tor Beeches, except perhaps Tomlinson who lived at Luton and who had promised to keep in touch but hadn't. In spite of the lack of privacy of communal school life, Richard had not been looking forward to having to share a cabin with anyone. But Dearest had been unusually insistent about it: as much, he thought, because she didn't want him to be lonely as because she was reluctant to spend too much of their money. She had this silly thing about investing some of it for him for after she'd gone, as though he wasn't ever going to be able to look after himself. It would be ages yet before he'd have to think about her going. Even at the time of his father's funeral, he had never imagined that a similar tragedy might strike Dearest. Or that she might be driven to doing something desperate—to herself. He simply assumed he'd earn his own money and keep his own family when he was older. He didn't want her to save any of the money for him. He just wanted her to be happy and secure. Without being consciously aware of it, Richard sensed that Dearest would like him to be husband as well as son to her. And now, for the first time in his life he was beginning to think ahead, to try to imagine himself at nineteen, at twenty-one, at forty, instead of being concerned solely with yesterday's prep, today's grub, and tomorrow's football match against Addiscombe Hall.

"So I spent six months in London, for the most part studying the work at the National Theater and the Royal Court," John said. "You Britishers don't seem to realize it, but your contemporary theater is the biggest single contribution you've made to Western culture in the last couple of centuries. Way out, man, way out. Isn't it a drag we didn't meet when I was in London?"

"Although the family lived in London, I didn't see very much of it. Tor Beeches was a long way away, you see," Richard said.

"I had a back room in Earl's Court that was no great shakes by any standards. Twenty bucks a week. That's what they charged. Twenty bucks. No cooking, no washing, and no visitors after eleven. How do you like that? No sex. And to judge by some of the things that go on in the London parks and on the subways, you'd think the British were sex mad. Do you dig sex?"

Richard felt his cheeks redden. The fact was, he hadn't been allowed to think very much about sex. Old Hickson had regarded it as something never to be used except in an emergency, like marriage. He'd been taught briefly about the birds and the bees, even rabbits, which were said to be pretty much like human mums and dads. He wanted to think about sex. He wanted to do something about sex. But he had this ridiculous thing of feeling ashamed every time it was mentioned, and had no logical reason why, except that grown-ups always thought it was something dirty. He remembered his dad once making a big scene about his wanting to use a public lavatory a day they spent in Brighton, telling him that people had evil minds which they spewed all over the walls, that it was always better to go at home if one could wait. Yet Old Hickson had always taught him it was bad for the bowels to wait, that one should get the basic bodily functions over with as soon as nature called or great digestive troubles would be caused in middle age. Grown-ups were so confusing.

"Well, do you or don't you?" John was asking.

He heard himself saying, "Yes, of course," then trying quickly to change the subject, like where had John been after he'd left London.

"I've been living in Paris since the fall. Sharing a couple of rooms off St. Lazare with a colored boy who's at the Sorbonne. You're not anti-Negro, are you?"

Here was another problem he had to tackle within the space of ten minutes. Father had often said there were too many blacks in Britain for a healthy economy, and Dearest had always thought it the wrong climate for them as the poor creatures were used to fresh air and sunshine, and, of course, they got diseases and spread them and it wasn't their fault, was it? And Old Hickson had positively avoided color. As far as Tor Beeches had been concerned, niggers grew copra in West Africa and cut cane in Jamaica, but never ever fancied a decent Oxford education for their sons or a white woman for themselves in the Bayswater Road.

"Of course I'm not anti-Negro," he said defensively. "Everyone has as much right to live as anyone else." And he hoped desperately that he would feel the same way when he was an adult.

John was a slender, almost hipless youngster, a few inches taller than himself. He looked older than twenty-three, but not much. His eyes were very dark and the hair was strong on his wrists. The blue stubble on his chin was disguised with flesh-tinted after-shave talc. Tightly fitting faded denims beneath a vast scarlet crewneck sweater gave him a bulk that was not his own. He wore a gold bracelet on his right wrist with his name on it; and his bony, long-fingered hands sliced the air as he talked, illustrating every sentence with a performance.

"Last summer I did Italy. Rome, Milan, Florence, Venice, Verona. Do you know Italy?"

Richard said rather lamely that he didn't know Italy, or France, or Spain, or Greece, or anywhere else. It was his first trip outside Britain, although his mother had had a winter holiday in Austria.

"With your dad?"

"Yes, of course," he said, shocked that anyone could think it might have been with someone else. And John rambled on about his Italian summer, and about Verona and the dazzling production he'd seen there of the two gentlemen from.

"Shakespeare is always better in translation. Divorced from archaic English the production flows, the actors are not intimidated, the whole complexity of his drama blossoms into life. That's probably why more Russian theater-goers see Shakespeare in any one year than the British. Are you anti-Communist?"

He liked John. John had a sense of humor and an involvement with life that he envied. But he wished he wouldn't keep raising issues like sex, and race, and religion, and politics, as though one had to have the computed facts down pat or be exorcised from the human race by the know-it-alls who got most of their information from the television pundits anyhow.

"I don't agree with anyone telling other people what they've got to do," Richard said. "If that's Communism, then I'm anti-Communist." He was a bit doubtful about his position, because history at Tor Beeches had somehow stopped at Queen Victoria and political science had got bogged down at about the same period. Communism, he gathered, could best be attacked with money, and one's best form of defense from it was prayer; but as to its nature, he was as ignorant as a witch doctor confronted by his first tablet of aspirin.

John went on, "I guess the whole of Europe'll be Red by the end of the next decade. Back home they've no idea of the strength of the Commies in France, or of the rioting in Italy. Bologna. Now there's a place as Red as the Kremlin. And my dad and his pals are still screaming about socialized medicine because they think it's going to do them all out of their jobs."

"Are you Red?" Richard asked suspiciously.

"Hell, no! I'm an artist. But if you're going to act, write, direct plays—anything like that—you've got to try to understand these things. Find out what makes people tick. I'm apolitical. That's what I try to be. But I'm against people being rich at other people's expense. And some folks back home would paint me Red for that."

Half a mile off the port bow they could see a couple of trawlers bouncing over the waves, making for the French coast. By screwing up his eyes, Richard could see the men stowing away their nets. The boats looked so small from the Observation Deck of the *Queen Dee* and the sea so vast. That was their life, every day, every week, every month, every year, bobbing over the sea, hauling nets, gutting fish, making money for bread and wine and women and children and fun and education and street lights and shoelaces and a roof over one's head. The awareness of work, the inevitable routine from which few could escape, flooded his mind for the first time. He felt sick at not knowing what his own lot would be, whether he would escape it, whether he should even try to. Would he still be wavering over a job at twenty-one, at forty?

"Jiminy, can my mother guzzle martinis!" John pressed his warm face against the cold glass to get a better view into the Americana. "Just look at them knocking it back with that crazy old military guy who looks like something out of a British war movie. Let's go in and bum a couple of shots. You do drink, don't you?"

Another awkward question. He'd already had too many for one morning. "Like a fish," Richard said lamely.

Raymond, the head barman in the Americana, was a plump

man approaching fifty; not fat, but portly, he would insist,
and not fifty yet because he had no intention of ever being fifty.
Every day he wore a clean starched shirt under his braided
royal-blue jacket, and every minute of the day he made sure his
bar stewards were working as a team intent only on convincing the passengers that the Americana was the most relaxing,
the most entertaining, the only bar to be seen in on the *Queen
Dee*. There were other bars. Benson lorded it over the monastical quiet of the Tudor Room, and Fred did nicely for himself in
the Smoking Room for'd on the Promenade Deck. But none of
them carried Raymond's rank. It was a rank he had created
for himself: for Mr. Lake, the chief barman in the first-class
restaurant, was senior to them all and supervised every one of
the ship's bars under the eagle eye of Purser Catering. But
then Mr. Lake was not in the fortunate position of making
such direct contact with the paying customers over such long,
elegant, remunerative periods. Raymond had a flair for remembering regular passengers by name, for never forgetting a
favorite drink once the face had ordered it, for convincing night
owls that the bar was being kept open just for them, for making the right introductions between bridge fanatics, for protecting those who chose to remain aloof from their fellow
passengers, for fixing this, for fixing that, for fixing everything. Raymond was the one member of the crew the Master
knew he couldn't get rid of out of hand, not without evidence
that would hang a saint. Raymond was too big an asset to B and
E Lines, and he knew it. His rackets were legendary, but never
too obtrusive. People liked giving Raymond money because,
in return, they left him feeling a little better than they really
were—morally, that is. For at heart Raymond was a very moral
man. And his reward was not less than three hundred pounds
per trip in gratuities. It was worth giving people a little more
than they expected for such pickings, particularly when the
company wouldn't wish it otherwise.

"There you are sir, madam, two more Dry Docks. You won't
get anything drier this side of Suez."

Mrs. Brewer screamed her delight, while Raymond turned
an inscrutable face to dispense the Colonel another Scotch and
his lady another white port.

"The Sikhs were a splendid lot of fellows. Hindi for disciple, you know," the Colonel expounded, splashing the smallest quantity of soda into his glass. "Tall. Bearded. Splendid physiques. Wore the five Ks. *Kes,* uncut hair. *Kacch,* short drawers. *Khara,* an iron bangle. *Kripan,* a sword. *Khanga,* a comb. Worshipped the cow, of course."

"Is that so?" Mr. Brewer said obligingly. He wasn't particularly interested in the British *raj,* but there was no doubting Colonel Jamieson had been and still was a top guy, and top guys always interested him.

"My stomach won't take curry," Mrs. Brewer said. "Isn't that so, Kenneth? Kenneth took me to the New York World's Fair and we went into the Indian Pavilion and I was as sick as a pig."

Alice said, "Tumeric has a purgative effect in hot climates. It was the only way to eat meat."

Mr. Brewer said, "Is that so?" and the Colonel went on to tell more romantic tales of the Empire. He even obliged with a rendition of "The Road to Mandalay" and then, when he sensed his American friends had had enough, abruptly switched the conversation to the City, and the empire builders in the world of finance.

Alice said, "If Ian hadn't invested what little money we had wisely, we wouldn't be as comfortably off as we are today. He's almost as familiar with Threadneedle Street as he is with Calcutta, aren't you, Ian?"

Ian said, "I have one or two small directorships, you know. A bit stacked away in communications, a few gilt-edged, and a rather interesting unit trust group. Freebody. You wouldn't be looking for an investment capable of yielding as high as fifteen percent on your capital, with security, would you, Mr. Brewer?"

Mr. Brewer was saying that the best he was getting out of his industrials was nine percent before taxation, that Wall Street had been depressingly sluggish for the past three years so far as he was concerned, that he'd certainly like more information on Freebody's if the Colonel would oblige, when John and Richard joined them.

John said, "Can I put a couple of shots on the check, Dad?"

Mrs. Brewer began fussing. "John, dear, you know how it distresses me to see young people take to hard liquor."

"So, who's young?"

Mr. Brewer said O.K. but try to make it one, son, and didn't kids drink Coke any more? The Colonel hid his displeasure at the interruption behind a cloud of cigar smoke. And Raymond said Yes, gentlemen, what will it be?

"Vodka. Well iced." John turned to his companion. "What's yours?"

"Cider," Richard said firmly.

Chief Officer David Welch returned to the bridge shortly after two-thirty, well fed. The previous evening he had had to be content with what the chef thought passed for a cold buffet, served in the officers' smoking room by Daisy Bell, and lunch had been his first good meal of the voyage—saumon d'ecosse fume, consommé Madrilène, delice de turbotin bonne femme, canéton rôti bigarde, pêche Midinette. Better than his usual pub snack, particularly as the 'fifty-seven Clos de Tart was *domaine* bottled and quite out of his price range on shore. For he was a man who enjoyed good living: and he was just beginning to realize how good the living could be on a cruiser liner like *Queen Dee*. He strode into the chartroom and cast an eye over the midday summary in the deck log. Steaming time: 15 hours. Distance run: 227 miles. Average speed: 15.17 knots. Engine distance: 248 miles. Slip: 7.2 percent. Average revs: 90. Day's consumption heavy oil: 44 tons. No surprises there. If she was on a scheduled mail line the speed would have been up and the distance covered nearly half again as much; but the company liked its cruising passengers to take things easy, nice and slow, gentle them along, so the sense of arrival would be that much greater. The amount of slip seemed a bit high, but nothing to worry about. It would take him a week or two, anyway, to get used to the old girl's susceptibilities. Better make a mental note to find out her critical revs, didn't want to be accused of shaking her to pieces and the passengers with her. He left the chartroom for the bright daylight of the wheelhouse.

"Good afternoon to you, Mr. Welch. Did you eat well?"

"Very well, thank you, Hewson." He couldn't be sure about the Senior Second Officer—whether, like the others, he had a built-in dislike for him just because he was standing in for their beloved Ben, or not.

"Some muck blowing in from the Azores. Langdon says to expect gale force eight, or more."

They'd alter course off Cape Finisterre to 180° true, and that would bring her broadside-on starboard to the full force of the Atlantic. For the present, she was pitching a little, but not enough to affect the comfort of the passengers. If the weather reports remained the same, tomorrow she would be rolling, and that would be a different story. Landlubbers always seemed to be more allergic to rolling than pitching.

The Chief Officer said, "Then the chef will have to go easy on the pork and trifle tomorrow."

"Would you be what they term a gourmet, sir?" He was standing with his back to the automatic pilot, which was computing, clicking, adjusting, as he asked. He was a stocky, dark man, a few years older then the Chief, but in the backlight he looked almost a youth.

"I like to know what I'm eating."

"Then perhaps I'd better not offer you one of these?"

He was about to refuse, but said, "What are they?" and reached for the offered packet of fruit drops, and the tension was broken.

Hewson chewed and said, "My wife's not a very good cook. I think she lives out of the deep freeze when I'm away. Poor bloody kids! But I insist on a roast and a couple of fresh vegetables when I'm home. You're a bachelor, aren't you, Mr. Welch? Bachelors always eat better, I reckon."

"You can call me David. Do we all have to be so formal?"

There was no mistaking the surprise on Hewson's face. "Yes, of course, David: but—"

"I sat on Rigg yesterday morning because he was doing something while he was on watch that was neither part of company nor harbor regulations for seeing to the security of the ship. I'm the new boy here, I know, and it's natural enough for the rest of you to resent it. It's not my fault Ben Wilson's on the sick list. But it would be my fault if I failed in my duty as Chief to run the ship as efficiently as he did. Harry, I'd like it to stay a friendly ship. Do you think we can keep her that way?"

"I think so," Harry said.

Out of the corner of his eye, the Chief saw the duty Quarter-

master raise his face from the radar sweep. The wine had loos-
ened his tongue. He hoped he wasn't sounding too eager for a
reconciliation. "I'll get a few winks before I take over, then.
By the way, does the company frown on its officers using
the steam bath?"

"I don't think there's any rule. But Wilkie says he can only
give us a rubdown if we go before noon. You haven't got any
fat to get off, have you?"

"No, but cleanliness is next to godliness, so I'm told."

When he got to his cabin he found a pale blue envelope resting against the bedside light. Inside was a piece of embossed
stationery filled with a spidery scrawl: "David—I think the
wretch who runs the Mizzen Club is waiting for this. When did
you say we were meeting for lunch?—Fiona." In the fold was a
check, not for three hundred or four hundred, but for three
hundred and eighty-two—the precise amount. No one could say
that Fiona Pratley wasn't generous when it pleased her to be.
Or indiscreet. Sir Gerald knew all about her carryings-on, of
course. He was an ass to put up with it. If his wife was to play
around as Fiona did, she and her studs would get a taste of his
fist pretty damn quickly. But then, he had no intention of doing anything so silly as getting married. Not when there was
so much of it around and he could happily go on driving without a license for the rest of his life if he felt like it. Eager
women like Fiona could be fun. Just fun. David had no illu-
sion that he was her first *divertissement,* and he didn't particularly care one way or the other. Why the hell should he? It
amused him to be wanted by women. He stood in front of the
bathroom mirror tweezering hairs from his nostrils and
thought about some of the silly bitches he'd had. June. Grace.
Delice. Then there'd been that crazy Brazilian who'd sent him
to her doctor first because she was so damned certain every seaman had the clap. Cynthia, the little blonde in Eastbourne
who was a lesbian. Her butch friend had been so mad when she
caught them spread out in the hollow on the Downs that he
thought he'd die laughing. Margaret—no, Marigold. Christ
what a name!—whom he'd had in the family car parked behind
her old man's house, who had said she was eighteen and no
virgin, but who had turned out to be sixteen and was. There
had been failures, but you just had to have the knack of blot-

ting the failures from your mind. What man wanted to think
twice about a bird who said no? Ouch! That bloody hair hurt.
Take more care with the next one. Gently with the tweezers.
Marigold had been hurt—like hell she had! He was well
equipped to hurt women: if they asked for it and then didn't
want it when they got it, that was half the fun. Now he'd made
his nose bleed fiddling with it like that. Why was he so damned
vain? Let the lousy things sprout if they wanted to. Come to
think of it, Marigold was the first woman he'd made bleed.
She'd been so scared when she saw the mess, being a virgin,
that he'd had to give her a wad of money to keep her quiet.
When all was said and done, he was a pretty generous type.
He'd often given them money when he had it: it was just that
he didn't always have it. In his youth he'd been what everyone called an easy spender; but in his youth he'd had all too
little of it to spend. Bristol was hardly a poverty-stricken area
in the buzz of the first years of war, but the streets weren't
paved with gold either. "There ain't no money in farming,
lad," his dad had said, and kicked him off the land into the
sea on account of him being the youngest son and what money
there was in farming would be going to feather-bed Roy and
his breeding sow of a wife. So, five years fighting for King and
country on H.M.S. *Manston* as a snotty-nosed petty officer, then
into the merchant service to sit for a mate's certificate. As everyone told him at the time, "Dave, the sky's the limit!" That, to
a seaman. No one had seemed to realize that the happiest time
in his life had been those youthful war years in the Navy. Ralph
Martin. Fat, happy Ralph, on night shore patrol in Alexandria,
squatting atop off-limits wog bars and hooking the lads by
their pants with a fishing rod in one hand and a flashlight in
the other. A couple of years of that life and brother Roy could
have had every lousy farm in Britain for all he cared. Then
the war ended and Roy made some clumsy attempt at reconciliation, offering him a job and a home and all that sentimental
mush. But he'd already decided on his future and it pleased him
to tell Roy to take a running jump at himself. He knew damned
well Roy had only made the gesture because he was feeling
guilty about sitting out the war years in a protected occupation, making an easy pile as he decomposed like his own com-

post. But the whole family was like that. Wanting exactly the same things to happen to them every day, day in and day out. No ambition. Not one of them. They were all such utter clods. He searched the bathroom cabinet for cotton to staunch the bleeding from his nose, otherwise he'd have it all over his shirt and two shirts in one day was one too many, even if he had just had a cool three hundred drop in his lap. And eighty-two. Christ, was Fiona mad about his lap! He'd sometimes wondered, when he'd seen the lean-limbed Latin lads flashing their teeth at the *signore* on the Mediterranean beaches, what it must be like to be a gigolo. He ought to be experiencing their sense of appeased vanity right now. But he didn't experience anything, not a bloody thing, except a vague feeling that he didn't fancy getting stuck up Fiona again. She could be fun for a short time, but after that she became a crashing bore. In any case, he hadn't actually asked her for the damned money —he hadn't made it a condition, or anything like that. Same with the commission. He hadn't specifically asked her to get Sir Gerald to throw his weight around the B and E boardroom. She had been generous enough to do it spontaneously. That's what he liked most about her. Her spontaneity. She'd probably scrawled out the check for no other reason than she wanted to be spontaneous. She'd probably have made one out for twice that amount to any old dodderer who came looking for a hand-out for the cats' home if the idea had gotten into her empty little head at the time. The money didn't mean a damned thing to her. All the same, he wasn't going to start making a habit of accepting money from women. It wasn't a particularly masculine thing to do. On second thoughts, he wouldn't accept this. The Mizzen Club could whistle for it until his salary came through at the end of the month. He was on the verge of taking the check from his pocket and throwing it away. But he didn't. He left it nestling there against a packet of indigestion tablets. There was no need to bank it with the Purser for a day or two anyhow. Maybe he'd be an idiot to bank it at the Purser's Office at all. That old quean Craddock would be wagging his tongue all over the damned ship in no time at all about how the Chief Officer was accepting money from, guess who?

"Three-fifty, David!" Hewson's maddeningly friendly voice

called to him from the other side of the cabin door. Ten minutes, and he'd have to take over the watch. Bloody hell, he'd
not gotten his nap.

One attraction that a *Queen Dee* cruise offered that was not
offered by B and E's competitors was the first-class restaurant,
which could accommodate everyone at a single sitting instead
of two. It was an attraction looked upon by the ship's officers as
a very mixed blessing indeed. Were the first-class passengers
divided into the sheep and the goats as the Assistant Purser
did the tourist, the socially disruptive, the jejune, the patently
obvious misfits could conveniently be herded together for the
first sitting, unseen, unhosted, and unmourned by both Master
and staff. But they were not. And Captain Corlett kept his first
dinner date with his passengers filled with the usual mixture of
disinterest, foreboding and a large pre-engagement Scotch. He
had at his table Sir Gerald and Lady Pratley, because as company VIP's they could hardly be seated anywhere else; Mr. and
Mrs. Kenneth Harrison Brewer, simply because they were the
only Americans aboard and the gesture obviously had to be
made; Mr. and Mrs. Paxton, two of the company's oldest customers whom, thank heaven, he liked; and a Mr. and Mrs.
Radford, whom he didn't know and had a gnawing suspicion
were only placed at his table because Mr. Radford had well
greased Craddock's palm. The first night everyone had dressed
informally: but tonight they were all dressed to the hilt. As
Mallory's publicity blurb so delicately put it, "It depends on
you whether you wish to dress for dinner or not. There are no
rules laid down. The majority of passengers in first class prefer
to do so, and so do some passengers in vessels having only one
class. In tourist class the majority do not dress for dinner." And
it was Lady Pratley's dress that caused the first *contretemps*.
It was a sheath of luminous emerald, set off by her bronzed
shoulders and the flash and dazzle of a diamond necklace and
an articulated gold bracelet. There was no doubt that her ladyship looked splendid. She even arrived at table determined to
please. But the dominating color in the brightly lit restaurant
was mauve—mauve drapes, mauve carpets, mauve lapels to the
stewards' white monkey-jackets. Even to the Master's unaes-

thetic mind, the clash was horrible. Convinced that even she could have nothing done to change the décor at a moment's notice, her ladyship retired with the sulks to change her dress, telling her husband that he was an idiot for not reminding her while she was in her bath that every damned thing was mauve —doubtless including the stewards' bollocks.

Captain Corlett did his best to make polite table talk. "Mrs. Paxton, this is the sixth time you've persuaded your husband to join our spring cruise, I believe."

Mrs. Paxton, a toothy woman in a black gown that made her ten years older than she need have looked, smiled at everyone and said, "Gordon persuades me, really. We're not very ambitious. Too old for adventuring, and it's all so comfortable and such good value, it seems silly to change if you can't be sure what you'll be letting yourself in for instead."

"What's your line, Mr. Paxton? I'm in automobiles myself. Dealer," Mr. Radford said. He was a stout, bald man with heavy glasses, Jewish the Master thought, and hoped he wasn't going to talk business every night.

Mr. Paxton said he was an actuary, and Kenneth Harrison Brewer asked did British companies refuse policies to persons known to be alcoholics? After that, Mr. Paxton and Mr. Brewer debated British and American insurance over the *hors d'oeuvres*, while Mr. Radford tried to interest the Master in some of the more revolutionary features of a new French coupé, leaving Sir Gerald to entertain the ladies.

"We were so cold this morning, standing about on deck for the boat drill," Mrs. Brewer said. "Kenneth said it's all like seat belts in an airplane. Seat belts, not safety belts: they're called that because it's all psychological or something."

"Of course, there are occasions when a ship's boats, however well designed, are no damned use, no damned use at all," Sir Gerald told her. "Can't get half of them lowered if the sea's too heavy. Even the most unsinkable boat can be a veritable death trap in certain conditions. Sixty-foot waves. Hundred tons of solid water. Gale-force winds. Send a small boat spinning like a top. No, in certain conditions, survival chances are much better staying on board. Assuming, of course, it's not imperative to abandon ship."

Mrs. Paxton shuddered in her black dress. "A disaster at sea must be a very terrible thing, Sir Gerald. Have you ever experienced one?"

"I've been through nearly everything in my time, Mrs. Paxton. Sounds frightening when you're sitting round a delightful dinner table like this, but going over the side's quite a simple operation. Nothing to it, if you keep your head. Jump into the water—never dive—feet together, one arm over your life jacket pressing it to your chest, and holding the nose. Swim away from the ship. Avoid oil fuel. Keep together. Make for the rafts or anything else that floats. And wait for help."

Captain Corlett was about to cut across the old fool's bow—he really should know better than to frighten the ladies like this—when her ladyship returned to the table, sheathed in what everyone accepted as off-virginal white.

"Don't listen to a thing the old coot tells you," she said. "The only time he's ever abandoned ship was when he fell over the side of a pinnace coming aboard. Have you told them about that, dear? You ladies all know what a pinnace is, of course?"

"My, but that's a lovely dress," Mrs. Brewer obliged.

"It's French, it's very expensive, and it makes me look an old maid," her ladyship said. "Davot. I tell you, never get a dress from Davot. It cost me the earth, and they wanted to fit an artificial bum to it because they said I was the wrong shape. I said, 'No you don't, the dress may be the wrong shape, but I'm not.' "

The Master couldn't decide which was the most disturbing influence at his table—Sir Gerald, or his lady. Dinner at last mercifully over, he escorted those who wanted to dance up to the Tudor Room on the Promenade Deck. The Paxtons had promised to meet a couple from Leaminster for a rubber or two of bridge, and the Radfords were heading for the cinema to see *Return as a Stranger* which they'd missed at home and wanted to catch because Mrs. Radford's sister had said Barbara Lake had never been better. Which left only the American couple and Sir Gerald and her ladyship to be escorted. As they entered the elevator, Chief Officer Welch followed them in together with three from his table—Pamela Westcott and a couple who introduced themselves as retired schoolteachers from up north. The Master was wondering how retired schoolteachers were able to afford first class accommodation on the *Queen Dee*, and was putting it down to a retirement gift from grateful constituents, when Lady Pratley caused the second *contretemps* of the evening.

"You found the check in your cabin, David?" she asked.

The Chief Officer looked momentarily like a kid caught stealing jam; but a second later he was saying with complete assurance, "Thank you, Lady Pratley. I've passed it on to the Chief Purser. You will get your receipt in due course."

Captain Corlett found it intolerable that the woman should be calling his Chief Officer by his first name in front of other passengers. The rumors about her ladyship were already proving to be truer than he feared. He said to everyone in general, "I am told we have the best orchestra afloat. I hope you're all going to have a very pleasant evening. I'm a bit old in the bones for dancing myself, but nonetheless, Mrs. Brewer, I hope you'll give me the pleasure of the first dance?"

Mrs. Brewer shimmered with pride. "I'd just adore that, Captain, if Kenneth will let me," she said.

They were leaving the elevator, but Lady Pratley, having created a situation, was not the kind of woman to let it drop without making the most of it. "Who's she?" she demanded of David, glaring at Mrs. Westcott, and when names had been politely exchanged, demanded, "Where's Mr. Westcott? You haven't dropped him over the side already, have you?"

Mrs. Westcott clenched her fists until the knuckles whitened. For what seemed like the millionth time she heard herself say, "He died last year."

The Chief Officer took her by the arm and escorted her across the foyer toward the Tudor Room as her ladyship put on her most brittle smile. "She doesn't look very merry for a widow. Poor little thing," she said.

The Master was unable to check himself in time. "Lady Pratley," he said, "Mrs. Westcott is not poor. You can see she is not little. And she is not a thing. She is one of our passengers."

The ship's orchestra, half a dozen musicians who apparently had never previously met each other, were doing their best to get on playing terms quickly, perched awkwardly on highly varnished beer barrels in a corner of the Tudor Room. The dancers, for the most part, were middle-aged or elderly couples, ladies with blue-rinsed hair and over-fed bodies, gentlemen with the hunted look of top executives uncertain that there wouldn't be a takeover in the board room during their absence. The ship's officers who were not on duty danced and made small talk with the unaccompanied ladies; and two secretaries from the Purser's Office, antiseptic in their navy-blue uniforms and short hair styles, made themselves available to the few lonely males with all the enthusiasm of vestal virgins. And beyond the warm fug of ye phoney bit of olde England, lay the wet darkness of the cold sea, broken only by the distant wink of the lights of passing ships and the circling sweep of lighthouses off the French coast.

"Are you looking for someone, Dearest?" Richard came up to her the moment she entered the room.

"No, I'm trying to avoid them."

"Same thing. You can't avoid them unless you know where they are. Who're you trying to avoid, anyway?"

She was trying to avoid Lady Pratley, but she didn't tell him that. "No one. I'm not really trying to avoid anyone."

"You are all right? You're not feeling sick or anything?" he asked, offering her his arm. He looked so gauche, wearing a tuxedo for the first time, stiff, blue-eyed, so incredibly fair-haired in the black jacket, and she wished she hadn't asked for his company. He was such a dear boy, so devoted to her, but she knew it wasn't good for him. Or for her.

"I'm very well, thank you, darling. The Chief Officer's been looking after me." She turned to her companion. "I'm afraid it must be a ghastly chore for you, doing your work by day and then having to look after lost souls like me at night."

The Chief Officer said no, it was a pleasure, which sounded sincere enough, and left her to Richard's care and attention.

"Shall we dance?" he asked her.

She knew he was terrified of dancing. The year before Arnold died, when he was sixteen, they had sent him during the Christmas vacation to have lessons. The Ticehursts' daughter, Sybil, was learning at the same time, and the families had hoped the youngsters would strike up a friendship. But there'd been some silly tiff over who was the mostest in the pop world.

Richard had insulted one of her idols, she had retaliated by calling him a public-school snob, and they'd never spoken to each other again. Worse, business relations between Arnold and Tim Ticehurst, who was very influential in Sunripe Mills at the time, had been strained to near breaking point. All over a guitar-twanging moron with long hair!

Richard asked, "Did you have the *tournedos* or the baked ham?"

"Steak. You know I don't like ham."

"The ham was smashing. Glazed peaches all over it. The steward gave John and me an extra helping. Don't Americans eat funny? John cuts everything up in little pieces, then shovels it in with a fork in his right hand."

"Perhaps you eat funny to him."

She was pleased he had met another boy about his own age. It was not natural for him to be constantly around his mother's skirts. And it was not natural for her to use him as a substitute for Arnold, although with his light complexion, full mouth and blue eyes, he was so much like his father when she'd first met him. They used to dance together at the Drive Hotel every Friday evening—Westborough's big hop of the week—with Arnold feeling so important because everyone knew him as the man who baked the Westcott Loaf. It made her feel dreadfully old to think back. To the youngsters Richard's age she was old —old enough to be their mother. Yet when she looked about her in the Tudor Room, at the sallow faces and blue rinses, she felt ridiculously young and wondered what she was doing there among them.

"Where's John now?"

"Gone to the flicks."

"Didn't you want to go?"

"Nope. It's only a deadly bit of sentimental mush with Barbara Lake."

He danced with her for half an hour. Then she wanted to sit and have coffee and almost at once they were joined by the Brewers, who were themselves tired of dancing and wanted to talk. Mrs. Brewer kept on about her apartment in Detroit with all the new gadgets, and when she was not going on about that she was about John: how she was just certain he was going to be something famous in the theater one day, not that they had encouraged it: how she was longing to have him back home, where Kenneth had already rented a small downtown apartment for him because, at his age, he would no longer want to be wholly dependent on them and he would be getting married soon—she was just sure he would—and Kenneth agreed with her, and they both hoped he'd give them oodles of grandchildren. And Richard sat and listened and thought about marriage, and if he'd be having oodles of children for Dearest to glow over when he was nineteen, twenty-one or forty.

"I think I'll go and meet John and find out how he enjoyed the movie," he said, when he could endure the tedium no longer.

Dearest said, "I'll be going to bed soon. The sea air's making me tired," and kissed him good night.

As he left the table, he heard Mrs. Brewer saying, "Such a nice boy. I do wish our John wasn't so unsettled. All those months in Europe, and we're lucky to get a card from him once a week. Isn't that right, Kenneth?"

It had been too hot for his liking in the Tudor Room and Richard walked out onto the deck to freshen up; but the night air was cold and it was spitting with rain and he soon changed his mind. He poked his head in the Writing Room. An old man with a monocle, reading a two-days old copy of the *Times*, was the only occupant. Several groups were playing cards in the Smoking Room up for'd. The Orchard Room was mostly filled with middle-aged women drinking sticky things like cherry or apricot brandy. He began to wish he'd gone to the cinema. Somehow, life on the *Queen Dee* wasn't the way he imagined it would be when he'd suggested the cruise to Dearest. It was very elegant and comfortable; but that kind of thing was all right when you were eighty—it wasn't what you were looking for at eighteen. He pushed open a door, and found himself in a deserted gymnasium, clinically white, with a dark blue floor, equipped with bars and rings and vaulting horses and rowing machines and climbing ropes. He walked over to a punch ball and began hitting it, gently at first, then with increasing vigor until he felt sweat sticking round his stiff collar. He heard a movement behind him and turned to see a steward standing in the doorway.

"I'm sorry, sir, but the gymnasium is supposed to be closed when there is no one qualified in attendance."

"I wasn't doing any harm," Richard said defensively.

The man was very apologetic. "I'm sure not, sir. But the door should have been locked."

He left the gymnasium to the steward's care, ill at ease at the way the man was "sir-ing" him. He'd done nothing to win the man's respect except to wear a new tuxedo. He remembered Old Hickson's lecture on the art of being a gentleman. "My boy, it's not the ability to treat some people well that matters, but the ability to treat all people exactly the same." That was crazy for a start. How did one treat a "sir-ing" steward the same as a cussing taxi driver? He walked down two companionways to B Deck and waited near the main entrance for the cinema to empty, killing time by window shopping in the ship's arcade.

"Hey, Richard! You missed the campiest thing. Barbara Lake sure knows how to send up a lousy script." John took a packet from an inside pocket of his jacket. "Gum?"

He took a piece and chewed, while John rambled on about the badness of the movie. It was, apparently, so bad it was good. John was still carrying on as they sat down in the Americana up on the Observation Deck and ordered a couple of beers.

"I'm pleased I missed it then," Richard said.

"Seth's just nuts about bad movies. Sees two a night if he can, mostly at the *cinematheque*—you know, goodie oldies."

"Who's Seth?"

"Didn't I tell you about Seth? I'm sure I did. The colored boy I've been living with in Paris."

Richard said, "I was going to have a holiday in Paris with a school party. Only Dad dying suddenly as he did, it wasn't possible."

"A school party! Oh boy, would they have been a riot! Twice round the Louvre, the gargoyles at Notre Dame, and an ice cream in a South Bank drugstore. Then home like good little boys, having kissed the Champs Elysées, kissed the Rue de la Paix, kissed the Eiffel Tower. Oh Christ, you can kiss Montparnasse!"

The beer was light and cold, German style, and they finished two glasses, and John suggested a third but Richard said no, he'd had enough and was going to turn in. John would have stayed up later, but he couldn't think of a damned thing to do except get drunk, and Richard didn't like drinking, and getting drunk alone was not much fun. He didn't have the money to drink away just like that anyhow, not without cadging a handout from the folks, which he didn't want to do, not when his freedom had been so hard to win and was so precious to him just the way it was.

"O.K., if that's what you want, we hit the hay."

Their cabin, for which the company had the audacity to charge a first-class fare, was amidships, for'd of the lower half of the swimming pool and immediately beneath the Tudor Room orchestra whose drum sounded in constant danger of making an unwanted descent through the deckhead. It was devoid of daylight, but fresh air hissed and gushed through a louvre. The small space was almost completely filled by two chintz-covered beds set on opposite sides, with two tiny wardrobes and a mirror between them. Richard carefully removed his tuxedo and placed it on a hanger. It was the first grown-up suit he had ever worn, and it was already a love-hate thing with him. As he put it away he looked at the frayed cuff on the herringbone jacket he'd worn almost every day since before he was sixteen, and wondered what clothes he'd be wearing when he was nineteen, twenty-one or forty.

"How did you put on so much muscle? You're not one of those fanatics for workouts night and morning, are you?" John asked.

"It just came," Richard said simply. "Rugger, I suppose." He was standing there naked except for his shorts—a blond, beardless head on a white, hairless body, molded and shaped by muscle that might inspire an artist. He was, as Dearest frequently told him, a beautiful boy.

"I used to hate games at school," John said. "I guess I was made for a life of lazy debauchery."

Richard kicked off his shorts and wondered if he'd ever play rugger again. Somehow life had come to a full stop for him and Dearest the moment Father died. It would have to start again soon: it couldn't go on in this anesthetic void forever. He squeezed into the small tiled closet with the pedestal on one side and a plastic-shrouded shower on the other, and brooded on what he was going to do about rugger, learning something more than he'd needed to know to scrape through his exams, finding a job he'd get a kick out of doing, making friends. The warm water gushed over his firm white body, the powerful spray stinging the upper part of his chest.

"Hey! Are you going to sleep under the shower, man?" John shouted impatiently from the cabin.

"There's room for two. Just. And you can rub my back. It's getting all pimply."

The dreaded curse of acne was already beginning to plague Richard's young life. Pretty soon he'd start shaving, and then his face would break out like Harry Kenton's, and no girl ever wanted to go out with a boy with a pimply face. Pimples, Richard thought, were the most dreadful disease one could catch. Worse than having to wear specs or braces. Just at the time one wanted to be most handsome.

"For crissake stand still or I won't be able to rub a thing," John said.

The two boys struggled together under the relaxing warmth —John tall and slender with curls of black hair streaked by the water down his legs and belly, vigorously soaping the English boy's shoulderblades. Richard laughed, wriggled like a fish, and tried to shout instructions through a curtain of water. Then John dropped the soap. As he recovered it from the tiled basin, he brought both arms up and around the other boy's body to soap his chest. Richard wriggled some more, muscles relaxed, white skin slippery with soap. He felt John's chin glance across the back of his neck, rough with unshaved stubble, as his body pressed firmly against his own. Then, what he was least expecting, happened. John's hands slid from his chest over the firm young belly muscles, to grasp, and rub, and coax him in a way no one had ever attempted before. For a few moments Richard remained in the embrace, his body taut and quivering under the torrent of water, numb to any sensation, either of pleasure or pain, affection or fear. Then, like an animal trapped by the hunter, he rebelled with mind and body, tried to break free, to make his escape.

"What the hell do you think you're doing?" he shouted, gripping John's wrists with two iron-hard hands and tearing them from the center of his being.

"Only having a bit of fun. Hell, I wasn't going to kill you. So what, I thought you were gay," John said.

"Don't touch me! Leave me alone!" Richard's voice was shrill now, like a girl's, as he stumbled naked and dripping into the cabin to towel himself back to composure.

When John came from the shower, Richard was lying on his back in bed. The American boy slipped on a pair of bright green pajamas and stood in front of the mirror for some time, drying his hair and combing and brushing and fussing over it. He hesitated, about to go to his own bed, but instead came and stood close to Richard.

"I didn't want to spoil things between us," he said. "I like you very much. It's just that I prefer boys for company to girls. I want to sleep with you. To get to know you better. I guess the answer's no, eh?"

Richard didn't even turn his head. His eyes were tightly closed. "You make me puke," he said.

"Oh boy, were you born at a very early age!" John said, and returned to his own bed.

It was a little after eleven o'clock when John turned out the light and, for all Richard knew, went straight off to sleep. But he couldn't sleep. He lay there in a strange bed, like when he was in the hospital for a couple of weeks after smashing up his right knee in the rugger scrum. Life was going on around him, but he was not a part of it. He heard occasional footsteps in the corridor outside and half-caught voices and laughter. Above, the drum kept up its incessant beat in the Tudor Room. Below, the *Queen Dee*'s engines pulsated and throbbed as she cut swiftly through the sea on her way south. People working, people talking, people playing, people loving. But his mind was filled vividly with two images from the past which, until tonight, he had forgotten almost the moment they had happened. Old Hickson throwing a bucket of water over two of the fifth-form boys he surprised interfering with each other in the sports pavilion: and the day they were mucking about in Selwin-Smith's dad's car in the garage, and Smithy said he'd show him how to get a fistful of pleasure, and putting action to words had begun a practical demonstration until Richard had left in disgust. Unable to sleep, he could think of nothing except those two sordid incidents, and of John's soapy hand trying to get him to experience something he had never experienced before, and wondered fearfully if he would want to experience when he was nineteen, twenty-one or forty.

Up on the bridge deck the Chief Officer was preparing to take over the four-to-eight watch from Harry Hewson. The Quartermaster had called him at three-thirty and again at three-fifty. He had bathed, shaved, drunk two mugs of strong black coffee from a bedside flask, and was in the chartroom running over the deck log, gleaning basic facts from course recorder and echo sounder, with a couple of minutes to spare.

"The muck seems to be blowing in earlier than we expected, eh Harry?"

"Last reports suggest that, yes, David. Barometer down to twenty-nine point eight four. Wind shifted westerly force six."

"Has the old man been alerted?" The Chief Officer looked up from the bright desk light over the chart table, one eye closed—a knack he had to prevent any momentary night blindness on entering the cloistered darkness of the wheelhouse.

"No, I haven't disturbed him."

"Why the hell not?"

The Second Officer's face hardened. "Because, sir, we never disturb the Master unless there's an exceptional change."

"Meaning that Ben Wilson didn't think force six with a forecast of a possibility of force eight imminent was exceptional?"

"Not for these waters."

"I'm sorry, Harry, but I was always taught to report any change in the weather to the Master, particularly at night if it changes for the worse. I'll ring him now, so if there's trouble for anyone, I'll cop it. Fair enough?"

The Second Officer said surlily, "Fair enough," and left the bridge, followed by the Fourth and duty Quartermaster. What riled Hewson was that the Chief was squaring his own yardarm, possibly at his expense. The old man wouldn't want to be waked at eight bells. Ben Wilson, Malcolm Rigg or he wouldn't have done so without some other element of possible emergency which made a decision from the Master imperative. But

David Welch was not Ben Wilson; he hadn't had Ben's years of experience, for one thing, and Hewson contented himself with the thought that the new Chief was playing it safe, for the simple reason he couldn't trust himself to play it any other way.

"Doesn't she appear to be yawing to you, Third?" the Chief asked Ron Tyson, the junior officer of the watch.

"Quite a bit, sir."

"That's what I thought. What's your time lapse on the auto-pilot?"

"Six seconds, sir."

"Let's try her at ten."

"Ten it is, sir."

The youngster leaned over the clicking mechanism to make the adjustment while the Chief returned to the privacy of the chartroom to call the Master. It was several seconds before a sleepy voice answered the phone. He took the weather report philosophically, and sounded grateful for having been alerted. What was their position? Were they on course? What was the state of visibility? The Chief satisfied him that there was nothing that should be done that had not been done, and with the muttered recommendation that he increase revs to ninety, the Master went back to his slumbers. There had been no trouble.

"Is the Captain joining us, Mr. Welch?" Tyson asked, shortly after he had returned to the wheelhouse.

"No, Mr. Tyson. Is there any reason why he should?"

"That's for him to decide, isn't it, sir?"

"Exactly. And I'm pleased you recognize just that." The bloody little bastard, trying to needle him: he'd better watch it, or he'd never know what hit him when Arkwright took over.

"It's always best to stick to the rules, sir."

The Chief Officer was about to choke him off, but the engine room was on the line, and he passed on the Master's orders to increase revs. For the next few minutes the changes in the old *Queen* were barely perceptible to the senses; but they were recorded in every detail by the myriad of man-made instruments. She kept to her course of 208° true, the yawing eased, and she made way from 14.8 to 15.5 knots, the wind and Atlantic swell taking her playfully along her starboard side trying to roll her in their sport. Any discomfort the passengers might feel was adequately corrected by the gyro-stabilizers; and at this time of night most passengers would be asleep—or should be. Chief Officer Welch knew that the Master's decision to push her just that little harder now was the sensible one. By dawn, if the weather worsened, they'd have to keep the passengers happy by easing her back to a more comfortable, time-consuming, speed. But for now, passengers and crew were protected by the officer of the watch, young Tyson, a burly bo'sun's mate, the gray-headed Quartermaster Climpson, two AB's, an efficient deck hand, a deck hand uncertified, an ordinary seaman, and a deck boy, watching in the darkness high aloft, watching to starboard and to port, faces glued to the fluorescent glimmer of the radar sweep, eyes on compasses, charts, direction finders.

"There's something coming into view," the Third Officer said, his face flickering a bluish-green over the screen. "Could be the *Bengal Castle.*"

"Let's take a bearing then. Has the masthead lookout spotted her yet?" The Chief Officer did not share youthful enthusiasms for radar. For one thing, it was pretty dicey in picking up a wooden hull; and for another, it had frequently been known to turn a blind electronic eye to even the biggest fully loaded tanker head-on. And the trained human eye could detect a change in the inclination of another ship a damned sight more rapidly than any box of tricks.

"One-nine-three degrees true by twelve miles, sir."

They kept taking bearings, sure now that the other ship would slip safely by in the night abeam to port, her lights radiating a friendly warmth across the swollen ocean. Again the Chief Officer compared compasses, checked the course laid off on the chart, and when he was satisfied with the state of things on the bridge began to make his rounds. Cursory they would have to be, like the Master's general inspection, but nonetheless efficient within their own limitations. Fire was not his primary concern—there was an all-night two-man fire patrol checked to precision by their timeclocks—but it was something he could not put from his mind. Fire at sea was the most dreadful hazard. He once saw a tanker at Milford Haven go up in a sheet of flames while she was discharging, half her crew trapped, the other half flinging themselves, burning flesh balls, onto concrete jetty or into murky water. He walked through the empty Smoking Room and thought of the times he had seen passengers throw lighted stubs over the side, to be blown back by a sportive breeze, to smolder God knows where. At this hour of morning, the *Queen Dee* was a floating specter, her public rooms silent in a subdued glimmer of light, the blue plastic corridors with their red floors diffusing into a purple haze. And when he paused, silence—except for the distant whine of a pump and the all-pervading gentle throb of engines. It was cold and windy on deck, even on the lee side, but it was his job to be there: to look, to check, to confirm, to be assured. To the east, the first silver of dawn was dividing the sky from the sea. He was passing the swimming pool, shrouded in flapping canvas, when he heard a patter of footsteps from behind the gentlemen's changing room and the muted closing of a door, almost lost in the whistling of wind through the rigging.

"Is that you, Jackson?"

He knew the moment he called that it wasn't, because there was no reason for any member of the watch to be there, or for anyone else for that matter at this time of night, in this weather, with the pool still empty. Then he saw that the changing-room door had been forced. His hand found a light switch and turned it on. The whole place smelled of damp clothing, a heavy body smell like that which hangs over streets neighboring a laundry. He pushed open the cubicle doors as he went in, one at a time, standing well back with each thrust. In the third he found what at first he thought was a girl, sitting cowed on the slat seat, long unkempt hair half hiding the round, ruddy face, and falling in tresses over the collar of a faded, food-soiled khaki parka. On the floor was a spread of newspapers and a single blanket. In one corner of the tiny cubbyhole was a knapsack, and on the seat, next to the girl-boy, an assortment of victuals—pieces of cheese, sliced meats, French pastries, biscuits, bottled beer, and a plate with the B and E crest on it. The Chief Officer needed no further evidence to know he was dealing with a stowaway.

"How long did you think you could hide here, eh?" he asked.

"I'm not hiding!" The voice was resentful, indeterminably feminine.

"You're not going to pretend you're a passenger, are you?"

"Find out!" There was a masculine harshness to the challenge, but he still wasn't sure.

"Even our most eccentric passenger is unlikely to prefer the dubious comfort of the gentlemen's changing room to his own cabin, particularly at this time of morning. You are a male person, I take it?"

The reply was impudent. "Why don't you find out? Or didn't your mother ever tell you the difference?"

"All right, on your feet! You're not staying here."

The ruddy face smiled behind the tousled hair. "Why, are you going to take me to your cabin? Do you fancy me? Is that it? You'll get yourself into trouble if you don't treat me properly. I'm warning you."

The Chief Officer found it difficult to control his temper. Bloody bastards! They thought the whole damned world owed them a living. If they weren't cadging free lifts on the highways, they were breaking into people's houseboats along the Riviera for free lodging and begging sustenance with their bodies or what little talent they had with guitars and chalks on their promenade pitches.

He said roughly, "Out! And bring that filth with you. You've been down to the A Deck pantry to steal the grub, I take it?"

The boy-girl said, "Get knotted!" and sat on the slats, making a two-fingered gesture.

The Chief Officer took a step forward and confiscated a cheese-encrusted clasp-knife. The creature was still gesturing him when he brought his right hand down across the ruddy left cheek in a stinging blow. "Now, are you going to do what you're told? Or do you want a little more warming up?"

The girl-boy whimpered. "You won't get away with this! You'll see. My old man'll raise hell when he learns how you've treated me."

He hurried the youngster out, with one hand on khaki shoulder nestled under a tress of matted hair. The feet were wrapped in tattered hand-made sandals, protruding from bleached blue jeans. "I assume you're one of the nonviolent types," he said. "Bone-idle, squatting at every street corner you come to, chanting 'We shall overcome'—or some such drivel."

"I don't think violence solves any problems," the boy-girl told him.

They reached the Orlop Deck by the midship elevator. Down there, deep below the waterline, where the engines were pulsing and roaring in the ears, the Chief Officer pushed the youngster into a metal-doored paint store full of tins and drums, and smelling of oils and spirits and tars and the bilge tanks immediately below.

"You lousy bastard, you're not going to leave me here!" the girl-boy shouted, twisting from his grasp and trying to run.

The Chief Officer dragged the twisting body back into the confined space and locked the door. For the next ten minutes he savaged into it with calculated ease, hurling the thick chestnut hair against the steel bulkhead, grinding the ring on his right hand deep into the ruddy left cheek until he had drawn blood, then fisting in beneath the lower ribs so that the mouth slobbered and dribbled bile. Finally, with the youngster swaying unsteadily in the parka like a giant bat, he brought his knee up into the crotch with all his strength. The bat screamed in agony and crumpled like a rag bag on the cold metal floor.

"Try screwing with that, boy—if you are a boy!" the Chief Officer said.

A moment later the man had gone, the metal door clanged and was locked from the outside. The youngster lay and cried with pain and fear as the *Queen Dee*'s engines throbbed and pounded all around. Up on the Boat Deck, Chief Officer David Welch filled his lungs with salty, beaten air. It was no longer dark. Billows of gray clouds raced across the sky from the west to meet the pale blue of dawn. He wiped a streak of blood from the back of his hand with a handkerchief. In another couple of hours the ship would be buzzing with the life of another day.

Lat. 43.45N Long. 9.14W

... *07:50 Accident boat stations practiced. Hands mustered wearing life jackets and instructed. Starboard accident boat manned, equipment inspected and found in good order. Starboard lifebuoy release gear tested and found in good order. 08:00 Correct time given to engine room. 10:20 Altered course 200° (Std.) 10:30 Divine Service conducted by Master in cinema. 11:40 Cape Finisterre abeam bearing 110° True × 11 miles. 11:45 Altered course 180° (Gyro) 191° (Std.) Compasses compared. Rounds made and all's well. Wind strong westerly. Heavy swell. Overcast with showers.—M.R.*

LADY PRATLEY was awakened at an ungodly hour on the Sabbath by the stamping of men's feet as they mustered for boat drill. She had had enough discomfort for one night, having been kept awake by Sir Gerald's snoring; and now, just when he had sunk beneath the blankets into his morning coma, a fusion of last night's gin with fresh morning air, there had been this stamping and shouting and chain-rattling. She was allergic to men, rough ordinary working men like the laborers who swarmed past her parents' house every day with their clownish limbs and primitive faces to clock in for a day's sweat and grime in the factory down at the end of the road. She never had found out what they made in the bloody place, she was that interested. Unlike her sister Patricia, who'd married a foreman, black greasy hair and a young body brutally swollen by beer, only to be stuck in Birmingham for the rest of her life breeding brats and getting as fat and ugly as her husband. Not for Fiona, Lady Pratley, *née* Florence Livett, called by all the kids and tradesmen and neighbors and schoolmarms and relatives in Pembroke Street, plain Flo. She'd grown up to hate noisy, stupid men. Her first schoolgirl crush had been for the slender dark-haired young man in the pin-striped trousers who super-

vised the serving of the gooiest of gooey cakes at the Fortune
Tea Rooms. Had she become famous instead of marrying Sir
Gerald, when they wrote her biography they could have said
in all truthfulness that that young man had been her ideal. Re-
fined, elegant, debonair, he was every inch a gentleman; and
she was sure that, given the chance, he would have been a slave
to her slightest whim.

"Gerry, do something about that dreadful noise those men
are making outside," she said.

He grunted and pushed two beady little eyes above the
sheets. "Did you say something, dear?"

"Yes, I did say something. I said, I want that noise stopped.
Now."

His eyes were red-rimmed and dewy with night secretions
as he reached for his wristwatch on the side table. "I expect it's
only some kind of boat drill."

"I don't give a damn what it is! It's disturbing me and I want
it stopped!"

"Perhaps it'll all be over in a few minutes," he said hopefully.

"You never do anything I want," she nagged. "Men are all
the same. They won't do a damn thing unless they're made to."

Her mother had nagged her father constantly ever since
she could remember. Why didn't he grow celery on the allot-
ment like other husbands did? When was he going to remember to fix the cellar steps, or was he going to wait until someone did themselves an injury? How much longer did he think
she was going to put up with his stomping into the kitchen in
his muddy boots? When the war came, the poor man made no
attempt to take advantage of his classified occupation; he was
up and out and having one hell of a time as a Desert Rat private
and would have been just as happy if he'd returned to
find them all blown to kingdom come. He'd been nagged so
much his senses had been anesthetized. His going off to the
war would have been another important chapter in her biography. It had made it so much easier for her to go off as well.
Patricia got married to her classified occupation of a husband
and mother tucked her hair in a snood and filled shells to drop
on the Hun. Both of them were only too pleased when little
Flo opted to migrate south and live with Auntie May, whose

two-hundred-pound chassis was dominating the dispensation of half the service canteen tea in London.

"Gerry, how much longer do I have to wait for coffee? You ordered it an hour ago, and that half-wit of a steward hasn't done a thing about it." She came from the bathroom in a sickly yellow terrycloth wrap. "Why don't you complain to the Captain, or something?"

He was waiting to use the bathroom, two white broomstick legs jutting from an over-short faded blue robe, his face the color of putty. "I'm sure he's being as quick as he can," he said to placate her.

"Well, he's not being quick enough. This is the most first-class suite on the whole bloody boat, isn't it?"

"Ship, dear. Not boat. Never boat."

But she wasn't going to be put off. She nagged him until he came from the bathroom half washed and got on the phone for the steward and stayed on until the breakfast trolley arrived. Addison was apologetic that it had been all of five minutes since the order was given: Sir Gerald was apologetic that Addison might think he was not aware that he was doing his best: and her ladyship said the coffee was cold, and bring some more that wasn't. Quickly. She curled up on one of the new plain blue bed covers, blissfully unaware that the harassed housekeeper had finally met her ladyship's pleasure by raiding the tourist-class linen cupboards, and nibbled at a piece of toast like an angry bird. It was cold and leathery. Addison could replace that, too. Then her eye caught the slip of paper on the trolley that passed as the ship's newspaper—news headlines gleaned from the B.B.C. by the radio office on one side, and a lot of tripe about B and E's services to passengers on the other.

"Gerry," she shouted into the bathroom, "why can't they provide proper Sunday papers?"

"Do be reasonable, my dear. We are at sea," he shouted back.

"I want the color supplements and the fashion pages," she said petulantly.

"Perhaps we can pick them up when we go ashore at Villefranche."

She got off the bed and stormed into the bathroom. "On Tuesday! Are you mad? I want to read them now!"

He said calmly enough, "I'm sorry, my dear, but you can't read them now, and that's the end of the matter."

"Why the devil did we ever come on this damned cruise?" she shouted into his ear as he gargled and spat the residue of last night's gin from his mouth. "Look at the weather! Cold, wet and bloody! I could be cold, wet and bloody all day as far as you're concerned, and you've got toothpaste all round your chin."

He said patiently, "The weather will improve soon. Be a dear and see if the ship's newspaper gives the time of Divine Service. It should be in there somewhere."

"Good grief," she said, "you're not going to drag me to church, are you?"

"It's my position, Fiona. You know perfectly well I must attend."

"For heaven's sake, stop talking about your position. It sounds filthy at your age. Like *soixante-neuf* or something else disgustingly French."

She hated the thought of going to church. Whatever people might say about her behind her back, and by all accounts they said plenty, she would never voluntarily play the hypocrite. Church, of one kind or another, had threatened to come between them right from the start. She, by birth and upbringing, was Catholic; he, by birth and upbringing, was Protestant. To her, going to church was an experience like making love, at the right time and under the right circumstances one felt better for it; to him, it was a duty, like paying taxes, honoring your father and mother, or sinking the enemy. They'd met in a club off Leicester Square. He was making one of his few London sorties of the war, cutting a dashing figure in his Navy uniform and looking for a little home comfort. She was dancing in the chorus, and singing a little when she had the chance, and keeping the boys company when they were lonely; but under the nicest possible circumstances, mind you, because Lew Trent who ran the club was a close friend of Auntie May, who would never in a month of Sundays let her sister's daughter go on the stage if anything worse than being buried alive by a wayward doodlebug was likely to happen to her. In those days Gerry had no knighthood and a crop of the cutest curly hair. To be fair, in those days she didn't need to make something of her-

self with the latest in foam-rubber uplift bras. Gerry had said
he was mad about her, and meant it; and she had said she was
mad about him, because she was supposed to be kind to the
boys and he hadn't done anything to harm her anyhow. Then
when she saw him again it was four years later and his hair
was falling like a stripper's feathers and she thought, my god,
you're older than my dad, you dirty old man. But he was so
kind and gentle, so distinguished and educated, and about to
become a Sir. She didn't have it in her to say no, not with fat
Auntie May and Mum in her snood trying to push her over the
brink so they could hobnob with the gentry. And there she was,
standing in front of the altar, not wholly unaware of the sins of
the flesh, dreading most the moment when the father-husband
would discover her lost virginity. But somehow he never did,
or if he did it was never mentioned. He'd needed a child and
he treated her nineteen-year-old nubile body as though she was
one and would never, ever, grow up.

"Bloody hell! That damned man did it on purpose. Look, my
finger's blistered." She dropped the silver coffeepot and its
steaming contents onto the carpet, where it lay untouched,
turning the elephant-gray camel-brown, and carried on demanding his sympathy.

"You *must* try not to be so impetuous, my dear. If only you'd
touched it gently at first, instead of making a grab for it."

"Gerry," she moaned. "*do* something. Get a doctor! I might
get blood poisoning. I'm never going to let that dreadful
man wait on me again."

"I'm sure he didn't mean it," he said to placate her.

"He did mean it! I could tell by the expression on his face
when he brought it in that he meant it. That man hates me,
Gerry. He hates me! I want him fired!"

Sir Gerald took her burned hand gently in his and soothed
it with his long, bony fingers, then brought it to his lips to kiss
the blister well. She stood there allowing the embrace as though
she were granting him a favor. It was the way she had treated
him ever since their first night together, for she had never
found him particularly attractive physically. During the first
few years of marriage she had teased him more than loved
him, letting him play with her body like a doll, childishly undressing it, bathing it, combing its hair, admiring it, and wrap-

ping it up again in new fineries. And her teasing had become increasingly cruel the longer she kept herself from the inevitable act that would make her dollish body woman. Yet he had never once tried to keep her from that act. Not once had he denied her the company of other men, if that company would relax her, make her happy. Right from the moment she had discovered his impotency, it had been like that. That long, sad night, following the day he had received his honor, bestowed for gallant service to King and country in his stone frigate way out in the wilds of Scotland. Sir Gerald. And she, Lady Fiona. She wanted so much for him to possess her, for all the wrong reasons, because she felt guilty at having a title thrust upon her, because he had done so much to make her happy and had received so little in return, for reasons confused, for reasons never quite understood. But he couldn't possess her. Nothing she could do would help him perform. And he had told her, gentle as a father, about his first wife, Ursula, whom he'd watched die in childbirth trying to deliver her first child. His child. He hadn't the will to risk it again. He was not a coward, but a gentle man. She'd often thought since then when she heard people ridicule his service career through jealousy or malice, that perhaps he'd avoided direct conflict just because he couldn't himself inflict pain or be the cause of it, just because he knew he would be impotent in action yet still love his country and the things for which it stood. Her burned finger wasn't burned very much, but she continued to pretend that it was, letting him soothe and comfort her and at the same time soothe and comfort himself, bringing his face gently to rest at the parting of her wrap and tenderly kissing her above her right breast. No more. But it was enough for him. And in its muted way, enough for her.

"I love you very much, Fiona," he said. "You're still very beautiful."

"So you should," she told him. "I'm more than you deserve, you silly old coot. Now, what are you going to do about that bloody steward?"

It was shortly after nine when the boy-girl was brought into the Captain's day cabin by one of the *Queen Dee*'s two Masters-at-Arms. Captain Corlett looked at the cold, bruised, hirsute creature, and felt a little disappointed that the last stowaway likely to feel the rough edge of his tongue looked more in need of sympathy than abuse. He tried to put himself in a sympathetic frame of mind, fighting thoughts of retirement, quelling his natural resentment at being confronted with the great unwashed, even discounting his regular Sunday irritation at having to abide the airs and graces of the first-class passengers dolled up for Divine Service in a way that so affronted his simple seaman's faith. But it was no good. The creature in front of him was failing abysmally to kindle any spark of understanding.

"Are you the captain?" the girl-boy spluttered.

"I am, and I want you to give me a full account of yourself."

"One of your officers beat me up and left me for days in some stinking hole down by the engines. I want to see a lawyer. He ought to be sent to prison for ten years for what he did to me!" The Master-at-Arms put out a restraining hand, and was immediately confronted by a tousled, ruddy face. "Don't you start! Lay off me, or there'll be trouble!"

The Master rang for Daisy Bell. "George, ask Mr. Welch to join us, please." And when the steward had left, he turned to stare some more at the wretched youngster. "I'm asking the officer who detained you to be present at the interview; then maybe we shall establish all the facts."

"There's a good chance of that, isn't there? You really think he's going to tell you the truth?"

"For a start, let's see if *you're* going to tell me the truth," the Master said, doodling a ballpoint pen over his desk pad. "What's your name?"

"Larry Hampton."

Captain Corlett heaved a sigh of relief. They had at least established the boy-girl's sex. "And your age, Mr. Hampton?" he asked, trying to check his sarcasm. Young people, he had learned by experience, were not susceptible to sarcasm.

"Seventeen." The youth hesitated. "Sixteen and a half."

The Master-at-Arms took a step forward. "With your permission, sir. I've been through his belongings. There's no passport. Apart from a few items of clothing he appears to carry nothing that might establish his identity except this notebook."

Captain Corlett took the dog-eared scraps of paper. "Larry

Hampton. Twenty-one Low Fell. Esher. Surrey. England. That's your home?"

"Yes. That's my home," the boy said sullenly.

"And you live there with your mother and father?"

"Yes."

"Do they know where you are?"

"No, they don't know where I am."

The Master's face tautened a little around the mouth. "And you're not concerned that they may be worried about you?"

"So, they're worried." He stood looking sullenly at the Master, refusing to answer further questions until the arrival of the Chief Officer helped him find his voice again. "That's him! That's the bastard who beat me up and left me down there in that stinking hole!" he shouted.

"Now understand this, young man," the Master said sternly, "you'll be put down there again if you don't cooperate with me in establishing all the facts I need to know."

"He banged my head about on an iron wall. Look, you can see where he messed my face up with his ring. Then he kept kicking me in the balls. I can hardly stand on my feet."

"Then perhaps you would like to sit," the Master said, indicating a chair. He turned to the Chief Officer. "Let me have your account of the incident, please, Chief."

"I was making my rounds at five-ten hours this morning when I discovered this person in the gentlemen's changing room near the swimming pool on the Promenade Deck. He had apparently broken in and was living on foodstuffs stolen from the ship's pantries. I asked him to account for himself. This he refused to do and became violent. I had to restrain him, sir. In the interest of the ship's safety, and his own."

"What about this?" the boy interrupted, pointing to his swollen cheek, dark with congealed blood.

"You fell down the aft companionway on B Deck trying to evade me, and struck your cheek on the handle of a linen-cupboard door. Don't you remember?"

"No, I don't remember! What I remember is you grinding that whopping big ring into my face."

The Chief Officer smiled tolerantly and extended both his hands. "You must be mistaken. See for yourself. I don't wear a ring."

The youngster protested that the Chief Officer was lying, but the Master, having no alternative but to support his officer, reminded the boy that he had committed an offense under the Merchant Shipping Act, that the police would be notified, and on his return to England a prosecution would doubtless follow. "I intend handing you over to the British authorities in Gibraltar and having you packed off home," he said sternly, elaborating the instructions for the Master-at-Arms. "Advise Gibraltar we'll be delivering him by ship's boat and the company may want to proffer charges. Until we get there, providing he behaves himself, fix him up with a DBS."

"What's a DBS?" the boy asked suspiciously.

"More than you deserve, lad. A spare berth in the crew's quarters for any distressed British seaman we need to help along the way. But watch it! Or you'll be back in the paint locker."

The moment the boy had gone, the Master turned his sarcasm on his Chief Officer. "I'm sorry the lad should have caused you so much trouble, Mr. Welch. One wouldn't have thought that such a long-haired weirdy could have behaved so violently."

"You could see for yourself how undisciplined he was, sir."

"Yes, indeed I could. And you decided to discipline him, is that it?"

The man refused to admit an error of judgment. "As I said in my report, sir, he became violent and I had to restrain him."

"For the safety of the ship. Is that correct, Mr. Welch?" The leathery face scanned the notes in front of him on the desk.

"Yes, sir. For the safety of the ship. And for his own safety. He might have broken a limb falling down a companionway. Or in the mood he was in, he might have gone over the side."

"As it was, he now has only a broken face." The small blue eyes shifted to focus on the Chief's right hand. "You may return now to your cabin, Mister, and replace your ring. Or do you wish to tell me that the ridge below the knuckle on your second finger was also caused while acting in the interests of ship's safety?"

The Chief Officer's face flushed with temper. "Thank you, sir," he said, in a voice calculated to display his contempt for the rebuke, and left the cabin.

Captain Corlett opened a fresh tin of tobacco and began packing his pipe. He wished he could deal with his Chief Officer as easily as he could deal with some wretched kid who'd run away from home. But he couldn't. Chief Officer David Welch was no longer a boy; he was a man, with a man's buffeting and cosseting by life. He might prove to be the best deck officer B and E Lines ever had, and he might not. But whatever personality limitations he possessed, he'd possessed them for a long time, and no homily now from the Master, or from any other senior officer, would change them. The man would defend his character like a woman her honor. It was, after all, the safety of the ship that mattered, not the comfort of some young lout who'd boarded her illegally. All the same, he had no liking for bastards such as Welch. They were the kind who would always press just that bit too hard, stop at nothing on the right side of the law to get a conviction if they were a cop, grind the smallest competitor into the dust just for the hell of it if they were in business. He wondered how many real friends a man like Welch had. Perhaps he thought he could get on without them. So unlike poor old Ben, who hadn't made an enemy in his life: then, in his prime, when he had every right to be thinking of taking over as Master, to be struck down with something so profoundly final as cancer. The love of God just didn't make sense. It made a mockery of justice. He sucked on his pipe and contemplated whether or not Ben would reap joy in the next world and his Chief Officer get his deserts, and told himself he was a sentimental old fool to admit in the space age that there was another world; but it was what he had been taught to believe when he was a lad, and now he was no longer young it was a comfort to go on believing it, even if it wasn't fashionable to do so. He began pacing the cabin, looking out occasionally at the leaden sea which was building steadily into great hills and valleys of water with the increasing force of wind. And when he had communed enough with nature, he knocked out his pipe. It was just the day for Divine Service. He'd try giving them a bit of hellfire.

"O most powerful and glorious Lord God, at whose command the winds blow and lift up the waves of the sea, and who stillest the rage thereof: we, thy creatures, but miserable sinners . . ."

There were about a hundred and thirty passengers gathered in the cinema on B Deck to partake of morning prayer. A few had come because without it they would not be sustained. Others were there to see who else was there. And the rest, unable to sun themselves on the decks, or to start drinking decently before eleven, were there for want of anything else to do. Richard comforted himself with the thought that he was there because it made Dearest happy. She had been to church regularly since his father's death, once every other week, and although she said she didn't think she could ever believe it all, it was, they both agreed, a nice thing to do. Although there was nothing particularly nice about standing in a cinema singing hymns and listening to the old codger on the stage stumble through the small print in the Book of Common Prayer.

". . . and that we may return in safety to enjoy the blessings of the land, with the fruits of our labors, and with a thankful remembrance of . . ."

Richard was far more interested in the girl standing next to him, trying to join the recorded singing of "Eternal Father." She was about his own age. Dark, with an oval face. Like a medieval madonna, he thought. But her clothes were not very madonnaish. Gray skirt, a striped dark-green, canary and beige sweater, dark blue leather jacket, knitted socks and beret in burnt-yellow. And she spoke French. He had heard her whispering in French to the gaunt, silver-haired woman who accompanied her. He couldn't keep his eyes off her. The clothes were real gear. He began wondering why he hadn't spotted her before; there were so few people his own age on board, he couldn't understand how he'd missed her. Then he remembered that Divine Service was for first and tourist classes together, a kind of token acknowledgment that all men were created equal. He began wondering if he'd see her again before next Sunday. Perhaps ashore, in Villefranche or Athens. It was just his luck that Dearest wanted to travel first class. How did one strike up a conversation with a smashing girl like that when one was in the wrong class? He let his eyes steal round to have another look at her. And she had slinky eyes, too. More. She had deliberately pressed her arm against his. There was no mistaking the movement. It was a come-on, all right. He felt his face go scarlet with shame. It might be a cinema, but it was supposed to be a church, and perhaps God could see.

"The Grace of the Lord Jesus Christ and the love of God, and the fellowship of the Holy Ghost, be with us all evermore. Amen."

They were coming out into the brightly lit shopping arcade, Richard with an image of Jesus whipping the Temple traders from the forecourt, Dearest on his left and this French chick with her Dearest on his right, when something came over him —perhaps Jesus—and he was asking *"Parlez-vous Anglais?"*

"Yes. I'm told I speak it very well," she said without false modesty. "I've been living in England for the past three years with my aunt. But you speak French, no?"

"Un peu." Then he stopped trying. "But I can't think in French. I'll have to live in France for a long time before I can do that, won't I?"

They were looking in the shops, instinctively not wanting to part, and the two adults were exchanging pleasantries, having nothing in common but aware that their charges were attracted to each other, calculating if it was prudent to encourage the meeting or, if it was not, if there was anything they could do about it anyhow.

Mrs. Westcott made the first move. "Richard, dear, the noise from those amplifiers has given me a headache. I'm going to my cabin to lie down for a while. What do you want to do?"

This was the first time anyone had come between him and Dearest. He felt it was his duty to escort her to her cabin, to make sure she had an aspirin, to be there to comfort her; but instead he let her walk away alone. He hoped like hell it was what she wanted him to do. "Would you like a cup of coffee?" he asked, turning his attention on the lovely little thing from France.

"I'd prefer a Coke," she said. And the worst was over.

She told him her name was Simone Otard. Her uncle was in the diplomatic service, attached to the Embassy in London, but at a very low level; and as civil servants were very poorly paid in every country of the world, that's why they were trav-

eling tourist class. It embarrassed Richard that she felt it necessary to excuse life on limited means. He'd thought so little
about money that although it would now be easy to ask Dearest
for a larger allowance than a couple of quid a week, he was still
wearing the gray flannels and the shirts and the herringbone
jacket he was wearing at Tor Beeches two years ago. He
wanted to buy new things, perhaps mad things like the Mods,
but he didn't know what; and his essentials, like socks and underpants, still came via one of Dearest's West End accounts.

"Where is your uncle now?" he asked.

"In London. Working. My aunt suffers a lot from bronchitis,
and the English winter was too much for her this year. The
doctor suggested a cruise. I'm looking after her. Isn't that a
nice job?"

Richard said yes, it was, and followed them through a watertight door aft to the tourist accommodation. He at once wished
he and Dearest were traveling tourist. It sparkled with life,
the public rooms bold and colorful in design, and the people
for the most part young and colorful to match. They sat at a table near a window, the aunt between them, looking out to sea.
This was a development Richard had not anticipated. He
thought the aunt was going to make some excuse to leave them
alone, like Dearest had. But she didn't. She sat right there between them like a big, black bird, and instead of concentrating
on how best to tackle her intrusion, his mind kept on making
up childish puns about *"la plume de ma tante."*

"My brother, Gaston, is at home now in Paris cramming for
his *bac*. Poor boy! We all hope he'll be going to the X. Papa has
a little influence, you see."

He came out of his daydream. "What's the X?" he asked.

"The Ecole Polytechnique," she said, surprised he did not
know. "It's the most important school in France. It's like finishing your education at Cambridge and Imperial College in
England, or Harvard and the Massachusetts Institute of Tech-
nology in the States. It combines the arts with the sciences.
Astrophysics. There's a good example of scientific culture
which enriches the mind."

The aunt sipped *thé au citron* and asked him if he had finished his studies and was he going into industry or government?
He said he was thinking very carefully about his future, which

was a lie, because he'd just been killing time, having given up the race for a university place and not certain which direction to take to equip himself for industry or government—or neither.

"What does your father want you to do?" she asked.

"I haven't got a father," he said, an edge to his voice that he hoped would hurt her more than her question hurt him any more. He was fagged out with people shedding crocodile tears over a lad without a dad, when for most of the time he had had one he hadn't seen him. When Richard hadn't been in the monastical seclusion of Tor Beeches, Dad had been in the monastical seclusion of his office, working like mad to keep him there. He hoped that when he was nineteen, twenty-one or forty, he wouldn't be on a similar hook, living just beyond his means, scratching away to make his kids better than himself. That kind of living didn't make sense. He found lots of things in the adult world didn't make sense which, he excused himself, was why he was so reticent to become a part of it.

"You poor boy," the aunt said. "How difficult for your mother." After that, she seemed to lose interest in him, sipping her tea and staring out at the sea, which one moment appeared to be on top of the ship and the next, underneath it, almost as though it wasn't there at all. Presently, after she had stared too long, the aunt said, "I'm not feeling very well, Simone. This movement is most vexing. I'm going to the pharmacy for something to calm my stomach. You stay here with your young friend. I won't be long."

The moment she had gone Simone said, 'Ah, *les croulants!* The same in Paris, London, Berlin, Rome . . . everywhere. They think we are all Peter Pans, and the world we live in is not the same as theirs. At the *loco* on the Rue Leoville there is a special enclosure for anyone over twenty. If I had my way, anyone over twenty would be kept out all together. Old people make me feel creepy, don't they you?"

Richard hadn't exactly thought about age, but he said, "They're all right if they let you run your own life."

She took out a packet of Gitanes. "You like French cigarettes?"

"I . . . er . . ." He was about to say he didn't smoke; but

how could he to this doll? He played it big and called a steward
for a book of matches.

"What's black and white and crawls along in the gutter?" she
asked him, and when he had no idea, laughed without spite or
disrespect, "A spastic nun!" And he told her the story of the
duck that couldn't get up for down, and realized her English
was not that good, and neither was his story, and began to feel
he'd never be able to cope with a girl who was so obviously—
how did she say it?—*dans le coup*.

"Let's get out of here before my horrid old aunt returns,"
she said.

He was a little shocked and wondered when he'd start treating Dearest like this. "If you think she won't mind," he said.

"Mind! She'll pee in her drawers!"

They left the Assembly Room and went aft on the Promenade
Deck, but it was too cold and windy to stay there more than a
few moments, to fill the lungs to bursting with spray-fresh air
and strain their eyes eastward for a first glimpse of Spanish soil.
But none could be glimpsed. The horizon was a mountain
range of leaden sea, scored by the wind like plowed and har-
rowed land. Simone lost her cigarette in a sudden gust, and
they chased it frantically along the deck, catching it in the scup-
per. They both made a grab for it, his hand touching hers, his
face a few inches from her face. She didn't seem to notice the
contact, but laughed and said she couldn't afford to lose a cig-
gie as her whole family was as mean as a Marseilles whore.
Richard had never thought about the parsimony of Marseilles
prostitution; he had never, in fact, thought about prostitution;
and all of a sudden the simple act of picking up a cigarette and
giving it back to her, crumpled but still alight, became a confusing, disturbing experience. The softness of her hand. A new
kind of smell, which might have been perfume, or a combination of the leather jacket with her own body smell. And quick
images of last night, of John touching him the way he had.

"Let's go play with the children," Simone said. "The old cow
won't think of looking for us there."

The Children's Playroom was immediately beneath the aft
docking bridge, overlooking the *Queen Dee*'s stern, thick with
cables and electric capstans. It was a clinically bright room, full

of balls and bricks and wooden trains and chalks and stuffed
bears and pictures of Donald Duck on the moon. A stewardess,
in hospital white and blue, was doing her best to prevent a
dozen youngsters from wrecking the train with the youngest
youngster in it. She seemed surprised by Simone and Richard's
presence, but was grateful for the distraction they created.
Simone took a moppet to a peg block where it could vent its
destructive urge with a mallet, while Richard was befriended
by two wide-eyed little boys whom he thought were twins but
who turned out to be strangers to each other.

"Whose daddy are you?" one of the little kids asked.

"I'm his daddy," Richard said, pointing to a teddy bear in the
corner.

"No, you're not!" the littlest one said, "because he hasn't got
a daddy. He told me so."

Richard had vague longings that he was not an only child,
that he'd grown up in a big family with little brothers and little sisters and big brothers and big sisters. He shouldn't have
tried to fool the child. It was looking at him with such a depth
of disappointment at the deceit that he was afraid for a moment it was going to cry.

"If poor Teddy hasn't got a daddy, we must play ball with
him, mustn't we?" he said.

He sat on the floor with the teddy between his legs, and the
two little boys rolled a red plastic ball for the teddy to kick
back to them. He felt a bit of a daddyless teddy himself, sitting
there in the playroom of the *Queen Dee* with months of wasted
time behind him and the prospects of more wasted months
ahead. Perhaps he should have another crack at his A levels
and then try for physics at Cambridge. It still wasn't too late.

"You make a good goal-keeper," Simone said, preventing her
charge from hammering a peg through the plastic floor.

"Scrum-half, actually."

"Will you play professionally?"

"I'm not that good," he said.

"What do you want to do?"

"Haven't given it much thought. Don't know what I'd be
good at. Probably make a boob of it, whatever it was."

"You? *Faire le bide?* Never!"

It was a funny morning, unlike any he had spent in his whole life, playing on a nursery floor in an Atlantic wilderness, his mind confused with thoughts of parenthood, of a French girl intent on being his first-ever date, of an American boy who was throwing everything out of focus by wanting him like boys wanted girls and being so decent about it. It was John's utter decency that most worried Richard. He was so unlike the perverts he'd been warned about; men who'd buy him sweets, take him for rides in their cars, or pounce on him like things that go bang in the night. He liked John. They were getting along just fine together, until—

"Richard, you are a fool!"

Simone was laughing at him. Suddenly he was aware of himself, the himself the rest of the world saw, rolling over the playroom floor with a giant teddy bear, oblivious of the two little kids staring at him with their big wide eyes, himself a little kid again. For one, quickly lost moment.

Business was brisk in the Americana. Mostly brandy to ward off the cold and settle the stomach. Raymond was in good form, a never-ending source of interesting, if useless, information as he supervised the dispensation and began working up the atmosphere to fever pitch for the midday ship's sweepstakes.

"There's a rogue born every minute, I say, Colonel. Only last trip we had to get rid of a couple of the lads for bleeding the monkey. They stole the best part of a cask of the company's own brandy before one of the pursers noticed someone'd been at it. Yes, there's a rogue born every minute. And they're not all this side of the bar."

The Colonel said, "The bounders. When I was on the northwest frontier, they'd have had their hands off for less. Not very practical though, eh? Not if you want any more work out of the blighters."

"No, sir, I suppose it's not," Raymond said. "Mind you, I'm a vindictive man myself. If someone did me some hurt, I'd be very vindictive. But I think I'd stop at hands."

On the far side of the bar several passengers were looking out to sea, watching the rise and fall of the waves, occasionally getting a glimpse of the blue-gray silhouette of Cape Finisterre. Sir Gerald had planted himself firmly in their midst, glass in hand, inviting questions and answering them almost before they had been asked. "That's her. The furthermost tip of Europe. If the visibility was better you'd be able to see more of the Spanish coast. Very much like Cornwall, of course, only more sun."

Doris Brewer's American voice asked anxiously, "Do you think the weather will start getting better now, Sir Gerald?"

They were all poised on his reply. Since they'd left Southampton the skies had been overcast, and now the wind seemed to be strengthening rather than slackening. What they all wanted of the spring cruise was sunshine: and they hadn't once yet seen the sun.

Sir Gerald said, "Halfway to Gibraltar now. Another couple of days and it will be all sunshine and blue seas."

"Another couple of days!" Mrs. Brewer wailed. "Kenneth, why didn't we fly to Ville . . . Ville . . . whatever the first stop is, and pick the cruise up there?"

"If you want my opinion," Sir Gerald went on, assuming that they did, "we'll be feeling the weather more for the next twenty-four hours. Been turning southerly most of the morning, taking the main force of wind on her starboard bow. Bound to roll a bit, although the stabilizers will help, of course. Not like a frigate in a high sea, though, Mrs. Brewer. I've known small craft running before the sea, broaching-to, and being capsized. Bow buries itself in the trough. Overtaking rush of water diminishes steering control, and that's it. Nasty business."

Mrs. Brewer agreed it was a nasty business, and if she hadn't been talking to royalty wouldn't have welcomed the answers she was getting to her questions at all. Sir Gerald was about to launch himself into a description of another navigational hazard when Raymond began tub-thumping for the final stages of the day's sweepstake. The bar was packed, refugees from the boredom of the windswept decks. Raymond beamed at his captive audience. It was going to be a good day.

"I've never gambled in my life before," Mrs. Westcott confided to the Colonel's wife, privately feeling that perhaps she shouldn't have started now, particularly on a Sunday. "I find it all so complicated."

Alice seemed to have the system at her fingertips. Everything depended on the previous day's mileage, and that would be relayed from the bridge shortly after midday, when the officer of the watch had made up the log. Tickets had been on sale at two shillings each since breakfast, and immediately after Divine Service a middle figure had been named and thirty numbers drawn, fifteen high field and fifteen low field, and anyone who wanted had put them up to auction and half what they got was theirs and the other half went into the pool; but Mrs. Westcott must have been born lucky, because she didn't have to bid as she was already in the high field.

"I see," said Mrs. Westcott, not seeing at all.

Raymond had a hot line to the bridge in his hand. "It's three-four-six, ladies and gentlemen. Some lucky passenger has just sailed three hundred and forty-six miles to get a jackpot of—" He put on a pair of heavy spectacles to read a note an assistant had pushed in front of him. "A jackpot of three hundred and sixty pounds."

There was a rustle as everyone checked their tickets. And Mrs. Westcott couldn't believe her eyes. She held the winning number. There would be smaller shares for ten others. Raymond would take ten percent of the stakes, which he daily assured passengers were dispatched to seamen's charities by none other than the Chief Purser—as though anyone would disbelieve a barman so patently honest as Raymond.

"I just can't believe it," Mrs. Westcott said. "I've never won anything before in my life. Arnold plays the pools occasionally, but he's never won more than a few pounds at a time. He only does it for relaxation. He works so hard at the office, you know. But I must be careful, mustn't I? Or it will go to my head and I'll get the itch, or whatever it is gamblers get, and it'll be the ruin of us all." Her voice was no longer saying what she was thinking, rattling on about things she thought people wanted her to rattle on about, while her mind was stabbed with repeated images of a taxi, of a living lovely Arnold being smashed under its wheels, once, twice, again, again, it never stopped hitting him, and she could see nothing but rubber tires, and blood, and her own vomit on her dress. She was being sick in public. Oh God, what a dreadful thing to do!

"Mrs. Westcott, are you all right? Ian, order her a little brandy. I think the surprise has been too much for her."

Colonel Jamieson lumbered through the crowd. They were standing in a circle around her, silly grins on all their faces. She wondered what Richard was doing. She'd share the winnings with him. He could buy himself lots of lovely things at the places they visited. Thank God, Arnold had left her Richard. Life had its mercies if one knew where to look for them.

"Here you are, Mrs. Westcott. This will soon have you back in the land of the living," the Colonel said, pushing a glass in her hand. "Nothing to be ashamed of. We're all feeling a bit squeamish in this weather, aren't we, Alice?"

She sipped the brandy slowly, forcing back the vomit. "I suppose I must buy drinks all round," she said. "Can someone . . . will . . ."

"Already done, madam," Raymond smiled. "Ship's tradition. I'll have your change, approximately three hundred and thirty pounds of it, in just a few moments. Is there anything else I can bring you? Olives? Crisps?"

"No, thank you." She sat, telling herself she should be madly excited at having won so much when she was least expecting it. But the money didn't seem to matter, the fun wasn't there any more. Perhaps if Richard had been with her instead of going off with that girl. Or even brother Fred, making his vulgar jokes after the first couple of pints. Fred would be better than this all-pervading loneliness.

"Mrs. Westcott, do you play bridge?" Alice asked. "Perhaps we could find you a partner. Ian so enjoys an occasional game with friends."

Captain Corlett was called to the bridge from the lunch table, just before his steak, by an urgent message from Second Officer Harry Hewson, who was at the time officer of the watch. There had been many occasions in the past when the authority of his command was needed on the bridge, to check a revised course laid off on the chart, the sighting of another large unscheduled vessel, a sudden deterioration in weather conditions; but he couldn't remember a previous occasion when he had been summoned from the table when his appetite so urgently needed to be appeased. It was good neither for the digestion nor for his temper.

"Sorry to disturb you during lunch, sir," Hewson greeted

him. "But I thought you should be alerted that the stabilizers aren't working."

"The devil they're not! What is it? Worn seals in the valves? Or an electrical fault?"

"Chief didn't say, sir. But he hopes to have them back in service within the hour."

"Hopes?" The Master was always testy before meals, and a steak snatched away before his eyes had made him doubly so. "Since when has the Chief Engineer been running the machinery on hopes? You can tell him I hope the engines are not going to quit on us as well. On second thought, I'll tell him myself."

But he didn't tell him for several minutes. Bob Herrington had been a good friend of many years' standing, and there was no point in giving him the edge of his hungry tongue for something he patently hadn't fixed on purpose and was doubtless sweating to put right. Instead, the Master did the practical thing of checking position, course, wind force and direction, current variation, and pondered the latest forecasts. When he did speak to the Chief Engineer, he was in an even temper again; but the news was no better for that. There was something wrong with the gyro transmission, and they'd be damned lucky to have the stabilizers working again that day—and perhaps not until they could call in a specialist's services at the next port of call.

"We'd best tack out of this beam sea," the Master told his Second Officer when he returned to the wheelhouse. "It'll put us behind schedule, but passenger comfort must come first, I suppose."

The wind and waves were thundering against the *Queen Dee*'s starboard freeboard with steadily increasing violence. Without her stabilizers, her roll was becoming more pronounced with every synchronous hill of water. If she were a smaller, more spritely ship, the bilge keels alone would be sufficient to reduce the rolling with an increase of speed. But the more sophisticated gyro-fins either worked as they were intended to work, or they were no damned use at all. The Master put on forty-five degrees of wheel to starboard, bringing her head toward wind and seaway, then, minutes later, reversed the wheel to complete the zigzag to port. When he was satisfied that the maneuver was reducing the extent of roll and that they were maintaining their mean course, he went over to the pub-lic-address system microphone on the main control panel be-hind him.

"This is your captain speaking. May I have your attention for a moment, please, ladies and gentlemen. As you are aware, the weather is not as clement as we might wish, but I have every reason to believe it is getting better. However, we are having a little difficulty limiting the rolling movement of the ship as the stabilizing equipment is temporarily out of action. This equipment consists of retracting fins which protrude from each side of the ship under the waterline amidships. The fins are controlled by two gyroscopes which decide the time of tilting and the amount of tilting necessary to counteract the rolling. It is these gyroscopes that are not functioning correctly. I want to emphasize that you are absolutely in no danger whatever. Every other piece of ship's machinery is functioning as it should. But until we are able to bring the stabilizers back into use or reach calmer waters, I regret you may experience a little discomfort from the ship's movement. Your cabin stewards will be pleased to advise you how to reduce the discomfort to a mini-mum."

Most of the passengers were at the coffee stage when the Mas-ter made his announcement. Had there been windows in the restaurant, all would have instinctively looked out to confirm that they were not sinking. Instead, they gazed morosely at the coffee cups and water glasses, convinced that every slight movement of the liquid from one side to the other was a sign of impending doom.

"Now in the U.S. Navy they favor anti-rolling tanks," Sir Gerald said, illustrating his lecture with a dessert spoon wedged precariously in a half-filled water glass. "Two tanks, you see, one on either side of the ship, and by varying the amount of water in each tank you can reduce the amplitude of the roll. Ingenious. Economic. And, I'm told, very successful."

Mrs. Radford said she thought it quite scandalous that the company could charge so much and then treat them to all the discomforts of a day trip across the Channel. Her husband said if the cruise didn't prove as beneficial to them as the brochure claimed it would be, he'd get a certificate from their doctor and sue the company for every penny they had. And Mrs. Brewer's husband said he guessed the Britishers would look after them all okay, and the best thing they could do right now was sleep off a damned good lunch—just in case it was their last.

They were leaving the table when Second Officer Hewson came from the elevators and stood briskly to attention before Sir Gerald. "The Chief Engineer's compliments, sir, and he asks if you would most generously allow him to avail himself of your experience. He understands our stabilizing gear is similar to that fitted in the *Ardmore*."

"Clancey and Moore? Capable of giving a torque of up to 144 foot-tons?"

"Yes, sir."

"Know it well. Of course, my boy, only too pleased if I can be of some assistance."

Lady Pratley cut across his bows. "Don't listen to the old coot," she said. "He doesn't know the front side of a stabilizer from the backside of a Sea Scout. And I'm telling you, he saw plenty of those when he was in the Navy."

Sir Gerald smiled royally. "Please forgive my wife," he said. "I'd promised her a game of cards this afternoon, and she's naturally disappointed that more important matters have come up."

"All right, you listen to me," her ladyship said. "This old coot sank more British battleships in the war than the Germans. If you let him loose in the engine rooms don't allow him near the plug, or whatever it is lets the water in, or he'll have us all down with him."

"Fiona, my pet," Sir Gerald smiled in anguish. "Why don't you spend the afternoon having your hair fixed, or a manicure, and I'll see you a little later?" He bowed himself away from the table and followed the Second Officer from the restaurant.

"How would you like it if your husband told you you looked a wreck?" her ladyship said, turning her attack on the nearest remaining victim, who happened to be Mrs. Radford. "Come to think of it, you are a wreck. Remind me to give you the address of a good *salon* when we get back to London."

The Chief Engineer was obviously relieved to see Sir Gerald accompanying the Second Officer. The Master had radioed London and the Marine Superintendent would be dragged from the seclusion of his Sunday dinner somewhere in the country and notified of the mishap. And the Chief Purser was even now notifying passengers that the Captain's cocktail party, traditionally held the third evening out—a kind of *hors d'oeuvre* to the more substantial Mediterranean fare to follow —had been postponed "owing to inclement weather." The Chief Purser had been at sea long enough to expect the worst, and to know how best to disguise it from the passengers with delicate phrases. By late afternoon, for all the canny touches the Master might give to the wheel, the customers' heads and stomachs would be getting the better of them; and Dr. Hammond, who at the best times was in everybody's mess but nobody's watch, would be rushed off his feet and making a pile for himself in the bargain, for all the ship's medical services were chargeable as extras. But worse would follow. They would have to steam full-ahead during the next couple of nights in order to make up for lost time, for to begin the scheduled stops late would foul up all the shore excursion arrangements, to say nothing of prereserved berths at Piraeus, Beirut and Naples. And if the galley packet proved right, there'd be at least a couple of hours' unscheduled delay at Gibraltar to put a stowaway ashore. If there was one thing that riled the Master, the Chief Purser, the Chief Engineer and every other old-timer on the *Queen Dee*, it was being expected to keep to a schedule like some damned bus service because the London moneybags said so. Not that the old man would take instructions from anyone if the safety of the ship was at stake. But since B and E had turned over their surplus tonnage to cruising, the holiday-camp mentality had begun to pervade everything. There was something positively indecent, the Chief Purser thought, in a gentleman like himself being expected to concern himself with the safety of donkey rides in Capri for a lot of middle-aged matrons with more money than sense.

"Sir Gerald, this is most generous of you to offer us the benefit of your advice," the Chief Engineer said, taking the claret-mellowed sea-dog by the arm. "It suddenly occurred to me that as you were advising the company on the *Ardmore* refit, you might not object to—"

"My dear Herrington, why should I object? In my advisory capacity with Fomona it's my duty and my pleasure to be of service to member companies whenever possible. Besides, between you and me, I find I don't make a very good passenger. Nothing to do except entertain the ladies."

The Chief Engineer was soon to discover that Sir Gerald was not going to be satisfied with merely giving advice. He was determined to take over the whole operation, delegating maintenance ratings as he thought best and proceeding to a complete dismantling of the port gyro hydraulic transmission unit. Men were recalled from their rest period. Sir Gerald donned a boiler suit. And the Chief Engineer fussed on the fringe with a service manual spread out in front of him, anxiously watching the removal of every nut and bolt and shaft.

"It won't be as difficult a job as I thought," Sir Gerald announced after the first hour, face red and wet with sweat, hands black with grease.

It was precisely at this moment that the Chief Engineer had serious doubts about his decision to seek Sir Gerald's advice in the first place. But worse was to come.

"Nothing wrong with the transmission," Sir Gerald announced at the end of the second hour, confirming what the Chief Engineer had anticipated from the start. "You know what I suspect? Wrong grade of oil put in when she was last serviced. Filter looks clean enough outside, but my guess is we'll find her completely stopped up on the inside with heavy deposits. Right. You two men, let's have a chain under there. Cradle her while I have a closer look."

"Won't you let me do it, Sir Gerald?" the Chief Engineer asked hopefully.

But Sir Gerald was already on his back, slithering himself into a position that would have been difficult for a man half his age. "Too much movement to get this lot realigned correctly." His voice came from the dark cavern of machinery, hollow and a little breathless. "Kindly ask the bridge to heave to with the sea lying on the bow." He didn't doubt for a moment that the Master might not want to heave to. It was an order he expected to be obeyed.

The request put Captain Corlett in a quandary. He was angry with Herrington for seeking Sir Gerald's advice without first referring the matter to him. If the Chief Engineer's staff was so underqualified that they couldn't fix the stabilizers themselves, then the proper course of action was to await instructions from London as to whether or not the work should be done at the next port of call. On the other hand, Sir Gerald was a close friend of Sir Edgar, and had apparently well satisfied the company with his supervision of the *Ardmore* refit. If the stabilizers could be brought back into action before the passengers succumbed to the worst of the westerly winds and mountainous sea, it would be at least a job well done, businesswise.

"Bring her round to two hundred and eighty, Second," he ordered. "Try holding her at thirty-five revs. Let's hope she doesn't start pitching too much."

Second Officer Hewson knew it was not an order the Master had given willingly. It was the first time in all the years he'd been sailing on the *Queen Dee* that he'd known Ted Corlett to allow anyone else to influence his judgment. He saw to it that the Quartermaster carried out the orders, and when the old *Queen* had her head toward the oncoming dunes of water, pitching gently but no longer in a roll, he went to lay off the course. It was all too common a mistake to make insufficient allowance for leeway, particularly in a prolonged gale, when in addition to the wind there were surface currents caused by it. Cases abounded of ships having gone aground through failure to make sufficient allowance for leeway in the course steered. He checked and doublechecked the figures. He was damned if he'd give that bastard Welch another excuse to choke him off when he took over the watch.

"Easy now! We're almost there." Sir Gerald lay on his back under the labyrinth of steel, the vast weight of the port gyro suspended above him with blocks and tackle. Farther aft in the machinery space the engines had quieted to a steady rumble. The ship's movement had steadied to a one-directional pitch of some fifty seconds' duration. It was just at this moment, when Sir Gerald apparently had everything under control, that the tackle slipped, paused, held for an infinite part of a second, and then let go the grim mass of steel with a metallic scream. At first the Chief Engineer thought it was Sir Gerald who had screamed; but the blow had been instantaneous, pushing the over-fed, under-exercised body to one side and leaving the left arm trapped under a shaft three times its own circumference. Sir Gerald lay there, face ashen, eyes closed, immobile.

"For Christ's sake, get the arm free before anything else shifts!" the Chief Engineer shouted, fearful that the next pitch might put the whole ship into another roll and Sir Gerald's whole body be crushed by a sideways movement of the disconnected filters. "And get the ship's doctor here immediately."

It took nearly an hour to free the trapped arm, four ratings working with crowbars and wrenches until their chests and backs sweated dark pools through their clothing; and during the whole time Sir Gerald, mercifully, remained unconscious, pumped full of morphine by the doctor, his head gently cradled in blankets by a nurse. By the time his plump, limp, boiler-suited flesh had been transported up to the quiet cleanliness of the ship's hospital, the Chief Engineer was quite certain of one thing. It was going to be a long time before the *Queen Dee*'s stabilizers were working properly again. They'd have to weather the storm without them.

Lady Pratley was under a hair dryer when she heard about the accident. "I want our own doctor flown out here at once," she told Dr. Hammond.

"I'm afraid that's not possible, Lady Pratley. We're not on an aircraft-carrier," he said, refusing to be intimidated by her ladyship's attack.

"Then he must be taken ashore," she said. "He's to have the best attention. I'm not going to have my husband butchered by some ship's quack."

"He *is* having the best attention. I've X-rayed the hand and arm, and I'm pleased to say there're no broken bones. The injuries—"

"Of course there're broken bones," she interrupted him. "At his age bones snap like matchsticks."

Dr. Hammond said patiently, "I assure you, Lady Pratley, there are no breaks or fractures. The damage is confined to lacerations and bruising, and a certain amount of shock. He was very lucky. I have him under sedation now, and it would be advisable for him not to be moved for perhaps a couple of days. But by the time we reach Villefranche he'll be running about in the sunshine like a ten-year-old."

"Good God! If you're going to rejuvenate him, I'm taking him out of here with me now," she said. "He's more trouble than he's worth as it is, without you giving him monkey glands."

Dr. Hammond said humorlessly, "You can see him for a few minutes, but what he most needs is rest."

She went into the tiny white ward and found him lying on his back with the freshly crisp linen tucked under his chin. He didn't see her at first, or hear her—the effects of the sedation or of age. She saw the pallor of his skin, the listless eyes, and realized more than at any time the sheer weight of physical age that separated them, and always had. "You silly old coot," she said. "Didn't I tell you you'd make a balls of it."

When Chief Officer David Welch went onto the bridge to take over the watch from Hewson, he found Captain Corlett still there personally handing out orders and glaring moodily through the clear-view screen at the gray wetness beyond.

"The old man's in a filthy temper, so watch out for his tongue," Hewson said as he finished making up his log. "We've been farting around most of the afternoon, and now we're back on course he's pushing her all out to make up time. To hell with passenger comfort!"

"They're a pack of fools in the engine room to have let that happen to Sir Gerald."

There was no mistaking the Second Officer's resentment. "Herrington runs the best engine room in the fleet. Most of his senior men have been with him for fifteen years or more."

"Perhaps that's the trouble." The Chief Officer looked around from the course recorder. "Perhaps they need some new blood down there as well."

The next hour passed in stony silence, Climpson at the wheel and Third Officer Tyson with his head stuck like an ostrich in the radar sweep; and on the starboard side of the wheelhouse, the Master, immobile, sulking or thinking or both and staring straight ahead, while the Chief Officer fought against the gloom by keeping up an almost constant telephone contact with the lookouts, a display of cheerful efficiency that rapidly developed into a battle of nerves between himself and the Master. And the whole time the *Queen Dee*, bang on course, cut swiftly through leaden sea, pitching and rolling in the wind-whipped beam, almost as though the Master enjoyed playing God, punishing the damned below in a hell of heaving, swaying, overheated plastic-veneered boxes for living.

"If you're afraid the for'ard lookout's lonely, Mister, I suggest you go up there and join him. Let him tell you when he has something to report. Bainbridge is a good man. I've known him since he was deck boy."

The Chief Officer had it on the tip of his tongue to remind the old sod that lookout efficiency could be greatly improved by encouragement from the officer of the watch: but instead he merely said, "As you wish, sir."

After a few minutes, the Master said, "You came straight into the service as a cadet from college, I take it. It's no longer fashionable for officers to earn their tickets the hard way. Up from the decks."

"I'm old enough to remember the war, sir. H.M.S. *Manston*. Discharged in forty-seven with rank of Petty Officer." It was on the tip of his tongue to tell him about their mad skipper, potting off floating mines at a couple of hundred yards' range, until the cook threw up in despair at ever serving dinner. But he kept his reminiscences to himself.

"We all remember the war, except the youngsters. You've weathered well. Or maybe you haven't had to work for a living like most of us?"

He saw Tyson look up from the sweep, embarrassed by the public caviling. "I've had my good times and my bad times, like most men, sir. I wouldn't want anyone to think I was born with a golden spoon in my mouth."

The Master pressed his face nearer the clear-view. It was as much a pretense as his Chief Officer's constant flow of calls to the lookouts had been. "H'm, h'm. I hear the annual subscription to the Mizzen Club is twenty-five guineas these days. Bit out of my range; but then I'm not single. Haven't been for forty-four years."

The Chief Officer could feel the waves of resentment breaking over him. The Master was still smoldering because he'd failed to get his whole life story out of him; because he was on more than nodding terms with both Sir Gerald and Lady Pratley; because he'd been put in the job without the Master being consulted; because he wasn't Ben Wilson; because he was there at all. Well, he *was* there, and he was bloody well going to do the job he was paid to do, and with luck he'd still be doing it when the old sod was decomposing six feet under. The other

officers, Hewson, Rigg, young Tyson, seemed to accept him even
if they didn't like him. Why the hell not! He knew his job, they
knew their jobs, and that's all the company expected of them.
But this old sod—the sooner Arkwright replaced him, the better. Len Arkwright was a good fellow: they saw eye to eye with
each other.

"Begging your pardon, Mr. Welch, but I thought you ought
to know that the passengers are not finding the conditions at all
comfortable." The Chief Purser's voice came through loud and
clear over the telephone from his office on B Deck. "Is there anything I can tell them? About weather conditions? Or the way
we'll be making for the next few hours?"

Captain Corlett could hear the conversation from where he
was standing near the clear-view. He turned for the first time in
more than an hour and took the telephone from the Chief Officer's hand. "Mr. Craddock, tell me your problem in ten words."

The Chief Purser said, "The movement's upsetting them,
Captain. In the tourist accommodation the stewards can't keep
up with the call for pots. It's going to be a thin restaurant for
dinner."

"Are you trying to give me orders?"

"Why no, of course not."

"Then to what do we owe the pleasure of this call?"
The Master's voice had a sarcastic rasp.

"I . . . I just thought you should know how the passengers
are."

"Thank you for the information. Now you can tell them that
we're trying to get them to sunshine and calmer waters just as
quickly as possible. And if any more of them think they can fix
the stabilizers, ask the doctor for a strait jacket and don't hesi-
tate to use it!"

That was it. He'd vented his temper on the one officer who
least deserved it. And although he hated himself for thinking
it, he was damned pleased Sir Gerald was in the sick bay with a
crushed arm. If he was the doctor, he'd have it off for him.

The restaurant was even thinner for dinner than the Chief
Purser had expected. After the first unstabilized onslaught,
those who would never find their sea-legs admitted defeat
and, with little spirit left in them for complaining to the pursers,

departed to their cabins with medicinal brandy and pills, in the vague hope that tomorrow the sea would be calm. Of the few who came down to dinner, half had not bothered to dress, and those who had were stoically going through the ritual because they had paid for first-class cuisine and were determined to have it, even if they threw it all up again afterward. The Chief Officer had only Colonel and Mrs. Jamieson, Miss Peebles and Mrs. Westcott at his table. The Aftons, teachers, were both confined to their beds, and the Earls, something in cosmetics, took one look at the menu and decided to adjourn to the Tudor Room for a quiet *Fernet Branca,* which they understood was just the job for such squeamish circumstances. Miss Peebles, however, was in splendid form. Not only did she go right through the menu, but did so while regaling the assembled company with a detailed plot outline of her next shocker which was to be about a lady social welfare worker who specialized in killing country parsons because of something one of them said (not did) to her as a child. Even the Colonel, one of her most ardent admirers, wilted over the soufflé during the fourth sacrilegious murder and took Alice off in search of a few rubbers of bridge. The Chief Officer looked across the vast area of unused table to Mrs. Westcott and wondered how much longer she would bear the brunt of Miss Peebles without wilting. He dreaded the thought of being left alone, defenseless, with that best-selling dinosaur.

Miss Peebles said, "What will you turn your hand to now that you've finished bringing up your family, Mrs. Westcott?"

Mrs. Westcott hadn't thought of turning her hand to anything, and said so, which was not good enough for Miss Peebles.

"I think it such a pity that these days people who do decide on families have such small ones," she went on with barren abandon. "After all, one child takes up as much of one's time as two or three, and it's just as effective in stymieing one's career. You ought to think about teaching domestic science. I know several colleges that are crying for the not-so-youngs with good family backgrounds."

The Chief Officer said, "I don't think you need to work for a living, do you, Mrs. Westcott?"

She smiled her thanks at him for the rescue operation and

said she was sure she'd always find something to keep her busy, even if it was only the housework.

"That is hardly the point," Miss Peebles said severely. "Women did not win their suffrage still to be dominated by the male half a century later. If you take my advice, you'll grasp your freedom with both hands. Get into a career, before it's too late."

The Chief Officer rose to his feet and said he had promised to initiate Mrs. Westcott into the mysteries of frog racing in the Tudor Room and would Miss Peebles excuse them? Miss Peebles, faced with impending isolation, ordered the cheese board and told the departing Mrs. Westcott that if she thought of anything else that might suit her, she'd let her know later.

"She's a bit much, isn't she?" the Chief Officer said when they were out of earshot. "I hope you didn't mind my making up that bit about the frog racing to get you out of it."

"Not in the least," she said. "I'd like to be initiated. I've never raced a frog in my life."

She realized too late that she had virtually invited his company, when perhaps he had more important things to do than look after a lonely widow. She told herself that in fairness she should plead a headache and let him off the hook, but she had been fighting against sea-sickness all day and had triumphantly beaten it, and now she wanted to enjoy her triumph.

On the way out of the restaurant they passed John eating by himself. "Richard's not sick, is he?" she asked anxiously. "I've been making him swallow tablets all day. They've kept me on my two pins."

John got politely to his feet. "I guess he's fine, Mrs. Westcott. He's gone to see the early movie."

"By himself?"

"I saw it last night, and they're not putting on a new show until tomorrow."

She could tell by the hesitancy in his voice that he hoped there were not going to be any more questions. Boys were all alike, covering up for each other's exploits. Poor John, all by himself. It was quite obvious that Richard had run off after the French girl he'd met that morning. Such a pity. If only he could be content with John's company. He seemed so young to be taking an interest in girls; but then, children developed so much more quickly these days. All the same, it hurt her to see Richard putting away childish things. Why did it have to end so soon? This mad, mad urge to be grown up. He was flinging himself into that sad, fast-moving, noisy world of teenage insecurity, full of so much disillusionment and heartache, and she, like every other mother before her, was powerless to protect him from it. Sooner or later he'd find the right girl, or maybe the wrong girl, settle into a job, become quieter, more mellow, contented with his lot, clinging to the few unshattered illusions that remained, like everyone else. No, she wouldn't want to relive her young life again: those dreadful in-between years, wondering how, when, and where one was going to be flung into the adult world.

"You'll have to find yourself a girlfriend too," she told John, and left him to finish his meal.

Few passengers had the stomach for frog racing, and after the first twenty minutes the red-faced young assistant purser who had been delegated to organize the meet was forced to admit defeat. Mrs. Westcott had lost two pounds, and the Chief Officer had won five. They were still standing at the table after the red-faced young man had packed up the cardboard reptiles, she at a loss what to do next, he wondering how much longer it was his duty to entertain her.

"Would you like to dance, Mrs. Westcott? Or maybe a drink?" he asked.

"I could do with a drink," she said. "But no dancing, please. The feet are willing, but I'm not so sure about the tum."

He took her along to the Orchard Room where, he said, she was less likely to feel the pitch and roll of the ship. She chose brandy with soda, and he took it neat. They sat in awkward silence while the steward served them, and remained silent for some moments after he had gone, neither knowing what to talk about now they were away from the social formality of the restaurant.

"I do hope I'm not keeping you from your duties," she said.

"I assure you, no. I've finished now until four."

"*Four?* In the morning?"

"Tradition, Mrs. Westcott. Chief Officer takes four-to-eight watch, morning and afternoon. They're the best times. Providing you don't keep too many late nights."

"You don't give the impression of being the kind of man who needs much sleep, Mr. Welch. Like my late husband. Arnold could sit up working on an idea for Dough Boy—he was in bread, you know—until the small hours, hardly get his head on the pillow, and then be off with a briefcase full of papers for a nine-thirty conference."

He hoped she wasn't going to carry on about dead Arnold all evening. There was something positively indecent about it, she looking not a day over thirty, fine auburn hair swept up in coils, a well-kept figure discreetly displayed by a long gown in navy and white crushed silk, with a son old enough to have kids of his own, and a husband little more than a year cold. Grass widows he could handle. Well. But the genuine thing had him all at sixes and sevens.

He said, "Is this your first sea voyage? I'm sorry, I asked you that last night."

"You must find it very confusing having to meet so many people as part of your job. I have a terrible memory for names. The faces I recognize at once, but I can never remember what they're called."

"My old man had an infallible method. He used an indelible pencil on them. They were pigs."

She laughed. "I can't imagine you as a farmer's boy. What made you run away to sea?"

"The war. It made a lot of us do things we hadn't planned to do."

She hoped he wasn't going to carry on about the war all evening. It didn't make sense, him in the Navy—how long ago was it?—twenty-five years? He didn't look much more than thirty now. Just out of the boyish stage, a man with eyes that didn't shift when you caught them, a man with the confidence of experience. He could have been only a kid, playing at war, like Richard growing up: pray God he and his generation wouldn't be involved in another holocaust. Occasionally, when she was alone, like this past year, she woke up in the early hours disturbed by some echo of the violence of the forties, unable to place the detail that something deep inside her was refusing to forget. Perhaps one of the great blessings in life was the ability to forget, really to forget, personal failures and disappointments, unkind words and deeds, periods of loneliness and depression, the death of a close friend or husband. If only she could be blessed!

"Do you like swimming?"

His voice cut through her meditation. "Very much. I was the half-mile backstroke champion at school."

"I don't think you'll be able to do half a mile in our pool. But it's not at all bad as ship's pools go. So I'm told. I'm the new boy around here, as you've probably gathered. If the wind drops during the night, the lads'll be getting it ready for the grand opening on Monday."

"What I'm really looking forward to is getting into the sea around Izmir. I'm told the water's warm, crystal clear, and calm as a millpond. I can't face putting a toe in the English Channel any more. These last few years my swimming has been almost wholly confined to the Bavistock Country Club."

"Old Bavers? Good Lord, I'm surprised we haven't met before. I've been a member for four years, or is it five? Fellow from Seaways Insurance introduced me. Clifford Martin."

Her face lit up. "I know Clifford. Played badminton with him at least a dozen times. And beat him. Perhaps you know the Humphries? Something or other in the B.B.C."

"I haven't had the pleasure. I can't get to the club as much as I'd like. This job makes me an unsociable bastard."

"Arnold thought it would be good for Richard if we joined. Meeting nice people with children the same age. It's a small world, isn't it? Sir Gerald and Lady Pratley are members, and do you know I never knew who they were until I saw her come down to dinner last night."

"How extraordinary!" he said, trying to sound surprised, not wanting her to guess that he knew damned well that Fiona was also a part of Old Bavers, that it was she who'd found him a convenient sponsor in young Martin.

Mrs. Westcott finished her brandy before he was half through his, and said she'd have another—for medicinal reasons. Then, after her second, she wanted a third—for fun. An hour ago he would have resented it, the way she was hanging on to him for company; but an hour ago he didn't know her so well. Now, instead of wanting to find the right excuse to ditch her, he was perfectly happy to sit in the softly lit seclusion and drink and talk and get to know her better. The women in his life had either been low-class sluts like Marigold or high-class ones like Fiona, depending on the bars or clubs where he'd picked them up. Officers were no different from ordinary seamen where the hazards of the job were concerned. It was a seaman's preordained lot to be lumbered with the wrong kind of woman, unless he wedded a willing little scrubber to tend the shore base called home and breed kids for him between voyages for God knows why. Mrs. Westcott was so unlike any other women he'd met. She wasn't making any physical demands on him. He could talk to her without worrying whether or not she expected him to make a pass. She was making an effort to sustain conversation, to understand him, to help him understand her, and that was something Fiona had never once tried to do, not even during their many long car journeys together. Mrs. Westcott had something he'd never experienced before, like a rare perfume, a kind of motherly virginity, and she fascinated him with her talk about badminton and other crazy English games, the Communization of underdeveloped countries, and the techniques of growing tomatoes, at which she had some expert knowledge.

"Big monstrous things. That's what people go for, so it's no wonder that they're stuffed like battery hens, tasteless lumps of red sponge. Unless you know the garden they've come from, you can't be sure of getting a good tomato anywhere these days. And the same goes for gooseberries. Now you tell me, Mr. Welch, when did you last taste a good goosegog?"

He found her very funny, trying to carry on a genteel conversation while getting pleasantly pickled on brandy. "I like goosegogs, but they don't like me," he said. "Here, your glass is empty. Let me get you another brandy."

"I almost wish the weather was rough every day," she said. "If I carry on like this I'll finish the voyage dipsy. I'm afraid I'm giving you a very bad impression, Mr. Welch. I'm not usually like this at all. My family always believed that gentlemen should hold their liquor and that ladies shouldn't be carrying any, anyway."

She knew what was happening to her, but she couldn't tell him, almost a total stranger, although he was a part of it, a part of her returning sensibility. For more than a year she had died a little, at first too grieved to make new friends, and then

too fearful of rebuff to make the effort. Now, all of a sudden, she
realized how easy it was to reach out and take a little of someone else's personality for oneself. For months she had told herself that Arnold would not want her to be locked away like this
in a prison of her own making, waiting until, if there be anything after death except oblivion, she might again share experi-
ences with him. If she had told herself once, she told herself a
thousand times that life must go on. But until tonight it had
stopped; and now, with the *Queen Dee* pitching and rolling
through a troubled sea, she felt a warmth and security that she
thought she had lost forever under the wheels of a taxi.

"Cigarettes were the cause of our family's downfall," the
Chief Officer told her. "Mother made a terrible scene when my
elder sister started smoking. I don't hold with such petty prejudices against the ladies myself. Although I think I'd draw the
line at them smoking cigars like some of the Dutch women."

"Or becoming sea captains?"

He laughed. "Good Lord, you don't mean that seriously, do
you? Shipping's about the only industry left that women
haven't got a foot in."

"There you are, you see. You are prejudiced. I knew it the
moment you went out of your way to deny it. Men are all alike
where women are concerned."

He laughed again. "Can you really imagine a ship this size
being taken round the world by an all-women crew?"

"No," she said, "but being a woman, I like to think it is possible."

"Being a mere man, permit me to tell you that I like you all
as you are. Illogical. Sometimes a little vain. Almost always
beautiful."

She sidestepped the flattery and asked him a direct question that he wasn't expecting. "Then why haven't you married
one of us, Mr. Welch?"

"Surely you've been told about sailors, Mrs. Westcott?" he
said, trying to joke his way out. "A girl in every port and a port
in every girl."

"Going to sea must be a very lonely life. For all of you."
She was suddenly sober again, full of the intense compassion
that often accompanies alcohol.

"Not really. There's always something to do. If not duty,

then pleasure. Are you sure you wouldn't like to dance now?"

"Yes, I think I would. I daren't drink any more tonight or I'll disgrace myself." She got unsteadily to her feet, and he had to hold her arm to prevent her falling. "The head is willing but I'm not so sure about the feet."

"It was the ship rolling," he lied, knowing damn well it was the liquor.

The walk aft to the Tudor Room was not easily negotiated, she dropping her evening bag, and he, on helping to pick it up, dropping her. The few couples they passed either pretended they were invisible or gave them that special look of condescension reserved for drunks. When they reached the floor, like the rest of the ship it was virtually deserted, the orchestra doing its best to make a cheerful noise, but to judge from the players' sallow faces a little under the weather themselves. He took her in his arms and she let him manipulate her around the floor like an outsized doll. A couple of stewards with nothing better to do stood watching the exhibition, amused, doubtless thinking that the Chief Officer was embarrassed when in fact he was finding his partner's abandon rather endearing. She was so obviously happy; and if the liquor had gone uncontrollably to her head, once she set herself firmly on her feet, only the nicest reflexes came to the surface. Like a child, she seemed quite unaware that she might be sexually desirable. She squeezed his hand in time to the music, clung to his broad shoulders when she stumbled, and giggled to herself at only half-explained memories that kept flooding through her mind; so that when his eyes could no longer avoid the barely concealed whiteness of her breasts held firm below the neckline of her gown, he looked at them without passion, satisfied by her sexless abandonment as no woman had ever satisfied him before. It was not until an hour later, after he had escorted her to the observation deck and seen her safely to her cabin door that he felt lonely without her. And he could have kicked himself for not even asking if she would like his company for the remainder of the night.

"Yes, sir, Mr. Welch, I'll have a bottle off the ice for you right away." Raymond was about to close down the Americana for want of custom, a thing he couldn't recall ever having to do at just eleven-forty-nine. By the slightest inflection of his voice he betrayed his surprise, not that someone should be ordering champagne at midnight, but that the someone should be the ship's Chief Officer. Raymond had heard through Daisy Bell's grapevine that the Chief was the kind of oddball who did things by the book on the bridge and with the tip of his boot when he was below decks. One thing was certain: the champagne was not for the poor bloody kid in the DBS. If the Chief Officer wanted champagne in the solitude of his quarters, a steward would take it to him; if he wanted it with one of the passengers, it would be served at table in this or one of the other bars; but if he wanted it in one of the passengers' cabins, flagrantly in defiance of company regulations and the code of a gentleman and a ship's officer, then he could still have it, only Raymond would do a little code-breaking himself to find out all there was to know. For Raymond had learned at a very early age that it was what you knew, not who you knew, that mattered. "There you are, Mr. Welch. Cold as an iceberg. Shall I put it on your mess chit?"

"No, I'll pay for it now." He glared at the barman, well aware of the hostility that existed between long-service staff and a newcomer like himself, trying to calculate just how hostile the man was. "What's the damage?"

"Twenty-eight shillings, Mr. Welch. I hope you enjoy it. It's very popular with the ladies, this one. Not too dry."

The Chief Officer dropped him thirty, and left before the provocation made him lose his temper. Raymond was not a man one would sensibly choose for an enemy, but there were limits to how much of his effrontery he was prepared to take. And that crack about the ladies was very nearly beyond the limits. He left the bar and walked for'ard along the deserted starboard corridor to the Rose Suite. He rang the bell and waited. Behind him he heard a door click and turned just in time to see a steward's face peering at him from the seclusion of his pantry. Damned impertinence! Without a doubt the man was one of Raymond's spies; well, he'd have it in for him, too. He was about to go back to put the fear of God in the bastard, but the door opened and Lady Pratley was standing there, robed in purple and white, her face shiny with overnight cream, her hair netted and rolled, and her temper at Force 8 rising.

"What the hell do you mean by ringing my bell at this time of night?"

He gave her his most disarming boyish smile. "Fiona! Surprise! I promised you a champagne party. And here it is!"

She looked at the frosted bottle in his hand and grimaced. "What, *here*? Now? Are you crazy?"

He said apologetically, "I didn't know you'd turned in. You're usually such a night owl."

"Well, either go away or come in," she said as he hesitated still in the doorway. "Sex, unlike justice, should not be seen to be done. I assume you haven't called to play tiddleywinks with me."

"Why did you bolt your cabin door this afternoon?" he asked sourly.

"If you knew it was bolted, you must have tried it; and if you tried it, you knew damned well why it was bolted. The poor old coot's hardly been in the sick bay a minute and you're down here with your tongue hanging out."

Most men were terrified of Lady Pratley. But he was not most men. He'd known her for the best part of six years, which was quite a time to know a woman who was somebody else's wife. He had long ago discovered that it was unwise to assume that her bite was worse than her bark. She enjoyed playing the bitch, enjoyed playing sex as other people played canasta; but in other ways she was an extraordinarily moral woman, if loyalty to friends, generosity toward people genuinely in need, regrets at having attacked the defenseless had anything to do with morality. Admittedly, the better side of her ladyship's character often got hopelessly confused. Like the time she stood surety for Bobbie Reynolds, only to find he *had* stolen Priscilla Mansell's bangles after all, so that her days spent in the corridors of justice ended only in vexing humiliation. Or the time she had donated a thousand guineas to the Society for the Rehousing of the Rural Aged, only to find them putting up an estate of rabbit hutches right next to the manor rose garden. Too late to stop the check, she had promptly demanded repayment of the money and had been equally promptly refused by the Society's general secretary, who had been brought up in the belief that a gift once given was given forever.

"How is Sir Gerald?" he asked, standing the bottle on a table by the sofa.

"Not well enough to come stomping up here till the morning. That's why you asked, isn't it?"

He denied it, although he did want to be sure the old man was unlikely to disturb them, or them him. "It was a bad show," he said. "Herrington must have let engine-room discipline go to hell for a thing like that to happen to anyone."

"He did the slipping. I told him not to do it. He thinks he knows everything about everything, and he knows nothing about nothing. The busted arm'll do him good."

"It's not serious, is it? I heard it was mostly bruises and a few abrasions."

She came out of the bedroom with a couple of glasses, the cream wiped hurriedly from her face, and her hair unnetted. "If they had it off for him, then I'd have to do all the check signing. Mean old buzzard."

He said awkwardly, "About the check, Fiona. I had to say something in the elevator yesterday. But I haven't cashed it. I can't accept it."

"David, you're a fool. Get it down to the Purser's Office first thing in the morning before I change my mind."

"But I can't keep accepting things from you," he protested. "I shouldn't have mentioned that bloody Mizzen business in the first place. They can fly a kite for their money."

"Then buy yourself something nice with it. Or buy me something nice. Or buy something for the old coot: nobody ever buys him anything these days, poor old devil." The next minute she was on the telephone to the sick bay asking a night nurse how the poor old devil was. "How do you like that? Sleeping like a baby," she said, coming back to the sofa. "He wet his bed like a baby a couple of months back. He's been in his second childhood since nineteen fifty-six, or was it seven? I think that was the last time he had a hard-on."

"You shouldn't talk about him like that to other people. After all, he *is* your husband," he said.

She didn't tell him that the abuse was because she couldn't bear to think about the old coot in pain, lying there, humiliated, in a hospital bed, no longer able to give the orders. "Well, at least the little night nurse is safe," she said. "Let's stop talking about him, can't we? The champagne will be warm and flat. Or do you prefer your champers after copulation?"

"You should know," he said, and made the pass she was expecting, leaning over her to nibble the lobe of one ear while his hand glanced the sheen of her robe to disappear into the warm nakedness of her thighs.

"Stop playing at it like a schoolboy, and come into the bedroom and do it properly," she said.

As he followed her into the bedroom, desire left him. He knew exactly what to expect. He had expected it all before. Half an hour ago he'd wanted it again, but now he felt he could sleep just as well without it. He watched her shake an assortment of tubes and packets of prophylactics onto the nearest bed from a small plastic toiletcase, pink and white with rosebuds. She did it with so little finesse, with the kind of clinical detachment reserved by young masseurs for crumbling ancient flesh.

"Take what you need," she said. "Damn beds. Look at them! Hardly big enough for a performing seal. What do they think people come on cruises for? Frog racing?"

He couldn't perform like this. She'd have to make some effort to excite him. The mere sight of her freckled body, its winter ravages concealed by ultraviolet light and tanning lotion, was not enough. She was altogether too bloody selfish in love-making. He hated her for the way she treated him like a pop-up toaster, to be replaced by the latest model as soon as he didn't pop up on command. He hated her for the way she somehow always played the masculine role, demanding that he suited her pleasure, not she his. He hated her for having more money than he'd earn in a lifetime, for having less sense in her rinsed, rolled, pampered head than he had in his own, for being old when he preferred them young, for being big when he preferred them small, for laughing at his toaster when it was down and he feeling down with it.

"If the bed's not big enough, you'll have to have it on the floor," he said, roughly pushing her to her knees before his falling trousers.

She twitched nervously, anticipating the ill treatment she so craved, her face buried in the center of him as he felled her to the carpet, rolling and struggling over the thick pile with

her in a web of shedding clothes as mouths and tongues gave
pleasure in the violence of weight, and sweat, and muscle. She
feasted on him like a hungry animal, fascinated by his size, like
a rabbit petrified by a shaft of light before the inevitable impact. The impact came. And she screamed. Not from pain, but
from a latent desire to let its bigness destroy her lust: to satisfy,
to complete, to compose, to return her to the land of gracious
living where, for a few more hours, she could forget the hip sex-
fix world of vaginal sprays, condoms and prophylactic jelly.

"Why don't you take your dentures out?" he said to humiliate
her. That's what she wanted more than anything, humiliation.
He felt her working on him for a second time. She'd been getting worse in recent months, unable to get sufficient satisfaction from him, exhausting him, boring him, making it sore in
the process. He wondered how many others she had had, and
let his thoughts wander among fantasies of her reclining on
an ottoman of pure silk impurely fondling the equipment of a
circle of men, young and old, black and white, drowning her in
a foaming sea of sperm until the billows of silk dissolved, disin-
tegrated, blowing like ashes across an endless mosaic forecourt from her palace of vice, and sweeping her away with them
into oblivion. And, as easily, she was swept from his mind, the
mechanical manipulation of his body giving him as little satisfaction as the morning evacuation of his bowels. In her place
was an image of Mrs. Westcott, her long auburn hair standing up like the heroine in some horror movie, spiraling stiffly
into the darkness of night, her face white, stifling a cry at the
sight of him over the bed bundling her ladyship like a laborer
bundling clay. And the cry made him laugh.

"What the hell's so funny?" she said, wrapping her legs
around his waist. "I told you these beds were useless. If they
had a plaque 'The Virgin Mary Slept Here,' I'd believe it."

He forgot her again, and pretended it was Mrs. Westcott lying under him, and wondered if she would be more satisfying:
not that she'd had Fiona's vast experience, but there was more
to sex than experience. Mrs. Westcott didn't move you sexually
when you first met her, but she was a nice person to be with,
good company, not to be laughed at as a horror-lady: it was
after she'd gone that one thought, Christ what a good lay! She
was a good person right through. "Going to sea must be a very

lonely life. For all of you." She'd pinned him down without wounding him. Instant analysis over the instant coffee. He knew that was why he let bags like the one underneath him now get the better of him. Here today, gone tomorrow, no roots, only a whacking big grappling iron with which he just about managed to cling onto some kind of life. What he really wanted was a wife and family, and a sense of belonging when he came back from somewhere—for however brief the stay—but to bring an end to this constant drifting. He was getting too old for it. Going to sea was a bloody lonely life. For all of us.

"You must be getting old. That was a bloody mockery." She pushed him off the bed and made for the bathroom. "You can tell this is a British ship. No bidet."

He took his clothes from the floor and called to her to throw him a towel. He ached. Twice was too much. She was right, he was getting old. Past forty a man started running downhill. Past fifty he'd probably lose the knack. What nagged at his mind was the thought that he might still have the desire. Christ, what a fate! Wanting it like mad but not being able to do a damned thing about it.

"Now I'm ready to guzzle the champers," she said, swishing from the bathroom in the purple robe.

He wedged the bottle between his legs and unbound the cork. When it let fly at the ceiling, the crude symbolism made her laugh like a child. For a moment, for all the wrong reasons, he found her attractive in spite of the crow's feet savaging her eyes, her brittle gaiety acting on his emotions like a magnet.

"We're going to have one hell of a time this trip, David," she said, gulping the bubbles and letting them explode in unladylike burps. "When we get to Athens we'll hire a car and we'll all go up Parnassus. Up the new road. The old coot will love that. He's got a thing about mountains."

The Chief Officer said tactfully, "You're the ones on vacation, don't forget. I have a job to do."

"That's right, David, so you have. Looking after me."

He smiled. "Now, do be serious for a moment, Fiona. It's only fair to Sir Gerald that you go places together. Particularly with his disability."

"What's all this disability bit? You make him sound like a prize bull that didn't jump the fence high enough. He's got another hand to pat a few bottoms with, hasn't he? He can look after himself. And I want you to look after me. In Athens, in Rhodes, in Beirut and in Naples."

He said firmly, "I'll spend as much time as I can with you, but I've got my duties to do."

"If I say so, you've got all the time in the world," she said, reaching out for him to replenish her glass. "Here's to adultery! Long may it teach us to love our husbands better."

"Good God!" he said, "I believe you really mean that."

"Yes, David, I do. The old coot is very dear to me. I think I'd kill anyone who really hurt him."

"You're a mad, mad woman, Fiona. I don't think I'll ever understand you," he said.

"Don't bother to try. I don't even understand myself. Who does?"

He stayed a few minutes longer, until the champagne was finished, and then said he must hit the hay. It was nearly one-thirty, and he had to take over the watch at four, sober and rested.

She walked him to the door. "David," she said, "you won't forget the *Torrance,* will you? I'm trying to forget it, but it isn't easy when you start making excuses for avoiding me. You must understand one thing about me. I'm a very greedy woman."

Greedy, and a bloody menace. As he walked up the companionway to his cabin on the Bridge Deck, he cursed himself for ever having responded to her glad eye that night in the bar off Jermyn Street. He'd have been better off buying himself a street-walker than gettiing fouled up with a nympho—and a rich nympho at that. There had been times when he wished she would tire of him, times when he wished he would tire of her —her money, her influence, her title, her easy body. But she'd had him hooked from the start, and every time she thought he was about to wriggle off it, she threw the *Torrance* at him. She really did love that pompous old bore of a husband; and she kept him around merely as a convenient satisfier. She'd be as well off with a donkey. Damn, damn, damn! He was in it up to his neck, and if he didn't take some effective avoiding action, that's how it was likely to be for the rest of his active life. He showered her sweat off his body and fell on the bed. A deck light cast wild patterns of rigging on the ceiling. He tried to think clearly about his future, to decide how best to out-maneuver the bitch, but the dancing light and shade quickly hypnotized him to sleep. His last thought was of her, astride his grappling iron, a silly grin of contentment on her face, his big pink hands round her throat slowly easing her out of his life forever.

In the wheelhouse Fourth Officer Tim Mathis gave Hewson the news that the Chief Officer had just turned in.

"Has he indeed!" the Second Officer said, face straining into the heaving darkness ahead. "Mr. Welch certainly believes in burning his candle at both ends, doesn't he? Let's hope before this voyage is over it doesn't go out on him."

"Yes, sir," Mathis said, returning his bright eyes to the radar sweep.

There was nothing for miles around, except the *Queen Dee* and the sea. Thirty-three thousand five hundred tons of steel and iron and wood and glass plunging her sleeping cargo toward the sunshine holiday of their dreams. Nothing quite equaled the wonderful atmosphere on a *Queen Dee* cruise.

Villefranche-sur-mer

THE morning sun danced like diamonds over the salted wheel-house windows. They were not, Captain Corlett correctly observed, properly clean. It had been one of many acid observations so far that morning. The first had been delivered to the Chief Officer who had handed over the watch to Second Officer Rigg at eight o'clock, wearing smoke-green glasses and dressed according to ship's orders of the day in white shorts and open-neck shirt. They had reached the sunshine at last and there was nothing about the Chief's rig that riled the Master. It was the glasses. "Is there something the matter with your sight, or with your liver, Mr. Welch?" he asked, not expecting to be advised, with equal acidity, that the doctor had prescribed them for ingrown toenails. Everyone seemed to be finding this a happy Tuesday morning except him. The *Queen Dee* was gliding gently through a crystal sea. Five miles to port was the bronze coastline of the French Riviera—St. Raphael, Cannes, Antibes, Nice: and beyond, the lower heights of the Col de Valberg, Col de la Cayolle, and the hazy majesty of the Grandes Alpes. In spite of an early-morning chill, the air was heavy with promise for a calm, hot day, and as the sun crept toward its zenith, the sky perceptibly darkened to a velvety blue.

"What does that idiot think he's doing?"

The Master walked out quickly on to the wing bridge to get a better view of a small motor yacht flying the French flag that was cutting across the *Queen Dee*'s bows instead of giving her passage astern, small as a fly, chugging south—probably to Corsica. He looked down through his binoculars and saw a man in a swimming suit at the wheel and a woman in the entrance to the saloon, breakfasting a baby in arms from her breast. If its father insisted on being such a bloody fool the kid would be lucky to be alive for lunch. It reminded him of the time Susan's husband had little Henry out of the rowboat on

Regent's Park lake and they all thought he was a goner. It seemed a lifetime ago now. Henry would be fourteen next month and expecting his granddad to bring him back something special from his last voyage. Heaven knows what! Perhaps an Arab camel whip with a dagger in the handle, in return for a pledge that it wouldn't be used on the Sealyham or mother's furniture. On second thought, he'd settle for a sheik's headgear. Much safer. He shook thoughts of retirement presents from his mind—those given and those received—and raised the binoculars on the port bow. A VC 10 was taking off from Nice Airport, banking over Cap Ferrat, and below it he picked out the pilot launch coming to meet them.

"Dead slow ahead," he ordered.

A telegraph bell rang. "Dead slow ahead, it is, sir—both engines."

The pilot came on board at eight-thirty, bringing with him the senior port official's compliments and a smell of garlic. The *Queen Dee* gentled herself toward the land, until her passengers thronging the decks could clearly see the traffic trailing along the Corniche du Littoral between the villas hugging the cliff face, decked with asphodel, rock roses and early jasmine. By eight-fifty she was positioned in the roadstead, and the starboard anchor let go to five shackles. In a few minutes the electrically powered port accommodation ladder would be lowered. A steady stream of launches would be coming out from the mole, for the mercenary French would not let the visitor use her own; and passengers, tourist and first classes, would be vying with each other to be first ashore. Unlike the Master, they would have forgotten the ravages of the voyage out by the time they had seen their first *bistro* and downed their first glass of Bellet.

"Let Mr. Craddock know that I'm breakfasting in my cabin if he wants me, Second," the Master said as he left the bridge. "And make sure my Chief Officer is aware of the fire drill this afternoon at sixteen-thirty before he starts giving anyone liberty."

"Yes, sir," said Second Officer Rigg, trying with two words to express his disappointment that the Master's last voyage should have got so fouled up in less than four days.

Captain Corlett was a man of habit. Breakfast, whatever the

circumstances, was at eight, unless, as today, he was needed to take command on the bridge. And breakfast, whatever the climate, consisted of porridge followed by fried bacon, kidneys and eggs, followed by thick buttered toast and chunky marmalade, all washed down with strong Indian tea and milk without sugar. Daisy Bell knew exactly how much salt to sprinkle over the porridge, when to bring in the hot toast, how to dilute the canned milk when fresh milk was not available, and when to talk or remain silent. Usually the Master read a book over breakfast, war memoirs, studies in English wildlife, or Trollope, whose *Barchester Towers* had become a kind of supplementary navigational aid every time the Sinai Peninsula came into view off Suez. But today when Daisy served breakfast, he was reading nothing, just sitting out of the direct rays of the sun, brooding. It was almost as though someone at the head office had carefully planned for the voyage to get fouled up from the start, as though they had put the new computer to work on it. Yesterday's figures for oil consumption, for example. Three hundred and twenty-eight tons from Southampton, when it should have been nearer two hundred and eighty—and would have been if he hadn't had to run her at an uneconomic speed to make up time. Damn the stabilizers! In his youth, passengers didn't know about such things and companies felt under no obligation to educate them to indulge such expensive tastes. And it was unforgivable that Bob Herrington should have allowed Sir Gerald to meddle as he did: even had his meddling been successful, it would not have been right. There'd be another delay at Naples, to have the damned things fixed properly for the voyage back. Then there had been the kid they'd had to put ashore at Gibraltar who, as it turned out, had a father in pet foods worth five thousand a year, unable to domesticate his son, but determined to fight the company every inch of the way for having laid a finger on him. The Chief Officer stuck to his story that the kid had fallen down a companionway, and the Master hoped for everyone's sake he kept stuck to it —not that he believed the man for a moment. Welch was a bully. He hadn't liked him from the start, and in some ways he was pleased to have it confirmed that his dislike was not merely rancor at the way the Marine Superintendent had gone about making the appointment.

His meditation was broken by Langdon coming down from the radio office and pushing a piece of paper in front of him. "I'm sorry, sir," the First Radio Officer said. "I know how you'll feel about it. All ship's officers will feel the same."

It was a message from Ben's wife. The exploratory operation had shown the cancer to be malignant. Mrs. Wilson, with the exemplary control of an officer's wife, had added, "Life now seems so very short for both of us, but every moment is vibrant with love."

The Master was not a sentimental man, but all the same he felt moisture flooding his eyes. "Thank you, Langdon," he said. "We all have to go some way, I suppose, but I hope mine's not like that. You can tell the other officers."

He poured himself another cup of tea and wondered what he could reply to Mrs. Wilson. A Trollope would be at a loss for words to express what he really felt. It was inconceivable that Ben wouldn't be leaning over the chartroom desk any more. And neither would he, come weekend after next. Life went on and on; one settled comfortably in a rut, then suddenly the rut was no longer there and life had disappeared with it. That damned cocktail party tonight! He'd put it off until it was in-evitable: smiling and drinking and making pointless conversa-tion with people he would never see again—or want to—when Ben, whom he did want to see again, did want to drink with, talk with, live with, was lying in a hospital bed, his rotting guts cut and slashed by a surgeon's knife. "Do have another martini, Mrs. Worthington-Smythe. Mr. Eggerton, I want to hear all about your stamps. My Chief Purser tells me you have one of the finest collections of Indian in Europe." The damned silly things people had to say and do for a living.

The Chief Purser provided the second interruption to the meal. He came in wearing his whites with the self-consciousness of a bank clerk, and this in spite of the fact that he'd been wear-ing them in sunny waters almost since he was a boy. "I wanted your advice on the rather delicate matter of Miss Liscon," he said, settling himself awkwardly in an armchair drenched in morning sunshine.

"Who the hell is Miss Liscon that I have to be concerned with her welfare?"

"Cilla Liscon. Model. She's traveling with her husband. Lester Dickson, the photographer. In 0.21. She's not only a model, if you know what I mean."

"Complaints?"

"Not yet, sir, but—"

The Master exploded. "For goodness sake, Mr. Craddock, you've been doing your job long enough to know there's not a damn thing I can do about it unless it's annoying other passengers, or there is watertight evidence from one of her customers."

The Chief Purser protested, "But she had *four* last night, sir, if Addison is to be believed. One of them Mr. Radford. From your table."

"If Mr. Radford's morals are not such as I would choose to emulate, that is his concern. And if she puts the squeeze on him because Mrs. Radford is also on board, then he's an idiot as well as a lecher. We've been through all this before. I'm not concerned with our passengers' morals, only their safety. If that is all you've come to tell me, good morning Mr. Craddock. Good morning." He saw the Chief Purser's face quiver with thwarted indignation; but he'd had enough damned bad luck already without getting himself and the head office involved with charges and countercharges, false arrests, slander actions, and anything else that might follow if he treated Miss Liscon as the whore she undoubtedly was. He tried to be all things to all people, but for his Chief Purser to expect him to play the avenging angel, with his career only two more weeks to go, was really too much.

The water was a calm, translucent blue as deep as the eye could see. But the launches, with their hard wooden seats, used more frequently for day trips to the Iles de Lérins, were rising and falling unnervingly against the lower steps of the accommodation ladders. For the inexperienced, it was an adventure in itself to make the jump from the solidarity of the *Queen Dee* to the bouncing tender. That the old *Queen* herself should have been rolling and pitching them into a state of misery barely two days ago seemed inconceivable.

"Will you be comfortable here, Dearest? Here, why don't you sit on my jacket?" Richard helped his mother to a seat in the fore of the boat.

"No, leave your jacket on," she said, fearful that a wayward breeze would give him a chill if he took it off.

There was not much room to sit even if the journey was a short one. Richard shepherded Simone into the seat next to his mother, and stood immediately in front of them, his feet between theirs. "This is smashing!" he said. "I can't wait to get my feet on French soil for the first time. It's almost as exciting as going to the moon."

Pamela Westcott felt ill at ease with Simone. She was a nice girl, and she was pleased for Richard that he had her company, but neither youngster really wanted her dogging them. They had both insisted she go with them on the tour, but then they were both polite children—too polite to tell her that they would prefer to be alone in the crowd. As the seamen pushed the launch away from the accommodation ladder, she had a sudden impulse to return to her cabin, to leave the young people to themselves.

"Good morning, Mrs. Westcott. This weather's more like it, eh?" Colonel Jamieson gave her a wrinkled smile. Alice was nowhere to be seen. Instead, he was accompanied by Kenneth Brewer and two sets of golf clubs.

"It's very nice," she said, anxious not to have to continue the conversation.

He kept smiling. "Alice enjoyed our little game last night. Perhaps you'll win it all back from us before we pass this way again."

"Perhaps I will," she said, fearful that Richard and Simone were listening. The little game had not been her idea of little. Ian and Alice had found her a partner, a Mr. Courtenay, who was something in the City, and after only three rubbers she was over a hundred pounds down; and by the end of the evening she had lost all her Sunday winnings in the ship's sweepstake— and quite a bit more. Mr. Courtenay had been very nice about it, but she couldn't help feeling that in some way he blamed her for his losses, which had been equally substantial.

"In Grasse you must buy some of the perfume, Mrs. Westcott," Simone told her. "The lavender essence is very good."

She did not think she was yet at the age to smell sweetly of lavender, but she said, "I'm sure it's very nice, dear. I always buy French perfume at home."

The launch came alongside the Port Health Office Mole, and as she put a foot onto the narrow wooden landing plank, she felt a strong hand steady her arm. She thought at first it was Richard, but as she reached the causeway she turned to see a tall lean figure in white standing beside her. When she got the sun out of her eyes, she saw it was the Chief Officer.

"Thank you," she said. "I seem to be surrounded by willing hands."

"Are you going on the coaches?" he asked.

She said yes, and perhaps it was the lack of enthusiasm in her voice that encouraged him to invite her to accompany him in a taxi to Nice. "I have some shopping to do," he explained. "That doesn't sound very masculine. But there were a number of personal things I hadn't time to get in England. The shops in Nice are very good. Perhaps—"

"I'd love to come," she said, glad of the excuse. She turned to Richard. "You'll be all right on your own, won't you, darling?"

He knew she was making the sacrifice for him, that she really wanted his company as she'd had it nonstop for the past year. But he'd promised Simone he'd let her show him France, or at least a little of it, and it wouldn't be right to let her down. It was awful being between the two women.

"Sure. I'll be all right, Dearest," he said. "Have fun looking round the shops."

The Chief Officer stood there, his hairy legs jutting powerfully from crisply laundered shorts, eyeing him superciliously, treating him like a child. He felt suddenly ashamed, for the first time in his life, at publicly calling his mother Dearest. He had a girlfriend now. He must be careful not to embarrass Simone.

"I'll bring your mother safely back to you in time for lunch," the Chief Officer told him. Richard hoped no one else had detected the contempt in the man's voice.

The coach started up the Moyenne Corniche, away fom the old-world port with its steep, narrow streets. The waterfront cafés were shaded by palm trees, and the bay sheltered by the wooded slopes of Cap Ferrat. As they climbed above the worn stone steps, they could look down on the plush blue sea, broken only by the dazzling whiteness of the *Queen Dee* with her scarlet funnel.

"It is beautiful here, isn't it?" Simone said. "But very enervating. Maybe that's why so many artists have chosen to live in this part of France. Renoir at Cagnes, Bonnard in Le Cannet, Picasso at Antibes, Vallauris and Cannes. Matisse spent the last years of his life in Nice, and designed the lovely little chapel of Saint-Dominique, in Vence. Do you like art?"

"Yes, of course," he said defensively, acutely aware of the limits of the British educational system and hoping like hell she wasn't going to interrogate him on the subject. But she did. During the whole drive up into the mountains behind Nice, and into the Gorges du Loup, she kept up an almost nonstop chatter about trends in French art since the Impressionists: how many living artists had become interested in local crafts, such as pottery: and what a pity they were staying less than a day, because she would like him to see Vallauris. The more she talked passionately about art, the more it reminded him of John talking passionately about the theater: and he didn't want to be reminded of John—not today, in the warm fragrant sunshine, in the company of such a smashing girl as Simone. When the weather turned for the better yesterday, he had roamed the decks, partly hoping Simone would have escaped from her aunt, partly hoping he would be able to escape from John. Not that John had said or done anything to offend him since the incident on Saturday. Indeed, when they turned in nights and got up mornings, he went out of his way to be friends. What worried Richard was that by all the laws of nature, as he understood them, John should have been ashamed to look him in the face on Sunday morning, but he wasn't; instead, Richard was the one with an unaccountable sense of guilt for being a prude, for rejecting friendship because he was afraid of accepting it on terms other than his own. And now he kept thinking about the off-hand way he had refused to play deck tennis with John yesterday afternoon. "I hope you're not going to start playing with yourself," John had said cheerfully, making the *double entente* painfully obvious. "You Britishers are all the same. If you have a prejudice you don't know why you have it, and you don't want to find out why you have it either." He didn't really blame John for slamming him down. Perhaps he deserved it. He'd taken the edge off both their afternoons by not playing tennis, for the alternative for John was partnering a lot of old married men who wanted to get their weight down. Richard wondered if he was going to be fat by the time he was nineteen, twenty-one or forty.

"It is wicked how ignorant people always think that artists are immoral. Morality is the hypocrisy of nations. Balzac."

Simone's voice rang through his left ear like a bell. "We read *Madame Bovary* at school," he said. "But I thought it was a bit soppy. All right for girls."

"That was Flaubert," she scolded.

The coach pulled up with a hissing of pneumatic brakes in the Gothic square of Saint-Paul-de-Vence. He was glad of the excuse to help her out into the sweet-smelling sunshine to hide his embarrassment. Everyone seemed to know more about things than he did. He was beginning to think he must have been the laziest kid ever to go to Tor Beeches.

"Let's keep away from the guide," she said. "They are always boring. They think they know everything but they know nothing. You discover things in life by . . . feeling them."

They saw the Tintoretto Catherine in the church, then walked through narrow, medieval streets toward the ramparts. A mixture of orange blossoms and roses was wafted by the breeze, blending with the smells of cottage cooking and the occasional patch of dogs' excrement between the flagstones.

"Did you know it takes twelve thousand kilos of roses to make just one kilo of perfume?" she asked.

"No," he said lamely, "I didn't know that."

She laughed at him; but it was a kindly laugh. "Richard, you are so English. You pretend you are a stupid boy, but you're not. You're a shy boy. Why don't you put your arm round my waist? I won't hurt you. You do want us to be friends, don't you?"

"Of course, Simone. You're the nicest girl I've ever met," he said anxiously.

"I'm the first girl you've ever met!" She pouted her lips and gave him a playful kiss on his right cheek, taking his hand and drawing it toward her.

"You're wonderful, Simone. Wonderful," he said.

A little way out of the village they glimpsed the snow-capped peaks. The sun beat on his fair skin and he wished he'd worn a hat. Simone wore a hat, a big flopping straw with a yellow ribbon that fluttered over her shoulders. And she had a sleeveless linen smock, bright with geometric blobs of color held together by bands of black—a piece of walking op art. He remembered those deadly afternoons his parents had forced him to dance with that horrid Sybil Ticehurst. He was not a public-school snob, whatever she said. Simone knew that. She wouldn't like him if he was a snob. Simone was quite the most wonderful thing that had ever happened to him. Her live young body moved gently under her dress as they walked, her soft skin a few inches from his face. Nothing seemed real any more. He had to keep reminding himself that he was in France, that every boy had a girl for company when he grew up. Except John. Hell, why did that screwball have to keep coming into his mind at a time like this?

"For lunch, you will come to Nice and eat with my aunt and her friends. It's a bore, but why should I be bored alone?" she said, planning his day. "Then tonight I will take you to a *loco*. Some place away from all the *moins de vingt dents*. You would like that?"

"I'd love that, Simone," he said, not quite sure what that was.

They found the path up to the Fondation Maeght, and she opened his eyes to the exciting forms of Miro and Giacometti against a natural backdrop of fir forests and hills. He began to understand what she meant by feeling art. Seen like this it was a part of nature, and both nature and art a part of them. He squeezed her waist with his hand and she smiled. A gentle, innocent smile of friendship. It was as though he had known Simone all his life, as though she was part of the family, a willingly incestuous relationship between brother and sister.

"Race you down the hill," she suddenly said, scurrying off over dappled tarmac. He heard his feet pounding the hard surface of the road, saw the leafy countryside flashing by, and he thought of the fields near Tor Beeches and rugger and the sweaty scrums and would he ever play again? She was two paces ahead, laughing, and he flung himself into a tackle without realizing that she was a girl. His weight threw her off balance and they both fell heavily against the trunk of an ancient fir. She took the worst of the impact, sandwiched between him and the tree. For a moment he thought he heard a rib snap.

" 'Struth! I really didn't mean to do that, Simone. I'm ter-

ribly sorry. I . . . I guess I don't know my own strength." He
could tell by her face that he'd hurt her, and he leaned forward
to kiss the hurt better, like when he had instinctively kissed
Mother the day he had accidentally splashed boiling milk over
her hands. His lips were going to her forehead, but she raised
her face so that her lips met his. There was more than touch to
the contact. It was as though all his nerves lay bare over the
petal softness of their two mouths, she taming his clumsy peck-
ing by holding his cheeks in her thin cool hands. Her breath
spread warmly round his nostrils and the moisture in her
mouth tasted pure and sweet. All at once, panic at what he was
doing flooded his body like burning oil: and he closed his eyes
in shame.

"I'm much better now," she said, gently pushing him away
from her. "I was afraid you didn't like me very much. Can I be
your steady for the summer? I expect to be in England with
my aunt and uncle unteel I 'ave zee English perfect."

"I've already told you, your English *is* perfect," he said,
amused by her deliberately thick accent. "Better than my
French. How do you say it? We *ça a fait tilt?*"

"We hit it off. H-h-h-hit."

They strolled arm in arm back toward the village. On the
outskirts they came across an old woman in a food-stained black
dress bending into the open bonnet of a prewar Renault. She
looked up as they passed, her face red with effort, and said
something in patois that Richard didn't pretend to understand.

Simone turned to him. "She is a very rude old woman. I've
told her not to treat a car like a donkey."

"Let me have a look," Richard said. "I think I can fix it for
her. Old Hickson had an old jalopy that kept breaking down
and I used to fix it for him. Saved him pounds in garage bills.
Tell her I'll get it going again for her if I can."

He threw his jacket on the driving seat and stuck his head
into the bonnet. It was almost impossible to see what should be
where for the caked mud and grease. The old woman kept
crowing, doubting his skill, fearful that he would do the precious mechanism some permanent injury. As he worked, the
sun beat on the back of his head until his face was blotchy red
like the old woman's. From time to time he stretched his back
and glanced across the road to where Simone was waiting for

him in the shade, and they exchanged quick, nervous smiles. He was worried because something inside his mind kept asking what she'd look like naked, and he had to keep telling himself consciously that it was wrong to think about her in that way. Yet. Unlike Tomlinson, who was sex mad, and used to come back at the start of every new term full of his exploits. He'd talk for hours in the dorm after lights-out, claiming he'd seen everything, done everything, just like that. But Tomlinson was a liar. Take that signed picture of Elizabeth Masters, posed with nothing on but a few feathers for one of her London cabaret shows. "To Tommy, with love from his Elizabeth." There'd been a hell of a row because some of the other boys also started putting pin-ups in their lockers, and Old Hickson had made them take them down. All except Tomlinson's Elizabeth. It turned out that she was his older sister, that the family wouldn't be paying his Tor Beeches fees if she wasn't stripping for a living. Nicely, of course, the family was anxious to point out; and not completely, because she was an *artiste*. Poor old Tomlinson was never quite the same again. The following term he returned with a different picture of Elizabeth, in black tights and a broad silk sash; and then, after one of Old Hickson's fireside chats, he seemed more interested in spies than in sex. All the same, everyone wondered if Tomlinson had ever had a girl, the way grown-ups did, and whether his sister really did take her clothes off in public, all of them. He looked up and smiled at Simone again. It would be terrible if she were to take her clothes off in public. He didn't think he'd like to see her naked. Ever. She'd be like a cherry tree without its blossom.

"That's it. Tell her to keep the choke out for a bit, and it'll be all right," he said, as the engine roared to life.

"Richard, you're absolutely covered in oil. I don't know what my aunt will say."

She came over to the thundering, shaking car. He was wearing an ordinary blue shirt with his gray flannels, the kind of shirt policemen or airmen wear, only they never wore them splattered with car grease and crumpled by sweat. There were grease smears over his face, and when he took out his handkerchief to wipe them away according to her instructions, his hands only made things worse. But he could tell that she admired him. So did the old woman, who was full of praise for *le jeune*

Anglais. He didn't want the old woman's admiration, but he did want Simone to think he was clever, that even if he didn't know all he should know about Chagall, he was with it where Renaults were concerned.

"I'll be okay if I keep my jacket on to hide the worst of it," he said, "and find a good loo where I can scrub my hands. I suppose they do have loos in Nice?"

They returned to the square with the sparkling fountain just in time to appease the coach driver, whose temper was mounting at the prospect of having lost them. Simone said to give him a couple of francs for his services as guide, although they hadn't availed themselves of them; and less than an hour later the man was obligingly dropping them near the old port at Nice before taking the rest of the party back to Villefranche to lunch on the *Queen Dee.* They walked past a carpet of yachts, moored two and three deep so that it was impossible to see the water, deck boys with naked brown torsos and old men in faded jeans busily scraping off last season's paint. Then into the shaded streets, past the boutiques with their impeccably dressed windows, drawing on local color with unerring taste. Momentarily they paused to look, pointing out to each other things that they liked, or didn't like, the things that they could or couldn't afford. She saw a shirt in pink and gray, all diagonals and circles. He said he liked it; and before he realized what she was doing she had bought it for him, and he was putting it on in the shop, attended by a dark young man all smiles and mince. It was the most spontaneous, generous, wonderful thing that anyone had ever done for him except Mother. And as he walked into the Hotel Splendide's loo to scrub his hands, he felt the most important, the most wanted person in the whole of Nice.

Simone's aunt was coldly pleased to see him. She welcomed the opportunity of showing off an English public-school boy to Monsieur Pelligrin and his wife, with whom she was lunching, but she left Richard in no doubt that he was not exactly expected and therefore should properly regard himself as being in disgrace. Monsieur Pelligrin, an old friend of the aunt's husband, was an official at the *mairie* who spoke English tolerably well but had no intention of doing so on young Richard's account. The aunt thereupon more than once alluded to Richard and Simone's friendship, and made plain her conviction that

youthful emotions were best kept under control by adult pru-
dence. "You will," she said to Simone, deliberately in English,
"spend the rest of the day with your aunt, won't you, dear?" He
felt like a pampered pedigree dog being fed bourride, arti-
chokes à la barigoule and Vaucluse strawberries, but there only
for the family to show off. He sat and ate the crumbs from
under their table and tried to follow the French conversation,
which began with the aunt's impressions of changes in the British political scene and ended with Monsieur Pelligrin's disapproval of the social changes along the French Riviera. He
didn't, for instance, like the Tropicana beach-cum-nightclub
west of Antibes with its floating Chinese junk and sand flown in
specially from the Pacific, where one could dance on metal
water lilies in pools full of fish and flowers. Richard thought
it sounded fun. And there was St. Tropez, which came in for
adult disapproval for its gaudy slacks, bare midriffs and tight
whatever-you-choose. "It is very much like Lourdes," Monsieur
Pelligrin observed. "The young people flock there with all
their worries and yearnings, expecting to be healed by the new
religion of glamour and pop stardom." And while the adults
talked, Richard and Simone ate in silence, occasionally exchanging furtive glances, he wondering what youth in general
had done to evoke such total censure. Perhaps it was just simply
that old people had regrets and not many more years of their
lives to lead.

"That's a lovely shirt you're wearing, Richard," the aunt
said, trying to sound magnanimous. "Did you get it in France?"

Simone said defiantly, "It's a present, isn't it, Richard? From
me."

The *Queen Dee*'s emergency signal boomed over the quiet
Mediterranean afternoon at exactly four-thirty. Heavy feet
pounded the decks, closing ports, deadlights, convention valves,
deck baffles, fireproof valves and watertight doors. Those passengers not spending the afternoon ashore had been warned
of the disturbance, but nonetheless there were a few timid souls
instantly prepared to meet their doom. A fire was presumed
to have broken out in the fore peak store, and all ventilation in
the vicinity was sealed off while two hoses were rigged in a matter of seconds and tested under pressure. The Chief Officer

moved briskly about the deck watching the Third and Fourth, who were watching the bo'sun and the certificated seamen. And while all this was going on, passengers lined the roped-off area like city crowds around a car accident.

"Let's have extinguishers D7 and D8 expended and recharged," the Chief Officer ordered.

"Aye, aye, sir."

A short distance away men were moving about in smoke helmets like cosmonauts. Others were manning the davits to lower the lifeboats to embarkation deck level and bowse them in. They worked to precision, smoothly, effectively, like circus acrobats. The Chief Officer watched with an eagle eye, his face set hard, giving no indication of his satisfaction at the way the exercise was going. All in all, it had been a very satisfactory day. He had not expected to meet Pamela Westcott going ashore, neither had he expected her to be so willingly parted from her son. It really was too sissified the way he kept calling her Dearest at his age. She'd told him herself while they were having coffee overlooking the flower market that she thought Richard had led too sheltered a life and that it wasn't good for him. Like hell it wasn't! Do the little bastard good to get stuck into some job or other. Clipping tickets on the buses if he couldn't do anything better for himself. Pamela realized this. She was a sensible woman—and a lovely one. He found it hard to believe that she was thirty-eight and had been through life with diapers, cooking for a hungry man and a growing boy, birthday parties, the Monday wash, death, about the lot life had to offer a woman. Walking the sunny streets of Nice, she had been more like an office girl worried at how to say no after a few drinks, yet anxious to make a good impression and excited by the prospect of her whole life ahead of her. Of all the women he had known—and he'd known plenty—she was the most fascinating. Simple. Open. Almost unaware of her good looks. Innocent, although she'd been married for the best part of twenty years. To Arnold. He must have been quite a man, keeping her faithful as he had. And there was no doubt in his mind that she had been faithful. Constantly. The word adultery would have been anathema to Pamela Westcott.

"Good God, don't those men know how to handle a hose properly?"

"Sir." The bo'sun twitched with anticipation.

"Under-run at shoulder height to expel the water. If I see a man use his feet on a hose again, he'll be logged. Is that understood?"

"Yes, sir."

Boat-station signals rang out. Crews mustered at their boats wearing life jackets. The Chief Officer, with the Second and Third, made spot checks on life-saving apparatus—a hand bilge pump here, a battery signaling lamp there. In a little under half an hour after the exercise had begun, the order "Hoist all boats!" was given. The power winches clattered into action, a cascade of noise over the afternoon stillness. The cradles holding the boats moved back slowly up the skids, their weight supported by wire rope an inch thick.

"Stand clear there!"

The Chief Officer flung himself toward number 5 boat, grabbing the startled seaman by his collar and jerking him free of the winch. From farther down deck it looked as though the two men were fighting, as their twisting, twitching limbs clambered from under the davits. The fall stranded and snapped in a snaking, screeching inferno of frayed wire, letting the boat overhead crash with a creak of timber on to its steel slide.

The seaman looked back to where he had been standing, the paint and metal scored by the rampaging wire. "Thank you, Mr. Welch, sir. I nearly had my chips then, didn't I?"

Second Officer Hewson and Third Officer Tyson fussed around the broken fall, contemplating how it might have happened.

"It happened," the Chief Officer said, "because rope inspection has not been thorough. The core had dried out. I want to know when it was put into service. Somebody should know that a wire rope has spent half its life when one wire of any strand is broken. I want every piece of wire rope and cordage on this ship checked before there is any further liberty for anyone. Is that clear, Mr. Tyson?"

"Yes, sir," Third Officer Tyson said.

"I'm beginning to think that whoever was Chief here before ran a very slack ship," he went on, letting his anger get the better of him. "I want it impressed upon every member of the ship's company that meticulous attention to detail not only protects equipment but will also save lives. Is that understood?"

"Yes, sir," Third Officer Tyson said. There was no mistaking his resentment at the way the rebuke had been delivered; but he was in no position to answer back. If Ben Wilson had a complaint to make to his fellow officers about the way the ship was run, he'd have made it in the proper way, later, in private, not in front of a muster of the ship's company. The plain fact of the matter was that David Welch was an officer, but no gentleman.

Captain Corlett received his guests for cocktails in the Tudor Room at six-thirty. For the officers, it was a mess-kit affair. The late afternoon sun was dipping behind Cap Ferrat. A few passengers were still around the pool beyond the wide sweep of glass, their bodies indecently white in the golden shades of evening or tinged red from overexposure after the cold English winter. Stewards in freshly laundered monkey-jackets moved silently between the guests with their trays, while Raymond, down from the Americana, supervised Benson's dispensation from the bar. Almost before it had begun, the guests clung nervously together in little groups, unwilling or unable to make the effort to mingle. The Master and his officers did their best to mix them, but after the first few drinks they gave up the struggle and left them on their islands, cruising between them to keep their inbred conversations politely oiled.

Lady Pratley arrived shortly after seven, escorted by a wan Sir Gerald, his left arm mummified in a sling. The Master immediately descended upon them, accompanied by a dapper little man with a hairline moustache and a pin-striped blue suit. "Sir Gerald," he said, "we are all delighted to see you about again. I hope the arm is giving you less pain."

Sir Gerald smiled royally. "Dr. Hammond has been most kind. The best possible attention, I assure you, Captain."

"Who's he?" her ladyship asked, a finger pointed at the dapper little man in blue.

The Master made the introduction. "I would like you to meet Monsieur Briçon. The company's agent in Nice."

"Well, you're a bore for a start," her ladyship told him.

Sir Gerald extended his uninjured hand. "Monsieur Briçon," he lied, "I've heard so much about you from Sir Edgar. It must be a very taxing task looking after the company's interests out here. I'm sure you do it most splendidly."

"It's a pleasure, Sir Gerald, a pleasure to be taxed for the company," the little man said, relieved that he must after all have misunderstood her ladyship.

But he hadn't. Worse was to come. "Do you like animals, Mr. Briçon?" she asked, a brittleness in her voice defying him to say no.

"Yes, your ladyship. Very much. My wife and I keep a cat. A rather special blue Persian."

"That's sensible. I'm telling you, never keep a dog. When I first married this old coot, we had an apartment in London and I had a dachshund. Then it got ill. It didn't like the climate any more than I did. The vet told me it was something to do with his testicles. Well, I didn't know what testicles were. You must understand, I am only a simple woman. So one day I asked the postman. I said, 'What are testicles?' and he said, 'Balls, madam.' Why didn't the damned vet say balls? Everyone knows what balls are. Then he said he needed a sample of his water. I ask you, have you ever tried getting a sample of a dachshund's water?"

Monsieur Briçon assured her ladyship no, and clutched a passing glass of Scotch.

"So I took him for a walk round the block with a frying pan. And I was just getting the pan underneath him when a policeman came up and asked me what I was doing. Wasn't it perfectly obvious to anyone what I was doing? I tell you, London policemen aren't as wonderful as everyone makes out."

Pamela Westcott's particular little island was with Mr. and Mrs. Brewer. They were drinking dry martinis and she was keeping to sweet sherry. Mrs. Brewer was saying how much Nice was like Miami, and they wouldn't have come all this way if it wasn't to see John. Mr. Brewer was saying the golf was worth the journey—greens so smooth you could skate on them —and he guessed that if he stayed a while in Nice he could get his handicap down to ten.

"Don't keep on to Mrs. Westcott about your golf, Kenneth," Mrs. Brewer chided him. "I'm sure she's not in the least interested in what you men get up to. It's such a pity John doesn't play golf. But he never has had an interest in games, not since he was a little fellow. He'd have been such good company for his father. We haven't seen him in all these months, and then he goes running off by himself, almost as though he wanted to get away from us. You know what it's like—well, of course you do, being a mother yourself. I do wish he'd start to settle down, begin to think about having a family of his own. Kenneth and I are getting to the age when being grandparents would make us feel young again. That's so, isn't it, Kenneth?"

Kenneth said yes, that was so, and added that all the same he'd been given a good game by Colonel Jamieson, who might be a diehard Republican by conviction but was nonetheless a fine old English gentleman with whom it was a pleasure to do business.

"I really don't think you should go investing any money in his Freebody Trust, or whatever it is he calls it," Mrs. Brewer whined. "He wants English pounds and not dollars, and with every respect to you, Mrs. Westcott, I think we ought to keep our money where it belongs, right back home. It wouldn't be patriotic to do as he suggests, Kenneth."

"But honey," Kenneth complained, "it's a yield of almost fifteen percent. With security."

Pamela Westcott was in no mood to think about money. She found herself wondering if hers was well invested, and something in the back of her mind started telling her it was Arnold's anyhow. Friends had suggested taking the bank manager's advice, but there was nothing very personal about the advice of a man she had only met once before in her life. Come to think of it, there had been very few men she had met. A few other wives' husbands, friends of Arnold. Mr. Pulbright, who was organizing the house move for them while they were away, elderly and ever so sweet. And now David Welch, who was more in her age group, mature, yet still with a boyish charm. It was quite something to be escorted ashore by the ship's Chief Officer. He had walked her around the old harbor, explaining the finer points of the private yachts and motorboats being made ready for the summer. Nice was a town of such contrasts. The Promenade des Anglais, ugly as Brighton; the Cimiez thermae, as Romanesque as anything in Bath; and the flower market, which might not be so large as Covent Garden but was eminently more visitable. Being with him, she felt more at ease,

more secure than she had for months. It had been something
she'd dreaded, this going out with another man for the first
time. She had a strange feeling that she might be hurting Arnold in some way if she chose the wrong kind of new friends.
They used to joke about voices from beyond, but she knew he
didn't altogether disbelieve it, and neither did she: lots of
little things happened in life that could not be explained logi-
cally, so why not big things as well? All the same, Arnold was
gone, and she preferred him to stay gone. She had Richard's
happiness to think about now. See him settle down in a job.
Take a wife. If she found companionship again it would ease
her fears of the future; but if she didn't, then she'd just have to
carry on alone—many other, younger women had done so. Nevertheless, she had returned on the launch across the short strip
of water between the mole and the *Queen Dee,* crystal and
blue as in any fairy tale, with ever such a little wish that the
Chief Officer might turn out to be her Prince Charming, that
she wasn't too old to start life all over again.

"If Colonel Jamieson's as good at golf as he is at bridge, he's
very good indeed," she said. "They won more than six hundred
pounds off Mr. Courtenay and me last night."

"My dear," Mrs. Brewer said, caught in midbreath, "we
simply couldn't afford that kind of gambling!"

"Neither can I."

Sir Gerald was knocking back the gin and talking to an over-
thin dark girl of about twenty-three clad in pink and black.
"The main danger of drifting ice is that it's frequently accompanied by fog. But you always know if the stuff's about if you
keep a sharp lookout. Ice blink, absence of any sea swell in a
breeze, or herds of seals and flocks of razorbills far from land.
Of course, you know for sure as soon as you spot calf ice, or hear
the stuff breaking up in the distance with cracks like gunfire.
Deadly things, icebergs. Seven-tenths below water. Spot one
bang-on and the only thing you can do is order full astern, because if you try to turn the chances are you'll rip your bottom
out."

"If Sir Gerald hasn't iced your drink sufficiently, Miss Liscon, please ask one of the stewards for more." The Master
edged into the conversation, eyeing the young woman with a
disarmingly paternal smile.

"Sir Gerald's simply fascinating, Captain," she said. "I had no idea there was so much to know about ships."

"Everyone's job is always fascinating to the other fellow," the Master said. "Your job interests me, Miss Liscon. Modeling, my Chief Purser tells me. But why should we all be talking shop? Everyone's here to enjoy themselves. You're not here to work, are you, Miss Liscon?"

For a moment her eyes blazed defiantly. "I never mix business with pleasure, Captain. But in the entertainment profession, pleasure is so often a business that it becomes ever such a teeny-weeny bit confusing."

"I don't confuse easily, young lady," the Master said severely. "And I trust you won't be confused either for the remainder of your voyage with us." And with that he was gone.

"Odd chap," Sir Gerald said. "Can't expect a man to be quite himself when he has retirement staring him in the face, I suppose. You won't have to worry about that for many years yet though, will you, Miss Liscon?"

"No, Sir Gerald," she cooed.

The Chief Officer presented himself at the party shortly after eight, just as it was breaking up. Before he had time to ask for a drink, Lady Pratley cut across his bows, rattling a Scotch.

"Where the hell have you been?" she asked. "The party's nearly over."

"You seem to forget I have a job to do, Fiona. I didn't hand over the watch to Rigg until eight. Ant then I had to struggle into my mess kit. I must be putting on weight." Her demanding attitude annoyed him, the more so since the Captain's cocktail was yet another job as far as he was concerned. The old man would rightly be annoyed if he didn't move around making the paying customers feel at home.

"What were you doing earlier, then?" she demanded.

"I had some shopping to do in Nice."

"With that dreary little widow. I saw you coming off the launch with her."

"She just happened to be returning by the same launch," he lied.

"How convenient." She helped herself to another drink, sipped it, and returned it to the steward's tray. "Tell Raymond or whatever his name is that I like it iced, but not watered."

The Chief Officer prepared to leave her. "We can talk later," he said tactfully. "I have to move around now and say hello to a few faces."

"Take me over to Monte this evening. I feel lucky," she said.

"Sorry, Fiona, no dice. I'm turning in early."

"With her?" Her eyes flashed jealously. "I've had a simply bloody day looking after the old coot, and I want to go ashore for at least a few hours."

"Then you'll have to go alone. You'll be quite safe. You're a big girl now."

"I've decided to stop payment on that check after all," she snapped as he walked away from her.

Mr. and Mrs. Paxton were standing close to her ladyship, talking to an oval-faced little woman who looked a bit like a nun who had lost her habit and a red-faced man whose face was mostly hidden in a ragged growth of ginger beard. "I really don't think I could go on living with *my* husband if he insisted on growing a beard," Mrs. Paxton was saying girlishly, the liquor getting the better of her.

Her ladyship broke into the circle. "Nonsense!" she said, arrowing a finger between her ample cleavage, "we all have beards!" The party was a bore, David was a bore, the Paxtons were bores, and she was going to give the lot of them hell.

Les Yé-Yé were packed like sardines on the underlit purple glass floor of the Discotheque Chouette. The latest *tube* was coming loud and clear from the amplifiers. Heads and hands kept time to the lusty beat, while a hundred mouths mimed the paean of a love lost out East where the West begins. Some vibrated on their feet over the luminous glass; others just sat drinking the hard stuff, like Coke or fizzy orange. The boys for the most part wore Italian six-button blazers, with American shirts and expensive *pulls* from England. The girls favored plastic jackets in gay colors, knitted dresses, or inexpensive mini-skirts worn with such style because they had been chosen with such care. The atmosphere was hot, the air heavy with perspiring bodies; yet to the *habitués* the Discotheque Chouette smelled like spring.

"*Ca chauffe carré.*" Simone turned from the girl next to her to speak to Richard. "You like it here, no?"

"It's smashing," he said. "There're lots of coffee bars with jukeboxes in London, but I've never got around to going to them, what with school, and then Father dying. But they're a real lot of weirdies around the West End. They take pep pills and other things."

"In England it is fashionable to *faire le bide,* how do you say, to be a deadbeat. No, the American word is better. A bum. In France, maybe there is not the need to rebel against conventions so much. But if a French boy were to wear his hair long it would be a big insult. People would not just stare, they would publicly insult him. So, we never have had Rockers although I think we are all a little bit like your Mods."

Richard bought her another Coke; and when she had finished it they danced again, crazy new steps, mad new beats. They talked to everyone, and everyone alked to them, and Richard suddenly discovered that his French wasn't as bad as he thought it was. He turned the pages of the latest *bouquin,* agreed that if Simone were to take up singing she would *faire un tabac,* and kept telling everyone he met that the place was *bath,* smashing, *c'est le pied.* For the moment, he had even stopped worrying about his battered herringbone jacket that looked like such a sad rag in contrast to the gay colors and smooth styles the French boys were wearing. Simone had one arm resting on his shoulder as they sat on the purple glass to listen to a new folk number. Then, in the hazy darkness on the far side of the cellar he recognized a familiar face. It was Simone's aunt; and behind her was his mother, looking like a plain-clothes sister of mercy. But there was nothing particularly merciful on the face of Simone's aunt.

"My horrid old aunt has a horrid old mind," Simone said. "I left her a note to tell her I would be here and there was nothing to worry about. I said you'd bring me back early. Oh, *les croulants!* They are all the same. You play fair with them and they spit in your eye. They think we are all drug addicts or sex maniacs. I'm sorry, Richard, it's all my fault. We'll have to go over and be nice to them."

Simone's aunt was nice-resistant. She spoke rapidly to

Simone in a French that Richard couldn't understand, and then she turned on him and said, "Young man, I forbid you to speak to my niece again. You are a very bad influence on her."

Richard mumbled, "Yes, ma'am," and exchanged glances with his mother, who hadn't said a word. She didn't have to say a word; he could tell that she was feeling wretched about the whole situation. The other kids walked around them at a safe distance, a few stopping to look at the horrid old aunt with amused, or puzzled, expressions. And when they left the Discotheque Chouette the kids parted respectfully as though there'd been an accident.

They walked down narrow streets toward the harbor in the hope of finding a taxi back to Villefranche. The night air was cool and gentle after the noise inside. Above, the stars, so white and bright, radiated their innocence over the ancient stones. They walked in silence, Simone and her aunt in front, Richard and his mother behind. Richard thought this must be rather what it was like to be arrested by a policeman, a kind of confusing wonderment at what it was all about and what was likely to happen next. Only he had no sense of guilt. None whatever. He wouldn't dream of hurting Simone. Why should he? She was the most wonderful thing that had ever happened to him.

"I had to come, dear. She insisted. I really don't know why. It looked like a very nice place to me." Mothers could be a great comfort at times.

They were getting into a taxi by the waterfront when he saw John. The American boy was leaving a bar, arm in arm with a French sailor. Why didn't he have a horrid old aunt, Richard wondered. There just wasn't any justice in the world.

Athens

THE *Queen Dee* berthed in front of the Central Customs House, Piraeus, at exactly four minutes to eight. The low shafts of morning sunlight were turning the scudding dust to gold. The buildings, public offices and private businesses alike were colorless with heat, paintless with neglect. On the quay, uniformed officials paced about their business while sallow-skinned women in black and small boys and old men in sweat-stained shirts scurried in their preparations to sell postcards, painted pottery, lace, copies of Byzantine jewelry, or suspect cameras and gold-plated pens to the arriving tourists. Bars, chandlers, stores stacked with seamen's clothing: the streets were full of movement, rising into the golden haze to the southern suburbs of Athens and the sandy brown and olive green slopes of Mount Hymettus beyond. The Chief Purser and his staff were in the crowded vestibule on B Deck, attended by three Greek immigration officials, exchanging landing cards for passports. The arrangement was always a passenger-irritant, in some ports more so than others, and the Chief Purser and his staff did their best to limit the irritation. Regular travelers knew that eventually their passports would be returned to them, but the timid were less certain of the security offered by one slender piece of card rubber-stamped "Valid until 13:00 hours April 21." If they were not back on board by lunchtime tomorrow they would not only have missed the boat but, it was sinisterly implied, they would be illegal immigrants and subject to immediate arrest, and possibly worse. The exodus from the dark vestibule down the canvas-covered gangway into the hot dazzle of the crowded quay, like gladiators entering an ancient arena, began as a trickle shortly after eight. By nine, when the first excursion coaches were due to leave, it was a steady flow.

Second Officer Hewson had risen at seven for berthing, having slept little more than a couple of hours after finishing his watch. He went to bed and got up with the Chief Officer on his mind. The man had a damned nerve the way he'd turned the whole ship upside down the last two days, having every inch of wire rope and cordage checked because of a single boat-drill incident. It wasn't so much the justification for doing it but the way he'd gone about it that got his goat. Implying that Ben Wilson had been a bloody inefficient Chief, and that he, David Welch, was a bloody efficient one. Efficient? Having deck space that should have been available for the comfort of passengers, albeit tourist class, monopolized for inspection. And prancing about the whole time as though life on the *Queen Dee* couldn't go on if it were not for him. If that were not enough, when he took over the watch the Chief Officer had had the nerve to tell him to instruct Mathis to take his four-to-eight in the afternoon for him as he had things to do ashore. Watch-keeping in harbor might be quite a different thing from watch-keeping at sea. Ben Wilson had been known to "have things to do ashore," and someone was always ready to stand in for him; but David Welch was no Ben Wilson. And never would be. It wasn't the ship he was so damned concerned about, but himself. He was a two-faced lying bastard. He'd made a stinking reputation for himself in less than a week on the *Queen Dee,* at least that could be said for him.

"Can I have a word with you about the course to Izmir, sir?"

The Master looked up from his breakfast tray. "Is it that urgent?"

The Second Officer was in no mood to take the hint. He was determined to talk. First about a course north of Andros and Chios. Then about current variations, estimated wind directions, forecasts, until the Master cut him short.

"Look, just what is it you have come to talk about? There's no need to start fencing with me after all these years."

"This is going to make me sound like a kid telling tales out of school," Hewson said, trying to make light of it. "I heard from Raymond that Mr. Welch spent the night with Lady Pratley in her cabin while Sir Gerald was in the sick bay."

"Raymond? The barman? An espionage agent?"

"Addison, one of the Observation Deck stewards, saw him go in. With champagne."

The Master found it hard to believe that an old colleague like Hewson should be so vindictive. "And you want to remind me that it's against company regulations? Is that it?"

The Second Officer was finding the whole conversation acutely embarrassing. "Not exactly that. I thought the situation was something that you should know about."

"The Chief hasn't altogether fitted in yet. He may have rubbed a few people the wrong way, but he's a good officer. Make no mistake about that."

"He's told Mathis to take his afternoon watch so he can spend the day ashore . . . with Mrs. Westcott."

That did make the Master jerk his eyebrows. "Mrs. Westcott? Huh! His amorous adventures are at least prolific. I hope he enjoys them." He intended that to end the conversation, but Hewson stood his ground. "I know you've told me all this because you expect me to do something about it. But put yourself in my position for a moment. Just exactly what would you do?"

"I'd point out to him that company regulations are every bit as important as international regulations," the Second Officer said. "If he *is* a good officer, he'll see it your way, sir. Otherwise, I'd relieve him of his duties for the rest of the voyage."

The Master shook his head sadly. "Be honest with yourself, man. Aren't you being just a bit narrow-minded, as well as perhaps a little jealous? I don't exactly hit it off with Mr. Welch; you and the other officers are well aware of that. But the company appointed Mr. Welch, not me. I'd have to have a damned sight better reason to relieve him of his duties than the fact that he's a little indiscreet where some of our female passengers are concerned."

"So I'm behaving like a school kid?" the Second Officer said.

"If you want my opinion—yes, I think you are."

The Chief Officer had sent a radio message ashore to have a self-drive car waiting for him on the quay. It turned out to be a scarlet coupé. He signed a couple of documents for the dark young Greek who had brought it and helped Pamela Westcott into the seat by his side.

"I think this is a wonderful idea," she said.

"David Welch Tours are at your disposal, madam. Where

shall it be first? The Acropolis? The Temple of Thesseus? Hadrian's Arch? Or the Agora?"

"The Acropolis," she said. "I've so looked forward to seeing it."

They arrived shortly before the first tour coaches of the day. For fifteen blissful minutes they had the shrine to themselves: even the photographers with their quaint wooden cameras and secret developing bags were too busy preparing plates and fluids for the day ahead to worry them. She sat on an ancient stone and just looked, while he moved around snapping her with a modern miniature.

"What do you think of it? It's rather splendid, isn't it?"

"It's the most wonderful thing I've ever seen," she said. "The pictures they use in the guidebooks don't do it justice. The proportions are so perfect they mesmerize you."

Still mesmerized, he drove fast along the Thebes road, overtaking the ramshackle public buses crowded with peasants and live chickens and bulky bundles. White beehives were scattered down the hillside like pebbles, and a heady scent of lemon and orange blossom hung over the car, almost as though it was deliberately following them. Near Thebes they paused by a monastery on the hill, blue and whiter than white. Among the trees in the monastery garden, a black-bearded monk in a stovepipe hat was peacefully digging in the flowerbeds in the shaded morning light.

"I wish we'd brought Richard with us," she said. "He's mad about fast cars. I suppose I'll have to give in to him when we get home and buy him one. He has his heart set on it."

"There wouldn't be room for him in this little beauty," he said. Then, so as not to upset her, he added, "I expect he's having a whale of a time with his little French girl."

But she knew otherwise. There was no mistaking the hostility of Simone's aunt, who was convinced he had been trying to lead her niece astray. She felt a twinge of sadness that Richard should be alone, but perhaps it was best for him; he couldn't be tied to his mother's apron for the rest of his life. Maybe he'd make an effort to speak to Simone again, in spite of the aunt's objections. She hoped so. For if there was one thing she was certain about where Richard was concerned, it was that he'd treat any girl as a gentleman should. That's why they had given him a public-school education.

"This must be a bore for you," she said. "Having done it all before."

"Only once before. Many years ago. I want to see how things have changed."

"Things always have changed. When I was younger they could never change fast enough. Now I'm beginning to feel that there is no such thing as a change for the better."

He blew the horn and swerved on a bend in the gritty road to avoid a couple of bell-ringing goats. "You're too pessimistic, Pamela. The world can still be a hell of a good place to live in. If you've got money and your health. Can't think of a better place off-hand."

The swerving car had pressed her close to him, and she felt the momentary tension of his muscles through his clothes. "I wish I could be like you, not worrying about things. But since I've been alone, things have been a bit . . . oppressive. Oh, look David! What right have I to be so humpy? It's heavenly."

A wood-and-plaster taverna lay beneath an arbor, and beyond, in a haze of blue and gold, the mountains rose up toward Delphi and Parnassus. They paused to drink ouzo, milky and cool. Outside, a shrimplike old man with several days' growth of beard was reading aloud from a newspaper. There had been a murder in nearby Levadia and other old men, unable to read, gathered round to hear about it, interrupting with questions and twitching the beads of a *komboloi* through their fingers as they listened.

"When this is all over and we're back in England, will you want to see me again?" he asked as they walked back to the car.

She hesitated for a moment, then said quietly, "Yes, I think so."

Her admission seemed to make him drive even faster. The warm dry air was chafing her skin and the throaty roar of the engine was sharing its nervous energy with her. Presently, he asked, "Do you like the Lake District?"

"Crazy, isn't it? England's such a tiny island, but I've never been there."

"I'll drive you there this time next year. The best time to see it is in the spring. That's a promise."

She began wondering what things would be like this time next year. The new house. How long Richard would want to be there with her before he started a career and went his own way. Who would share it with her if he didn't. But her eyes wouldn't let her mind concentrate. Suddenly, they were there. Delphi. Floating placid and ethereal above the Amphissa plain, carpeted with gray-green olives for as far as the eye could see.

"Okay, let's rid ourselves of this twentieth-century marvel and take a walk into antiquity," he said.

They left the car parked against a stone wall and strolled toward the ruins. A tall young Greek in very short shorts insisted on guiding them. They saw the Castalian spring, the tiger-striped Tholos, and walked over the sun-baked remains of the Temple of Apollo. When he was not guiding them, the young man man was singing.

"What's the song?" she asked.

He spoke English hesitantly. "The fish. It cannot live out of water. The Greek. He cannot live without liberty. Greek boy always sings, to forget he is poor boy and suffers."

"It's a lovely song, isn't it, David?" she said.

He said "yes," but without much enthusiasm, as though the guide had served his usefulness and should be away.

The young man said earnestly, "You like consult oracle?"

She laughed. "What will happen to me if I do?"

"Very little," David said, "unless you know how to interpret the guts of some sacrificed animal."

She gave a little shudder as they stood before the ancient stone, and he put his arm around her shoulder. The young man realized that they wanted to be alone, and a moment later he was gone, tumbling back toward the road like a sun-tanned spider. They turned from the ruins and sauntered up a bridle path into the mountains, between cool, tall firs, disappearing into the dozing sun-flecked shade. There was a strange aromatic stillness such as she had never experienced before, and when they paused to fill their lungs with the gentle mountain air, they were in a cocoon of silence.

"This must be what death is like," she said, and there was

nothing he could add because he knew she had struck a pain-
ful echo of the past.

They walked back to the sunshine and into the village, with
its row of modern hotels perched high over the sea of olives.
In the far distance the bay of Sálona was glassy in the midday
sun. They were poised looking down on the world like birds
when the young man in very short shorts greeted them again.

"All is new. Last century French archaeologists move people
from Temple of Apollo and pull down houses. Now everyone
live here. Kastri. Hotels good but better you eat my house."

Pamela looked back at the two shining rocks of Phaedriádes.
"We couldn't possibly impose on you like that," she said.

"Try saying no," David told her. "He'll exhaust us before we
do him."

The young man said, "English very good people. Saved life
of my papa during war."

She didn't ask how, but insisted that they couldn't impose on
his family's hospitality.

"You eat well at house of my papa and mama," he said, and
his bronzed smile told them they couldn't say no again.

The house was old and small and clean, a little way from the
road, shaded from the fierceness of the sun by a clump of olive
trees growing behind it on a ridge. Papa had apparently departed some time during the night with a mule and an English
lady who wanted to be up Mount Parnassus in time to see the
sunrise, and they weren't expected back until nightfall. Mama,
fat, in a washed-till-worn black dress, was turning chunks of
skewered meat over a charcoal fire. There was a skeleton-frail
old woman squatting on a stool in the corner, and three young
children. Impossible to say whose. Smoke curled from the open
grate and vanished through gaps in the tin roof and holes in
the stone wall.

The grandmother quivered to her feet and came toward
Pamela. "Come," she hissed in English as faltering as her bodily remains, "come and make your water."

When she returned from the primitive closet, the room was
full of people smelling pleasantly of earth and animals, drinking retsina straight from the barrel. Pamela and David were
instantly a part of the family; and always had been. Mama
came around spooning out great helpings of moussaka from

an earthenware dish and the young man in very short shorts
pressed them to accept the titbits of skewered meat. Someone
started singing. There was at once a rhythmic clapping of
hands. Several of the men were dancing. The young man in
very short shorts kept pouring retsina. And although it was
still early in the year, the wine, the meat, the acrid smell of
burning charcoal, the loud voices, and the warm air wafting
dustily in through the door, closed in on them with claustro-
phobic intensity.

"I'm afraid it's a little overpowering, David," she said.

He saw her face draining of color and was afraid she might
collapse. "The lady's not feeling very well," he said to the
young man. "She's not used to drinking retsina."

She wanted to walk slowly back to where they had left the
car, but the mother insisted she rest awhile. There was a small
bedroom behind the kitchen, built up on the ridge, the
wooden floor scrubbed bleach-clean, the iron bedstead covered
with fraying white lace. In one corner there was a marble table with a chipped jug and basin. On the damp stained walls,
once papered with pink roses long unrecognizable except
where protected by a worm-ridden chest of drawers, there
were sepia photographs of three men in army uniform, echoes
of two wars ago. The windows were opened inward; but the
shutters were closed and the room was pleasantly cool and
dark, smelling of hand-washed linen and lavender polish.

"Rest here awhile," David told her, "and I'll go collect the
car."

He left her lying on the bed, her long auburn hair like glowing coals in the darkness. When he returned with the car the
kitchen was empty except for the old grandmother. The village
street had been deserted, even of tourists. Everyone was at
siesta. Under trees, or lorries, or vines; in chairs, or blanket-
covered stone floors, or beds. He wondered whose bed had
been surrendered for Pamela—by the look of it, the mother's.
The grandmother nodded her head in sleepy recognition as
he entered. In the bedroom, Pamela was sleeping. She had let
down her coils of hair and it floated gently over her mustard
and green striped dress, to come to rest on the ancient lace. The
creaking of the door roused her.

"How're you feeling now?" he asked.

"Much better. But my mouth feels like the bottom of a parrot's cage. I'd give anything for a cup of tea."

He returned to the kitchen. The grandmother was dozing. He shook her gently by her bony shoulders. "Tea," he said. "I want tea."

She seemed to understand him, and he returned to the darkened room.

"This is absolute bliss," she said. "Why can't I live up here, always?"

"I hope I've pleased you," he said, leaning over to kiss her forehead.

She didn't resist him. Instead, she smiled and whispered, "I'm so pleased I met you. I didn't know it was possible to be as happy as I have been today. Thank you, David."

The grandmother crept into the room. "Tea," she said, holding a rusty piece of iron before her like a cross, and proceeded to fit it to the inside of the door.

"I'm afraid she doesn't know English as well as I thought," he said. "You won't get your tea."

"It's not important," she said.

When the old woman had gone, he returned to the bed and sat by her side on the squeaking springs. He wondered how far he dare go without offending her: she was so unlike any other woman he had known. He watched her body breathing under the thin dress, and when he could resist it no longer, asked "May I?"

"May you what?" she said, but she already knew the answer, lying quiet as a doe as his hand released the side zipper of her dress and crept through cotton and silk to caress her warm flesh. "Be gentle with me, David."

He eased her clothing away until she was naked, her skin tinged with the ruddy glow of two days' sunning around the pool. She lay quite passive, like a young girl fearful that any gesture on her part would be immodest. He fumbled frantically with his buttons, like an inexperienced youth, fearful that any delay might break the spell. His body was hard and muscular, not overdeveloped, that of a man who does an active job; but not once did she open her eyes to look at it. There was no sound anywhere in the house except for their steady breathing. Outside, the scraping of cicadae in the pines and a distant goat bell. She could feel his stiffness throbbing against her thigh, but still she made no movement. He took her hand and brought it down to feel him—sensitive, questing fingers that stayed frozen where he'd put them. She moaned a little, and his hand explored her body, moved through her pelt of pubic hair and was soon moist with love. He pressed his face to her right breast, a breast losing a little of its youthful firmness, spotted with two small brown moles an inch beneath the nipple. As he took the nipple in his mouth, her hand began exploring him, cool and delicate. And all the while she kept her eyes closed. He leaned slowly over her, parting her legs with his right knee and bringing his face close to hers, burying it in her auburn hair, moist with the heat of the day and perfumed with something delicately musky. For a moment he was about to plunge into her, seeking to make her scream with pain and squirm with pleasure as he had done so many women: but he hesitated, and was gentle with her as she had asked, coaxing their perspiring bodies into union with all the skill he used to coax a ship into harbor.

"Kiss me, kiss me, David," she breathed when she thought she would burst with his invasion.

His lips closed over hers, their teeth grated together; then his tongue thrust forward into her mouth as he drew his arms under her armpits to hook his body to her shoulders in a vise-like grip. The bed sagged and squeaked, and she lay prone under his weight, eyes closed, wondering how many times before two people had come together over its rusting springs, how many women had labored on it in childbirth, died on it in pain or peace. For a few brief moments it became her bed, the bed that warmed her in winter, nurtured her in sleep, and comforted her in loneliness. Then she had to think desperately of other things than David: his weight was too much, his size was too much, his violent spasms could be borne no longer and, having allowed him to go so far, she fought within herself to keep from screaming to him to stop, stop, stop, no David, not so hard, darling, I can't stand any more, deeper, deeper, oh hurt me, please, please hurt me, ah . . . ahhh!

He found a towel hanging at the side of the marble table and used it to dry his slackening flesh. "Thank you, Pamela," he said. "I needed that."

She opened her eyes but still she did not look at him. While she was putting on her clothes, she said reflectively, "I hope I wasn't a great disappointment. I've never been with any man other than Arnold. I'd begun to think I would never go with another man. Perhaps I shouldn't."

"Why ever not?" he asked, pushing open the shutters on the golden haze of late afternoon.

"Sons of eighteen don't usually take kindly to mothers who . . . well, you know what I mean."

"It's life, isn't it? Kids just have to grow up and get used to it, or lump it."

"I wouldn't want to do anything to hurt Richard," she said. "Young people have enough problems as it is these days."

He lit a cigarette, and as they prepared to leave the room he passed her her handbag. "I'd leave them a couple of hundred drachmas," he said. "It's quite enough. Put it under the washbasin."

Richard sat near the back of the coach with Miss Peebles. He had not chosen to sit with her, but by the time he had joined the coach it was the only seat left. The fact was, he was indifferent to joining any coach. He had hung around the quay for more than an hour keeping an eye on the tourist-class gangway, hoping to see Simone leave the ship. In spite of her horrid old aunt, he half hoped it would be possible for them to get lost together in Athens, maybe forever; and he wondered what it must be like to elope, to leave home and friends. And while he wondered the vendors were constantly trying to make him part with his drachmas for sunglasses, postcards, painted pottery or phony old coins. The first thing he learned about Greece while waiting on the quay was the irritating way they had of saying "nay" when they meant "yes." The second thing was that they coaxed you into buying something whether you wanted it or not, which was how he found himself with an embroidered belt he thought of giving to Simone in return for the shirt. But Simone did not turn up. The last tour coach was about to leave. He hesitated, wondering whether or not to go looking for her on board, but decided instead to do Athens,

Corinth and Mycenae for four pounds ten with lunch thrown in, although if he stayed on board lunch would have been free, part of the fare.

"These people have absolutely no road sense," Miss Peebles complained.

The coach was being propelled by a demon driver in a red shirt. The road out of Athens was narrow and twisted, full of bicycles, donkeys loaded with freshly cut grass, herds of sheep and goats, besides dogs, people, lorries, and other coaches. Olives, vines, cypresses, bougainvillaea flashed past as they careered through the obstacles, with glimpses of distant mountains and the spectacularly blue Saronic Gulf.

"Is this your first time in Greece?" Miss Peebles asked.

"It's my first time out of England," he said, hoping that she wasn't going to insist on talking all day.

"I first came here as a girl," she said. Richard had visions of an English virgin in bloomers interrupting some ancient stonemason who was putting the finishing touches to the Parthenon, in order to ask questions. "I am well traveled. A writer has to be. But I don't travel well. I have a delicate constitution."

Miss Peebles sat back in her corner to contemplate the effect of her carefully turned phrase. Richard said nothing, but thought about Simone and what she might be doing—shopping with her aunt in Athens, reading on deck while her aunt sipped camomile tea, splashing in the pool while her aunt kept a protective eye on her. He fingered the embroidered belt in his pocket, and wondered if he would ever be able to pluck up sufficient courage to give it to her. The coach bounced into a gleaming white fishing village, horn blasting, and jerked to a halt a few paces from the sea, lapping gently over a beach of flat gray stones. When they got out, instead of a salty, fishy smell, the air was impregnated with the warm scent of wild sage.

"We stop half hour," the demon in red announced. "You see church, buy souvenirs, drink Coke, or swim sea."

Miss Peebles, who was tired of being told that Corinth had pioneered public conveniences and that the Nemea wine was the blood of Hercules, and who was not feeling particularly religious that morning either, wandered off along the hot stones in search of a secluded cove from which to swim. Richard walked through the blinding, reflected sunshine, wishing he had bought sunglasses as well as the embroidered belt for Simone, past a shop selling hand-woven bags and goatskin rugs, past a ragged-sail windmill, to the small tile-domed church. It was, he thought, all rather like a stage setting for an opera, and was not surprised to find a man in glasses so dark he could hardly see, keeping people away from the best view in the village, while an American film unit photographed a blonde girl being dragged through the dust by her hair toward the church by an unshaven gentleman in tight faded blue jeans and a dirty and torn vest. A few locals were watching the performance, but it turned out that they were waiting for permission to enter the holy shrine and the film unit was more of an irritant than an amusement for them. Just like a film, Richard thought, life was constantly taking on new dimensions of unreality for him: the hot dry climate, the unfamiliar language, the houses, and the people to whom he could never belong, although he didn't feel that he belonged anywhere, even England, with school a thing of the past, and now the prospect of returning to a strange new house, and Mother beginning to take on new male friends, just as Tomlinson had told him she would. He was really on his own at last. Life would never be quite the same again.

Down by the little harbor he saw two men and a boy helping a sick old man in a canvas chair out of a caique. Fifteen to twenty people were gathered around. A big-eyed boy with a battered tray of iced Cokes told him that the old man was coming home from a neighboring island to die. Women in black sobbed dolefully as the invalid was lifted through the shallow water to the shore by the two men, thigh-high in the water. The wailing reached a crescendo when the dying man was laid on a stretcher to be carried by his brothers to his house between the slipped fishing boats and the drying nets. Richard shuddered feverishly in the heat of the day. When his father had died, it was all so remote, the clinical disposal of the body like a top-of-the-bill conjuring trick; but now, for the first time in his life, he felt a part of the act of dying. He had resented his father's death, as though he had done it to him and Mother on purpose. Now, as he watched the peaceful old man on the stretcher, bleached of life like the sun-hot stones, he was

filled with terror at the civilized injustice of death by war, by
murder, by the wheels of a taxi, and hoped he would also make
the gentle journey into oblivion in the company of those who
loved him, like this earthy old man. He had a momentary image of Simone, old in Grecian black, before his mind was
jerked back to reality by the shouting of English voices from
the tour coach. Miss Peebles had found her secluded cove, but,
it appeared, a couple of urchins had found Miss Peebles, and
while she was immersing her secret body in the warm, motionless water, they had scurried off laughing with her clothes. Her
wails from behind the rocks were like those of a mother superior reciting graffiti from the walls of the convent loo. An
English gentleman with a ginger moustache set off in search
of the young thieves but returned a quarter of an hour later
empty-handed, while the demon in red made the more practical gesture of taking a traveling rug from the coach and throwing it around the rock with the professional ease of a museum
attendant covering a priceless relic for the night.

The priceless relic rejoined the coach, wrapped in an itch-
ing tartan. "How can I possibly go into a restaurant and eat
lunch like this?" she wailed.

"It'll give you a jolly good story to write about," Richard
told her.

"I never," said Miss Peebles with shocked indignation,
"write about myself."

After that she was quiet for the rest of the day, sitting moodily in a corner of a none too clean eating establishment picking
at shrimps, or traipsing around the Lion Gate in Mycenae and
entering the tombs of Agamemnon and Clytemnestra like a
banshee.

It was early evening and the sun was making a blood
bath of the distant Cyclades when she suddenly turned to him
and asked: "Are you a Christian?"

Instinctively he replied, "Yes."

"In that case, young man," she said with a severity that was
disturbingly sincere, "think carefully of what you have seen
today and ponder what happened to the glories of the ancient
world when Christianity reared its ugly head."

He was ill equipped to argue. He sat looking at the shadows

flashing past the window and contemplated the most confusing thing anyone had ever said to him.

Captain Corlett was not looking forward to dinner. He had never been a fancy eater, and in all his years at sea the number of occasions on which he had been lured to dine ashore could be counted on the fingers of one hand. And since the company had turned the *Queen Dee* over to cruising, he had become even less enchanted with setting foot ashore. If anyone had business to do with him, they could come on board and do it. Otherwise, the fewer foreigners he saw the better. He didn't like their food, their climate, or their habits; and it was beyond him why so many people wanted to spend so much money mixing with them.

"This is a most unusual experience for me," the Master said, closing his eyes in horror as the taxi swung to port beneath the bows of an advancing bus. "It takes a man of great determination to get me to set foot ashore, Sir Gerald."

"I always tell Fiona that the best number for a dinner party is two—me, and a damned good headwaiter," Sir Gerald said, protecting his injured arm from the jolting of the car. "But tonight is something special for both of us. It's our wedding anniversary. Don't ask how many years. Too many. And how better to celebrate than in the company of a very good friend?"

"Stop making speeches and make sure the taxi's going to the right place," Lady Pratley told him. "Why should I want to be reminded of marrying you?" She turned to Captain Corlett. "Who wants to celebrate twenty wasted years? Forget the anniversary. We'll celebrate your retirement instead. Other people's disasters are so much more amusing than your own. What are you going to do when you haven't got a boat to play with? Run a troop of Girl Guides? That's what this old coot would like to do, but I won't let him."

The Master thanked her for reminding him of the awful finality of his last few days of command. If it was an event to be celebrated, he would choose to celebrate it with Ben Wilson, Harry Hewson, and perhaps young Rigg—but not in the company of these two. He wished now that he had risked offending them and had refused the invitation.

They had been sitting in the chandeliered silence overlooking Constitution Square waiting for service for the best part of half an hour. "I think the dark little chappie over there is supposed to be serving us," Sir Gerald said.

"Short arse, long handle," her ladyship muttered. "Try clicking your teeth, dear. You click them enough when we're eating at home."

Sir Gerald clapped his hands instead; but the dark little chappie was apparently deaf, or totally absorbed in watching an omelet on the service table slowly freeze itself to death. "The Greeks like their food cold," he said. "Something to do with the climate."

"Well, I'm not Greek and I like mine hot," she complained. "Go over and pinch his bum, or we'll go some place else. This is not the only place to eat in Athens, is it?"

The Master said not to worry on his account as he was in no hurry, and wished it was already tomorrow and another day.

She opened a petitpoint evening bag and rummaged for cigarettes. "Look at this silly thing. Not even room for a packet of French ticklers."

The Master was finding her ladyship as terrifying in private as she was in public. If a woman without a title carried on as she did, she'd be lucky not to be arrested before the end of the day. He offered her a light, but she insisted on finding her own. Finally she produced a gold and diamond gadget with a watch set into its base.

"How very beautiful," he said. "I've never seen anything like it before."

"You can have it," she said. "As a retirement present from me. I'm tired of it. Anyway, it's vulgar."

He handed her back the lighter with a polite smile, saying it was not quite the right thing for him, and hoped she would soon tire of showing off.

"Give it to one of your girlfriends then," she said. "Or do you prefer little boys?"

Sir Gerald had attracted the attention of the headwaiter, who in turn attracted the attention of the dark little chappie from the dying omelet. The menu was exhaustive but uninteresting, the kind of cuisine offered by any and every de luxe hotel from Athens to Zanzibar. The only thing Greek was the wine, and that her ladyship refused and ordered Scotch.

"I can't help admiring your dress, Lady Pratley. The colors are so unusual and so becoming," the Master said, clumsily disguising his effort to make polite conversation.

While he was speaking she moved Sir Gerald's wine glass to the edge of the table, in direct line with the waiter's approaching service of the entrée. A moment later the red liquid came flying, soaking into the clinically white tablecloth like blood and splashing over the bodice of the so-unusual-so-becoming dress. The dark little chappie looked in horror at what he had done. So did the headwaiter. So did the Master. So did Sir Gerald.

"Madame, I am most terribly sorry! I assure you—" the dark little chappie stuttered, expecting a torrent of abuse.

"It's not your fault," she said with affected charm. "This old coot shouldn't have left it there. He's always doing things like this to humiliate me in public." She turned on her husband. "What do you want me to do? Sit here and show the world my bubbies while someone gets it dried?"

Sir Gerald flushed with embarrassment and oozed charm. "Fiona, my dear, we are entertaining a very important guest. If it was my fault, I apologize. What more can I say? Perhaps the waiter can oblige you with a clean serviette."

"I'll oblige myself, thank you very much," she snapped. "I'm not having little short-arse touch me."

Her ladyship was supplied with a pile of clean serviettes and amused herself for several minutes dabbing, bunching, rubbing and salting the stain dry. "Now you can tell me that you'll give me two hundred guineas for a new dress," she said. "Mrs. Bartholomew can have this one, if she can get in it. Here, let me feed you, you big baby, you'll never manage it like that."

He let her cut up his food, and when she was about to fork some of it to his mouth, he said, "Thank you, my dear, but I still have one hand. I can manage it very well now."

The Master said, "I understand that Sir Edgar is modernizing head-office methods by bringing in a computer. Thank God, I won't be here to be at the beck and call of a mechanical moron." It was, he hoped, a gambit that would get the conversation back to the polite table talk where it belonged.

"It's bound to come sooner or later," Sir Gerald said. "A lot of captains resisted radar in the early days. Now they are grateful for it. What little I've seen of the City, there's a lot to be done by way of tidying up administrative methods. We're in the computer age now, Captain."

"It's a pity they didn't compute us," Lady Pratley said, blowing cigarette smoke across the Captain's face. "Every time I say something wrong he beats me. Look, you can see how my nose is bent. Last month he gave me a black eye. He should have chosen *me* by computer, then instead of beating me he could have smashed the machine."

"You mustn't believe everything Fiona tells you," Sir Gerald said with a strained smile. "It's just her sense of humor." He ate a piece of the chopped-up meat and hoped she had finished showing off for the evening. She was worse than she had been for some time, and he wondered why. It wasn't as though he had wished an unwanted social engagement on her, as was sometimes necessary; she had suggested dining Captain Corlett, and she had insisted it be tonight, before the cruise had gone any farther. The whole thing was her idea.

"When you've been at sea as long as I have, you get used to some pretty tall stories, Sir Gerald. But not so charmingly told," the Master said.

"Tell me, Captain, does your Chief Officer tell his tall stories charmingly?" she asked.

"Welch?" The Master sipped wine nervously, not anxious to be drawn into any conflict of personalities which could better be dealt with in the privacy of his cabin. "I've only known him a few days. I don't think there are any stories Mr. Welch needs to tell me."

"Why don't you ask him about the *Torrance*?" she said, flicking ash over the remains of her salad.

"Fiona," Sir Gerald said sharply, "I don't think the Captain wants a secondhand account of what is already history." Now, too late, he could see her tack.

"I would have thought Captain Corlett would be very interested in knowing his Chief Officer's little secret. Well, it was quite a big secret really. Fifty-eight lives and the ship's cat. Poor wives, poor little children left all alone, poor cat!"

"Fiona, I forbid you to say more! You've been drinking too much." But he knew she would say more. The affair had lasted six years, which was her longest yet, and for some reason or other David had steered a wrong course and now she was about to cut him adrift. She could be superbly cruel. To other people. He watched the Master's furrowed face as she vented her childish jealousy. It was quite a performance, and he had to admire her for it. His bandaged arm gave him a twinge of pain and he wondered, now she had so spectacularly abandoned David, who the next would be.

Richard followed the crowd from the point near the Acropolis where the coaches had dropped them. Between the darkened buildings a mirage of gold light appeared, floating in the sky, shrouding the Acropolis like a ghost, and was gone. They were, he thought, like a herd of cows being driven in before dawn for milking. They stood in the darkness somewhere between the Propylaea and the Parthenon; even the mirage of gold was no longer there to comfort them. Then, suddenly, in a torrent of recorded sound and a dazzle of colored lights the monuments, buildings, and gardens that once were old, were laid out before them as new as the kinkiest op art. The tour program had assured them this was a marvelous display "the majestic rhythm of which harmonizes with the grandeur of the surroundings to evoke the spirit of classical Greece." Richard didn't know much about classical Greece. Tor Beeches had taught him a little about Plutarch, Plato, Helen of Troy, Zeus the Olympian top god, and how to live a Spartan life and be happy. It was sufficient to sense that the ancient stones were going through a nightly agony, like a Bach score rendered by a pop group, or Goya's *maja* admired only for her nakedness. The whole thing was disastrously wrong. He felt ashamed to be there, and after the first few minutes he wanted to leave, and would have done so if he hadn't suddenly seen Simone's dark oval face reflecting a ghastly bluish light. For a moment he thought she was alone and his heart fluttered with excitement: but her aunt was there after all, standing a few paces behind, raptly attentive to the changing pattern of light and sound. He stood, wondering what he dare do, driving visions from his mind of going up and abducting her from beneath her protecting aunt's very nose like they did in the movies. And while he was thinking, he was drawn toward her, step by step, as to a magnet. He could try being nice to the aunt, convince her that he was not really a bad influence on her niece. Then he took another look at the aunt's grim face, as ancient as the floodlit ruins, and decided against the attempt. Click. The magnet had worked. He was there. He had taken Simone's arm and she, with a little start, allowed him to lead her through the crowd away from the ancient aunt. He had abducted her, after all: at least to the other side of the arena.

"Richard, do be careful," she said. "She'll be awfully mad if she sees us together again."

"But why? We haven't done anything wrong. Doesn't she understand that?"

"She's like all grown-ups. She expects us to do something wrong at any moment. She hasn't stopped talking about the *loco*. She was quite convinced it was full of drug addicts, and that if I stayed there a moment longer I would come out a *putain*—you know, a call girl, or worse. I tried to explain that it was my idea we went there, but that only made it worse. It would have been bad enough if you'd tried to lead *me* astray. Richard, I must go back to her."

"Does that mean I won't be able to see you any more?" he asked lamely.

A burst of white light momentarily lit her face, and he saw her eyes were filled with moisture. "She has been ill and it is my duty to look after her," she said. "I have to do as she wants. Don't you understand? I *have* to. She has forbidden me to go anywhere without her until we get home. You wouldn't want me to deceive her, would you?"

He was about to say yes, but he knew he couldn't deceive Mother if she asked something of him. Not yet, anyway; and he hoped he never would, the bonds of love were too great. "No," he said quietly, "if you have to look after her, you can't deceive her. Here. I've got you a present. I hope you like it."

She took the embroidered belt from his nervous hand. It looked pretty tatty in the darkness, but she embraced him ea-

gerly for it, pressing her hot young lips against his soft beardless face. "Oh, Richard!" she said, "it's the most wonderful
thing anyone has ever given me! I'll wear it all day and
all night. I'll never take it off. Even she won't make me take it
off. Ever."

"Write me when you get home," he said. "Perhaps some day,
some place, we'll meet again." It seemed a manly thing to say
when he had it in mind, but it came out like something from
a movie he'd once seen. Then she was gone in the darkness to
rejoin the horrid old aunt. He was left alone to the final moments of splendor of *son et lumière*, feeling as empty as the
brassy noise and convinced that his first love would also be his
last.

Cabin for Two

"WHAT the heck happened to the Greeks in the last two thousand years?" John peeled off a sticky drip-dry and prepared for
the shower. "All those gorgeous hunks of men you see in their
statues, and when you hit Athens, what do you find? Freaks.
Ugly, dirty little freaks. There's not a good screw among the
lot of them."

"Do you judge every country by whether or not you find people who share your tastes?" Richard asked him.

"They share my tastes, okay, but I didn't find a damned
thing I fancied. I'm very particular."

"So it seems," Richard said acidly. He was angry every time
John mentioned sex, simply because he rattled on about his
somewhat prolific love life without any sense of shame, while
Richard felt acutely embarrassed every time he thought about
his penis performing any function for him other than urinating. He'd always been taught to refer to it as his penis, and he
had a vague feeling of evil when other words for it flashed
through his mind.

"The best thing about the whole stopover was the production of Euripides' *Medea*. And the folk dancing. Trust you to
be a sucker and go for the *son et lumière*." John was shouting
to him from under the gushing water. "How're you making
out with Simone? Any chance of shacking up with her yet?"

"She has to look after her aunt. She's an invalid and—well,
she takes up most of Simone's time."

"She's a selfish old cow! She's no more of an invalid than I
am. You're not going to let her come between you, are you?"

"She's already come."

"Which is more than I have. Look. I haven't had a good
screw since Villefranche, and that was four nights ago. You'd
probably like it if you tried it." He stood in the cabin drying
it on a towel under Richard's nose.

"Stop being beastly. You only do it to annoy me. I know perfectly well that you're not as bad as you pretend you are."

"You mean you hope I'm not. Richard, you gorgeous creature, let me show you just how bad I can be!" And without warning he flung his naked body at the frightened Richard, popping buttons, tugging cloth, trying to get the other lad as naked as himself.

"Stop it! Don't touch me!" Richard screamed, his whole body shuddering in a nervous spasm. But John carried on playing, boisterously making a pretense of passion, laughing without malice at the English boy's wounded pride. Then, as suddenly as he had begun, he stopped, standing back to observe Richard's disarray.

"I'm sorry, you really are scared. Have you ever thought you might be gay without realizing it?"

"No, I haven't," Richard said angrily. "It's just wishful thinking on your part. I don't want to be gay. Thank you for the invitation."

"I knew a guy back in the States, a young actor, playing stock, who swore to everyone he wasn't. Poor kid didn't want to be. Public opinion doesn't make it easy to play the martyr. Finished up being bled of every dollar he earned by a headshrinker."

"Well, I'm sorry, but I just happen to think that people like you are suffering from a disease, and it's better for you and everyone else if you get yourselves cured." He was undressing to change into his pajamas, and felt as embarrassed doing it in front of John as he would had Simone been in the tiny cabin. "Don't you think you'd be happier in the long run if you went to a head-shrinker and then, perhaps, got married to a nice girl?"

"Like Simone? No thanks, ducky, I'd prefer a nice boy."

"Oh, crikey, you really should do something about that glandular condition of yours. Every time you sneeze, I bet you get an erection."

"What do you suggest I do about it? Take snuff?"

Richard jumped into his bed and switched off the light, to retreat into a womb of darkness. "You make me puke. You must have been debauched by a dirty old man at a very early age. Something awful happened to you to make you the way you are. It isn't as though you haven't had a good education. Your family's well off. You don't have to drag yourself in the gutter."

John fumbled for his pajamas in the darkness. "Dirty old men don't make kids homo. You either are or you're not. Like a four-leaf clover. Most people don't find anything revolting in that. It brings them luck. So, I make you puke." He folded himself into the bed and lay on his back, silent for a few moments, listening to the distant murmur of the *Queen Dee*'s engines. "When I was seventeen I had a girl. Living at home, in the family, it seemed the thing that was expected of me. Her name was Jeannie. Pretty little thing, with hair as golden as yours. Sorry, that wasn't meant to be a pass. We got on swell in a neutral sort of way. Then one night she hinted at what her girlfriends told her about how their dates necked with them in a downtown drive-in. And I gave her that line about being virtuous until maybe one day we'd get married. It was some time later that I realized it wasn't virtue. Indifference. Just simply indifference. Jeannie was fun. I like lots of girls I've met. But not one of them's ever turned me on." He reached out to the side table for cigarettes and matches. For a moment the flame illuminated his face, thin and pale in the flickering light, in spite of the past week's sunshine. He drew deeply on the cigarette, blowing the smoke upward into the darkness. "Detroit's not a good place to grow up in. It was a sheer accident that I met this Swiss geologist in a drugstore, a very good-looking boy a few years older than me, very manly, very tall and with a perfectly wonderful body. And golden hair. I'm mad about golden hair, as you know. He asked me back to his room. He was conducting some sort of survey at City Hall. Suddenly I felt him grasp me in his arms and kiss me. I was shocked and pleased all at the same time. Then it became a romantic passion. I was just crazy for him. He told me that I'd be better off away from home, growing up without inhibitions, being really free; after all, we yap enough back home about the 'free world.' That's why I went out to Frisco. After Hans had gone back to Europe. I cried. Like a girl, I suppose; but they were real tears all the same. My folks never knew. They still don't know. I guess it would break their hearts if they knew I was gay. They keep telling me I'm the right age to get married and settle down." The cigarette smoke started him coughing, and after the second spasm he stubbed it out half finished. "I should try to give it up. Smoking, I mean. Being gay's no real problem. The important thing is not to cure, but to understand, to learn to live in the mind and body you've got, because you're unlikely to be issued another. The quacks, medics or head-shrinkers, only have to deal with homos who have a guilt complex on their back, the guys who are ashamed of being themselves. Hans always used to say that you never really know a person until you've slept with him. He's right, of course; and homos are just like everyone else, looking for the lasting, permanent relationship. It's all there, from platonic love to lust, getting mixed up in a whole complex of emotions and needs, from a simple take-it-or-leave-it screw to the most bizarre vice. There are the strong or weak, healthy or unhealthy, whatever your sexual pleasure."

"Aren't you ever going to let me get some sleep?" Richard protested. "Whatever you do with your boyfriends, it's unnatural, it doesn't interest me, and I don't want to know any more about it."

"Hear no evil, see no evil, speak no evil, and you think that lets you out of the responsibilities of living? There's only one thing in the universe that's unnatural. A work of art. Unless, of course, you consider stuffing Strasbourg geese for their liver, forcing grit into oysters for their pearls, battery-feeding hens for their eggs, is unnatural. I might give you a point there. But I'm more concerned with man's inhumanity to man."

"You mean man's inhumanity to queers, don't you? For Christ's sake, shut up and let's get some sleep!"

"Do you believe in marriage?"

"Of course, everyone does." He corrected himself. "Most people do."

"Okay, let's approach it from that angle. Biologically a woman only needs to get screwed once a year to cope with all the kids she can reasonably breed. If she gets more, then it's fun and games. Nothing wrong with that, I say. Do you?"

"I've already said I believe in marriage."

"And if people have fun and games outside of marriage, it's wrong?"

"Yes."

"What kind of wrong?"

Richard felt himself being trapped. He said cautiously, "It creates all sorts of problems."

"The whole act of living creates all sorts of problems. For every married man or woman who commits adultery, I bet there's another whose marriage legalizes all kinds of vices it pleases them to indulge. Is it wrong to fancy girls in leather boots if you're not married, but okay if Miss Whiplash is your wife?"

"You're mad. You're absolutely stark, staring mad. If you don't shut up I'm getting dressed and going on deck."

"What kind of an education did you have if it closed your mind to ideas? This whole conception heterosexual people have that they are 'normal' gets me. It's only a matter of habit. Like smoking. It's all because of what grown-ups teach you when you're a kid. Pop culture does nothing but teach heterosexuality, in songs, magazine advertising, movies. But if a boy, or a girl, in spite of these pressures, turns out to be homo by nature, all society can think of doing is blame modern novels, French movies or some dirty-minded adult who taught the wrong things."

"Well at least it's not inherited like VD. But I still think it's a disease, and I don't want to catch it." He twisted in his bed and pulled a pillow on top of his head to block out any more of John's chatter.

"I assume you don't want to catch cruelty, rape, drunkenness, or dishonesty either. They're all personality weaknesses, known, I'm told, even in the realm of holy wedlock." He lit another cigarette, unable to sleep, determined to talk, even without a listener. "I read in a paper the other week that scientists have discovered ways in which a woman can be made to re-fertilize herself. Sort of battery hens, poor dears. Don't you ever think about animals? There are always more males than females, yet the females needs so little goo to start breeding. What are all the unwanted males supposed to do, sexwise? Of course, man is brilliant. When he domesticates them, he castrates the lot, one cock, one bull, one stallion per farm. Neat, simple and unnatural."

"Oh, crikey! You're not going to distort Darwin this time of night, are you?" The pillow had just been a pretense. He was still listening, attentively now.

"No, because I think human beings possess something more important that animals don't. We share with animals their basic sensual pleasures, but in addition we have the ability to love. Love. The most abused word in the English language. It's bounced about left, right and center in the drivel that passes for popular songs; but just once refer in public to one man's love for another man, and there's a shocked silence. Like you were the first guy to drop the H-bomb."

"Two men sleeping together doesn't seem right to me," Richard said.

"But will you accept that it not only seems right, but *is* right for the two men who do?"

"Maybe."

John said nothing for several minutes, but lay there smoking, the red glow moving around in the dark like a firefly, until Richard began to think the American boy had the admission he wanted and had ended the conversation. "I was thinking about Greece," John said. "In their conception of beauty, the man was naked and the woman always draped. Christianity produced the fig leaf and the naked dame, and your great Queen Victoria added the finishing touches to stamp out any remaining public recognition of homosexuality. Yet if you re-late every period of great development in the arts anywhere in the world with social customs of the time, you'll find being gay was the latest, the campest. Everyone who's civilized today admires Greek art, but how many accept that the whole way of life was civilized, including the men loving boys?"

"You've got a marvelous line in propaganda," Richard said. "But I just don't want to be loved by a man. I don't want a big hairy body all over me. I want to love a girl. Someone soft, and delicate, and lovely."

John laughed nervously. "Thank God, you're not sexless. I'd begun to think you were. You just suffer like so many peo-ple from this vast conspiracy to convince kids that de-sire can only be satisfied by the opposite sex. When they find it can be satisfied by their own sex they get frightened out of their wits. It wasn't so many years ago that boys were dressed

on the stage as things of beauty. The great age of the *castrati*.
These days we are taught to ridicule them, to pity them. What
kind of an education is that?"

"You object to farmyard animals having their balls lopped
off, but not to performing bears . . . I mean boys. I really do
think you're crazy."

"Look, answer me a few more questions, and still tell me I'm
crazy. The western countries are against polygamy and its har-
ems but how many ordinary people protest at adultery, call
girls, strippers? They accept them as part of their system. Do
you really think most men today want women as mothers for
their children? Nuts! They want a lot of Brigitte Bardots, sex
symbols, and line up in the drugstores for their contraceptives-
for-fun. Unless they're Catholic, in which case they try to figure
out a rhythm-method chart and line up for confession. Is a
woman's function in life always going to be confined to painting, powdering, and wearing the latest come-hither clothes to
attract the male? If women want to be treated as equal to
men—and why not, they're part of the human race—then they
must accept the possibility that they'll lose out in the game of
love to a male rival."

"You certainly hate women," Richard said.

"I hate hypocrisy, not women. When you were in Nice, did
you see the photographs outside some of the nightclubs? I saw
one place displaying pictures of a man and woman dancing.
They were having sex really. He was all between her legs, pushing her about in exotic poses. Titillation for the normals. But,
oh boy, are the customers in disgrace if they want to do anything about it! It's all one big business racket angled on guilt.
The normals love reading and talking sex scandals simply because they are substitutes for their own dull little lives. The
convention is that if a man and woman allow themselves to get
into a situation in which he could seduce her, it doesn't matter
a damn whether he actually screws her or not. It's appearances
that matter to the normals, not motives."

"I thought I was going to have the chance of answering the
questions," Richard said.

"Can you think of any better answers?"

"I hadn't thought about your kind of people at all until I

came on this cruise and found myself having to share with a queer."

"Richard." John's voice was quiet across the darkness of the cabin. "I hope, if you do find you prefer male to female companionship, you won't mind people using that word to describe *you*."

"I'm sorry," he said, no longer wanting to hurt him.

John was coughing again. He impatiently stubbed out the cigarette and lay on his back, arms under his head. It was a warm night and in spite of the punkah louvres the portless cabin was uncomfortably close. He pushed off the blanket and settled down again to sleep: but he was too restless, too frustrated. "Love's a funny thing," he said. "As soon as you really love someone you want to be gentle with them, careful not to hurt their feelings or their bodies. You've got to have sheer selfish animal passion to get a good fuck. I guess there's more passion than love in the world after all."

"You've never really loved anyone. You just make passes at everyone you fancy."

"I think love grows out of abated passion. As Hans said, you never really know a person until you've slept with them. I think I love Seth. He has a body as smooth as black silk and as tough as old leather. But I know it can't last. I'll probably go back to the States in the fall. I've an offer with a stock company in Frisco. He's studying medicine and wants to practice in West Africa. That's life. But I'll probably meet the right partner one day. I know gay people who've lived together happily ten, twenty, thirty years. Better record than many hetero marriages."

"Don't you believe in chastity?" Richard asked.

"Who the hell does these days? And if you want my opinion, I think masturbation really is queer." He twisted about trying to make himself comfortable, while Richard lay listening to the squeaking mattress. "I hate sleeping alone. It's the most unnatural thing in the world, for man or woman. And knowing you're over there makes it just hell."

Richard said firmly, "I'm afraid you'll have to get to know me without the benefit of Hans's advice."

"Do you like me a bit more than you did, or do you still want to go on avoiding me for the rest of the voyage?"

"I like you, John," Richard said. "I think I like you very much. I hope it's not pity."

"I can do without pity, thank you very much. Pity the poor devils whose wives make their lives such hell they end up scribbling obscenities on shithouse walls, or molesting little boys. And give every honest homo a bad name."

"I'd never really thought about sex being so complicated before tonight." Richard, too, was beginning to feel the heat, and he kicked the blankets off his bed.

John said, "I hope you won't ever confuse being homo with being effeminate. It takes all kinds to make a world. I've known six-foot marines who are as gentle as kittens in bed. I wish I had one now."

"Stop trying to shock me. It's not working any more. Aren't you ever scared of being blackmailed, or being picked up by the police?"

"It's life, isn't it? You've got to live with it." There was no trace of rancor in his voice. "There are some people who seem made to hate. They hate Jews, they hate niggers, they hate us, they hate themselves. You can change the law in those countries still so backward as to try to legislate one's sexual preferences, but you'll never change hate. It's there. Everywhere. But it doesn't hurt when you love someone."

Richard didn't reply. He felt incapable of responding to such overwhelming confidence in living. He lay in the darkness listening to John's heavy breathing, wishing vaguely he could creep into the other boy's bed and satisfy him. It was flattering to be desired so much; and he felt oddly in the wrong for saying no. But deep down inside, he felt a repulsion at sharing a bed with another man. Habit, education, animal instinct, religion or inhibition or both—he didn't know the reason. But he knew he was normal: and he hoped he always would be.

Izmir

THE *Queen Dee* slid down the Gulf of Izmir during the early
hours of Sunday morning, leaving Mytilene to the north. A
few of the more enthusiastic passengers had risen to greet the
dawn, standing along the port side of the Observation and
Promenade decks in the purple moments before sunrise. In the
far distance the sea and sky were knit together by the black silhouette of mountains on the Turkish mainland. They waited
for half an hour, staring toward the east; and then, bang on
time, the fiery rim of orange rose in majesty, filling the sky
with morning blushes. Minutes later, as far as the eye could
see, there were mountains, clear, sharp, stark against the azure
sky like improbably-colored postcards. Half involuntarily
someone cried, "It's a miracle!" and a passing deckhand smiled
with smug satisfaction, convinced he had arranged it all for
them. But there were others among the *Queen Dee*'s passengers who were incapable of rising to greet the dawn, or to greet
anything else for that matter. They had shared the spectacle
of the previous afternoon's cruise through the Greek islands,
and they had shared the spectacle of the sun dropping silently
into the wine-dark Aegean; but they had done so with
groaning bellies. One by one they took to their cabins,
all of them squeamish with thought-pictures of the previous
week's gales in the Bay of Biscay, which until this moment
had happened to other people, in another ship, in another century. By midnight the bugs were doing their worst, except to
those well-traveled souls who made the discomfort of their
friends and relations none the easier by singing the praises of
precautionary doses of iodochlorhydroxyquinoline. It was a surprise and an annoyance to the stricken passengers that they
should be laid low, but not to Chief Purser Leslie Craddock
or to Dr. Hammond who, in spite of preliminary warnings in
the ship's newspaper that traditional Greek cooking should be

eaten with caution, were all too familiar with the bouts of gas-tro-enteritis which always followed a call at Athens. In all, seventy-two passengers were laid low, none of them a part of the hygienically conducted shore excursions, but all of them with unhappy memories of drifting from taverna to taverna and mopping up the ouzo and retsina with dishes of tara-mosalata, stuffed aubergines, and shrimps fried in batter.

Pamela Westcott woke at eight. Everything was uncannily quiet. The *Queen Dee* lay at anchor in the roadstead. The sun streamed into the cabin, unmercifully blinding her as she lay physically and mentally exhausted by the excursion to Delphi. In the evening David had brought her down from the mountains, and they had had a quiet supper together in a *boîte* overlooking the Acropolis, danced a little, drank a little, romanced a little, walked as once she used to walk over the downs near Westborough with Arnold, and returned to the ship shortly after midnight. The morning sickness on Saturday she had put down to the simple biological fact that she had not had sexual intercourse for longer than she cared to remember. She had been very practical about it. Soda water, weak tea, and dry toast for breakfast; and then she had spent the morning sitting in the shade watching the enchanted isles drift by, each with its own style, its own particular mystique. But at lunch-time she was still not feeling at all well and she had sat facing the Chief Officer, trying to eat, trying to keep up an intelligent conversation with the Jamiesons and the Aftons, trying the whole time to avoid his soft brown eyes which kept saying, "I want you again, and I'm going to have you, you know."

"How about a Spithead pheasant for breakfast, madam?" Hyslop asked, offering her the Sunday menu.

"Good heavens, what on earth's that?"

"Bluejacket's name for a kipper, that is," he said with a perky smile.

"I certainly don't want kippers," she said "I don't think I want anything except a cup of tea."

"Now you mustn't spend all day in bed, madam. It's glorious outside. You'll feel better when you're up. Take a couple more of them tablets. Have a little scramble on toast. You'll be eating like a horse again for lunch, beggin' your pardon, madam."

"That's all right, Hyslop. I'll try to eat a little. But nothing heavy. Would you mind closing one of the curtains? The sun's overpowering this morning."

"Certainly, madam. I'll soon have everything tiddley for you."

"Tiddley?"

"Neat and tidy. Shipshape."

She smiled. He was making a superb effort to snap her out of her morning-after. "I think the only naval term I know is 'all at sea,' and that's about how my stomach's feeling this morning. I really should have been more careful what I ate."

"You probably know a lot of old navy terms without knowing you know them, madam. Most people do." He started busying himself about the cabin, adjusting details, moving bits and pieces, doing nothing really other than being there because he thought the lonely lady needed a little morning chatter. "Take 'the devil and the deep blue sea.' In the old wooden ships the devil was a large seam near the gunwale. To be between the gunwale and waterline was a pretty precarious position. Or 'no room to swing a cat.' Now that's one you must have used. The cat-o'-nine-tails which couldn't always be swung for punishment in the enclosed spaces of the old men-o'-war. Or 'chock-a-block,' full up, from choking the luff of a block and tackle."

She tried to listen to him, but her mind was too confused by other things. The Chief Officer had chocked her block and that was for certain. She must have been mad to let him do it after knowing him for less than a week, and at her age, when in a few more years it would be time to think about what her mother always called with awful finality the change of life, as though at a predetermined time one's whole bodily functions lurched off in a new direction with you after them, trying to keep up. She had no right to be young any more, although she wanted to be. Desperately. That one glorious day up in the mountains at Delphi had convinced her that she was still too young to start getting old. Yet she felt ashamed for being happy. She liked David; but she didn't love him . . . yet. And she couldn't understand herself for letting him know her physically before he even knew her properly socially. Why, he hadn't even visited her at home. Oh dear, life was so confusing.

Home wasn't there any more. It was being moved right now by sweet Mr. Pulbright.

"You talk about something being 'A-One.' Well, that's the top seaworthiness classification at Lloyds. You talk about 'bilge,' a lot of nonsense. Did you know that the origin of 'to blow the gaff' probably lies in a ship revealing her identity by hoisting her colors at the peak of her gaff? When you say something's 'copper-bottomed,' you're really talking about the days wealthy owners could afford to copper the hulls of wooden ships to protect them from water parasites. 'Bitter end,' the piece of loose rope after belaying. 'Money for old rope.' Now that doesn't need any explaining, does it, madam?"

She said mechanically, no, it didn't.

"And there's 'to shove in your oar' or 'to swing the lead.' "

His Cockney voice seemed to emphasise "shove in," and she thought about David, lying on top of her, naked. But she didn't want to remember anything crude about it. She had to think of the incident as something wonderful and beautiful. Yet the whole thing could be reduced so easily to the squalid if she lost her head about it. As it was, they hadn't taken any contraceptive precautions. She really must be mad, behaving worse than a young girl, and she old enough to have a grown daughter if she didn't already have a son. She'd heard jokes about eligible widows going off to the Mediterranean and kicking over the traces: "kicking over the traces" wasn't an old naval expression, was it? Perhaps she should ask Hyslop. She couldn't believe it was really her, lying there in the luxury of a first-class cabin on the *Queen Dee,* mistress of the ship's Chief Officer, it was all so appallingly wicked and she really shouldn't be enjoying it. She should be thinking about how best to end the affair. But she wasn't. She wasn't doing that at all. She was thinking about what would happen next, when and where David and she would be together again, and whether he would continue to be gentle with her, and whether he would grow to love her and she to love him. Life really was beginning again. And she couldn't stop it, maybe because she didn't want to.

"Breakfast, madam. Will you take it in bed, or shall I leave it on the side table?" She hadn't even noticed Hyslop leave the cabin and return with the tray. "Try the eggs, madam.

They're delicious. Laid specially for you this morning by the ship's hen."

She laughed. "Thank you, Hyslop," she said. The world could be a wonderful place. Ordinary people could be so kind, so generous with their emotions.

Richard came to see her while she was trying to stomach the scrambled eggs. He was full of youthful uselessness in the presence of illness, ambling around the bed like a large dog trying to wish her well. "You have taken your tablets like the doctor ordered?" he asked. "Are you sure there's nothing I can get you?"

"No, thank you, darling. I'll probaby be all right again by lunchtime. Then I can go ashore for a bit and see what Turkey's like."

"Shall I stay with you? Perhaps you'd like me to read to you or something?"

He suddenly made her feel very old. "I don't need to be read to," she said. "Besides, there's little in the ship's library worth reading. A few grubby travel books, some Dickens in such small print it would make you blind before you got halfway, and two by Miss Peebles, but they're out, of course, and anyway I don't think I'd like what she writes very much.'

"I'll stay anyhow, so you don't feel lonely," he said.

"No. Please go ashore and enjoy yourself. You may see Simone." She could tell at once by his expression that she'd said the wrong thing. "Buy me some genuine Turkish delight."

"I don't think I'll ever see Simone again," he said, and she wanted to laugh at his youthful dismay.

"Surely it's not as bad as that, is it? Why don't you speak nicely to her aunt?"

"Simone says that wouldn't do any good. But she's promised to write to me when we get back home."

She held his hand and patted it affectionately. "Faint heart never won fair lady. Still, Simone's probably right. She must do as her aunt wishes, although I must say she seems to be a very unreasonable woman. I mean, it isn't as though you're any old hobbledehoy."

"Did you ever have an aunt who tried to stop you seeing Father?"

"We had something worse. We had a faithful old master

baker who had your father supervising the mix at four every morning." She saw he was taking it seriously, which she hadn't intended. "Richard," she said softly, "you are happy, aren't you?"

"Yes, of course, Mother," he said earnestly, not wanting her to see that he wasn't. "It's a lovely cruise. If I never have the chance to travel overseas again, I'll have seen and learned things I'll remember all my life."

"Don't be such an old pessimist," she scolded. "I'm sure you'll have plenty of other opportunities to travel. It's not like when I was your age. Young people seem to go round the world these days as though they were born with jets on their feet. Now, be off with you, and have a wonderful day. Why don't you keep John company? He's such a nice boy."

"I'll see," he said. He was about to leave, but hesitated awkwardly in the doorway. "Can I have some more money, please? I got confused with the drachmas. I didn't know I was blowing so much."

He seemed too old to be taking handouts from his mother; but he was not earning for himself and the money was there, although she had no idea what was the right amount to give an eighteen-year-old son, particularly if he began courting. "You'll find some over there in my handbag," she said. "I think it's Greek, but they'll change it for you."

He rummaged in her bag until he found several notes folded behind a small mirror. Slipped in between them was a photograph of a man and a woman standing next to a white-skirted Greek Evzone on guard before the Royal Palace in Athens. The man was the *Queen Dee*'s Chief Officer. The woman, his mother. "Are you going to go on seeing him?" he asked.

"Why? Don't you think I should?" she asked anxiously.

"That's up to you, isn't it?" he said. "Maybe you need another husband. I don't think I need another father."

Captain Corlett had spent most of the previous day in his cabin thinking and brooding and reading a little Trollope, except for the few hours he was on the bridge commanding the *Queen Dee*'s course out of Piraeus and seeing her safely through the busy island shipping lanes. He was well aware of

Lady Pratley's motives for telling him what she had about his
Chief Officer's past, which more properly should have been
disclosed to him by the company's Marine Superintendent;
and he was equally well aware of Hewson's motives for bringing to his attention his Chief Officer's weakness where women
were concerned. Welch had an unfortunate knack of rubbing
people the wrong way. Some of the younger men might be jealous of his success with women, and the older ones resented the
way he used his authority to run the ship; but whatever their
motives, the inescapable fact was that with every day that
passed the *Queen Dee* was becoming less of a friendly ship.
In all his years at sea nothing like this had happened before. If
the vindictive Lady Pratley chose to spread her poison else-
where, the situation would get worse before it got better. He
was well aware that the situation demanded firmness and tact
on his part; but he resented having such a situation to deal
with, particularly during his last few days of command. It
would be so much easier to forget what her ladyship had said,
to forget what Hewson had said, to accept the Chief Officer
on his present showing as a man of proven ability, and let
the whole matter ride until the end of next week when Arkwright would take over command and create a whole new set of
personality conflicts anyhow. So on Friday night Captain Corlett decided to sleep on it. On Saturday morning he decided
to raise the matter with Welch . . . in the afternoon. But
he'd slept on it again, and now it was Sunday and in a few
hours he would be conducting morning service in the cinema
for the handful of devout souls who had not gone ashore, and
his conscience was troubling him. His old man had beaten the
Word of the Lord into him and sent him off to sea at a tender
age with an education based squarely on never putting off
until tomorrow things that should be done today. In the end,
old-time religion got the better of *laissez-faire*. Shortly after
Welch came off his four-to-eight watch, the Master summoned
him into his presence.

"Sit down, Chief," he said. "There are one or two things
that you and I have to get straight."

"Very well, sir," the Chief Officer said, sinking into the chair
and crossing his legs with defiant ease.

"When you joined the ship's company on April the tenth—"

"Ninth, to be exact, sir."

"Just eleven days ago. You may remember our first conversation together."

"I remember you were naturally distressed at having to have a replacement for Ben Wilson at all. I've done my best to run the ship efficiently. It takes a little longer than eleven days to get to know a ship thoroughly."

"And men, mister. It takes a little longer to get to know men."

"I'm afraid I don't follow you, sir."

"Really. Then see if you follow this. Your appointment was made by the head office on a recommendation from Sir Gerald Pratley. Sir Edgar being this year's chairman of Fomona, a word in his ear was no doubt a very powerful recommendation indeed. It was, of course, a mere coincidence that you happened to be a personal friend of Sir Gerald . . . and Lady Pratley."

"That, sir, is quite an unwarranted remark. Repeated outside this cabin it would be slanderous."

The Master paused in the center of the cabin to light his pipe. "There's no need for us to lose our tempers. I haven't accused you of anything yet. I merely want to establish facts. I thought it was common knowledge that you've known Sir Gerald and Lady Pratley for several years."

"So? Even seamen have friends."

"You know Lady Pratley very well, don't you?"

The Chief Officer got to his feet, raising his voice. "What the devil do you mean by that? I don't have to take that kind of insinuation from anyone—even you!"

"I understand that you spent Sunday night with her in the Rose Suite. While Sir Gerald was receiving attention in the sick bay."

"Who the hell told you that?"

"Is it, or is it not, true?"

"It's a lie! A stinking, filthy lie! Who told you? I'll give the bastard the hiding of his life!"

"But you did go to her suite that night?" the Master persisted, sucking the pipe into a crackling glow.

"No. Now who are you going to put up to saying that I did?"

It was an intolerable situation—the senior officer, the man he had most to rely on, telling lies like some petty thief. And he had a damned good suspicion he was only doing it to show his contempt. The man knew that to prove it he would have to go through the whole squalid procedure of producing witnesses from among the stewards. It was as childish as what the butler saw. But an admission on the Chief Officer's part was essential if he was going to prevent a deterioration in the situation, which at best would damage the company's public image and at worst could endanger the lives of the company's passengers.

The Master said, "You will not, I hope, deny that on Friday you instructed Fourth Officer Mathis to take your afternoon watch. In order that you might spend the whole day ashore with one of the passengers who dines at your table."

"I find this line of questioning insulting and infantile. You're treating me like a criminal because I choose to change the duty roster in order to have a few hours off to which I am perfectly entitled."

"So you don't deny you spent the day ashore with Mrs. Westcott?"

The Chief Officer walked over to the desk and helped himself to a cigarette from a silver presentation casket, a gift to the Master from the B and E board after twenty-five years of service. "Why should I deny it? Mrs. Westcott is very good company. Unlike most of the other old bores."

"Has no one ever impressed upon you that close personal relationships with any of the passengers is not in the interests of a well-run ship?"

"Hell, that's all right for kids. You're not seriously trying to tell me how I should run my own life, are you?"

"No, Mister. But I am telling you how you should run this ship. At least, while I'm Master. You can perform any hanky-panky you like during leave, but not while we're at sea. Is that clear?" He reached out to draw one of the curtains to shield the cabin from the heat of the sun as it got round westward.

"Clear, and unreasonable, sir," the Chief Officer said. "And now if you have nothing more to get straight with me, have I your permission to catch up on some sleep . . . alone?"

The Master was bitterly aware that the younger man had little respect for his authority. In a few more days he would have no authority left: Arkwright would have stripped the day cabin of any remains that a personality could stamp on it in a quarter of a century, and would no doubt be cracking jokes with the *Queen Dee*'s new Chief Officer about how things used to be done in the old days, the days of Ted Corlett and Ben Wilson. He said, "Before you go, I have another matter I want to get straight. It concerns the *Torrance*."

"You must have it in for me, to have gone to the trouble of finding out about the *Torrance* so quickly," he said, his right cheek twitching nervously.

"I don't have it in for you. I don't have anything in for anyone. I try to play god as well as God does. You can thank Lady Pratley for telling me about the *Torrance*. Perhaps now you will do me the courtesy of telling me about it for yourself."

"The bloody bitch! I should never have got involved with her in the first place. That's what becomes of being nice to the upper classes. I suppose she painted me as black as she possibly could?"

The Master said quietly, "I am not interested in gossip, Mr. Welch. Only facts."

"The *Torrance* was a Hemsley Lines vessel. Cargo. Seven thousand tons. I was Master at the time, and had been for four years. Filthy night, off Santander. Broke her back on the rocks. It was shortly after that I met the Pratleys. And joined B and E. The bloody bitch, telling you all this! I thought she had confidence in me."

"Am I to have confidence in you? That's what counts, isn't it?"

The Chief Officer leaned across the desk to shake ash into a tray. "The company has. The Marine Superintendent knows about the *Torrance*. You don't think I could keep it a secret from him, do you? What the hell, I don't *need* to keep it a secret from anyone! I'm not the only Master to be slammed down by a court of inquiry. If we were all kept off the sea for the rest of our lives every time something goes wrong, there wouldn't be a ship anywhere in the ocean!"

"Nevertheless, it was something you didn't think I had a

right to know about?" There was no mistaking the resentment in the older man's voice.

"It was not like that at all, sir. I knew you were retiring at the end of this voyage. And it's sort of a new life for me. There are some things best forgotten, and the *Torrance* is one of them. I think that's how the Marine Superintendent saw it. Otherwise I'm sure he'd have filled you in more than he did. They seem to be very happy with the appointment at the head office. For my part, sir, I'm very unhappy you don't share their confidence in me. It's not my fault Ben Wilson had to be replaced. I'm sure he was a splendid fellow. I feel sorry for the poor devil, as sorry as anyone can feel for someone they've never met."

The Master didn't believe the bastard's sincerity, not for one moment did he believe it; but he chose to accept it. Some of what Welch had said made sense. There were many good ship's officers who had accident records. Life was learned by experience; but, just the same, he doubted if his Chief Officer was the type of man who would learn by experience. A few more days and he'd be Arkwright's problem. Then Hewson's nose would be put out of joint well and truly. It wouldn't surprise him if the Second Officer applied for a transfer to another ship. Hewson wasn't a fighting man, and he could hardly blame him. The whole business was appallingly squalid. In the old days a man like Welch would never have got where he had in the merchant service. But times changed, and not always for the better.

He made a final effort to end the interview on a point of achievement. "May I have your word that, until we return to Southampton, you will discontinue philandering with any of our female passengers?"

There was a suspicion of a smile on the Chief Officer's face as he replied. "You can rely on my discretion," he said. "I think my interest in the company's welfare is more long-term than yours." He knew he'd got the better of the old sod.

Richard was too late for the excursion to Ephesus, so he would never see the harbor into which Saint Paul sailed and walked along the marble street. And the tour to Pergamon had been canceled, due to there not being a minimum of thirty passengers well enough or willing enough to trek up the mountain crag to see the site of the famous library confiscated by Anthony after Cleopatra had lost hers in Alexandria by fire. He was about to walk from the ferry pier to see the town by himself, when he heard John's voice calling him from a private launch coming alongside the landing stage.

"Hi, Richard! Wait for us!"

A couple of brown-skinned Turks in ragged baggy trousers ran forward to secure the boat. Then Richard saw Lady Pratley flutter forward from under the awning, a handbag on one arm and John on the other. She paused to pay the boatman, and a handful of banknotes were caught by a playful breeze to be scattered like manna over the waters. John did his best to catch them, but without success, and was only able to save what remained by grabbing her ladyship's bag and snapping it shut. He hesitated to haggle a price with the boatman, but she dragged him away.

"Do come along," she said. "I haven't all day. There's plenty more where that came from. It's only money." She left the boatman and several small boys fishing like mad for the floating pieces of paper. "I'm borrowing your friend to come on a shopping excursion," she told Richard. "You don't mind, do you? That old bore of a husband of mine hates shopping, and I want to buy lots of madly exciting things." She pounced on a terrified small girl carrying fish in a flat basket on her head. "The shops. Which way shops? Why you no speakie English? You no go school? You play pokey-pokey with boys instead?"

Richard wished like hell he hadn't missed the coach to Ephesus. Lady Pratley's showing off made him squirm. He'd never seen anyone behave with money like she did. It reminded him of the almost worthless bits and pieces of drachmas he had scattered before a beggar in Athens, to get rid of them. He'd felt rather noble about the gesture at the time. He'd never given a beggar anything before. But he realized now it was all an emotional cheat. He hadn't given the poor blighter anything of value to himself.

"How did you get lumbered with her?" Richard asked when her ladyship was out of earshot.

"She heard my folks planning to lunch with that crazy old

English colonel and his wife at some place along the coast. Kusadasi, I think it's called. Dad's got some kind of an investment deal in the works with the old boy. I was coming ashore anyhow, so when she pounced I could hardly tell her I'd set the day aside to climb Everest. For Christ's sake, stick by me! She's more than enough for two. But you must admit, she's the campest thing since bell tents."

It was, Richard thought, a pretty eccentric shopping expedition. Lady Pratley strutting off the pier in a tight-fitting linen two-piece, all scarlet and white, dragging a small fishy girl unwillingly behind her in order to be shown the shops. John in even tighter blue jeans, wearing bug-eye sunglasses and mincing along with her ladyship's handbag on his arm. And himself, conscious of the old gray flannels which he'd had the last term he was at Tor Beeches and the new pink and gray shirt, all diagonals and circles, that Simone had bought for him in Nice, and wondering what Simone was doing now and if she was thinking of him as he was thinking of her.

"I thought this was a center of ancient civilization," Lady Pratley said as they hit the heat reflecting from the blocks of modern breeze-and-plaster buildings. She took one look at the sparsely treed promenade, at the Turkish families sitting sipping cay from painted glasses, at the American servicemen's wives lugging babies to the shore to bathe, and plunged across the road after the small fishy girl into a shaded side street. "It's neither ancient nor civilized. I don't know why I allowed you boys to drag me out on this wild goose chase. I should have stayed round the pool on the boat."

John said that most of old Izmir had disappeared in wars and revolutions. Alexander the Great fought for it; Homer lived in it; Marcus Aurelius rebuilt it after the earthquakes had destroyed it; it was Byzantine, Crusader, Venetian, Greek and now Turk.

"No wonder it's a bloody mess," her ladyship said, as the small fishy girl deposited them on the steps of a mosque with a triumphant smile of achievement. It was not where her ladyship wanted to be deposited at all and she told the small fishy girl so in no uncertain terms. But the child had lost interest in conducting them any farther. Her ladyship gave it a fifty-lire note, which to judge by the crowd that instantly gathered was a fortune in any language, and the next moment they were being unceremoniously jostled by begging hands and grinning faces until they were lost in the noisy confusion of the old market. It was a vaulted labyrinth, dark for lack of sunshine, yet bright with fruit and vegetables, smelling of fly-blown fish and meat, the ancient flagstones treacherous with decomposed vegetation and butchers' swill. Once in, her ladyship wanted to get out, but the getting out was the more difficult as they were swept along clinging to each other in panic by a crowd of Turkish housewives going about their business in all directions at once. Suddenly, she saw a dark Aladdin's cave of carpets and rugs, large and cool, and smelling of pregnant goat. Inside they were received by an over-fed man with milky white skin, and eyebrows and moustache as black as burnt cork.

"I want a bedside rug in blue and white with dolphins on it," Lady Pratley said, making her requirements known with the assurance of a Knightsbridge veteran. But communication was not going to be as easy as it was in London, although the owner, in his vast balloon of black pleated trousers, aided by a covey of under-fed young men, was determined that the welcome English customer would always be right. Within minutes the cavern was a flapping, flying, dusty inferno, as the over-fed one displayed the intricacies of weft and web, the priceless greens and turquoise, and interpreted the meanings of traditional native designs. But no dolphins, blue, white, or any other damned color. She saw something which looked like a dragon and said she'd have it if they had it in a smaller size, and with the body in blue instead of red. After much arm-waving, the under-fed ones were sent off into the labyrinth of vaulted passages, while a small boy with innocent eyes and a knowing grin served black coffee from a swinging brass tray made in Birmingham. Her ladyship was about to depart, having by now lost interest in the acquisition of any bedside rug, when the under-fed ones returned laden with blue bulls, blue serpents and a blue Medusa; but convinced that none was suited to her boudoir, she swept from the cavern amid flapping arms, flying carpets and wet, sad eyes.

"What about buying some hand-beaten silver jewelry?" John asked hopefully.

"A lady never buys jewelry: it's given her," she said. "In any case, I've done enough shopping for one day. I want to sit down."

But to find her ladyship a place to sit was not easy. They eventually found their way out of the market by following a woman laden like a donkey with panniers of purchases: and there, almost as though it had been built to order, was a caravanserai, cool and quiet, with an inner court of creeper-covered sandstone. She didn't want to partake of anything, she just wanted to sit, but to oblige the waiter they ordered cay. A dehydrated little man with defeated eyes and a worn suit several sizes too large for him shuffled up to the table and threw a glass of some fearful-looking liquid at them. But no one bothered to move, it was so obviously a sealed joke glass. The little man tried to sell the glass, then offered a bunny that jumped at the end of a rubber bulb, but aware from the start that he wasn't going to make a sale, and fearful of the waiter's impending wrath, he shuffled out into the blinding sun.

"Tell me," Lady Pratley said, "I'm a very curious woman. Are you two lovers?"

"No," Richard blurted out with a finality that ended all further discussions of the proposition.

"But you're gay," she said, pointing a bony finger at John. "I knew it the moment I set eyes on you."

"Get you! Who do you think you are? Mother Earth?"

Richard began to wish he'd never got involved in the shopping expedition. He had never dreamed that people could banter such secret things in public. Lady Pratley looked at him with amused eyes.

"Perhaps you haven't made up your mind what sex you are yet," she said.

Before he could reply, she had gone off into the interior of the caravanserai in search of a loo.

"What a man-eater," John said when she had left them.

"Well, at least she's normal," Richard said acidly.

"Ducky, she's more than normal. She's abnormal."

"It must be awful for Sir Gerald," Richard said. "He has to live with her twenty-four hours a day, more or less. I wonder why he hasn't divorced her?"

"Maybe he loves her. Or perhaps he can't be bothered, things being so complicated in Britain. It's easy in the States. In Arizona you can get a divorce for a crime against nature. So remember. Keep off the grass."

Lady Pratley returned from the loo, followed by a big man in a red fez who was shouting at her in Turkish while she shouted back at him in English. It appeared that she'd got her "His" and "Hers" hopelessly confused and he, being a foreigner, was no respecter of titles.

"Let's get out of here," she said, throwing some money on to the table. "If he was a gentleman he'd have pretended he didn't see me."

"I'm surprised you've never been raped, carrying on the way you do," John scolded her.

"Oh, fiddledeedee! There's no such thing. Never believe a woman who says there is. You can run faster with your skirts up than your trousers down."

They left big red fez telling the waiter and a couple of his cronies about the scandalous conduct in the caravanserai loos, and made their way to what appeared to be the center of town. Cars were vying with each other to make the most noise and, with the sun climbing toward noon, it was becoming intolerably hot between the white-walled buildings. Suddenly they came across a skyscraper hotel and a cluster of shops crammed with the usual tourish bric-à-brac.

"That's the rug I want," her ladyship said, pointing to an orange and crimson monstrosity hanging in the window. It was, Richard knew, genuine Hong Kong and cheaper in London; but within three minutes flat he and John were struggling with it like a giant sausage out of the shop. Five minutes later her ladyship had purchased a dozen silk squares, a musical cigarette box for Sir Gerald with "A Souvenir of Izmir" stamped on it, a sulky-faced doll of indeterminate sex, and a vast hand-woven basket which she said was destined to do great things in the bathroom at Hadsham Manor as a receptacle for soiled linen. Then they began looking for a taxi in which to return the loot to the *Queen Dee*. But taxis were not to be found. They wandered for several minutes, the boys getting hot, she getting bad-tempered, until they at last found one standing on a corner outside an art dealer's shop. A tall, thin American, with a tiny straw hat precariously clinging to his head, was supervising two porters who were about to load a bulky, shrouded purchase into the ancient car. Her ladyship descended.

"No, you don't," she told the startled American. "Ladies first. And I'm a lady."

They were bundling the purchases into the commandeered taxi when John said he had to see a man about a dog, and while Richard was chiding him for leaving him in the lurch, Lady Pratley was trying to give the taxi driver directions by sheer lung power and finger work of dubious propriety. Finally the taxi rattled forward, Richard alone with her ladyship among the bric-à-brac, they hoped in the direction of the ferry pier.

"Are you afraid of women?" she asked.

"No, of course not," he said.

"Well, where are they all? A handsome fellow like you should have them on both arms. And legs."

"I have a girlfriend at home," he lied.

"Wait until we get to Naples," she told him. "I'll introduce you to lots of Italian girls. They're the most passionate in the world. I should know. Nearly all my friends seem to be Italian. I go to Italy at least twice a year."

"Thank you, but that may not be possible," he said evasively. "You see, I have to look after my mother."

"Really? I quite thought she was capable of looking after herself. Very nicely."

The men were having a predinner drink in the Tudor Room. Outside, their womenfolk were round the pool, or in it, as the sun sank into the still waters of the gulf. The last launch would be leaving the ferry pier in fifteen minutes, and by dinnertime the *Queen Dee* would have weighed anchor and be steaming into purple night toward Beirut and the farthermost end of the Mediterranean.

"When I was a lad," Sir Gerald was saying, "we used to play cricket in church. During the sermon. A run for every 'Jesus,' two for every 'Christ,' a boundary for every 'Lord God Almighty' and out for the 'Holy Ghost.' "

Colonel Jamieson was drinking Scotch like a fish. "Those were the days. When village life was village life. None of this mollycoddling with central heating for the cottagers, cars to take them into town, or the telly. I remember the joy of returning to Sedley for my leave, after sweating it out in the filth of India for a couple of years or more."

Sir Gerald looked out to the pool and saw Fiona lifting her brown body from the tepid water, glistening healthily in a simple lemon one-piece costume. She still had a splendid figure for her age, better than some of the gawky, diet-starved girls in their teens and twenties; but the trouble was she knew it. She was too body-conscious, she lived on too physical a level to be altogether wholesome to the average Anglo-Saxon mind. He dragged his attention back to the Colonel. "Sedley. I had no idea you were familiar with that part of the world. Still unspoiled by the ravages of progress, thank God. You're not familiar with English village life, Mr. Brewer. We old fogies mourn its loss."

The ladies were beginning to join the men, the inexperienced tired and blotchy with sunburn lotions, the experienced radiant with their first week of good living in warmer climes. Colonel Jamieson's tired old face fussed around Alice. "What'll it be, my dear? Your usual port?" Mr. Brewer helped Doris into a chair. "The doctor orders martinis. Bring the sparkle back to those travel-weary eyes."

"Benson, they're on me," the Colonel called across the bar. "All round. For everyone, friend and foe alike. Mr. Brewer and myself transacted a little business today. What is it you Americans say—clinched a deal?"

Mr. Brewer modestly said he hoped his investment in British stock would be profitable to all concerned, and the Colonel suggested that Sir Gerald might also be interested in the Freebody Trust. Sir Gerald was about to say he left it to his broker to be interested for him, when the Assistant Purser interrupted the party to ask Mr. and Mrs. Brewer if they had seen John on board. The moment he asked, she panicked at the thought of some disaster.

"There's no need for alarm," the man assured her. "He was not on the last launch. We're in radio contact with the shore authorities and when they locate him, he'll most probably come aboard on the pilot's launch. I just wanted to make sure that he hadn't in fact already returned and we'd failed to check him off."

But by the time they had assembled for dinner, John had not come aboard on the pilot's launch, or on any other launch. He had not been located. Mr. Brewer was demanding he be allowed ashore to find his son, and Mrs. Brewer was saying that it would create an international incident if the ship left without him. But the ship did leave without him. Three-quarters of an hour late. And Mr. and Mrs. Brewer could not even appeal to the highest authority for the simple reason that the highest authority instead of being at table, was at that very moment on the bridge, commanding the *Queen Dee* out of the gulf and across the waters to another country. So they flapped frantically around the Chief Purser at his table; only to find that the Chief Purser was not flappable. Mr. Craddock assured them with stoic calm that everything would work out all right in the end, that their son was not a child, that Turkey was not a hostile country, that even while at sea the *Queen Dee* would be in contact with him if he was there to be contacted. Finally, in desperation, he said, "The *Queen Dee* is not a prison, Mrs. Brewer. If your son *wants* to rejoin us, our agent on shore will make every possible arrangement for him to do so."

"But suppose something terrible's happened to him?" Mrs. Brewer wailed.

"Madam," he told her majestically, "in all my years at sea, I have never known anything terrible happen to anyone, although there have been many times when I wish Providence had been tempted."

Eventually the Brewers returned to their table to peck listlessly at food, comforted by platitudes from the Paxtons, the Radfords and her ladyship. Matters were not helped when Richard came over from his table, unaware of the news, to ask if anyone had seen John as he didn't want to eat alone. Then his mother joined them, anxious as any mother to add her consolations.

"You were with him today," she told Richard. "When did you last see him?"

"We went shopping with Lady Pratley. Then John left us

somewhere in town. He said something about going off to find a genuine Turkish bath."

"A bath!" Mrs. Brewer moaned. "What's wrong with the baths on the ship? He has a shower in the cabin, hasn't he?"

Richard said rather lamely that John wanted to see the real thing; and then the Chief Officer turned up, having done what he had to do on the bridge, and feeling he should now do something to comfort the distraught parents, particularly their being foreign.

"We're in constant radio contact with the shore, Mrs. Brewer," he assured her. "He hasn't been admitted to any hospital. The police haven't picked him up, or anything like that. He probably mistook the time. He's been living in Europe several years by himself now, hasn't he? He's not like many youngsters. I'd have thought your boy was more than capable of looking after himself."

Richard caught the Chief Officer's eyes as he spoke. He knew on the Villefranche mole, when he'd called his mother Dearest, that the man was contemptuous of him. The same insolent look was there again. That special contempt men reserve for those they think are effeminate. He wanted to look away, but instead he stared the man out, hoping like hell there was no serious chance of his becoming his stepfather. What right had people of David Welch's age to want sex anyway? It was disgusting. He looked at the Paxtons, the Radfords, bald Sir Gerald—all anesthetically packaged in their evening finery—and wondered if they still gave rein to their animal lusts. He knew damned well why John had missed the boat. He hadn't gone off to the baths just to get clean. And he felt acutely ashamed that one day, when he was nineteen, twenty-one or forty, he would be like the lot of them.

"I feel so sorry for you," Pamela Westcott told the wretched Mrs. Brewer as she prepared to let David escort her back to their table. "I don't know what I'd have done if it had been Richard."

"Richard's not the kind of boy to get himself into scrapes. Are you, Richard?" the Chief Officer said. "You're too sensible. Like your mother."

It was, Pamela Westcott thought, a lovely thing to have said. David was really a very lovely man. She had rested all day, let-

ting the little brown pills ease her back to a state of inner cleanliness, and wondered what it would be like when she saw David
again, whether there was anything between them to be nurtured and cared for in the hope that it would last, or whether
Friday had been an afternoon of sheer folly, there in the sublime Delphic heights, the wish fulfillment of a silly woman.
She watched him eat. Big masculine strokes with knife and
fork. He looked so handsome in his uniform. She tried to resist the physical urge to be possessed by him again. She was,
as he had said, a sensible woman. Companionship, tender love,
gentleness, emotional security—these were the things Arnold
had given her for nearly twenty years, and these were the
things she was finding it difficult to live without. If there was
to be another man in her life, he would have to be like Arnold. But there was nothing actually wrong in him being physically more demanding as well.

"Is it true we'll see camels in Beirut?" she asked.

Beirut

WAITING for the *Queen Dee* to berth at Beirut were customs officers, health officers, immigration officers, several armed policemen in thin khaki breeches, their shirt sleeves rolled high above their biceps, two police wagons, a Detective Superintendent from Scotland Yard, and John. They were standing on the sun-bleached concrete like troops lined up for inspection. It was a little after eight before the first gangway was down, but it was a full hour after that before John was allowed on board or any other passenger was allowed off. And then the first to disembark were Colonel Jamieson and his lady, together with a police escort. The old boy carried himself with blimpish dignity, pausing for a moment in front of one of the Lebanese police to adjust the man's Sam Browne, not from arrogance in the face of adversity but from sheer force of habit. Someone, somewhere should have sounded the last post; but no one did, and all was silent except for the impatient revving of the wagons.

"What a way to go!"

The Master was talking to himself as he stood alone on the wing bridge, looking down on a tiny moment of British history. He had been alerted by radio the previous evening that the arrest was to be made; but it was only when confronted in his cabin that morning by the Detective Superintendent and a Lebanese officer that he was told why. Warrants had been issued. The Scotland Yard man had been flown out at taxpayers' expense. And the old Colonel and Alice would presently be facing charges of fraud, embezzlement, false pretenses and forgery; all said to have been committed in London and at sea on a number of other cruise liners during the past three years. They were certainly throwing the book at them. And the surprising thing was nothing would have happened if it had not been for Raymond. It all stemmed from something the

[196

Queen Dee's chief barman had said, consciously or unconsciously, to a Greek immigration officer in Piraeus. The Yard
men had congratulated Raymond on being so astute and the
Master had mumbled a noncommittal "good show." He had
never quite imagined Raymond as a champion of law and order, and he had no intention of panegyrizing the man now. If
the truth were known, the Colonel and his lady had been
queering Raymond's pitch, fouling up some of his deals. And
the line between Raymond's deals and sheer bloody fiddling
was hair thin. By the time it was his turn to retire he would
have amassed half the wealth of the Orient to ease the pangs,
for Raymond was worth more, moneywise, than nine out of
ten of the passengers he so lovingly served. His integrity was
based on just that: it paid him to keep his nose clean. A barman could be a man's best friend, or his worst enemy. If the
Master had had his way, the Colonel's worst enemy would
not have been allowed to hang around the cabin door while
the Detective Superintendent rummaged, turning up bundles
of forged share certificates, marked cards, the usual stock in
trade. But this was the detective's show, and he had to let
him do it his way. The old boy had looked immeasurably
sad as he stood there supporting Alice amid the turmoil of little personal things. A rhinoceros-hide cigar wallet. Rolls of
gray lisle stockings. And Raymond hovering there the whole
time—the humblest of hypocrites. The Jamiesons were not
big criminals; but big enough for Scotland Yard to apply for
extradition orders. Neither were they the only criminals on
board, the Master had no illusions about that; but they were
the only ones likely to have the law breathing down their necks.
The small fry, like Cilla Liscon in cabin 21 on the Observation
Deck waiting to be called, with a "husband" ready to squeeze
a little hush money on the side if the opportunity presented
itself, would go scot-free. So would the petty thief, the small-
time gambler. Local police didn't want to know what went on
on a visiting British ship, and no Master would choose to play
avenging angel unless forced to do so for the good of complaining passengers or the safety of his ship. Captain Corlett had
seen it all going on around him for more years than he cared
now to remember. He consoled himself as he turned the blind
eye that a fool and his money were easily parted. Not that he

had any regard for the criminal who made crime a business. Embezzlement was every bit as vicious as a crime against the person. All the same, as he looked down from on high over the sun-baked quay where the old veteran of India was being manhandled into one of the police wagons, he felt a little sad at this ignoble end of a pukka sahib.

"What the heck happened to you?" Mr. Brewer asked his son the moment he could get to him. "You've had your poor mother gray with worrying about you."

"Hell's bells, Dad," John said. "I've been away from home for three years now. Not just three days. I can take care of myself."

"Mothers still worry about their sons if it's thirty years. You should know that. And what was that you told Richard Westcott about a bath? If the plumbing in your cabin's not working the way it should, call the steward and have it fixed. I'm paying enough for it."

"Yes, Dad, you're paying enough for it," John said and went to kiss his mother back to blue-rinsed security, telling her how he'd missed the boat on account of his having lost his watch and then having missed a bus from downtown to the ferry pier. The Turkish authorities were just great, fixing him up with temporary travel documents, helping him with air reservations from Izmir to Ankara and Ankara to Beirut, and here he was, exhausted. And broke.

"Your father was swindled by that dreadful old Britisher," she told him.

"Beware of respectability. It's the oldest con in the world," he said, and left her on her way to the Purser's Office with Mr. Brewer to find out if their dollar travelers' checks had been cashed by the dreadful old Britisher, and, if so, whether the police would be able to recover their money. Six other first-class passengers had similar problems. The dreadful old Britisher was a smooth operator.

"What happened to you?" Richard asked as John came into the cabin to shower and change his clothes.

"If I told you, you'd blush to the roots of your you-know-what," John said. "But I had a great time, man. Even if I did get rolled for my watch. Beirut's the greatest. I hit it just after ten last night and met this Arab guy. Aziz. He's going to take me some place to smoke hashish through a hubble-bubble tonight. Coming? Or are you chicken?"

"I'm not chicken," Richard said indignantly. "I'll try anything once."

"Anything?" John asked, amused by his friend's confusion.

"Anything I think I'll like."

The fact was, Richard had just discovered that he wanted John's company. The previous night, instead of relishing having the cabin to himself he'd wished John had been there to share it. He missed John talking away about the importance of Strindberg in the development of modern drama, the wonders to be seen in taking an old jalopy from Detroit through Illinois and Kansas to New Mexico, or the thrill of putting on one's first pair of skis in the mountains around Chamonix, until they both fell asleep. Richard admired John enormously for the way he grasped life. He seemed to know so much, do so much; and Richard wanted to know it and do it, too; and wondered if he ever would. He thought glumly of family friends who lived out their simple uneventful lives, drugged by work and worry and the English climate into a state of bovine acceptance of their lot. Like sweet Mr. Pulbright who was moving house for them. Well, he wasn't going to accept. The first thing he wanted when he got back to England was that car, small and powerful and fast and utterly utterly beautiful. And if Mother wouldn't or couldn't buy it for him, then he'd take any job where the money was good and have a down payment on it within three months. Then he'd get a hi-fi, buy lots of clothes like John, go places like that *discotheque* in Nice, meet girls like Simone. He was missing so much. He'd seen nothing of the world through the tall leaded windows of Tor Beeches, only the damp dun moors, the village with its one pub and two shops, and the yellow van that came from town twice a week to deliver grub. And back home between terms, nothing had ever happened; it happened to Mother and Father, but never to him. He had experienced summer afternoons by the sea at Westborough, winter nights at the London theater, days around the museums, evenings playing Monopoly, only through them. Even watching television at home, indiscriminately, because it was a forbidden vice at Tor Beeches except for the tacitly permitted "mind-improvers,"

was a second-hand depressive like watching other people at
tenpins. He hero-worshipped John simply because, like John,
he wanted to experience living for himself.

"I'm going to get a car when we get home. You don't mind,
do you?" he told his mother as they sat in the excursion coach
waiting for it to leave the quay.

"You must be careful," she told him. "The roads are so dan-
gerous these days. You will promise me you'll be careful, won't
you?"

It had been as easy as that. He wondered how easy other
things would be. When he wanted to go away weekends, when
he had a girl of his own, when he wanted a place of his own,
if he took a job Mother didn't understand, or made friends she
didn't like.

"Look, dear. Simone and her aunt are joining us. Perhaps
we can have lunch with them." She seemed to have her
heart set on getting them together again, perhaps to absolve
her conscience.

The cream and chrome coach with a sun-filter roof bounced
through the harbor gates and plunged its passengers into the
mystic East. A world of quiet, unshaven men, sipping mint tea
in the paintless, paperless, glassless street cafés. A world of crip-
pled people begging for their living, and dehydrated mules
humping for theirs. Between the narrow passages leading
into the *suqs,* the tourists glimpsed sunlit mosques with fragile minarets, seraglios with graceful arcades and domes, and
colonettes of icing sugar delicacy. The streets were heavy with
sandaled dust, bright with robes of many colors. Uncomplain-
ing women were carrying large bundles for dignified men in
ragged clothes, everyone walking on pavement or road alike,
indifferent to either the power or the importance of the gaso-
line engine. And at every street corner on the way out of town,
sun-baked boys and toothless men traded stems of dates, salted
sunflower seeds, and water-cooled slices of coconut.

"It's all a little dirty," she said, just as Richard was about to
say how marvelous it all was.

The road climbed the first ridge of mountains, green from
winter rain, and the promontory of Ras-Beirut was below them
with the Crusader castles of Sidon to the south and the ancient Phoenician ruins of Byblos to the north. Presently they

had left the coast and were descending into the fertile plain of Beqaa. It was shortly afterward that they saw their first camels, five strung one behind the other, lurching along the side of the Damascus road.

"I wonder if I shall ever see Japan or South America," he said, suddenly aware that the world was very large and only a very few of its inhabitants ever got around to seeing much of it.

"I don't think I'd like to go that far," she said. "There are so many foreigners everywhere."

They reached Baalbeck shortly before eleven and were organized by a sinister little French guide who stood under the shade of a white parasol and lectured them on the history of the broiling ruins. The pink granite laboriously brought from the north coast of Africa for the Propylaea "for the safety and victories of our lord, Caracalla." The six columns that remained of the Temple of Jupiter Heliopolitan soaring sixty-five feet into the ageless blue of the sky. And the Temple of Bacchus, with its rare example of the Roman use of Oriental stone craftsmen.

Near the exit gate Simone was having a ride on a threadbare camel, tended by an Arab with teeth as yellow as those of his beast. Her aunt was trying to take photographs and having difficulty operating the camera.

"May I help you?" Richard asked.

The aunt gave him the camera with ill grace. "Don't drop it," she said. "And return it to me the instant you have finished."

Richard dissolved into the private world of the view-finder. Simone was fresh and lovely, hair blowing gently in a mountain breeze, like a girl in the toilet-soap-of-the-stars advertisement. When he had taken several pictures she shouted, "Come up and I'll take one of you." The Arab grinned toothily as he helped them change places, all the while prodding the beast into bending its knees. They stood close together for a few seconds, he asking her if she was having a wonderful time, she assuring him that she was, and telling him ever so momentarily with her eyes that it would be better still if he were around. The next moment he was sitting high up on the camel, looking down at her. Then her aunt returned to retrieve the camera and walk her back to the coach. He wondered how many pictures she'd made, and how many more she would have made if she hadn't been led away, and if he would ever see any of them.

"I do think her aunt is unreasonable," his mother said as he half fell, half jumped off the ill-tempered beast. "I intend to talk to her about it. I don't think it's right to interfere with young friendships of the proper kind in the way she does."

He was about to say that if she felt like that she might have said her piece at Nice, in the *discotheque,* when it mattered, instead of conniving with the old woman as she had, treating them both as though they had been caught *in flagrante delicto* committing some heinous crime. But he didn't say any of it. He held his tongue, not wanting to hurt her, hoping that she would be weak as she always had been where making moral decisions were concerned, and that she would leave him to sort out his own life, his own car, his own place, his own girl, his own wife, his own family. The Arab was holding out his hand and displaying his ghastly teeth. He dropped a little baksheesh into the hand and returned the grin.

They returned to Zahleh for lunch, sitting in the shade by the rushing waters of the Barduni gorge, a *mezzeh* spread before them in a score of dishes and milk-cool arak with which to wash it down. Several coachloads of American tourists flashed by, whisking the occupants back to their air-conditioned hotel shells for food, clinically separated from the dangers of European or Asiatic eating and the dirt of living.

"This is a fabulous country," he said. "It doesn't seem possible that you can swim in the sea before breakfast and be skiing in the mountains by midday."

"I don't think I dare eat this," she said. "I do wish they'd give us something simple like chicken sandwiches. We get so much rich food on the ship."

Richard was whoofing away a dish of *hommos,* Arab style with paper-thin bread, when she asked, "What are you going to do with yourself this evening?"

"I've promised to go ashore with John," he said, half expecting her to want his company to see the show out at the casino.

"I'm so pleased," she said. "I don't want you to be lonely.

But you won't do anything foolish, will you? Like missing the boat."

"I suppose you're going to see *him* again," he said, and she felt the resentment in his voice go right through her.

"Is it that you just don't like David? Or aren't I supposed to have friends?" she asked. The gap was widening between them, more rapidly now each day they were isolated from familiar places and familiar faces and familiar things. He might be married by this time next year. Young people did things so quickly, so impulsively. Losing a son, gaining a daughter, it was a tiny facet of dying.

"I don't mind who you see. It's none of my business anyway, is it?"

It was the second time he had made his protest. And she felt a little frightened at what she was doing.

Richard dined with John on board, and the two young men left the ship well fed to meet Aziz at nine, in the Bar Nautique off el Borj, the throbbing square heart of the old Moslem city. The narrow street of peeling stucco, with its fluorescent-lit barbers' shops, seedy hotels, and cafés full of silent men, was packed with tourists, pimps and scavenging dogs. The bar had a mural of a bosomly mermaid caressed by the waves, and Aziz had a long, serious face, with big, serious eyes, and a little woolly hat that was as old as he was young.

"Give me three pounds and I buy beer," he said.

They sat and drank three beers at a pound each, Lebanese pounds, three to the American dollar. John asked Aziz what he had done all day, and the man told him sleep, but tomorrow maybe he find work portering on the harbor. Or the day after.

"When did you arrive?" Aziz asked Richard. "By air or sea? Which hotel you stay? How much charge for room? You have mama, papa? Brother, sister? Friends? You are here for work, or tourist?"

It was a thoroughly professional once-over and the man went through the lot despite John's protest that what the heck, he'd already told him he was from the same ship. Richard answered all the questions as though they had been directed at him by Old Hickson. Aziz seemed pleased that he had already visited Baalbeck, telling him he had a brother there, but it was

too cold in winter, and had he been to the quarry to see the
Hajar el Qubleh, the largest hewn stone in the world?

They finished their beers and Aziz said, "You want smoke
hashish now?"

"Sure, man," John said. "Lead the way."

Richard knew this was the moment to stay, but he didn't.
Outside the bar they were joined by an unwashed boy with a
big head and small body who had been waiting on the curb
with the scavenger dogs. Aziz said his name was Hooda, and
he was a good boy as he didn't steal.

"Gimme pound," Hooda demanded of Richard with out-
stretched hand.

"Why?" Richard demanded right back.

"You see. Gimme pound!"

Aziz nodded that it was the thing to do, and Richard did it.
The boy grabbed the grimy note and scurried to the kiosk on
the corner. He returned with a tablet of chocolate and a satisfied grin.

"Swiss," he said. "Good. You have."

They were munching chocolate as they bundled into a battered black service-taxi, Aziz in front, John and Richard behind with Hooda between them. Aziz spoke Arabic to the
driver, offered him a cigarette, and exchanged a joke.

"Give me two pounds for the driver," he said.

Hooda pointed at John. "You like boys." He turned to Richard. "But you like girls. Aziz say." He laughed and munched
chocolate and put his arm around Richard with the sexless affection of a kid brother. "I like you. You English. I learn speak
English capitano oil ship. Me wash clothes."

The car rattled over a cobbled street, under the high wall of
the free zone, and north along the Tripoli road, past rows of
simple dwellings luminescent beneath the canopy of diamond
bright stars. Hooda's voice pealed with childish laughter, and
Richard picked his fingers with worry for what he had let himself in for.

Aziz leaned over the front seat. "When we get out of car, you
no speak any English," he said. "Many bad people not like
English or American. You understand? Boom!"

The taxi dropped them where the brick houses ended and

the crude huts of boards and corrugated iron began. After a few paces they had left the street lights behind. The air was heavy with highly spiced cooking and stale garbage. Occasional glimpses of life in oil-lit shacks behind sackcloth entrances or ill-hinged doors—sad families around tins of stew, an old man reading a crumpled newspaper through a broken glass held in a shaking hand, a woman combing long black hair by an up-turned soap-box covered with little pots and packets of cosmetic. Aziz led them to an oasis beyond the slum, a dusty clearing with bushes, two or three palms, and by one of the palms a bigger, taller shack, lit more brightly with acetylene. Several men shuffled around in the darkness, the silence broken by the sound of someone urinating on the brick-hard earth. Some little distance away, the gaunt silhouette of a bedding factory, and high in the sky among the stars a flashing neon sign. Sleep Comfort. Sleep Comfort. Sleep Comfort.

"Give me five pounds for pipe," Aziz said.

Inside, the hut was filled with men sitting around the walls on upturned boxes, old stools, or cross-legged on scraps of paper. Smoke swirled in the bright blue light, acrid, burning the eyes, choking the lungs with its crematorium stench. The floor was strewn with spit-sodden sawdust. The walls barren except for a Coke poster, healthy boy in beach shorts, healthy girl wet with salt spray. Drink Coke. Drink Coke. Drink Coke.

"You talk now," Aziz said. "These good people. Hashish make them much happy."

A pipe was already doing the rounds. A man with a big black unkempt moustache passed it to Aziz, who passed it to Hooda, who passed it to John, who passed it to Richard, who passed it, passed it, passed it. Glass bowl of bubbling water, globe of smoldering weed, rubber tube, fluted mouthpiece, make plenty beautiful music, suck, bubble-bubble, inhale, hubble-hubble, breathe deeply, breathe deeply. Then cough and spit your guts out. Choke for air. Struggle to retain bile. Spit long dribbles of phlegm from lips to sawdust between parted legs. Now their communal pipe was being prepared. A small piece of something slivered and dropped among the glowing twists of tobacco. And the pilgrims started off once more along the road to elation. Quiet, gentle men, contemplating fantasy on earth, reaching through the physical pain and squalor for the sublime afterdeath, but all of them lacking the courage to die now. Sleep Comfort. Sleep Comfort. Sleep Comfort.

"You plenty pleasure," Hooda said, passing the pipe to Richard.

He sucked in, tried not to inhale, but the kid was watching and he couldn't funk it. He swallowed the vile smoke like medicine and coughed it back again like a cat choking out fish bones. His whole body was pulsing with heat and nervous tension. He felt more miserable than he did happy, more here than there. The men looked at him with disinterested eyes, gave him disinterested smiles, and sucked and spat their way to cheap oblivion. He'd imagined it would be paradise on a silken pouffe, soft lights, relaxing music, belly dancers. His head was bursting with pain. The salt-sprayed girl was belly dancing with the healthy boy all over the wall. Sucker, the boy said, sucker. Drink Coke. Drink Coke. Drink Coke.

"Gimme two pounds," Hooda said.

"What for?"

"I buy Coke. You drink Coke. Good."

"Drink Coke! Drink Coke! Drink Coke!" Richard shouted, getting to his feet and staggering from the acrid dazzle into the clean warm air of night.

"Hashish good. You feel good soon," Hooda said, coming into the darkness with him. "We take you place plenty girls. Much love."

Several minutes later John emerged pretending to be higher than he was, followed by Aziz, who paused to secrete a piece of the precious joy-weed in the fold of his woolly hat. They all filled their lungs with freshness and, marginally different than when they arrived, wandered through shantytown back to the brightly lit main road.

"Give me two pounds for taxi," Aziz said.

They were driven fast and dangerously back to el Borj, Aziz telling John he would show them a good nightclub, Hooda cuddling Richard and telling him they find him very good girl. Clean. The mad driver, shirt-sleeved and oily with sweat, left them by a yard filled with much-traveled buses and patiently waiting people, peasants from distant villages, the men with battered brown suitcases secured with string, their women standing sentinel behind their yashmaks. A few paces beyond the yard a flight of stone stairs led around an apartment house to an upper room, the door signed in Arabic hieroglyphics and protected by a hirsute man in a soiled turban.

"Give me eight pounds. Drink included," Aziz said, taking the money and giving it to the turbaned one.

The room itself was like a recently evacuated government office. A once pleasingly plastered ceiling was festooned with faded flags and naked colored bulbs. The length of one side, a plain wall of indeterminate color; along the other side, vast open windows, arched, looking out to a panorama of stars and mosques and the palmy streets below; the tables covered with unwashed plastic, attended by hard mission-hall chairs. And at the far end, in a pool of white light from a battered spot, a small band of native musicians accompanied a plump woman in veils who was dancing and singing. They found a table and were presented with four tumblers stacked with ice cubes over which an unshaven man with dirty fingernails poured a small measure of a fiery liquid said to be "weeskee." Some fierce perfume was fighting the fetid breath of the men sitting next to them. Drums and tambourines. The atonal voice soaring to nowhere as the veiled one quivered fleshy folds behind the gauze.

"Give me four pounds. More drinks," Aziz said, taking the piece of secreted joy-weed carefully from the fold of his woolly hat and proceeding to break open four cigarettes, carefully paring the sticky brown substance into the tobacco and handing the reformed cigarettes round the table with solemn grace.

"Girl good. Very sexy," Hooda said to Richard, quivering his own body with mock modesty. He turned to John with hopeful eyes. "You like me? We go. Make love."

Aziz smiled with the tolerance of age for the impatience of youth. "I know what he likes," he said. "Take you place plenty men and boys. All night. Twenty pounds. Do what you like."

A dark-haired girl with vermilion lips, her bosom hanging free behind a thin blouse of emerald silk, came and sat, uninvited, unwanted, but hardly unnoticed, next to Richard.

"Gimme five pounds," Hooda said. "Weeskee good."

Richard counted out the notes. He had about thirty left.

Not a great fortune, but the girl put her hand gently on them, and on his, and smiled.

"She no speak English," Aziz said. "She say she like you very much. Her name Rima. She make you plenty happy."

Rima was trying to make him plenty happy in public, and he told himself he was not to blush, to be a man of the world, start living a little. The liquor hit him like a sledge-hammer right on the crown of his head. Rima smelt of sugar and spice. "Nice, nice, she do nice things," Aziz kept saying, impassive, gently, wanting to please. The boy, Hooda, young—maybe no more than twelve—with the face of an old man between bursts of smiles, urging "She good. Me knows. Make plenty love." And John, relaxed, drinking in the atmosphere with the foul liquor, as at home here in a sweatshirt as he was in tuxedo in the first-class restaurant in the *Queen Dee*.

"If she's not your type," John said, "there's plenty more. Just clap your hands, man. Hooda seems to like her. He's an ambidextrous little clod, isn't he? All the Arabs are."

Richard knew damn well that John was amused by his predicament. He'd planned it this way. He just sat there gulping the raw liquor and trying to keep a straight face as he watched the girl crawl all over him. How the hell could he get out of it? It wasn't that Rima wasn't smashing—it was quite simply he didn't know how to cope with *any* Rima when it was made so embarrassingly obvious what coping involved. Sleep Comfort. Sleep Comfort. Sleep Comfort. The drums pounded in time with his throbbing head. The girl's soft, cool hand was stroking his golden curly hair, her fingers following the outline of his ear, her eyes looking deep into his, her lips moist and moving almost imperceptibly toward his cheek. He'd have to say yes, go through with it, find out what it was like, or queer John would never stop laughing over him. And he would never stop crying over himself. This was it. He had to stop playing the boy and pretend to be a man.

"She's wonderful," he said. "She's just wonderful."

A few minutes later they were all leaving, back to the yard of much-traveled buses, Rima holding onto Richard like a little girl with a big doll, Aziz in earnest conversation with John, and Hooda skipping impishly between them talking sex like algebra. "We give your friend good time. We do bang-for-bang. Plenty fun." They led him down narrow ill-lit streets, the noise of the city constantly echoing beyond the walls and left him with her in an apartment house doorway beneath illuminated signs painted in Arabic and English . . . Lilia, Qamar, Shama, Jemmil, Desiree, Rima. As he followed her up the stone steps he heard John's departing voice calling after him. "I'll be thinking of you! Have fun!" It was all a bit like the family farewells when he returned each term to the arms of Tor Beeches. And now, like then, he felt alone and defenseless from something that was new and strange. He heard Rima slip the lock on the door. The room was lit by a small orange light. It was as he imagined a nun or prisoner's cell, the abode of anyone confirmed or confined to institutional life. A small window high up, too high for any view. A large low bed, all cushions and silk. A tired mat on a tiled floor. A deep basketwork chair, coming apart. Small table full of small things. A white washbasin staring into the darkness like a glass eye. On the wall, a paper print of a long-legged belly dancer—revealing, revolting, receiving the stains from a hundred naked backs that had leaned against her inky limbs.

"Make love." Rima knew no other English.

"Where?" he asked, not knowing what to do now he was there.

She kissed him as he stood, shivering a little, in the center of the hotly humid room. Lips soft. Breath sweet. Hands gently bringing his hands up to parted blouse, to cup large soft globes of womanflesh. Then head pressed gently down. Receiving flesh. Sugar and spice. Mewling and puking in the nurse's arms. Lips on large brown tit. Sleep Comfort. Drink Coke. Sleep Comfort. Drink Coke. She was naked, lying back on cushioned silk, beckoning with parted legs. He stared, transfixed, stiffening, wanting, not daring, and finally buttoning and fleeing.

He was tripped on the first flight of steps, sprawled against a crumbling wall, was raised to his feet again by a little man with enormous hands. "Give me twenty pounds!" Money flying, feet flying, down narrow alleys, blue, green, red grotto rooms, fat half-draped women waiting for custom on tatty couches. Domes of *hammams* echoing the unspoken love of male ablutions like cathedrals filled with incensed rites. A wall stained with the piss of ages. One-legged man selling halawa.

The Bar Nautique. Mermaid caressed by the waves. Safety. Drink Comfort. Sleep Coke. Drink Comfort. In the distance, a wailing Arab song from a crackling radio, like the distant call of the faithful to prayer from the midday minarets. And here, near, inside of him, a sickening awareness that he was running away from living, that he might never be born.

The Chief Officer changed his number-ten rig at nine-thirty, and by ten, in civvies, was escorting Pamela Westcott into the Club Indigo opposite Pigeons' Grotto on the fashionable Corniche de Chouran. Gentle, seductive music; gentle, seductive lights; gentle, seductive liquor. They floated over the highly polished floor, weaving between graceful people used to luxury and projecting their elegance with a cultured snobbery inherited from a distant past under French mandate. English voices, French voices, German voices, sometimes the sound of Arabic; the Club Indigo might well have been in Paris, London or New York.

"A penny for your thoughts," he said, when she had not spoken for a full five minutes.

"Twopence. Inflation, you know." They laughed, and she said she was sad that this was as far as the *Queen Dee* was taking them: that she wanted to see Egypt, the Red Sea, the Indian Ocean, a sampan off Singapore. "It's not fair that we have to head back to gray old England so soon."

"You don't have to," he told her. "You've no ties. You could leave the ship here if you wanted, and take another, or fly to all the places you want to see."

"Don't be silly, David. You know that's not possible."

"But why not?" he insisted. "While you're still young enough to enjoy it. You've got the money. And there's no one to tell you how to spend it."

She held him closer to her, hoping he would spend the night with her, would possess her again, that his appetite for her would never be sated. "Don't joke," she said. "You know life isn't that simple. There are always ties. I have to think of the future. There's the new house I haven't even really seen yet. It's in such a lovely part of Reigate. And I have to see Richard settled into a job. He's at such a difficult age."

"I wasn't joking. I don't believe in living with the past. If you really want to see more of the world, that's what you should do."

"I wouldn't want to keep traveling by myself. And Richard has his own life to lead. You see, David, I'm rather a lonely woman. I think you realize that."

"Yes," he said, and brought his lips close to the lobe of her right ear in the indigo darkness. "But you don't need to be. You can offer a man . . . so much. I know that, don't I?"

When the music stopped he wanted to order more drinks, but she said no, the place was too European, she wanted to see something Oriental. "Take me," she said, husking her voice, "to the Casbah!"

They found a place by the tiny harbor of Minet el Hosn, a dilapidated wooden pier built perilously out from the rocky shore with a vibrant view of the moonlit mountains curving to the north, and the winking lights of jets zooming in and out of Khaldeh Airport to the south. The Cabaret Nils was run by a German quean, possibly a former Nazi, although no one ever asked him that. Paint was flaking from the ceiling, half the bulbs in the brassy festoons were burned out, and lying behind the wall brackets were pieces of candle in readiness for the next power failure. Between two bird cages, long devoid of life, was a work of art hopefully titled "Paris au Printemps," depicting young lovers sipping an aperitif at a boulevard café under cherry blossoms in the shadow of the Eiffel Tower. An occasional cockroach ventured inside from the kitchens to keep the customers company. Outside, posters in several languages announced a "typical Lebanese folkloristique entertainment." The entertainment consisted of a dozen girls and boys singing wild mountain songs while dressed in costumes more *Mikado* than folkloristique. And seated at the tables, sipping iced beer, were a score or more passengers from the *Queen Dee*—among them the Aftons, the Earls, the Radfords, Miss Peebles, and Simone and her aunt.

"Why, Mr. Welch! You didn't tell us you were spending the evening ashore," Mrs. Afton said, nudging her husband to make room for the newcomers at their table. "Do come and join us, Mrs. Westcott. We've had the most exhausting day, but quite wonderful. I have all the Phoenicians and Crusaders and Romans and French and Arabs and Turks hopelessly jumbled, I'm afraid."

The last thing the Chief Officer wanted was to flaunt the affair under the noses of other passengers, and he knew she didn't want that either. Unlike Fiona, who would have relished such a situation, Pamela was visibly embarrassed. And there they were, trapped, unable to leave before they had properly arrived. So they sat for a while, sipping beer, making small talk between folkloristique songs and dances, and waiting for the first opportunity to get out.

"But we don't dispute that God gave them the Promised Land. All we are asking is that they show us the lease." The old German, Nils, was huffing and puffing at the bar, putting on his pan-Islamic act for the benefit of the tourists, paying the daily penalty of being a foreigner in a foreign land.

"It just doesn't seem right that Jerusalem is divided in half," a little woman, hot in tweeds, was moaning. "What our dear Lord must think, men falling out even over His birthplace."

"His death place," Nils corrected her. "It's an overrated city, anyway. Only fit for dying in."

Two folkloristique boys were slapping each other's thighs while a buxom girl put her song into full throttle. As she was hitting the highest note, a heavy freckled hand clutched at the Chief Officer's shoulder. "It is David Welch, isn't it? The Master of the *Torrance*? I've waited a long time to meet up with you, mister!"

He looked up to see a red-haired man, sturdy but not big, dressed in a crumpled linen suit, tieless, with a many-colored striped shirt. He wondered who the hell he was, and asked, "I'm afraid I haven't had the pleasure, Mr. . . . er . . . ?"

"Findlater. Greg Findlater. Gary's brother."

His mind raced back to that dreadful night of December 3, seven or was it eight years ago? Second Engineer Gary Findlater. The last of fifty-eight to die. "This Court wishes to put on record its appreciation of the commendable presence of mind and initiative displayed throughout by the Second Engineer, and further, it wishes to . . ."

"You don't deny that you are David Welch, do you?" the red-haired man asked. "I knew the *Queen Dee* was putting in

today, and I was told you'd be aboard her. Chief Officer. Fine
bloody Chief Officer you make for any ship! You're not fit to
shovel shit on a Dutch barge!"

"David, who is this dreadful man?" Pamela asked.

"He's crazy. He must be crazy," David said. The *Queen Dee*
passengers had lost interest in the entertainment and were
looking at him as though he had two heads. He said as calmly
as he could to the red-haired man, "If you think you have reason to pick a quarrel with me, this is neither the place nor the
best way to do it."

"I'll pick a quarrel with you, you bastard!" The man was
standing in a space between the tables, preaching to the crowd.
"Don't you people know who you're sailing with for Chief
Officer? You've got Mr. Bloody David Welch. That's who
B and E Lines have given you. Mr. Bloody Welch. A yellow
bastard who put his own skin before his ship and his crew. The
sod who broke the *Torrance*'s back on the Pacas rocks because
he was too bleeding drunk to skipper her properly."

The Chief Officer said firmly and clearly, "I must ask you to
moderate your language in front of ladies, sir. I must also remind you that the accusations you have just made against me
are slanderous. Perhaps now that you feel better for having
made them, you will leave, and allow us to enjoy the rest of
the entertainment."

The Aftons, the Earls, the Radfords, Miss Peebles, Simone
and her aunt looked first at him and then at the red-haired
man, expecting an explosion.

The red-haired man said, "Come outside, you bastard, and
I'll give you the hiding of your life!"

"I have no intention of taking unfair advantage of your age.
Besides, I have absolutely nothing to fight about. Now be a
good fellow, and go away."

Hearing the disturbance, Nils came over to the tables with
two of his waiters. He said something to the red-haired man in
Arabic. The man paused to spit on the floor at the Chief Officer's feet. And then he was gone.

The Chief Officer smiled at the gesture. "You can't be liked
by everyone in this world," he said. But he could tell from the
eyes around him that the incident had left its mark. Perplexed
eyes, puzzled eyes, worried eyes, frightened eyes. Even Pamela.

She had quite unconsciously moved her chair a few inches from his.

Nils gave them all a flabby smile. "Mr. Findlater has worked in Beirut for many years," he explained. "Buy. Sell. In the free-trade zone. He's not a bad man, you understand, but a little crazy. He's a very good friend if he likes you, but if he doesn't like you—" He waved both arms in an expressive gesture. "It must be the English climate that made him like he is. But, please, forget him. Drinks on the house for everyone. You are here to enjoy yourselves."

David and Pamela enjoyed themselves for a few more minutes, and then they made their exit. The moment their backs were turned to walk away, David heard the hushed undertones of whispered scandal above the folkloristique song. What, he wondered, would they get their teeth into first— Pamela or the *Torrance?*

He put his arm around her and was relieved that she didn't shake it off. "I'm sorry about that, Pamela. What would you like to do now? We could try somewhere else, or maybe you'd prefer to return to the ship?"

She said it was too soon to start the journey home to England. Somewhere else. Couldn't they find somewhere genuinely Oriental? They found a taxi driver who spoke good English and told him what they wanted. He zigzagged up hills and down narrow streets, slipping American pop records into a car-player to serenade them.

"I hope you didn't believe what that man said. You could tell he'd been drinking," David said.

"Must we even think about it?"

But he obviously wanted to think about it, and to make sure that she was thinking about it from his point of view. "A captain has to take ultimate responsibility. In that sense, I suppose I was to blame. But so many things happened on that night which were beyond anyone's control. He made it sound as though I killed his brother in cold blood."

She always warmed toward Arnold when he was fretting over something, like the night she sat with him holding his hand like a child when the public health officer, tracking down a typhoid outbreak, thought it had been traced to a carrier in the bakery. And now she was warming toward David, taking his hand in hers in the back of the taxi, and saying, "Don't fret about it. It's something which happened long ago. I'm sure it won't ever happen again."

"I think you understand me better than any woman I've ever known," he said. "I hope we can make this something permanent."

"I hope so, too," she said quietly.

He drew her lips to his and kissed her. "I'll have to get up at three-thirty or I'll miss my watch," he said. "And that means waking you. Do you mind?"

"I wouldn't want you to be accused of two crimes in one day," she said.

The taxi dropped them by the Suq des Orfèvres, and the driver pointed to a dimly lit entrance. "There very Arab. Song, music, drink, no tourists. Real Beirut."

He hesitated at taking her inside, but she said she'd never forgive him if he didn't. The arched hall was packed with men drinking coffee and smoking hookahs. At first she thought she was the only woman, but then she noticed a few French Lebanese with their wives, drinking local wine, and one or two overdressed tourists showing off with iced arak. A woman in a sheath of yellow and green silk, with the throaty voice of a Spanish gypsy, was belting out a plaintive song accompanied by an old man on a *quitara*. Stale tobacco smoke, the aroma of fresh coffee, all blended with a penetrating smell of musk.

"David, this is absolutely marvelous," she said, childishly delighted. "It's like something right out of the *Arabian Nights*."

He wanted her to be happy, to forget the squalid incident at the Cabaret Nils, to be ready to let down her long auburn hair for him again, to let him try this time to raise something more than passive passion in her. The warmth of night and the heady smells filled his nostrils. He felt himself stiffen with anticipated pleasure while he told himself frantically that he was no longer a kid and should try to control himself like a man, and what the hell was he going to do if he had to stand up. He concentrated on ordering iced beer, told her what little he knew about Arab music, which was little indeed, and asked her if she was the musical type, doing the London rounds of the Proms, the Garden, the Wigmore Hall. He listened to her

talk and instead of thinking about her body, which only excited him, thought about her money, and wondered exactly
how much of it there was. How much dough did she get out of
Dough Boy? Was she likely to play the jet-set Lady Bountiful
like Fiona? Or would he have to marry her in the old-fashioned way for her dowry? He thought it would be the latter.
She was a very beautiful old-fashioned woman. Of course, he
was missing out somewhere. Sex-plus-cash didn't equal hap-
piness-plus-security; but he could always live in hope that the
missing link would forge itself one day.

"Who knows, I might grow old and start loving you for your
mind."

"David, are you sure you're all right?" she said anxiously.
"You're not making sense. I said, I wish we were staying another night. I hate the thought of turning around and going
back."

He snapped out of his reverie. "I wonder what I'd do with
you if we did stay another day? I know. Take you out to the
casino. The biggest sheiks in the Middle East play there. I'm
sure you'd break their banks. And their hearts. You were born
lucky."

She gave him a girlish laugh which betrayed an encroaching
double chin. "You really think so?"

"When we get home I'll introduce you to the Mizzen Club.
I'd like to see you break their bank."

She was suddenly serious. "Just because I won the ship's
sweepstake you mustn't think I'm lucky by nature. For myself,
or for anyone else. I'm not really a gambling woman, David. In
any way." She looked nervously over his shoulder. "That red-
haired man's here. I think he's coming over."

But he didn't come over. He stood in the doorway with three
other men, watching, waiting. Sooner or later they would have
to leave, and when they did—

"Mr. Welch and I have a little business to complete, haven't
we, Mr. Welch? I suggest we all leave quietly in my car. You
don't want to involve the lady in a public brawl. The company
wouldn't be very happy about that, would they? And neither
would the lady."

There was a malicious glint in his red-haired face. The three
other men, Lebanese, dark, one of them quite young with a

harelip, all dressed in dark suits, smelling of cheap cologne, closed in around them. They hustled them through the dimly lit exit, into the side street, and into a waiting car.

"I'm sorry to have to involve you in this, Pamela," he said. "The man's quite insane, but for the moment there's nothing I can do but humor him. If they do anything in any way to harm you, I give you my word the *Queen Dee* won't leave port until every one of them has been brought to justice."

It was sheer flamboyance on his part, for he was damned well aware who it was being brought to justice. The car drove through the *suq,* across el Borj, and drew to a halt at the side of a bar in a narrow street of peeling stucco. The men piled out, taking David with them, leaving her in the back of the car alone, except for Harelip.

The red-haired man said politely, "I assure you, madam, you will come to no harm if you wait in the car with my colleague. It is better there for a lady than in the bar, and Ghossein will be respectful of you in every way."

"No, David! Don't go with them! Don't let them separate us!" she pleaded. But he didn't seem to hear her.

"Would you like a paper to read?" Harelip asked politely.

The Chief Officer was filled with a fatalistic impotence. He let the three men hustle him to the back of the bar and down a flight of dark, twisting iron stairs, into a foul-smelling basement. The red-haired man paused in the bar to feed coins into a jukebox, flooding the building with canned American noise. Boom-twang-wail. Boom-twang-wail. It thudded through the basement ceiling, sending shock waves of sound down the slender flex to the blinding, swinging, naked light bulb. The concrete floor was sweating with humidity. Several crates of empties stacked at one end. A broken table, encrusted with dust. A long-forgotten camel saddle. Boom-twang-wail.

"I'm going to give you a chance, a very sporting one," the red-haired man said. "You broke the *Torrance*'s back, and my brother's back, and now I propose to break your back. I hope for your sake you know a little judo. It will make it such an uninteresting exercise if you don't."

The two dark-suited men stood sentinel by the door, and the red-haired man began stripping off his clothes as casually as though it were a bathing party. When he saw that his oppo-

nent was standing indolently against the broken table, he said,
"Well, come on, man! Or do you want them to prepare you for
the slaughter?"

"You're insane. You're quite insane. I'm leaving here and
taking the lady back to the ship, and neither you nor these two
thugs are going to stop me!"

But the two thugs did stop him. He saw their grinning faces
as they twisted and tore him from his clothes. He was already
sweating when they flung him into the center of the cellar,
naked except for his underpants, to face his red-haired adversary. Physically the two men were unevenly matched. The
Chief Officer taller, younger, his body lithe and muscular and
perhaps fifteen pounds heavier. The red-haired man sturdy,
showing his age, his pink freckled skin hanging from what was
once a solid frame, paunching over the elastic waistband of
his shorts. But the moment they were locked in action, there
was no doubting the older man's superior skill. He played
with the younger, better-equipped man like a cat with a
mouse, countering his holds, ducking the blows from his flying fists. And ever so slowly, minute by minute, the red-haired
man built up a crescendo of chops on neck and chest and belly
that took the wind out of lithe muscular David and slowed
him down. Boom-twang-wail. The dark-suited men grinned.
Naked feet padding over a concrete floor. For a few moments
blows of retaliation, a twisted arm, a fist in the red-haired face
that seemed to draw blood and temper with it. But almost immediately the red-haired hands gripped his naked loins, lifted
his body high to glance off a glaring bulb, to send the room
spinning with light, then thwack back on the sweating floor.
Pained silence. Grunts. Again. The wall hurtling, spinning,
advancing like a lightning flash. Boom-twang-wail. Eyes ablaze
with sexless lust. The red-haired knees up into his crotch, once,
twice. Can you take more, you bastard? Bodies slippery with
exuded sweat. Limbs alive with pain. Mind numbed with
agony. And the red-haired ape, astride his victim like a crab,
thighs gripped under arms, sitting gallantly in the saddle
while his victim's chest ground into the concrete, wriggling,
struggling, chafing flesh, twisting, doing everything a man can
do to ease the pressure on the back, the back, the back. *Tor-*

rance. Boom-twang-wail. Wail. "My back! Stop! Stop it! God, no more! You're breaking my back!"

The red-haired man flung the folded legs contemptuously to the floor. He kicked the limp body over onto its back and paused to knead his foot into the soft meat beneath the white underpants. "That's one for the ladies! And now, Mr. Bloody Welch, I feel better. I've been waiting to get you, you bastard, for a long, long time."

It seemed like a lifetime waiting in the car next to Harelip, not talking, heart beating, fearful of what was happening to him, to her, in this dreadful, dirty city. Then at last the three men came out of the bar. Without David. The red-haired man sweating a little, mopping moisture from his freckled forehead, but as polite with her as he had been from the start.

"I apologize that we should have inconvenienced you, madam," he said. "But I assure you it was something that had to be done."

"What have you done?" she demanded. "David. Where is he? You haven't hurt him?"

"We'll drive you back to the ship," the red-haired man said. "It's better that way."

But she refused. She struggled to get out of the car and he indicated to Harelip not to stop her. She ran through the bar and down the twisting iron stairs. And she saw his white body, limp, dirty with the filth of the cellar, twisted in agony on the concrete under the blinking swinging light. "Oh, my God! They've killed you!" Instinctively, like an animal sniffing around the corpse of its kind, she sniffed around David until he stirred, opened pained eyes, tried to smile, awareness creeping back, making an effort to pretend it was not he who was humiliated so. Boom-twang-wail. Several minutes later she managed to seat him on the edge of the broken table. She fussed him, loved him, wept over him, and helped him limb by limb to ease on his clothes and cover his broken pride with man-made plumage.

"I'll call the police. Why didn't somebody *do* something?" she said.

He could barely speak. "No. No police. Help me to the ship. If you love me, Pamela, no police. An accident. It was an accident. I fell down the aft companionway on B Deck. Stow-away. Trying to catch a stowaway. Larry Hampton. Struck my cheek on a handle of the linen cupboard. Don't you remember? Accident. Tell everyone it was an accident."

She half pushed, half pulled him up the twisting iron stairs. And there in the bar, staring at the bosomly mermaid caressed by the waves, drinking by himself, was Richard. Never before had she so desperately needed to see her beautiful son.

"Richard," she said. "Please, please darling, help me. There's been a most terrible accident."

They left the Bar Nautique under the impassive gaze of the sallow-faced barman, wiping glasses with a grimy cloth, the Chief Officer leaning heavily on Richard's broad young shoulders, Pamela flapping nervously around looking for a taxi. There was no sign of the red-haired man and his friends in the narrow street of peeling stucco.

"If this is going to be my new father," Richard said, "I hope he's not going to make a habit of coming home blotto."

The one-legged man came up trying to sell his halawa. A small boy sitting on the curb grinned a friendly we're-all-peo-ple-of-the-world grin as the procession limped by. And in the distance an Arab song reached for the sky. Boom Comfort. Twang Sleep. Life was one long accident.

Bath for One

He got through the four-o'clock watch with the aid of a shot of morphine from Dr. Hammond. It cost him five pounds for the shot and another five for the man's silence. The *Queen Dee* would be in her berth until nine, waiting for the passengers who had made the long pilgrimage to the Jordanian side of Jerusalem. And in those early hours before dawn, the Chief Officer dragged himself twice from the bridge, along the decks, and down to inspect the gangways and check the moorings. It was sheer masochism that he insisted on doing it himself. "Fancy me going arse over tip down a companionway!" he told Third Officer Tyson, making as light of it as possible. "And all I copped was a bruising. Nothing that a good steaming won't work out." But by eight, when he handed over to Rigg, the effects of the drug were wearing off and he felt like death. He tried to eat breakfast but couldn't stomach anything. In a few hours they would be starting the voyage back, and he hoped for Christ's sake the old man wouldn't want him on the bridge until his afternoon watch.

"What can we do for you today, Mr. Welch?" Wilkie asked as he hobbled into the Promenade Deck steam bath.

"A long, long, soak and a good workout. So I hope you're feeling energetic."

The man gave him a friendly enough smile. The Beirut incident had obviously not gotten around the ship yet. But the wagging would start soon enough, and then he'd know who his true friends were. Those who weren't for him were against him. When Len Arkwright took over, that would be the time to show anyone who was against him that they'd made the wrong bloody choice. He'd soon have any bastard who didn't see things his way to heel. There was no reason at all why the *Queen Dee* shouldn't remain a chummy ship, providing he and Arkwright lost no time in deciding who they wanted around them to be chummy with. Let the wagging start. The *Tor-rance* incident had to come out into the open sooner or later and now was as good a time as any. Hewson would be the first to turn, of course. The bastard already had it in for him because his sex life didn't measure up to the till-death-do-us-part bit of his own. Well, sod you, Hewson! You can be the first to go.

Wilkie said, "You've got the place to yourself today, Mr. Welch. I doubt if we'll have any customers till we get to cooler waters. They don't know what's good for them, do they, sir?"

He went into the nearest cubicle to strip off his starch-stiff whites. On the back of the door, under a plastic cover, was a Notice to All Passengers—"The B and E Lines respectfully draw the attention of all passengers to the regulations laid down by . . ." The type, the company insignia, the legal jar-gon—for a moment he thought it was that bloody report of the court inquiring into the *Torrance* affair. The Merchant Ship-ping Act 1894. Report of Court No. P 19765 M/V "Torrance." In the matter of a Formal Investigation held at Church House, Dean's Yard, Westminster S.W.1. on the 9th, 10th, and 11th days of June 1960 before Hubert Chatterton, Esq., Q.C., assisted by Captain P.H. Mills O.B.E., A.R.I.N.A, Dr. Jacob Mannering M.A., Ph.D, M.R.I.N.A, Mr. Ralph Stevenson O.B.E., into the circumstances attending the loss on the 3rd December 1959 of the British motor vessel "Torrance" in the Bay of Biscay, as a result of which 58 members of her crew lost their lives. The Court having carefully inquired into the . . .

Getting his clothes off had shaken him up again. It was sheer hell getting to the showers. And when he raised his hands to adjust the flow of water, shock waves took him from under the arms, sweeping over his chest and belly to tremble in his testicles.

. . . The "Torrance" was a steel single screw cargo vessel, having two decks, and was built in 1943 by the Garfield Ship-building Corporation, New York, U.S.A. She was of all welded construction with transverse framing throughout. The regis-tered dimensions were 432.6 ft. x 58.0 feet x 36.3 feet. The ton-nages were—gross 7492.14, net 4514.18, underdeck 7043.28. The "Torrance" was classed 100 A1 with Lloyd's Register of Shipping. The last special survey in this connection was held at . . .

The lapping warmth of the water was forcing the tortured muscles to relax. That bastard Findlater, setting him up like that. It was a bloody unfair advantage he'd taken. He remembered Gary once saying his brother had won a southern area championship. Bloody unfair. For something that didn't even happen to him anyhow; and an age ago. Some people sure carried a chip. He couldn't even remember what hero-brother looked like all those years ago. He had been Master of the *Torrance* for three years at the time, and Gary Findlater had been Second Engineer for two. They'd hardly exchanged a dozen words with each other, not because he had any reason to cold-shoulder Gary, but ship's engineers always were a race apart, keeping themselves to themselves like lousy Seventh-Day Adventist. Ouch! He gritted his teeth as he forced his muscles to lift his arm and turn off the water. He should have got Dr. Hammond to give him another shot. He picked up the wrap and staggered toward the steam room.

. . . was making for Tunis and thence farther east, carrying a general cargo, including some livestock. She was under the command of her Master, Captain David Welch and, in addition, carried a crew of 12 European officers and 53 Pakistani seamen. Her draught on sailing was 20 feet 3 inches forward and 23 feet 9 inches aft. She was well found and fully provided with life saving equipment. Early on the morning of the 3rd December, during the Second Officer's watch, the "Torrance," which was proceeding in a westerly direction, reached a position . . .

The steam hit him in the face and momentarily took his breath away. His body shivered with the sudden change of temperature and the shivers made him gasp with renewed spasms of pain. God, he'd like to get back at that red-haired bastard! No one could humiliate him and get away with it. No one! He'd think of a way to get even. Something would turn up sooner or later. It always did. He laid the wrap along a tiled step and gently eased himself onto his back. Hell, the bastard might really have broken it. He might be dead, just another two-day sensation for the popular press to spew out over a few million breakfast tables.

. . . was then northwesterly of gale force and the vessel took a heavy sea which shifted the crated cattle and disturbed some deck cargo and also lifted No. 2 lifeboat and holed it. The lifeboat was lashed down and plugged and the Master decided to alter course to bring the wind and sea forward of the starboard beam. It was intended to make good a course of 204° true, but the Court is left in doubt as to what, if any, allowance was made for compass error or leeway. Shortly before handing over the watch to the Chief Officer at 16:00 hours, the Second Officer laid off a dead reckoning position on the chart. The Second Officer gave evidence before the Court, but did not recollect this dead reckoning position . . .

Would the damned pain never shift? Sweat and steam, lying supine, breathing gently, one leg raised, the ugly streaked-blue bruise on his thigh staring into his face. The time on *Manston* when Harper had a stinking cold on his chest. That wouldn't shift, either. They'd tried to get rid of it for him by cupping. In the morning there'd been a red ring on his shoulder, and that nit of a lieutenant thought it was teeth marks, carrying on like a banshee about there having been a woman on board and if not someone had been trying to commit arson. Oh, Christ, that was a laugh! Big, burly Harper and this nit going red in the face at the situation he'd created for himself. Ouch! Damned bruises! He had one on his right arm, too. Must have been where he landed on the edge of the table. Now, a little gentle exercise under steam heat. A-h-h-h, that was better. He might get by without another shot after all.

. . . The Master told the Court that, at about 19:15 hours after finishing his evening meal, he left his cabin and went to the chartroom expecting the Llanos light would be seen. He said that he looked at the radar and saw what he thought to be the echoes of an island on the last range ring on the screen. Realizing that his vessel, which was making for a position 15 miles north of Gijon, was very considerably eastward of her intended position, the Master decided to alter course to starboard. He therefore marked on the chart a position 4 miles westward of the Pacas buoy. About 15 minutes later the light of the Pacas buoy is said by the Master to have been sighted 5 to 6 degrees on the port bow. Shortly afterward he went below, giving orders to be called when the light was abeam. At about 20:25 hours the Master felt the ship shudder and heard a noise. He went up to the bridge and, very shortly afterward, realized that the vessel had broken in two . . .

Standing up gently in the swirling steam, he mopped the sweat from his skin with the cotton wrap. Outside he could hear Wilkie sluicing down the massage room. See if you can touch your toes. Slowly. The fireworks were less severe. Now up. Once more. Hands up. Higher. Stretch. Those years with the Hemsley Lines after his discharge from the Royal Navy seemed an age ago now, yet he still remembered Robbie Wymark's round pudding of a face as though it was only yesterday. There was a man who could hold his liquor. Ten pints of draft stout without batting an eyelid. He was a good man, Robbie. It was through him he came into Hemsley. It was through him he jumped from First Mate of one of their coasters bringing tomatoes from the Channel Islands to Master of the *Torrance*, in five years. Or was it six? Anyway, Robbie was a good man. He was designated manager at the court of inquiry, and afterward, when it was all over, said simply, "David boy, it happens to the best of us." Just like that. No recriminations. A good fellow. He spread the wrap on the tiles for a second time and lay prone, tucking his head in his arms, receding into the hot darkness. Beads of condensed steam dropped from the ceiling, stinging his back and preventing him from being lulled to sleep.

. . . After the vessel had broken in two, 10 persons, including Captain Welch, were left on the forward part. The radio aerials had parted and no signals could therefore be transmitted on the main or emergency sets. Whilst the No. 3 lifeboat was being lowered the portable transmitter kept in that boat was lost overboard and, consequently, no radio signals were ever sent out. No distress rockets were fired. The No. 3 lifeboat was successfully launched with 3 persons in it but they were unable to prevent it drifting away in the heavy sea and the remaining 7 persons on the forward part, including Captain Welch and the Chief Officer, then launched an inflatable life raft. This was quickly holed by jagged edges of the broken vessel before it could be got away. Those in No. 3 boat were able to pick up Captain Welch. Attempts were made to row the boat to the raft, but it disappeared and its remaining six lives were lost. Those in No. 3 boat let off flares during the

night and were rescued by the S.S. "Trader Pat" at about 04:45
on the 4th December . . .

The swirling water was choking him, filling his lungs, sucking him down, down, down. He shot off the hot tiles, face from
armed darkness into steaming whiteness. He could have
sworn he saw Gary Findlater sinking there beneath him,
trapped screaming beneath his naked wet body. He picked up
the sodden wrap, wrung it dry, and wiped himself down again.
It was every man for himself. That's how it always had been,
and that's how it always would be. If you were going to be
scared about what happened to the other guy, you'd never
rocket to the moon, drive a bus, or ride a tandem. It had happened, and it was just not his fault. If hero-boy Findlater had
been Master, the same bloody bad luck would have dogged
the voyage. And how would that red-haired nut-case of a
brother feel about that? He flung the hot wrap around his belly
and left the steam for a rub down. He hoped Wilkie knew his
job. He wanted his muscles to be done some good. They'd already taken enough punishment for a lifetime.

. . . When the "Torrance" broke in two there were 55
persons on the aft part, but no deck officers other than one cadet. There being no explosion, the instruments in the engine
room were undamaged. Second Engineer Gary Findlater displayed commendable initiative. He at once stopped the transfer pump and started the condenser pump, anticipating an
order to stop the engines. The Fourth Engineer reported to
him that the stokehold was flooding and he started the ballast
pump and endeavored to ring the bridge. Failing to make contact, he ordered the door to the tunnel closed and proceeded
toward the bridge to report personally to the Master. He found
the vessel had broken in two. Returning to the engine room he
ordered the engines to be stopped and had the main condenser
circulating pump put to the bilge injection. Next, he ordered
the rest of the engine-room staff to go to their boat positions.
His own boat was the damaged No. 2 on the port side. He began to prepare it for launching with four Pakistani members
of the crew. Other crewmen were having difficulty on the starboard side launching No. 1 boat as its aft davit had jammed.
Second Engineer Findlater assisted in clearing the davit and,

when the boat was swung out, returned to his own boat station . . .

"You've some nasty bruises there, sir," Wilkie said.

"I fell down the aft companionway on B Deck. I'm surprised you haven't heard about it yet."

"You won't know you've got them when I've finished with you, sir."

The man sluiced hot water over his chest and legs, cold over the crown of his head. Wilkie's body was marble smooth from years of steaming, chubby as a baby from overdrinking. He hitched the towel tighter round his waist, rinsed out the cotton wrap and flung it in a snake coil over the Chief Officer's vitals. The pain stabbed him like a dagger.

"Take it easy!" he yelled.

"Weren't sliding down the banisters at your age, were you, sir?" Wilkie asked. It was as near as he dare go to calling the Chief a liar.

. . . As No. 1 boat was being lowered, its aft part fell away and it was left swinging on the falls for several minutes before it broke free. Of about 40 persons who had been in the boat and were thrown out when it fell away, only 8 were able to get to it after its collapse into the water. Severely damaged by swinging against the ship's side, it was soon water-logged. During the night several people in the boat died from exposure, and shortly before dawn the boat capsized. Only three men were able to hold on to the grablines in the heavy seas until they were picked up at about 05:10 hours by the "Trader Pat." Of these three, only one Pakistani Able Seaman survived the ordeal. After the No. 1 boat had been lowered, several members of the crew, including the Chief Engineer who had been off duty and sleeping at the time of the impact with the rocks, were left on the aft section of the "Torrance." During the night unsuccessful attempts were made to attract the attention of passing vessels by means of torch and rocket signals. The aft section began to sink at about 01:45 hours and the damaged No. 2 lifeboat was let go. Efforts were made to free the cattle in the crates on deck. The water, however, was a quarter way up from the base of the funnel. Second Engineer Findlater was seen to be swept overboard by a beam sea.

Shortly afterwards, probably at 02:15 hours, the aft section sank. Second Engineer Findlater was able to grasp a floating bale of cattle food and cling to it until he was picked up by the "Trader Pat" in the morning. He died later in the day from exhaustion. The Court finds that the loss of . . .

Wilkie's fingers were working over his body with the gentleness of a woman, soothing and toning wrenched muscle, frisking firm hairy limbs like a sculptor gauging his final touch. If he asked the man if he ever played queer games, he'd deny it. Most men would. There were times when everyone was expected to lie. Which was why the court was so bloody unreasonable going at him the way they did on his evidence. Of course he'd told the Master of *Trader Pat* that an explosion in the old girl's guts had burst her in two. Of course he had said later that if there were no explosion, then the weather had battered her in two; that the first light he had seen had been Llanos and not Pacas as the court alleged; that the *Torrance*'s radar range was twenty-five miles when he knew damned well it was thirty-five; that he had made sure every lousy Pakistani on board knew where the spare life jackets were stored. God Almighty, what did they expect him to do? Go like a lamb to the slaughter? As Robbie had said, it could happen to the best of us. The man's hand was as near to his crotch as he dared. He was certain the bastard was queer. Well, he wouldn't get any joy out of him. Not that in his younger days he hadn't played. On the *Manston*. In Pompey. The equipment was too bloody fouled up now by that sod Findlater. Why the hell had he done it? He was probably one of those kinky types who really thought he was avenging justice, that the sun shone out of his arsehole for what he'd done. Like the three smug-mugged assessors who'd been so quick to concur with the judge's report.

. . . It has been customary in cases of this kind, when the Minister has asked that certificates should be "dealt with," for Courts holding Formal Investigations to suspend the certificates of Masters adjudged culpable. Presumably it has been thought that suspension does some good. What good it does is less easy to ascertain. There is no statistical evidence to support the proposition that such suspension has a deterrent effect on others. It may be that this way of dealing with such cases has become a ritual. If a suspension is imposed which allows a Master to go to sea again within a short time, it may give the impression that the fault in respect of which it was imposed is not a grave one. If the suspension is long enough to hurt, it may result in putting its victim so much out of the practice of his profession as to impair his efficiency for the future. There are undoubtedly cases in which certificates ought to be cancelled. This is not one of such cases, taking as we must into account the prevailing weather conditions which were severe and Captain David Welch's previous good record. The Court, constituted as it is for the purpose of this Investigation, is not persuaded that good will accrue to anyone as a consequence of suspending the Master's certificate. The folly and error of his behavior calls for the strongest possible censure and the decision of the Minister to order an Investigation deserves the complete support of the Court. By his recklessness, Captain Welch has caused the death of several other valuable and experienced officers and a crew of knowledgeable and well-trained seamen. He has struck tragedy into the lives of many families and it is a scar he will wear on his conscience for the rest of his life. Taking this, and our earlier statement into account, the Court will confine itself to the considerable expense to which the whole community has been put in exposing these errors. Those who make necessary the expenditure of large sums of public money for these profitless purposes must be made to contribute to the expenditures that they have brought about and the Court has, in the appropriate form, ordered that Captain David Welch pay the sum of £750 on account of the expenses of the Investigation. It is often emphasized that one of the purposes of these inquiries is to see, if possible, what lessons may be learned from the casualty under investigation. In the opinion of this Court, the only lesson to be learned from this casualty is that shipmasters should regard the radar screen merely as a navigational aid and not an adequate and reliable substitute for the human eye and longer established and proved methods of . . .

He was back in the shower room, taking it cold, icy fingers up and down his spine, trying to sing, to shake off the past, in order to return to the bridge ceremonially cleansed. Robbie Wymark had told him the court had let him off lightly. Perhaps it had; but it didn't seem that way at the time, or now.

The old fool who had represented him more or less implied it
was better than he deserved; but he wasn't the one about to
lose his job. Hemsley Lines, not surprisingly, was reluctant to
give him another commission, even though Robbie had put in
a few good words for him. Or said he had. And 750 quid became a dominating factor in one's life when one was unem-
ployed. Finally, he'd taken a drop in rank and salary and fer-
ried passengers instead of tomatoes across the Channel for British Rail. And he spent his leave doing either London or Paris,
trying to work it out of his system with liquor or whores or
both. It hurt because deep down inside he knew he was wrong,
which was why he had to protest his innocence so loudly. At
one time he thought of chucking the sea altogether and going
back to the land. His old man was still running the farm with
the help of brother Roy and his currant-eyed wife, and
although he could hardly expect the prodigal to be welcomed
with open arms, there was a pretty good chance that family
ties had not been irretrievably broken. But he didn't go back.
One night he drifted into that tiny Jermyn Street bar,
and there was Fiona, just waiting for someone who wasn't a
bowler-hatted pansy with a tightly rolled joystick. Fiona was
good for him, and he was good for her. She'd had it in a way
she'd never had it before; and for six years the chemistry
worked when, looked at rationally, most people wouldn't have
given it six months, she being beyond her prime, he being
about to reach his. But she was good fun. Not the clinging type.
She was a kind, and at times a very generous woman. Perhaps
he was an idiot to have—

"Are you ready for your towels, sir?" Wilkie was standing
there to swathe his nakedness in billows of freshly laundered
white. "You may still be a little stiff tomorrow, sir. If I may
suggest it, half an hour in the gymnasium on the rowing machine will do the trick. You're basically in good shape. Very
good shape. Don't want to start letting yourself go to seed yet,
do you?"

He put on his white shorts and tabbed shirt and went out to
the Promenade Deck. The sun stung his arms and legs with
blistering intensity. The *Queen Dee* was cutting swiftly
through a gentle sea. Beirut was a memory on the distant horizon. Soon they would be able to see Cyprus off the starboard

bow. The pool was crowded, all shapes and sizes sunning themselves on mattresses and being served cooling drinks by high-collared stewards. Lady Pratley was queening it over them all with Sir Gerald, sweating pinkly, at her side. The Chief Officer knew damned well she'd seen him from behind her dark glasses; but she preferred to turn her head. A lot of people were going to start turning their heads during the next few days. If he was going to keep the job, he'd have to start playing it cool. Hold out till this bloody cruise was over and Arkwright was in command. Len Arkwright was like Robbie Wymark. They were both damned good fellows.

Rhodes

THE first sight of Rhodes was enough to make Sir Gerald think of England. And wish he was there. Surrounded by sunbleached islands, with the primeval Turkish coastline to the north, it was a sea oasis of brilliant flowers and fragrant breezes. He knew many of the Cyclades and the Dodecanese from his Navy days; but fate had never previously brought him to Rhodes. It was even more lovely because he had found Beirut unendurable, his only shore excursion having been to an American bar in one of the skyscraper hotels along the Corniche de Chouran where he thought he would best avoid the wogs, but failed, and was surrounded. He breathed in the perfumed air wafting across the bay, and was anxious to get ashore to see what the ship's newspaper had described as "the myraids of butterflies which, when disturbed, rise in a cloud and vanish as quickly as they appear." There had even been a photograph of the vanishment.

"God, my hair's a mess!" Lady Pratley said, looking anxiously in the dressing-table mirror. "There's absolutely no one in the ship's *salon* who knows a thing about hair. You really would think the company could find one experienced person to look after its passengers, wouldn't you?"

"Yes, dear," he said, padding around behind her, nude, looking for his underwear beneath a discarded blanket.

"I'll have to have it fixed properly in Naples. Remember to have someone radio ashore and make an appointment for me. Anselmo in the Via Brazzi. I know he's good, and if he's not he can't be worse than this. And do put some clothes on. You look revolting enough dressed."

He had asked her to ease his injured arm through the sleeve of a fading maroon sports shirt. "I still think it's fractured," he said.

"Nonsense, you old worry-guts. It's bound to take time. I'm

sure Dr. Hammond's a very experienced doctor. The company wouldn't have given him the job if he weren't." She had on her skin-tight pink slacks and was too worried over what best to wear with them to think that perhaps the company's choice of medical aid was no more reliable than its *salon* service. "And keep it in the sling or it will never heal."

"All the same, I think I'll get a second opinion when we berth. The English hospital in Naples is absolutely first class." He didn't really think it was first class. He wasn't really worried. He simply wanted an excuse to avoid the complications of meeting her Italian friends. Almost as soon as he'd married her she'd gone off on an Italian kick, and the thought of traipsing around Positano, Amalfi and Capri with a lot of Ferrari types frankly terrified him. A quiet day in hospital was an infinitely preferable alternative.

"Fernando probably knows a good whorehouse, if you'd prefer that," she said. "You won't get much joy out of the little English nurses. Is there any more coffee in the pot?"

He opened the lid. "No, dear. You've had it."

"I haven't had it! Call that steward, Addison or whatever his name is, and order some more." She looked out to the recreation deck below where half a dozen early risers were playing tennis in the shade of the Boat Deck superstructure. The *Queen Dee* was at anchor less than a mile outside the old Mandrakio harbor, and the first of the launches was already landing at the quay. "Why did you have to book a suite overlooking a tennis court? It's worse than living at Wimbledon."

"Forget Wimbledon and tell me what you've planned for today," he said, struggling to hitch his trousers with only one hand.

"It looks as though this morning is going to be taken up presenting one old ruin to another. You're sure you feel up to it?"

"You know perfectly well I am," he said, refusing to let her hurt him.

"I'm not lunching ashore, that's for certain," she said. "I don't want the runs again. And this afternoon you can take it easy in a deck chair with the paperbacks I bought you in Beirut. They're not sexy, so don't start panting for them. I'm not going to have you getting a heart condition."

"And what are you going to do this afternoon?"

"I'll probably go ashore again and find myself a quiet beach."

"You're sure you'll be all right by yourself?" he asked anxiously.

"I may not be by myself," she said. Addison came into the room with more coffee, but she made no effort to change the conversation: rather, she welcomed an audience. "I might as well tell you. You're bound to find out sooner or later, you old coot. The American and English boys are taking me. I'm sort of their fairy godmother. I think that's rather cute, don't you?"

"Will that be all, sir?" Addison asked, removing the empty jugs.

"Yes, thank you, Addison. Unless her ladyship has a sudden whim for sarsaparilla."

Addison took a startled look at her ladyship blinking blandly in the mirror. The beginning of the voyage home was always a testing time for the stewards, knowing where they stood, what to expect by way of gratuity for services rendered. Rows were usually the fatal sign. If a steward could be put in the wrong, and replaced, the shysters among the customers would convince themselves no tips were necessary. They were worse than the "I'll see you're all right" brigade on the first day out, the "I'll give you damn-all at the end" bastards.

"I said that would be all, Addison," Sir Gerald barked.

"Yes, sir. Beggin' your pardon, sir. Thank you, sir," he said, disappearing backward through the open door.

The moment the man had gone, Sir Gerald turned on her fiercely. "Don't you think you've caused enough trouble for one voyage? The *Torrance* business is all round the ship. You crucified David. Quite unnecessarily, if you want my opinion. He's a damn good fellow. Knows his job. The judge put the whole matter in a nutshell when he summed up at the inquiry. I can't understand you. You're all over people one minute, then drop them the next."

"There you're wrong as usual, my pet. I'm never over them. I'm under them. You know, the good old-fashioned under." She saw she had hurt him at last: but almost before she had enjoyed her success remorse set in, and she added, "Anyway, most of the time they drop *me*. Who wants a fairy godmother when she's forty?"

The island was not like England after all. Nonetheless, it justified its claim to beauty. The Colossus had gone from its position astride the harbor entrance, narrow enough to support a big man or wreck a carelessly navigated ship, and in its place were two bronze stags. The medieval walls and moats were draped with flowers, pigmented with such intensity that they glowed like burning coal. Scores of tiny cafés, gently bobbing private yachts, and, where nature did not suffice, whitewashed cannon balls completed the decoration. He wanted to wander up steep narrow streets and past the inns of the Knights of St. John to the Palace of the Grand Master, but she refused. She said her feet were killing her. So they hired a car and demanded to see the whole island in two hours flat.

"What are they staring at? Anyone would think they hadn't seen a pair of trousers before," her ladyship said, staring right back at a group of black-beetle women who had been rudely shocked by her shocking pink. "You're a lot of silly old women! Don't you know that girls should wear the trousers to keep it warm? All the works are packed inside. And men should wear the skirts. Mother Nature wants it all to hang out in the fresh air, you see. Oh, why bother! They're like a lot of children."

He anxiously helped her into the car and closed the door on her, relieved she was once more in her own private world where she could nag and fret and laugh and cry and fornicate as she pleased without the public world having to be importuned. He looked from the window on to the hot countryside as they climbed the mountainous road toward Lindos and wondered, not for the first time in his life, why he had ever married her and, having married her, not cast her adrift long ago. She was so unlike Ursula, who had come from good British stock, landed gentry, not very fashionable these days, subjected to popular ridicule and political abuse, but Britain wouldn't have been Britain without their kind. Ursula had been thin and gentle and delicate, the perfect English rose, almost too timid to exchange more than a dozen words with strangers, and consequently, it had to be admitted, not the best choice for an officer's lady. But was Fiona any better? Aggressive, determined to follow no code of conduct other than her own, her quick tongue all too quickly dissipated the favorable first impressions of her brittle good looks. He knew damned well that people gossiped about her behind her back; worse, she knew it and enjoyed it. It was an essential part of her life, to shock. But it had been an acute embarrassment to him on many occasions; like the time when a rear admiral had taken him to one side in the Ritz grill to say, "Pratley, some wives are like children. They are better seen and not heard." No one would ever have had cause to speak that way about Ursula. She was so delicate, in mind as well as body, that what he had done to her was all the more unforgivable. Perhaps if they had consulted a doctor when they were married, they would have known in advance that delivery could never have been easy for her. But to see her in such agony, through him, for him, struggling to give him his child and tearing herself apart because of her physical incapacity, refusing to the last moment every medical aid because she so desperately wanted it to be a loving, natural thing, their apogee. That was 1939. He'd just been promoted to commander and Europe was about to be plunged into a holocaust. All that seemed so trivial at the time compared with dead Ursula, and had remained so for many years. He was in such a fatalistic mood when war came that they could have put him to patroling the Western Approaches for all he cared. But it had to be a stone frigate in Scotland, such was the luck of the draw. And up there he saw dead Ursula and their unnamed child in every scurry of highland mist.

"What are you thinking about? Why don't you talk to me?" Fiona asked.

"About the war, dear. I was just thinking about the war. It all seems so far away now." It would have been cruel to have said Ursula, he was thinking about Ursula, and the son he almost had. It was all right for one partner in marriage to be cruel; but not two. It couldn't work at all with two.

"I should never have married an old bore like you. You haven't any past glories, so what do you think about anyway?"

The villages were picturesque and Lindos, high over the southeastern shore, cluttered with pottery, an Acropolis, and a Byzantine church, was the most picturesque of them all. She bought an enormous urn which she said would make a use-

ful present for someone and left the driver to struggle with it
into the front seat of the car. Fifteen minutes after they had arrived they were off again, winding up Mt. Prophet Elias
through cedars, pines and cypresses. When they got to the top
to see the view, she decided she wasn't going to get out of the
car after all, and left Sir Gerald to see it by himself. He returned, lonely, and they started on the journey back into the
valley.

"I hoped this cruise was going to bring us closer together,"
he said. "But it hasn't, has it? We're just as far apart as ever."

"You're right here, next to me. I'm showing you the island,
aren't I?" she said, fending off any serious conversation.

"Fiona, I'm well aware of what a failure I've always been to
you, physically. But I've tried to make a go of everything else.
I've tried to give you everything you've ever wanted."

"That's it, now tell me I'm spoiled."

"You were a beautiful woman when I first married you.
And you still are. Isn't that worth spoiling?"

"Well, if you put it like that, how can I argue with you?"
She looked out of the window and obligingly gave a royal wave
to some village children as they passed. "But must you go all
broody on me? Why here, of all places? You know how I hate
your big thought sessions."

"It's the Westcott boy you're after this time, isn't it?"

"I told you, I don't want to talk about it. Stop irritating me,
Gerry."

"He's only a lad. He's much too young for you."

"He's a very big lad. I hope."

"You're old enough to be his mother."

"So, I'll mother him."

He said, exasperated by her apparent indifference, "Fiona!
This time you're playing with fire!"

She laughed a little nervously. "What's that joke about rubbing two Boy Scouts together? Oh, do stop fussing, Gerry. It
won't hurt him to learn a few advanced facts of life."

"Just this once. For my sake, Fiona. Don't!"

But even this once she was determined not to give in. "I'm
not going to cut his body up into little pieces and post it to his
mother as a birthday present, or anything way out like that. I
won't hurt him. That's a promise. I won't hurt him!"

He said with tears in his eyes, "I wasn't thinking of him, my dearest. Can't you understand that? I wasn't thinking of him. I don't want you to get hurt. I couldn't bear to see you hurt."

"Oh, fiddlesticks! You're saying hurtful things to me all the time. You never stop. How on earth do you think a young hopeful like Richard could possibly hurt *me*?"

"He might say no."

They were standing in the valley, a little way from the road. All around them were tiny spring flowers, and from moment to moment, in sudden bursts, the butterflies flashed into the air in a rainbow cloud. Even she was enchanted. They seemed to be performing just for them.

"Poor little blighters! Only live for a day," he said.

"I wish I was a butterfly," she said wistfully. She put her arms gently around him, careful not to hurt his damaged wing, and kissed the side of his cheek where it was warm with sunlight. "I love you very much, you silly old coot. Never forget that, will you?"

Junior Second Officer Rigg came off watch at noon in a filthy mood and handed over to Senior Second Officer Hewson who was in little better temper. One of the launches returning from the quay had overshot the mark and been jammed by the current under the accommodation ladder, fortunately without any passengers in her since at that time of day the passengers were all heading for shore. But the Chief Officer had held Rigg directly responsible for what was essentially the bo'sn's mate's mistake. And Hewson had received a handwritten note, not even the courtesy of a verbally delivered request, telling him his log entries were getting more illegible every day, and to please watch it. The Chief Officer had at least had the common decency to use "please." But as Hewson had said as he took over from Rigg, "The man's got court-of-inquiry jitters. He got a public dressing-down in Beirut and now he's going to take it out on us."

The officers' smoking room on the Bridge Deck was fuller than usual. No one said it in so many words, but they all knew they had gathered for one purpose only—to discuss the Chief Officer and to contemplate if, and how, the Master would deal with him.

"They'd been told there was a three-knot current running," Rigg said, fixing himself a Scotch and soda. "It was a bastard as it was, this morning, to lay anchor head-to-stream. They should have laid a tide spare forward from the outer stringer of the ladder. Parsons has sailed the Mediterranean long enough by now to know you never trust it any more than any other ocean."

Tyson tried to divert the ill humor with reminiscence. "You remember, Riggie, when the old man fouled her up off Gibraltar?" he said. "Tidal stream then was little more than half a knot. But he had it up her tail and she swung athwart stream. Cable-holder brakes wouldn't hold, ran out to a clench and parted before he could turn her head-to-stream. It can happen to the best of us."

But no one wanted to be diverted. Langdon, the First Sparks, had a complaint over the Chief Officer ordering him off the air to send a maintenance rating aloft to check the forward steaming light, just at the time he knew damned well Langdon had the bulk of passenger business and greeting messages to transmit.

"I'm in his watch, so I get the worst of his tongue," Tyson said bitterly. "But one has to be fair to a bloke. I mean, he knows his job, there's no doubt about that. He just won't give you any damned credit for knowing yours."

"You mean to tell us you think the chewing-out he gave you at Villefranche over the cordage was justified?" Riggie asked. "Like hell it was!"

"Justified or not, what do you think the old man's going to do? There's not a single passenger who's not talking about the *Torrance* affair or the account that silly old cow Miss Peebles has been giving of his row with Findlater's brother in Beirut."

"I lay five to one the old man won't do a thing," Langdon said. "So long as Welch keeps his nose clean on the bridge. Would you risk a head-on collision with the Marine Superintendent over one of his bright-eyed boys a week before your pension was due?"

But Langdon lost. The old man had already done something. They went down to the sparsely filled restaurant for lunch, and the Chief Officer was not at his usual table. He was not at any table. Second Officer Rigg discreetly asked the Chief Purser if Mr. Welch had gone ashore, and Leslie Craddock, who was first to get everything from the bridge on Daisy Bell's grapevine, took Rigg to one side, his heavy glasses twitching happily on his grog-blossom, and explained in detail the scandal of the day.

"Mr. Welch will not be dining in public for the rest of the voyage," the Chief Purser said. "If any of the passengers ask questions, they're to be told that changes in the duty roster make his absence at usual mealtimes unavoidable. I don't think even the Earls are stupid enough not to know the real reason, although I did hear her say at table the other day that she thought croutons were a game they played on deck."

"The old man blew his top, then. I'd like to have been there," Rigg said. "Doesn't do the company image much good, though, does it?"

The Chief Purser shrugged his shoulders expressively. "That's my problem. But the interesting thing is, Mr. Rigg, suppose our Chief Officer doesn't choose to be confined to quarters?"

"That's a point. I wonder how far he dares buck the old man. I think he's had it where the Pratleys are concerned. But, how well does he know Captain Arkwright? The Marine Superintendent isn't wet behind the ears. He must have known about the *Torrance*. But will he continue to turn a blind eye to it if he doesn't have Sir Gerald breathing a recommendation down his neck straight from the connubial bed? The plot thickens, as Miss Peebles would say."

The Chief Purser said piously, "Mr. Welch may be a good officer, Mr. Rigg; but he is a very stupid man. A very stupid man."

John spent the morning with his parents doing the island in one of the tour coaches. He loved both Europe and his parents; but the two together were more than flesh and blood could bear. Europe fascinated him for its constant changes of people and scenery and climate; life on the Loire, the Rhine, the Po, and the Danube was so incredibly individual, yet each river and its peoples was no more than a few hours away by train or road. Unlike back home where you could travel for days with never a change of language and seldom a change of scenery. But change irritated his folks. It was the curse of being adult. His mother was positively hostile toward simple people who couldn't speak American, was just not interested in food or liquor she hadn't eaten or drunk before, and saw poverty in everything that didn't reflect, however distorted, the American way of life. And although his father was not so aggressive, he left no doubt in John's mind that he saw Europe as a quaint backwater that was good to photograph during a few weeks' vacation, but in all other respects an economic mess and a potential trouble-maker warwise.

"Why don't you come back to the States with us, John dear?" his mother urged, oblivious to the irritation she was causing the guide who was trying to interest them in the Temple of Apollo.

"Not yet," he said firmly. "Please do try to understand. I'm not ready for it yet. When I do come home, I want to be secure in myself. Know exactly what I want to do. I think it'll have to be the theater, and if it is, I'll be the best. I promise you that, Mother. Whatever I do, I'll give the best there is in me."

His father studied a bas-relief, moved by his son's sincerity. "It's a hard life for all but a very few. Not much money in it. And after the education we've given you—"

"I'm sorry, but we've been over all this before and I don't want to go over it again now. Money's not the only thing that makes me tick. If I haven't got it, I haven't got it. But I don't think I could live without a symphony by Beethoven or a play by Shakespeare. But you could. The both of you."

"All right, son. I just hope you're never hungry, that's all." His father shook his head sadly, unable to comprehend, and followed Mrs. Brewer toward the sacrificial altar.

They returned to the *Queen Dee* for lunch. John went down to the cabin to shower away the morning dust and sweat. Lying in the center of his bed was an envelope, the kind anyone could pick up free in the Writing Room. He thought at first it was a message from Richard, backing out of the afternoon swimming party with that camp bit of British aristocracy, or saying he'd be late, or something like that. But it wasn't. Inside was a single photographic print, badly processed, but all too appall-

ingly recognizable. It showed Aziz, Hooda, a Lebanese sailor
and John, doing things with and to each other, which, before
lunch, a couple of days later, took on an entirely new dimension
of human achievement. At first he was amused to know he
looked like that when he was being screwed: then he was
mildly revolted at being reminded of sex before lunch when
quite another appetite was rumbling to be satisfied, and, as
suddenly, his temper quickened at the thought of who the hell
had had the bloody nerve to take the pictures without his permission anyhow. Richard? Surely not. The idea was as improb-
able as it was funny. He was laughing to himself as he turned
the print over. On the back was scrawled in pencil, "There
are four more even better. If you want all five negatives leave
five hundred dollars behind cistern in men's lavatory in cinema during last performance tomorrow. Or the pictures will
be presented to your parents as a souvenir of the cruise."

He was still staring at the chalky image when Richard came
into the cabin. "Rhodes, Izmir, Athens, Beirut . . . they're
all beginning to look alike to me," he said. "Are they some of
your dad's snaps? May I see?"

Suddenly John felt guilty without quite knowing why. "No,
it's only a postcard I'm sending to an aunt in Cincinnati," he
said, stuffing it quickly into the hip pocket of his jeans. He
was mad at himself for not practicing what he preached. He
should show the picture to Richard. "Me. On the *plage* at
Beirut. Enjoying the local customs." But he didn't, any more
than newly-weds would want to show their friends picture souvenirs of the intimacies of the honeymoon. Yet love in all its
guises was as much a part of living as riding donkeys on the
sands, rolling naked babies over bearskin rugs, or all the other
idiotic stances in which human beings were constantly prepared
to be publicly remembered.

"What shall I wear this afternoon?" Richard asked. "I
won't need a jacket, will I?"

"For Mother Earth? Are you kidding?"

The swimming party was conducted with the same ceremo-
nial attention to detail as tea at Henley. Lady Pratley turned
up with a vast wickerwork hamper, an assortment of brightly
colored towels, a portable changing tent, a portable record
player, a portable canvas chair, a straw mat, a box of various lo-

tions, and a plastic bag crammed with enough swimsuits to stock a shop. She was, as she pointed out to both her escorts as they struggled under the load, a very fickle woman. Once ashore, they found an obliging taxi driver who whisked them to a secluded bay of golden sand and delicately colored shells and left them, miles out of town, not certain as to whether they'd end the afternoon thanking him for the revelation, or cursing him for having caused them to miss the boat. It took nearly an hour to settle her ladyship and furnish the rocks with the record player, the tea set, and a formidable array of sunning requisites. And when she was settled, reclining in an emerald bikini in all her bronzed splendor on the straw mat, a molded piece of matching emerald plastic protecting her eyes and nose from the ravages of the sun, she demanded to be entertained. Records interspersed with silly chatter and cups of tea and *Queen Dee* cakes. But although her chatter was silly, it reflected a lively interest in the things most people forgot about after they were twenty—the urgency of protest songs; the fun in wearing switched-on clothes that made all the switched-offs green with envy; doing something about starving black babies; not doing anything about the future, like a dull job with security at sixty-five. She was so different from when she was with Sir Gerald, sparking off ideas, sending up everything, including herself, yapping away the years till Richard could no longer look upon her as Mother anything.

"Don't you ever go to the all-night jazz clubs in London?" she asked him.

"Not yet. They didn't give us much of a chance to do that kind of thing when we were at Tor Beeches."

She made a rude gesture with her fingers. "That to the British public school system! What are they trying to teach you to be? Monks? You come and spend a weekend at the manor sometime, and I'll drive you down to London and show you a place where you can hear the coolest music this side of heaven."

"I'll drive *you*," he said anxiously. "In my new three-litre coupé. I'm getting it as soon as we get home. Mother said so."

"Good for you! It'll be fab, zooming down the Mile End Road for a jellied eel supper, won't it? You like jellied eels?"

"I don't know," he said, "but I can always try, can't I?"

"We can always settle for the Savoy Grill," she said. "Now tell me all about your car. I'm sure it's going to be a beauty." She was, she thought, making surprisingly good progress for one afternoon.

John saw through her ploy from the moment she started on the starving children of Africa bit. He knew quite a bit about fly fishing himself. For the past half hour he had been left out of the conversation. Once she'd said to him, "Now, let's listen to the flip side, John." And that was all. She had the old pro's touch—there was no doubt about that. She was snake-charming Richard with the calm certainty of a leathery old fakir. Richard couldn't help being normal, of course, but if his graceful young body really found Mother Earth attractive, then it was one of the great mysteries of life why he had carried on the way he had that night under the shower. John still had doubts. Richard had told him yesterday that he'd had a smashing time with the girl they'd picked up for him in Beirut. But smashing what? He was still the kind of boy who thought hymens were something you sang in church. The Britishers were sure born at an early age. Richard still wouldn't know if he was animal, vegetable, or mineral by the time he was nineteen, twenty-one or forty.

"Richard, bring that *bombe* of mousse and do my back for me, please. That's it. The one with the orange and white stripes. Behind the tub of cold cream."

John left them anointing each other's backs. She was too rapt on gauging Richard's reactions to the touch of her skin to notice him leave. The water was warm but nonetheless refreshing, busy with small fish basking, yet not too busy to receive him into an isolated world of utter purity. He swam some distance from the shore until he was over a sudden depth to one side of a craggy rock, his body turning a sunless white as he floated above the bottomless blue below. He wanted to block out everything from his mind and commune with nature, but that damned photograph kept reflecting across the surface of the water. It must be a joke. Respectable married men who fancied schoolboys might get blackmailed for indulging their *recherché* tastes, but not people like himself, devoid of respectability, wives, employers or, in this part of the world at least, the law to worry about. It was all so petty, threaten-

ing to tell his folks. Who the hell could be doing it? And how
had whoever-it-was got hold of the pictures in the first place?
He didn't remember anyone taking pictures. They'd gone to a
small hotel in a cul-de-sac behind the Place Riad Sohl. Perhaps there had been a room with a two-way mirror that was
used for trapping international spies. It was all so utterly ridiculous. But weren't the greatest tragedies in drama based on
situations which, when analyzed, could be reduced to the ab-
surd? The maddening thing was that whoever had left him the
photograph had picked his one vulnerable spot. His parents.
He'd made the break from home after a series of arguments
that had too often descended into abuse, and the break
had been as difficult for him as for them, on account of his being
the only child. He'd never go back now. They knew it.
He knew it. But neither admitted it. He was gay, and always
would be. He'd hang on somehow in the world of the theater,
not because it was an escape from a dreary normality but because he felt a burning urge to create, to fashion something of
beauty, to show off his personality to the world around him, a
substitute for his lack of desire to breed babies in his own
image. Maybe ultimately this would be a better, more reward-
ing choice for them and for him. But parents were parents, full
of love and good intentions, however misguided; and his
mother was miserable enough, failing to coax him home. The
photographs would shock them, destroy dreams and hopes that
one day the framed picture over the hearth would be of John
and Mrs. John and the little Johns, their grandchildren. He
didn't want that to happen. He didn't give a damn who else saw
him being screwed by an Arab; but not them, he'd do anything
to prevent their being hurt, particularly if the hurt was of his
own doing. He had to get the pictures from whoever had them.
There was no alternative. He didn't feel particularly noble,
like going to the cops. How did one go to the cops on board the
Queen Dee anyway? And he didn't have much confidence in
old Captain Corlett's ability to handle the matter, even assuming he was sympathetic enough to want to handle it. But God
knows where he'd find five hundred bucks. The study grant he
was getting from the States just about covered food and lodging. Having to fly from Izmir to Beirut in order to rejoin the
cruise had wiped out most of the gift his father had given him

the day the folks arrived in Europe. It would be a screwball situation to try to squeeze five hundred bucks out of them in order to pay for their peace of mind. He just couldn't do it: he couldn't demand any more handouts from them, not for anything. He had to run his own life, his own way. The lousy bum who was twisting his arm had made one miscalculation. He was assuming that every American who hit Europe was stinking rich and that just because his folks were paying his first-class passage they would give him first-class dough any time he cared to ask for it, or that he was the kind of guy who would ask for it. So, what to do? He didn't have the five hundred bucks, and there was no immediate prospect of earning it either. Of course, he might be able to coax Richard to earn it for him off Lady Pratley. The sheer stupidity of such a situation, the thought of Richard as a call boy waiting in sheer silk lingerie by a white telephone, made him laugh so much he swallowed water. Ugh! it was salty as hell! He was letting the whole situation develop in his mind to monstrous proportions. It was all madly camp really. He'd play it that way. He'd leave a note behind the cistern instead of the money. Perhaps he might get to meet his blackmailer. The guy might be quite a dish. He might even settle for something other than money.

When he came out of the water, Richard and Lady Pratley were sharing the same straw mat, drinking in the sun. He playfully shook water over them. "Aren't you two ever going to get some exercise?" he asked.

"Richard," she commanded. "Get some exercise."

He rubbed his eyes to get John in focus. "Why the hell did you have to wake me just when I was dreaming of a steak smothered in mushrooms for dinner?"

"Some dream," John said, pulling him playfully off the mat and whipping him with a towel to make him run.

For several minutes the two boys exercised. Running, jumping, doing handstands, attempting cartwheels. And her ladyship sat there sipping lemon tea from a flask and pretending Richard was fighting over her. Presently John chased him into the sea. When he came out she threw him a towel to dry himself.

"Why have you got muscles and he hasn't?" she demanded.

Richard shouted through the engulfing towel. "John's the

studious type. I was playing rugger twice a week until last spring."

"I can see you've been playing something," she said, looking at him till he froze like a marble statue, uncertain how, standing there in only an ice-blue brief, he could prevent John laughing at him. "I've never watched a game of rugger in my life. You must take me to Twickenham some time. I think it's such a manly sport. It develops the biceps to such an enormous size. They are the muscles that run down the back of your legs, aren't they?"

"No," said Richard awkwardly. "They're these. In the upper arm. See?" He flexed them for her.

"Tell me, Lady Pratley," John asked. "Have you ever come across a case of only one ball?"

Pamela Westcott had a perfectly awful dinner. The food was of its usual excellence and the service was faultless; but the company became more cruelly oppressive with every course. Over the *hors d'oeuvres* Mrs. Earl remarked on the Chief Officer's absence from the table, and hinted darkly that she had heard that the Beirut incident was going to cost him his job. Over the entrée Mr. Afton referred, hypothetically, of course, to the number of men who must have had their careers dashed by a woman's influence. And by the time they had reached the dessert, Miss Peebles was ready to move in with vague references to religion, and marriage, and the tragedy of young people being involved in their parents' divorce, adultery, separation, death, and other of life's matrimonial disasters. No one actually said so, but they all made it perfectly obvious that they thought she was personally responsible for the *Torrance* disaster and was probably a Jonah who would have them all floundering on the next reef they came to. Her first reaction was to ask the headwaiter to move her to another table, perhaps one she could share with Richard; but she decided against it since it would display a moral weakness, against which she knew she had to fight. What was more, it would not be fair landing herself on Richard again, just when he had made a good friend of the Brewer boy. People could take such pleasure in being cruel when they knew other people were at their most vulnerable. The cruise had seemed such a sensible idea at the time, but it wasn't working out at all in the way she had hoped it would. Instead of returning to the new house in Reigate relaxed, relieved of all the tensions that had weighed her down since Arnold's death, she was going back with a whole new set of problems. Richard, who was growing up so quickly, and wouldn't want to depend on her for anything much longer. David, who was becoming a complex, dominating part of her life, and the *Torrance* with him. She so disliked scandal, and it was too terrible for words to find herself becoming the center of one. She declined the Aftons' offer of a little bridge and decided on an early night. She lingered for a few minutes on the Observation Deck, watching the thick purple water shimmer by as the *Queen Dee* headed westward into the night between the hundreds of tiny, lonely islands. Could an island ever feel as lonely as she? Perhaps it would be better to end it all. She would have done so months ago if it hadn't been for Richard. He had needed her then; but his need was becoming less urgent every day, and with that severance her own isolation was crowding in on her oppressively. When she got to her cabin the first thing she wanted was to part the curtains, fling wide the window, and let in the cool night air. But she couldn't. For the simple reason that the Chief Officer was seated there in the armchair with a bottle of Scotch in his hand.

"Good heavens," she said, undecided whether or not she should be pleased at his presence, "what are you doing here?"

"Visiting. I know where they keep the passkey. One of the privileges of being Chief Officer. Can I pour you a drink?"

She said nervously, "Are you sure it's wise for you to be here?"

"Wise?" He looked at her incredulously. "What the hell do you think I've got to be afraid of? That poor old devil Corlett, who'll be on the scrap heap next week anyway?"

"You have sort of been banned from mixing with the passengers, haven't you?"

"There's no point in colliding with him head on. It suits my purposes. More time to myself . . . and with you. You don't think I enjoy dancing and prancing in front of the paying customers, do you? Dreary lot."

He got to his feet and tried to embrace her, but she resisted him. "It makes it seem so squalid, meeting in my cabin like this. Like a couple of misbehaving children."

"I always misbehaved when I was a child, didn't I tell you? My mother used to send me to bed with only bread and water for supper. I'd get my own back by hanging over the banisters and calling, 'Mum, can I have some more water please?' Then I used to wet the bed." He turned on the smile which so many women had found irresistible. "You will have that drink, won't you?"

"Well, just one," she said, "seeing you've brought it all the way from Scotland."

He went into the bathroom for a couple of glasses, and when he returned she had kicked off her shoes and was sitting on the bed wriggling her feet. "It's the hot weather. It makes them swell up like balloons," she said. "They've been giving me hell all day."

"Let me soothe them for you," he said, taking her right foot in his hands and massaging it. But the moment he got playful with her she scrambled from the bed and paced the room in her long white gown, shaking her auburn hair angrily, like a cornered animal. Somehow he had to snap the bond that still linked her with dead Arnold. And it wasn't going to be easy.

"I hoped you wanted my company for my mind as well as my body," she said, and he could barely conceal a smile at the schoolmarmly way she scolded him.

"But I adore your mind," he said. "It's got little tresses of rich auburn hair all over it."

"David! I don't feel in that kind of mood tonight. Can't you see I'm worried about the way things are turning out?"

"I tell you, there's absolutely nothing to worry about. Nothing. Here, drink up!"

But she was not so easily put off. "I'm not concerned with whether or not you wrecked a ship. But I *am* concerned with whether or not you're likely to wreck my life. And Richard's."

"What a crazy thing to say! Isn't that just like a woman? *My* this. *My* that. Can't you see, it's *our* life that matters? If I could foretell the future, I wouldn't be pushing this ancient pile of steel up and down the Mediterranean. I'd be a business tycoon on the way to making my second million."

"I only want to be reasonable, David. You must see it from my point of view. I've lived a very . . . well, sheltered life. Before my husband died, I'd never even thought of another man in an intimate sort of way—you know what I mean. I've never been an emancipated woman like Lady Pratley. You'll never find me the least like her."

"I should hope not!" he said. But he'd made his protest too late, and in the wrong way.

"So the stories about you and her are true," she said.

"I've known Fiona *and* Sir Gerald for some time. Yes. What stories are you prepared to believe about me? I didn't think you were the kind of woman who listened to gossip."

"I'm a one-man woman, David. I'm not a prude, but I just don't happen to fancy promiscuity as a way of life. I don't think I could live for long with someone who didn't share that point of view."

"Darling Pamela, of course I respect your point of view. I respect everything about you."

She said, almost with brutal firmness, "I didn't say 'respect,' I said 'share.' "

He drank heavily. "I've already said I can't read the stars, just navigate by them when I have to. I'd like to share everything with you. Don't you realize I'm mad about you? I'd even try to be a good father to Richard."

"Is that a proposal? You see how innocent I am. I might not recognize one when it was made. My husband did it rather romantically. In the best room. I think there was even an aspidistra in the window. I come from that kind of a family."

"Yes, I suppose it is a proposal. I'm more innocent than you, you see. I've never been married at all. All these years driving without a license, and I haven't been caught in the act yet."

It was the kind of crude joke brother Fred might make. "So this little blonde piece said I weigh eight stone twelve, but eight stone nine stripped for gym, and I said why bother with Jim while I'm here?" She thought of Fred and the rest of the family on her side, and what remained of the family on Arnold's side, and wondered what they'd all be saying behind her back if she was to take another husband, even a ship's Chief Officer, which wasn't even common, like marrying a sailor.

She daren't go through with it. But how was she going to get out of it? She had to break off the affair now, before it was too late. Her mind formed a mosaic of possible maneuvers, but they all became hopelessly jumbled.

"No," she said, which was the simplest, most direct approach.

"No what?"

"No marriage," she said, and added, "I'm sorry," which was fatal, because it gave him just the opening he needed to get his foot into her door and wheedle and coax and flatter and cajole and plead until she was back again where she began, with a vague yearning and a frightening void of confusion.

"People like me don't have any real roots, nothing deep we can hold on with," David said, his voice as persuasive as an Irish brogue. "While I've been working ashore with Sir Gerald, I've kept a small place going in Pimlico, just for weekends. But the rest of the time it's been a matter of living aboard, or in some miserable hotel room."

"A naval officer's life always seems so glamorous," she said.

"Pamela, I'd chuck the job tomorrow for the opportunity to settle down. You don't think I want to become a crusty old sod like Corlett, do you? If I had the money and the right woman behind me, I'd start my own business. Or manage a pub. Not in London. I'm not really a night owl, you know. Some small place. Lewes, Guildford . . . or Reigate would do me fine."

"We'll have to see how things work out when we get back to England," she said, knowing deep down inside her that things couldn't work out, and hoping that on their return he wouldn't try to make them.

"Let's drink to that!" he said.

She had never been a heavy drinker. Once, at Bruce's wedding reception, she had overdone it, mixing spirits with champagne, and she had vowed she would never let herself get tiddley again—it was too awful. But the last few days she had drunk more than she had ever drunk in her life, and always with him. At least it was better than becoming a secret drinker and having everyone talking about the secret drinking behind your back. But Scotch was a man's drink, and she wished there was something else, that they could be seated comfortably again in the Orchard Room drinking sociably, in public, instead of in this squalid way like that dreadful Cilla Liscon, behind locked doors.

"I really think I've had enough," she said, pushing the bottle away.

"Nonsense. You can never have enough of a good thing," he said, pushing the neck of the bottle into her glass.

"Don't you have to be going soon?" she asked anxiously.

"Not until this is finished." He looked at his watch. "And not for another three and a half hours. Have to be in quarters ninety minutes before four-o'clock watch. Company regulations. Those I keep. I may have to be with the company a very long time. Or will I?"

He put an arm around her waist and kissed her cheek, but she was still dreadfully frigid, wriggling out of his grasp, pretending she didn't want affection, unable to snap some bond inside her that would set her emotions free. And when he tried to kiss her again, on the lips, she nervously put the glass between them and swallowed the liquor in great gulps.

"You'd have thought the company could have afforded radios in the first-class cabins for the price they sting you. Then we could dance," he said.

"The proper place to dance is in the Tudor Room, isn't it?"

He smiled again. Ravishingly. "Pamela, my dear, you are so middle-class you're funny! Why do you have to be so proper about everything? You can dance anywhere you feel like it. Even without music."

"I don't think—"

"Let me do the thinking for you tonight. And I think you feel like it, only you won't admit it. Even to yourself."

He put down his glass and reached out for her. Again she resisted, fighting both him and the drink. He caught the back zipper of her gown and tugged it. As she pushed herself from his grasp, the shimmer of white silk fell forward and down, trapping her in folds at her knees, exposing her freshly bronzed skin firmly held in bra and girdle. She dropped her glass, tried to run from him, stumbled, and fell sprawling over the Scotch-soaked carpet. He followed her down, spreading himself over her, trying to twist her to face him, mussing her hair, snapping the flimsy straps.

"No, David, no! Stop it! You're behaving worse than an animal. Let me go! Do you hear? Let me go!!"

She fought him frantically with animal panic, escaped his weight upon her and ran, breasts swinging free, to the safety of the bathroom. She slammed the door in his face and bolted it. Away! You must go now! He couldn't be anything other than a gentleman. No one would dare molest her here. But he banged on the door, excited by a mission only half completed. Shoulders, heavy breath, thin wood, small bolt, crash—and he was with her in the moist tiled privacy, touching her again, clawing at her like an animal, removing her last vestige of clothing, drawing her naked into an embrace with the coarse weave of his mess kit. His large pink hands grasped her head like a ball, fingers twisting through coils of knotted auburn hair, while his mouth descended on hers, forcing her to respond, refusing to acknowledge the fight that was still in her. And when he had quieted her, he soothed her with questing hands, sitting her astride the bath-stool and kneeling before her to excite her with his mouth, his lips, his teeth, his tongue. So he debauched her with play until, herself an animal, quivering with desire, craving satiation, she willingly helped him shed his uniform. At the sight of the purple bruising along his right thigh, she moaned and kissed saliva down his throat. She felt him, caressed him, admired him, and they stood together under the shower, soaping each other, filling the vast pink bath with luxuriant suddy water. Bodies slipping hard muscle receding flesh mouths globes stem hot breath sensitive skin eyes wide delight hands eager grasp legs wrapped heads tumble rumble rollick frolic spume sperm splash spray play. The bond had been well and truly snapped, and dead Arnold was well and truly dead.

Naples

CAPTAIN CORLETT awakened at six-thirty on the morning of Saturday April 28, and the first thing he saw staring at him from the other side of his cabin was the canteen of cutlery. His heart sank before its glistening splendor. It had been presented to him six hours earlier by the Chief Purser on behalf of the entire ship's company, the highlight of a gala dance on the Promenade Deck to mark his birthday, his retirement, and the climax of the *Queen Dee*'s spring cruise. He had forbidden the family to observe his birthday for the best part of twenty years. He had no wish to be annually reminded of doomsday. Sixty-five and out, on to the scrap heap, in his prime. He hadn't had a day's illness that he could remember since a childish dose of measles in 1911, or was it 1912? But the canteen was a gesture of respect and affection and he had to accept it with good grace, together with Leslie Craddock's fussy little speech about father figure, loyal service, lion of the sea, never a word in anger, loved by the youngest member of the crew, and other such claptrap. The passengers had enjoyed the excuse for yet another round of drinks. Sir Gerald, either with insensitive exuberance or calculated malice, had led the singing of "For He's a Jolly Good Fellow." And Mrs. Brewer, who was a motherly soul and not to be criticized on that account, had burst openly into tears. If all that was not enough, he had to cut a monstrous cake shaped like the old *Queen* and play hell with his digestive system by eating a fruity slice of it at half past midnight. It was the kind of thing that would never have happened when they were making the passage to India, accompanied as it was by all the wild gyrations which these days passed for dancing, in which he was expected to take part, until the celebrants nearly had him in the pool. It was neither a truly auspicious occasion, nor a welcome one.

Daisy Bell shuffled around with a breakfast tray. "You may

[254

like to know, sir, that the Chief Officer asked to contribute to
the presentation," he said. "Mr. Craddock wanted me to slip
you the word. So you'd know it was unanimous."

The fact that the Chief Officer had not alone refused a contribution only betrayed another of the man's character weaknesses. The Master was not the least comforted by being
slipped the word, but under the circumstances he had to grunt
his gratitude.

Daisy Bell took it as the cue for which he had been waiting
for weeks. He touched his long-ago receded forelock and asked,
"Begging your pardon, sir, but would you know what the company intends to do where I'm concerned when you're gone?"

"I'm afraid I don't, George. It's really Mr. Craddock's responsibility. Have you spoken to him about it?"

"No, sir. I thought perhaps you had. You see, sir, I've only
six years to go before it's my turn. I'd like to spend them on
Queen Dee. Only you know what they say about new brooms.
Captain Arkwright may not want me."

The Master was washing the sleep from his eyes in the
bathroom. In the mirror he saw the steward taking his uniform from the closet and laying it out ready for him to put on.
In all these years he had gleaned shamefully little information
about the man's private life, except that he was single and had
a married sister in Scunthorpe with whom he spent most of his
time ashore. It was probably a damned sight worse for a
man like Bell to be tossed on the scrap heap, without even a
canteen of cutlery with which to remember past glories.

"I'll have a word with Captain Arkwright myself, George.
Does that make you feel better?"

"Yes, sir. Thank you very much, sir. I really don't think I
could work another ship, not at my age. And as captain's tiger
it would be a bit humbling to go on ordinary cabin service.
Not that I'm a proud man, you understand, but—"

"Yes. I understand. Now, will you please leave me to finish
my ablutions?"

The Master was in the wheelhouse by seven. It was one of
those lingering Italian mornings when the sun seemed too lazy
to burn away the dawn mist. Salerno was on the starboard bow,
a thin ghost of silver. The sea was so still that, in spite of the
few early risers among the passengers and the deck crew mak-

ing ready, the old *Queen* was a bit of a ghost herself, floating empyreally across the waters.

"Visibility's not all that it might be," the Chief Officer said. "I've had her reduced to forty revs since o-six-hundred-hours."

"Thank you, Mr. Welch."

"We should be berthed about forty minutes behind schedule. I've had them radio ashore to request additional immigration staff. With luck, all the tour coaches will be away on time."

"Uh huh." He was damned if he was going to say "good." The Chief Officer was showing off, making efficiency a vice, trying to put the Master in the wrong and himself in the right. Visibility was not all that bad. It was being overcautious to reduce to forty. He'd have chosen sixty and reduced now, as they approached the bay with its numerous small fishing vessels. There was no reason at all why they shouldn't have berthed bang on time, at eight o'clock. Request additional immigration staff indeed! Mr. Welch would be running the whole Italian Department of Immigration as well as the *Queen Dee* if they were fool enough to give him an inch. He was still brooding on the man's arrogance when the pilot came aboard. The minutes ticked away, the noisy mess that was Naples began to engulf them, and, just as the Chief Officer had predicted, the first gangway was down at eight-forty. The Master had arrived in his very last foreign port of call. Ever. Next stop, England. And eternity.

"With your permission, sir, I'll make sure there's nothing I can do on shore to help Mr. Herrington," the Chief Officer said. "If I know the Eyeties, they'll hold up the stabilizer repairs for a couple of days if they can squeeze a few more lire out of it."

"Good. I was about to suggest that myself," the Master said.

He was about to suggest it for the simple reason he didn't want to give the Chief Officer any further excuses for his philandering. He watched the man leave, then packed a pipe and exercised himself on the Bridge Deck for a few minutes, looking at the ships large and small, old and new, steel and wood, that stood in the murky waters of the *stazione maritina* like the herbaceous borders and hardy perennials that would soon be under his command around the small red-brick house on the edge of the North Downs, just outside Ramsgate. Pray

God he'd have the good temper to endure it. He allowed the
Chief Engineer a decent time to get a preliminary report from
the company's agent on the state of the stabilizers, then got
him on the phone.

"Can you tell me yet how long it will take to have them working properly again?"

"Ten hours, they think. Maybe eight."

The Master sighed with relief. "Fine. It'll make for
happy faces in London on Monday morning." It would have
riled him to have to drag the Marine Superintendent from
his Sunday dinner to report a delay in arrival time. The
Queen Dee was working to a tight schedule from now until
the end of the season. She had to be eighty-five percent full to
break even, and no one could blame passengers for canceling
bookings if departure times were haywire. A day lost could
not easily be made up on turn-round. A day lost was five thousand quid lost. And masters who lost days were not popular
with their companies, even if they had just been given a canteen of cutlery and were in line for a gold watch in the board
room from Sir Edgar's gracious white hand. For there was one
thing on which Captain Corlett was determined. He was going
to hand the *Queen Dee* back to her owners just as he had
taken her out, bright as a new pin, and bang on time. And it
would take more than a fouled stabilizer to stop him.

Richard woke to a full realization of one of Old Hickson's
favorite metaphors. He was, he had to admit, on the horns of a
dilemma. The day in Izmir, when John had involved him in
the shopping excursion and then ditched him with her ladyship, he had said yes to meeting her Italian friends; but at the
time he had not actually meant it, because he thought she
didn't mean it either. But she did. And now he couldn't get out
of it, not that he was all that sure he wanted to get out of it.
He had never met anyone quite like Lady Pratley before. She
didn't react to life, she shaped it for herself. She didn't take
anything seriously, unlike the rest of the *croulants*. She refused
to grow up, to give in to the onrush of time: and it was how
he hoped he would be when he was nineteen, twenty-one or
forty.

"Say hello to Rossana. You can kiss her if you like. She enjoys being kissed."

The girl who met them was small and dark-eyed. She wore the simplest white dress and just one piece of jewelry, a cluster of real diamonds. She was perhaps twenty-two, no older, and the moment he saw her car, yellow, with black leather seats and white-walled tires, he had no doubt about what he wanted to do. This would be better than any old conducted coach tour. Meeting real Italians, guest at a nobleman's private villa. He had to start acting the equal of everyone he met: it was one of the most important ploys of living. If he didn't, he might as well live the rest of his life under a stone. And now, seated with Rossana and Lady Pratley in such a super car, was as good a time as any to begin.

"See Naples and die! That's what you English say, isn't it?" Rossana asked as they throttled through the harbor suburbs, a pall of chemical smog eddying in the hot, confining sunshine. "The real saying is 'Videre Napoli et Mori.' Mori was a little village loved by a fifteenth-century poet, Iacopo Sannazaro. Poor old Iacopo wouldn't have had much love for this twentieth-century mess, would he?"

"It's not so bad," he said, far from convinced that it wasn't.

"The Neapolitans are all a lot of thieving bastards," her ladyship assured him, putting out her tongue at a passing cyclist by way of confirmation.

The two women resumed their chatter, partly in Italian, which her ladyship appeared to speak like a native, leaving Richard to watch the scenery as they sped along the bay, the sea to their right and the fertile mound of Vesuvius to their left. He was disappointed that the volcano was not belching fire and brimstone. Soon they were under the morning shadows of Monte Lattari, speeding through Sorrento, whose ugly modern houses left him with precious little desire to return. And then, as they came over the promontory, there was the sun dancing on the sea and Positano reaching down a chasm of rock to play with it.

"To have a place in Positano is like having a cottage in Sussex in England," Rossana told him. "It is very Italian to come here when everything is too complicated in Rome."

"It's very beautiful," he said, relieved that she had decided to speak to him again in English.

The Saracen houses looked pasted on the mountain. The *duomo,* with its gleaming ceramic cupola, seemed to be physically holding the whole village together, as though without it, it would slip, forgotten, into the silken sea.

"It's your day. What do you want to do with it?" her ladyship asked him.

"Whatever you like, Lady Pratley," he said. "Please don't let me keep you away from your friends."

"They'll have to do what we want. We're the guests, aren't we? And stop calling me Lady This and Lady That. It makes you sound like a bank clerk. What's wrong with Fiona?"

Count Melchiorre Fernando Amaducci's villa was perched in Positano *alto,* quietly Roman among the bouganvillaea. The Count was a frail, elderly man who seemed to be visibly shrinking in his clothes. He was something to do with high finance, but Richard never quite found out what. He was the kind of man who never had need to do anything with money, except spend it pleasantly on living a contented life where he chose, among people and things that pleased him. The villa itself was as ancient as its owner, shrinking a little in the clothes of an overgrown village—German bibliophiles, French musicians and the remains of Russian and Polish aristocracy. The Count's guests were all Italian, young and old boys, young and old girls, some married, but to whom Richard quickly gave up guessing: the relationships were as infinite as the stars and, seen from afar, as fragile.

"*Eh! Benvenuta Fiona cara. Che piacere di rivederti! Non credevo che verrebbe il giorno nel quale ci rivisiteresti di nuovo!*" the old man said, escorting them into the villa.

"This is Richard," she said. "He doesn't speak any Italian. I must teach him what I know, mustn't I?"

"Fiona has taught many people many things," the Count said, with just a flicker of an amused smile. "You must try to be a good pupil, young man."

"I'm sorry I don't speak Italian, sir. But I can speak a little French." Richard was blushing as the other guests came forward to be introduced.

"It's nothing to be ashamed of, my boy. You can't be expected to know everything at your age. What is your age?"

"Nearly eighteen, sir."

"Ah, quite a fledgling. *Chi non ha vergogna, tutto il mondo é suo,* as we say in Italy. He who is without shame, all the world is his."

"Stop teasing him, and try to find out what he wants to do now that he's here," Lady Pratley said, flinging her arms rapturously around an Italian girl whose body was too large for her dress. "He won't tell me a thing. Maria, darling! It's been simply ages since you've visited us in England. Why? The old coot hasn't done anything to upset you, has he? Because I'll have his hide if he has."

Planning the day raised no end of complications. The Count suggested taking one of the cars to Amalfi and Salerno and back via Pompeii. Toni, a young man from Florence who wasn't married, suggested taking one of the boats to Capri; and Ricardo, a young man from Grosseto who was—but appeared nonetheless to be unattached—suggested Vesuvius as it was in good rumbling form that week.

"It's not likely to blow up, is it?" Richard asked.

"No more than the rest of the world," Ricardo said. But his idea lost out, and they settled for nothing more adventurous than the beach, making the procession to Positano *basso* via the piazza. Outside the school of hand-made lace a row of old women were giving free advice to the white-and-gold police force. They padded down a precipitous alley drenched in the aroma of flowers and bad drains, and were presently on the narrow strip of gritty sand where the *bagnini* charged visitors enough for a few hours' sunshine to keep the whole village prosperous during the deserted winter months ahead. But the Count and his party were not tourists to be chivvied and clipped, particularly as the aging little man had a vast fiberglass launch moored on the jetty with powerful twin engines that sent her zooming across the water in an angry white-crested roar. Tourists and peasants alike watched the little *grande signore* entertaining his guests, with a mixture of fear, envy and admiration. Richard had a most exhausting morning trying to water ski, helped by Rossana, encouraged by another girl whom he thought was her sister but who turned out to be her mother, and admired by her ladyship who told him dreamily from the cockpit while sipping a *negroni* that he looked just like the boys in American movies when he was up, which, he calculated, was about one minute in every ten.

"When I first came here this was a village of fisher-folk," the Count said as they trundled up the hill for lunch. "My friend, Chizzi, the artist, you know his work maybe, lived here then. He tried to form a society that would prevent tourism savaging into antiquity. Of course, it was doomed to failure. What defense is there from the vulgarian with money? Fortunately he died a few years ago. He couldn't have borne to see Positano today."

After lunch Toni insisted that Richard should see Pompeii and offered to take him in his Maserati. Then Maria wanted to go and her ladyship, irritated that it wasn't her suggestion in the first place, decided to take command, and piled into a car that was already a tight fit for three, next to fat Maria. Toni was everything Richard would like to be, or thought he would. An after-shave charm, driving a fast sports car in jeans and bare feet, surrounded by beautiful girls and rich parents. The typical *giovani leone*. Woosh! He had it made.

"They even had road problems in those days," Toni said as they walked from the Basilica into the Via Marina. "You can see where the wagons have left deep ruts in the stone."

Richard was appalled by what had happened on August 24 in the year A.D.79. Seeing a simple thing like a carbonized loaf of bread, an earthen wine pot, or an election slogan scratched on a wall, was so much more real than any history book. A shower of pumice stone seven or eight feet high, a breathtaking cloud of water and ashes, and a whole people and their way of life was buried and forgotten for nearly two thousand years. He looked down the narrow street between the roofless buildings to the slumbering giant that had vomited nature's wrath. "It must have been like a little atom bomb," he said.

Lady Pratley had paused to pick the blooms of a few wildflowers struggling for life through cracks in the ancient stones. "Which of the countries we have visited have you liked most?" she asked him.

"This," he said after a moment's hesitation. "Italy."

"That wouldn't be because it's my favorite, would it?" she

asked, deciding she didn't love the flowers after all, and scattering them around the feet of a bronze satyr.

"I always like the place I'm in at the moment best," he said evasively. "Except when I was at school. I didn't like being at school very much. It was so far from anywhere. Like living in another world."

Toni and Maria could be heard calling to each other around the peristyle of a minor temple. Their feet scurried into the distance. When they rejoined the rest some time later they had four bottles of iced *chinotto* for refreshment. They put the empty bottles on a wall and flung ancient stones at them until they fell with a clatter into the Casa della Caccia beyond. An unshaven keeper in a worn uniform waved a deprecating finger at them.

"You're a silly old fool!" Lady Pratley shouted after him. "Someone ought to throw stones at you! Hasn't anybody ever told you that unless you behave like little children you can't enter the Kingdom of Heaven? Huh, I bet it's pretty crummy up there as well."

The keeper obviously hadn't understood a word of English. He gave them a decayed grin and went back to the shelter of his faded wooden hut.

"Come on," she said. "Let's do the snob part of town."

They came to the House of the Vettii, so named from the seals of two freedmen found in it. At its entrance a painting of Priapus was discreetly screened by a twentieth-century blind. Inside, elegantly proportioned, was a garden with fountains, and leading from it a dining room painted with the infant Hercules strangling the serpents, Pentheus slain by the Bacchantes, Hephaestus binding Ixion to the wheel in Hades. It was, Richard thought, an odd choice of decoration to eat with. They were about to leave when Lady Pratley ushered him through the kitchen, its utensils still there from an age of Roman culinary splendor, and beckoned a keeper to unlock the door of a small adjoining room. Inside the darkness were the remains of a past age of erotica. Its first effect on Richard was to remind him of his dead father, the way he'd carried on the day Richard had wanted to use a public lavatory in Brighton. People had evil minds which they spewed all over the walls. Yet he saw nothing evil in these faded images of love, a communication between foreign tongues, an invitation to the delights of the flesh. The proper place for them was next to the kitchen. John. What was it he'd said? "I think love grows out of abated passion . . . you never really know a person until you've slept with them." A girl, her lower body coupled with a bearded man, had long ago flaked away to leave their heads floating through space, forever smiling at each other, reminded him of the dark-haired girl with vermilion lips from whom he'd run away in Beirut. Rima. He wished now that he'd stayed with Rima. To find out. To discover something about himself, for himself.

"Which position do you like best?" Lady Pratley asked. "I like them all myself."

At about the time Richard was looking up at Vesuvius, Pamela Westcott was looking down from it, standing near the crater, hot, tired, and intensely lonely in the company of Miss Peebles. Disappointed by the lack of anything spectacular, Miss Peebles was taking her disappointment out on Mrs. Westcott and about a hundred and twenty other passengers who were making the excursion. At thirty-five shillings a head, it represented to Miss Peebles a scandalous surcharge for a view which was no better than many other views of which they had had a surfeit in the past few weeks.

"It's nice to be able to say you've walked over the crater of a volcano," Pamela said by way of appeasement.

But Miss Peebles was not to be appeased. "I can walk over the ancient Druids at Stonehenge any day of my life. And it doesn't cost me a penny."

"But the sun's not out like it is here," Pamela consoled.

They were waiting for the chair lift down to the coaches when Miss Peebles vented the worst of her spleen. "Now that the Chief Officer has been put properly in his place by our Captain," she said, "I so hope you will think seriously about your position and will benefit from the . . . er . . . unfortunate predicament in which he has placed you. There is too little chastity in the world today. Marriage is not the be all and end all of life. I've never once regretted not marrying. Of course, it's not possible for everyone to turn their hand to the pen; but you're still young enough to take up a useful hobby. It isn't as though you're wanting for money. I wonder, have you ever thought about weaving?"

"No, Miss Peebles. Strange as it may seem to you, I have never once thought about weaving. Or the pen."

She met David at nine under the walls of the Castel Nuovo. He had spent the day on board, to be at hand in case of complications that might delay the repairs to the stabilizers. She had seen Caserta and its Royal Palace in the morning, and Vesuvius and Miss Peebles in the afternoon; and waiting on a street corner to keep a dinner date was admirable therapy for all four of them. It reminded her of when she used to wait for Arnold, under the wall of the Methodist Church in Westborough, only the nights then were not so warm or the odors so pungent. The assignation had been her idea, not his, devised to avoid any embarrassment it might have caused him if they had met on board and left the ship together. A secret trysting place was so romantic. It was years since she last fluttered with excitement in this way. But as she repelled the bold looks of passing Neapolitans, she couldn't help thinking that Miss Peebles had a point, albeit a teeny one, about weaving and the pen.

"Sorry if I kept you waiting. What's it going to be? An expensive meal on you, or a cheap one on me!" he asked as he joined her in the shadows.

She thought at first he was joking, but he wasn't. "Why are you so obsessed by money?" she asked.

"I have debts and I have expenses, and a Chief Officer's pay, after deductions, is a damned sight less than a cabin steward can make if he plays his cards properly."

Their taxi nosed its way down the Via Roma, vibrant with the brashness of life lived on the streets instead of behind closed shutters. The Neapolitans wore their emotions like a rash: and they were every bit as catching. "Are you playing *your* cards properly with me, David?" she asked.

"Love is too beautiful a thing to reduce to the squalid level of commerce," he said. "You can have anything I've got at any time, just for the asking. You know that, don't you? But right at this moment, until my monthly check comes along, I haven't got very much."

She wanted to eat in a *trattoria* off the Via Magnocavallo, crowded with fat *mamma mias* and their devoted offsprings. But he insisted on a *ristorante* in the Corso Umberto, which had more mirrors and potted plants and fewer families, where they ate *trattoria* food such as fettuccine alla marinara and the inevitable dolce washed down with a bottle of Lacrimae Christi.

"When we get back, England will be just at its best," she said. "Young greenery. Winter a forgotten thing. Life starting again, even more beautiful than before. The countryside full of such gentle hope. It's nice to see foreign places, but I don't think I could live anywhere else than damp old England."

He was eating ravenously, as though he was not properly fed on board. "What's Reigate like? I only know the West Country myself."

"Like most provincial towns that have become overpopulated. But there's still room to breathe in the countryside around."

"And the new house?"

"It's mock-Tudor, I'm afraid," she said. "As the real-estate ads say, two bed., two liv., kitch., bath. All the essentials. And a garage, which will be fine for Richard's car when he gets it. He's so set his heart on one. I suppose it's inevitable at his age, although I won't have a moment's peace of mind while he's out in it."

He helped himself to a thick wedge of Gorgonzola. "You're making the boy a present of the car?"

"Yes. Why not? He's my son."

"We don't want to spoil him, do we? He's old enough to get stuck into a job of his own. Give him the down payment and let him work the rest off for himself. I assure you, it'll be better for him in the long run."

"Why?" she asked. "Were you spoiled by an expensive present?"

Perhaps she was tired, had soaked up too much sun, had seen too many strange places; but the fun of the past few days had evaporated into the heavy Naples air. Instead of finding her bearings again, she had lost them. The brochure had promised that she would be cosseted and pampered by the ever attentive but unobtrusive services of the ship's staff. Never in her wildest imagination would she have dreamed who might be doing the cosseting. David was so certain of himself, and having made more progress with her in a week than Arnold had made in a year, she supposed he had a right to be. But his charm was skin-deep. She was beginning to see that now. He would be as capable of cosseting some other lonely woman tomorrow, if it suited his purpose to do so. The fun had evaporated simply because she knew this and, worse, knowing it, still wanted him to possess her physically, even to the point of talking about the new house and how Richard would react to a new father. She had somehow agreed to marrying him without having yet agreed with herself that she wanted to remarry. Anyone. There was no pleasure in making decisions, not the kind of decisions that could affect one's whole life, and that was exactly what she had to do, here, on this hot, noisy, sultry evening in Naples.

"What would you like to do now?" he asked as they milled through the evening promenaders in the Galleria Umberto.

"I'm happy just watching," she said. "And listening. They talk with their hands more than they do their mouths."

They strolled for some time, between Italian women with large rounded breasts and thick black hair mussed by the evening breeze, between sharp-suited men with mirror-shiny shoes of the thinnest leather, between dirty kids asleep in each other's arms in gutters, or gnawing into pizza as large as themselves with firm white teeth. After a while, without again consulting her wishes, he called a taxi and had them whisked away beneath the skirts of the new Naples, sitting open-legged on the Sant' Elmo heights like an old whore, and along the Via Caracciolo, past neon signs and swish hotels, until they found a club that caught his fancy.

"Local color's all right for the first few minutes," he said, "but after that it sticks in your gullet. Particularly in this cesspool. It would have been a damned good thing if the Allies had razed the lot of it to the ground in 'forty-three. I tell you, there's no love lost between the Neapolitans and the rest of the Eyeties. Thieving lot of bastards."

The club was a little larger, a little noisier, and a little duller than the Americana on the *Queen Dee*. She wished she'd insisted on being escorted back to the ship. But instead she fell in with his wishes, drinking, dancing, drinking again, dancing again, until her feet could barely support her and her head was reeling. Between dances he kissed her, screened by a vastly vulgar menu; and between drinks he groped her all over the floor, behind nothing except his self-assurance that he was doing what she wanted, what she expected, what she would allow, and go on allowing so long as it suited his purpose to possess her as he had possessed so many nameless, breast-less, countless, humorless, toothless, graceless, hapless women before.

At last, unable to stand the tedium any longer, she said, "David, I want to leave now, please."

"But the night's still young, Pamela pet," he said.

"Well, I'm not so young. And don't 'pet' me. I don't like it," she snapped.

He brought his lips close to her ear and whispered, "It's too late to be seen together going to your cabin. I saw a nice little hotel a couple of blocks back."

She pushed him away from her, unable to bear the closeness of his flesh. "Not that again. I don't think I ever want that again. Not from you, David. Maybe someone else. But not from you."

He controlled his temper with some difficulty. He was not a man who could take a slight with good grace. "I gave you a good time the other night, didn't I, little Miss Soap Suds? It could go on like that. Forever. I'd try always to satisfy you. To make you happy. Honestly I would."

"I don't want to discuss it any more now, please," she said. "Perhaps when we are back in England we'll both see things differently. But right now . . . I don't think it's your fault . . . I've just been a rather stupid woman . . . trying to have something I should know doesn't exist any more . . . for me."

For a moment he thought there was going to be a crying scene. He fawned around her, trying to please, suggesting they go back and stroll through the *galleria* for some fresh air, un-certain as to why his charm had evaporated so quickly. Perhaps she was tired, had soaked up too much sun, had seen too many strange new places. She would be better again back on board, and better still once he was calling on her in Reigate, intro-ducing her to the Mizzen Club, giving Richard some fatherly advice on how to handle the new car. She needed familiar surroundings. That was it. She wasn't the kind of woman who traveled well.

"*Quarantamille lire, signore,*" the waiter whispered, slipping him the bill.

He handed her the piece of paper. "Can we cover it?" he asked.

But they couldn't. She was down to her last few lire and her traveler's checks were secure in her cabin; and what few lire he had were mixed with several crumpled Lebanese notes of small denomination. The waiter produced the headwaiter, who produced the manager, who was not in a mood to be clipped by tourists—particularly as their apparent relationship had little appeal to his Catholic soul. He was on the verge of losing his temper with them when David remembered the three hundred and eighty-two pounds.

"Look," he said, waving the check under the management's nose. "This is worth more than six hundred thousand lousy lire. And I give you my word it won't bounce, because it's been signed by British nobility."

But it was no good. The manager was determined to deal with the matter constitutionally. And that meant seeking police assistance. Three dark-eyed policemen with amused smiles sorting out a simple matter of how the nice, very welcome English guests might best be assisted to pay their debts. But all Pamela Westcott could see, written in their notebooks, flashing from neon signs as they were driven back to the harbor, etched in the angry furrows on David's face, was the casually scrawled signature across the bottom of the three hundred and eighty-two pounds check. Fiona Anne Pratley.

Fiona Anne Pratley had her arm through that of Richard Barcombe Westcott as they strolled along the road that circled the village. After a while they began to meet the same people again. He felt as though everyone in Positano was looking at him, expecting, wanting him to look at them in return. He tried to slip her arm out of his, but she wouldn't let him. Two spaghetti-plump youths, their sculptured hair moist with sweet-smelling oils, smiled at them sweetly, knowing more than he knew, and not caring.

"After you've been in Positano a few hours you realize you can do nothing without everyone knowing about it," she said. "But they can do nothing without you knowing about it. So you perform for each other. I think it's rather fun, don't you? Like charades at Christmas."

"It depends how good you are at acting," he said. Some musicians were playing Vivaldi in the courtyard of a crumbling villa, surrounded by elderly ladies and a few squatting British weirdies who were bumming around Europe.

"Do you like music?" she asked.

"A little. I had a season ticket for the Proms last year. I took Mother. I think it did her a lot of good." The Vivaldi floated like birdsong between the palms. "It was a bit of an effort, going out to the Albert Hall every night, instead of just listening to it on the radio. But I don't regret doing it. It was jolly good."

"The things we regret in life are not the things we do but the things we don't do," she told him. "Never forget that, young man. We only live once. Now, end of lecture. What about buying me a drink in Enzo's?"

They sat in the crowded cellar that was once a boathouse and listened to a fruity-voiced singer with a guitar dreaming his way through *"So' 'nnammurato 'e te!," "Anema e core,"* *"O sole mio"* and other loves that whispered the arrest of time. And she sipped imported whisky and gave him Strega which, she said, would be good for his potency. He sat and became one with the crowd—comfortably dressed Italians, several coolly dominating Swedish girls, and two Germans attempting to organize everybody.

"Would you like to dance, Fiona?" he asked.

She was pleasantly surprised. He was beginning to behave as a good escort should behave. "I'd love that," she said, "if we can find ourselves a space."

They were pressed together on the tiny floor, he mellow with dinner, she warm with desire. They exchanged a few words, but he was thinking not of her but of the Count, and the bitter apéritif they had drunk together in his study before dinner, so reminiscent of Old Hickson in his study, only at Tor Beeches there was tea and sweet buns. "Young man," the Count had told him, "you will learn in life that the only way to judge your fellow human beings is by their capacity to love. Laughter, good manners, music, fine words, eating, resting content . . . they are all a part of love. In Italy people love all the time. Even I love, because it keeps me happy at seventy-four. To be in love is the only time in a man's life when he can forget that of his nature he is alone, that neither religion nor science can bridge the gulf between human hearts, that he may live in company but he must die in solitude. Caresses and kisses, and gentle looks and whispered assurances, are mere inventions to hide our shame in loneliness." There had been only awful warnings delivered among the damp mustiness of Old Hickson's study. But this evening, a little wizened stranger had momentarily instilled into him a new kind of terror, a terror that he would never grow up, that he would never be accepted as one of them, have the capacity to make friends, to make love, to shake free the embryo of youth and be a man with all the pain of decision, responsibility and error, striving to know another soul as he knew his own.

"You were miles away then," she said. "Am I boring you?"

"No, of course not, Fiona. This is wonderful. I've had the most wonderful day. I can't remember when I've enjoyed myself so much."

Then he did something she was not expecting him to do. He kissed her. A quick peck on her right cheek, his eyes roving among the other dancers to make sure his theft had not been seen. Gerry was quite wrong. He wasn't going to hurt her. He wanted her like mad. She felt so young again, the music of happy voices around her like those golden days of girlhood in wartime London, held floating through life in the strong arms of a bronzed *giovani leone* with a fair flouncing mane.

"Take me home," she said.

"Home?" he asked, an amused smile on his face. "Where's home here?"

"Bed."

He was an awkward lover, too eager in case he failed, too reluctant to relax and learn. At first too coy to remove his clothes, the next second gamboling into bed like a forward making a touchdown. He smothered her face with beardless kisses, while her hands read the exciting braille of his muscular young limbs, his body hairless as a girl except where he was growing as a man. Like a groom, she had to guide the stallion to his target. Unable to control the violence she had let loose, she lay under him as his firm white teeth bit into her neck, not once, but twice, thrice, harder, deeper, she screaming, waking the villa with her joy. Sleep Comfort. She felt his whole body stiffen over her in priapic splendor and thought he was expended, ready to run guiltily back to his room. But he stayed, lay limp while she kissed it back to life, then started once more from scrum to touchdown. Lust: in all its purity of youth. Love: she thought of Gerry, that dear old coot, and yearned now for his age beside her. The free potent youth performed for her bond of impotency. Her bony hands held his marble smooth waist. Grind. Pleasure. Sleep. Forget. Comfort. Stillness. All is love. And the bed was dead.

He was awakened by a shaft of sunlight through the shutters. She moved in her sleep. He froze, defenseless in his nakedness between the sheets. Her waking hand reached out to feel if he wanted more; but he no longer wanted what he'd had. The savage beam of sunlight wandered over the morning heaviness of her eyes. His teeth marks showed purple around the sallow folds of her neck. God, what possessed him to do that to her? She looked worse than he felt.

"Love me. Love me, Richard," she murmured.

Before she could touch him again, he scrambled from the bed and went into the bathroom. He switched on the light and was ashamed by his own image in the mirror. He stayed under the purifying water as long as he dared, soaping, scrubbing, and soaping again. Then he returned to the bedroom, hoping that by some miracle she'd be gone. But she wasn't. She was still lying there moaning for him gently.

"Do you know it's only six o'clock?" she said, vexed by his eagerness to leave her.

"I always get up early," he lied. He reached out to the bedside table for his wristwatch. The one with the spaceship which appeared to float in space to indicate the seconds. The one his father had given him the Christmas before he died. What would Father think of him if he could see him now?

"What on earth are you going to do between now and breakfast?"

"Go for a walk. I may never see Positano again. I'd like to see it by sunrise."

As he was walking toward the door, she said, "Richard, don't you want to kiss me good morning?"

"No, thank you very much, Fiona," he said. He was the model of politeness. Gently, he opened the squeaking door. A few moments later she heard his footsteps on the gravel courtyard. And he was gone. This was the moment that hurt most.

"Oh, Gerry, Gerry, Gerry, you dear old coot," she whimpered. "Will it never end?"

Lat. 35.92N Long. 5.73W

. . . Compasses compared. Rounds made. Correct time to Engine Room. 16:30 All electric W.T. doors operated. 16:45 Gibraltar on bearing 093°(T) × 27 miles. 17:00 Reduced to 76 revs. 17:15 All boats except Nos. 2, 4, 6 and 8 swung out and lowering gear greased. 19:10 Cape Trafalgar on bearing 085° (T) × 19 miles. Alter course 291° (Gyro) 299° (Std.) Wind light NWly. Slight swell. Overcast.—D.W.

THE *Queen Dee* had passed that way before just two weeks previously. Now, with her seven hundred and twenty-eight passengers rested and for the most part content, she was heading back through the Gibraltar strait for the gray of the Atlantic and the chilling summer breezes of England. The day before there had been a final, lingering pause, a farewell to the sun, as the old *Queen* waited patiently at anchor off Ibiza. Her passengers had trekked over the mountain to the little white village of San Antonio and watched the foot-stamping Ibicenco dancing in San José, or just mooched around the Levente Promenade buying the last of their souvenirs and learning to drink wine Spanish-style from a *porron* in the fishermen's bars. And today, cutting quietly through the western Mediterranean, surrounded only by azure sea and sky, the Promenade Deck pool had been almost unbearably crowded as the disciples gathered to make their final act of obeisance to the Great God Sun.

John and Richard returned to their cabin from an early lunch, intending to change and play a little tennis before the courts became intolerably crowded. But lying on John's bed was an envelope, and in the envelope was a note which, the moment he had read it, sent him flying from the cabin without even pausing to give Richard the most flimsy excuse. For several days John had forgotten the blackmail threat. He had dismissed the whole thing as a joke, or, at worst, a bluff. But the new note was neither funny nor silly. It said bluntly, "You will find another interesting photograph in your mother's evening bag. There will be no further warning. Leave the five hundred dollars beneath the stationery in the drawer of the desk nearest the library in the Writing Room at ten tonight." When he reached his parents' cabin, he hesitated, hoping like hell they weren't there. But they were still lunching and he had to find a steward and think of a pretext to have the door unlocked. He found his mother's evening bag in the wardrobe, and inside he found himself, and Aziz, and Hooda, and the sailor. And again he was ashamed. When he returned to his own cabin, Richard was lying on the bed reading.

"Something up?" he asked. "You ran off like a startled rabbit."

John said nothing for a few moments, but twitched about the cabin in a pretense of tidying. "What is it you Britishers say? I had to see a man about a dog."

"Then let's go up on deck and punish a few racquets."

"Later," he said, seizing on a green sweatshirt and trying to worry a food stain out of it with his toothbrush.

"Well, what do you want to do now?" Richard asked impatiently. "Talk?"

"You can talk if you want. I don't mind."

"I can't just lie here and fill in pregnant pauses like a D.J. What do you want me to talk about? Politics? I read in a paper some time ago about an American student, in Philadelphia I think it was, who threatened to burn himself to death like a Buddhist priest if the United States Government didn't change its policy in Southeast Asia. And he was immediately sent five thousand boxes of matches by different people. Five thousand! I think that's dreadful, making fun of someone's feelings that way, don't you?"

"Yeah, I guess it's dreadful."

"Oh, crikey, what's bitten you? It's nothing I've done to annoy you, is it?"

John stopped twitching and sat on the edge of his bed. "I'm sorry. It's not your fault. I'm just being a damned hypocrite, that's all. And after the way I lectured you the other day!"

"What the heck are you talking about?"

"This!" John threw the photograph on to Richard's bed.

The picture neither repulsed nor angered Richard. He sat fingering it while John unburdened himself with tales of blackmail and family love, none of which seemed to involve him because all he heard echoing in his mind was the parson thundering from the granite chapel pulpit at Tor Beeches, "Judge not that ye be not judged!" And when John pleaded for sympathy, he gave it readily because the picture might well have been of himself, naked on a bed in Positano. He wouldn't want his mother to see a photograph of that either, not because it would hurt him but because he knew, too late, that it would hurt her.

"If I had a regular job, the skunk would threaten to send them to my boss too," John went on. "Giving people like me a square deal so far as the law is concerned doesn't solve any problems. As long as society treats us as inferiors, there'll always be someone to turn the screw at every opportunity."

"I don't treat you as an inferior," Richard said. "Honest. And I don't think your parents would, if you told them about it. If they didn't want to understand, then perhaps they deserve to be hurt. Love doesn't seem to have much to do with sex . . . it's . . . so much bigger."

"Oh Christ, you're beginning to sound like a lonely-hearts column!"

"Lady Pratley said something important to me the other night. At least, I think it's important. We don't regret the things we do—it's the things we don't do that make us unhappy. In other words, I suppose it's better to do wrong things than not to do things at all."

John screwed the green sweatshirt up into a ball and flung it into an open drawer. "How did you make out with Mother Earth in Naples? Did she surround you with lots of luscious chicks, or did you have to make do with her old bird cage?"

"I'd rather not talk about it," Richard said, blushing a little. "If you don't want us to talk about you any more, let's play tennis." But he knew that neither of them was going to enjoy the game.

Captain Corlett had been standing on the bridge from early morning until lunchtime, and after lunch he was back in almost the same spot, saying barely a word to any of the ship's officers, and looking not out to the open sea ahead but always back, back into the vanishing blue of the Mediterranean, back into deep echoes of his past, back into youth, into ambition, into achievement, into that void when ambition has been fulfilled and achievement won, and life is beckoning another of its kind into its final berthing place. Rigg had asked him his opinion of a passing French liner which they were seeing for the first time; but he hadn't wanted to give it, and the Junior Second Officer discreetly left him to his solitude. And after lunch, Hewson had tried to get him talking about the old days of the India run; but he resented any encroachment into his private thoughts, and as good as told Hewson so. Then, when the Chief Officer came to take over the watch at sixteen hundred hours, the Master disappeared abruptly into his day cabin with only the curtest nod of recognition.

"Christ, he's taking it badly," Hewson said.

"We all have to come to the end of the road someday," the Chief Officer said, running through the deck log. "He doesn't have to make it a personal vendetta against me, does he?"

"Doesn't he? Hasn't it occurred to you, Mr. Welch, that he might think you have been deliberately trying to buck him?"

The Chief Officer looked disparagingly at the log entry. "Your handwriting still doesn't seem to be getting any better, Harry. What do you use? An old toothbrush?"

The Master sat at his desk, called Daisy Bell, and ordered tea. He tried to concentrate on paperwork, but it was no use —he was a piqued old man and he had to admit it to himself, even if he would admit it to no one else. He was fighting off retirement like a disease instead of welcoming it as the opportunity to start a new life. He should try to be positive, think of the things he wanted to do, wanted to learn, wanted to see in the years ahead. But he couldn't think of a damned thing he wanted, except to go on being Master of the *Queen Dee*.

The phone on his desk buzzed. "Chief Purser here, sir. I thought you should know that the check for three hundred and eighty-two pounds which Lady Pratley drew in favor of Mr. Welch is to be stopped. She told me of her intentions just a few minutes ago."

"The devil she did! Has Welch been running up any other

debts I should hear about? Facilities ashore? Mess bills?"

"We don't have a record of any. I think a number of his expenses—car hire in Athens was one—have been charged to Mrs. Westcott's account."

"Good God! The man's an absolute menace where women are concerned."

"What do you suggest I do with the Naples account? I can hardly charge that to Mrs. Westcott, can I?"

"For goodness sake, Mr. Craddock, do I have to be involved in every detail of such a squalid matter? Slam it back at him. And if he won't meet it, or can't, then surely you know who to refer the matter to in the head office."

The Master banged down the phone. The Chief Officer's philandering was intolerable. That night in Naples, he'd been awakened from his sleep in the small hours of the morning by an Italian policeman politely asking for confirmation that the man they had escorted back to the ship was in fact the ship's Chief Officer. Mrs. Westcott had been scarlet with embarrassment, and no wonder. As for Welch, he seemed to have no shame at all, flashing Lady Pratley's check about, insisting that he accept it on behalf of the company and authorize the Assistant Purser to pay out umpteen thousand lire to appease the club manager for the lavish entertainment he had apparently provided for them. It was intolerable, intolerable, intolerable! He had known Mr. David Welch for just over two weeks, and that cocky smiling face would stick in his mind for the rest of his life, more permanently than Leslie Craddock's, or Harry Hewson's, or Bob Herrington's, or Ben Wilson's. If only the damned man had had the common decency to go down with his ship.

"Man overboard's a nasty business. A ship like this, cruising at fifteen knots, fellow drifts twenty-five feet per second," Sir Gerald expanded, buoyed by predinner cocktails and a little more than a bottle of Château Haut-Marbuzet '62. "Fellow would be abreast of the screws in no time. No point in stopping engines. Neither is there point in trying to swing the stern away by giving her full wheel. I've known many a good man get sucked into the race and be cut to pieces. Nasty business."

The Master never liked his dinner table being disturbed by reminiscence of the more unsavory kind. He could see that Sir Gerald, not the most tactful of raconteurs, was beginning to distress Mrs. Brewer and Mrs. Paxton, and decided to cut quickly across his bows. "In my experience," he said, "a man will probably float aft and clear of the screws even if no avoiding action can be taken. My officers are instructed to increase speed the moment the alarm is given, then go into a turn and commence picking-up operations. I think I've known a dozen to go overboard for one reason or another in my time. And we only lost one of them."

"Suicides? Or were they pushed?" Lady Pratley asked.

"They went overboard and they needed to be rescued," the Master said pointedly. "People on a pleasure cruise are hardly likely to be suicidal."

"Poor dears," Lady Pratley said, ignoring his point. "Fancy being rescued after plucking up so much courage to do such a thing."

"Of course, Captain," Sir Gerald said, "you have had only the limited experience of passenger liners. Now during the war—"

"During the war, Sir Gerald, the *Queen Dee* was trooping in one Mediterranean convoy after another. You, I believe, were grouse shooting!"

It was an unforgivable way to speak to a passenger, particularly a very important passenger. The Master knew it, Sir Gerald knew it, and everyone else at table knew it. Only no one, least of all Sir Gerald, had the audacity to do anything about it.

Mrs. Brewer was first to break the silence that followed. "This cruise has done Kenneth such a world of good," she said. "Before we came to Europe, he was so run down with overwork. He wasn't sleeping at all well, and his snoring kept me awake until it nearly had me running up the wall."

A chilling Atlantic breeze had forced the evening dancers from around the Promenade Deck pool into the comforting fug of the Tudor Room; and unless tomorrow's weather along the Portuguese coast held, the pool itself would be closed down, drained and covered for the rest of the voyage. The Assistant Purser was organizing a carnival dance, desperate that end-of-cruise gloom should be forestalled until the last possible moment. Officers in white mess kit flashed between bronze-backed women. And the ship's orchestra did its best with a reprise of Spanish and Italian dance tunes.

"Fiona, you know how much I dislike dancing," Sir Gerald said. "I'd much rather we made up a four at bridge. With the Paxtons maybe?"

"I want to dance. And bridge would be a misery for all of us while you're still slung up like that."

His arm was better. Dr. Hammond had suggested it might now come out of the sling. But he had insisted on a specialist's attention while they were in Naples, spending most of his time ashore in the chloroformed purity of a hospital on the hill. Not because he really thought it was fractured, it had not pained him for a couple of days, but simply because he wanted the excuse to leave her and the Westcott boy to their own devices, to cry a little over an injured arm and forget the deeper ills. The night he spent alone on board had been the worst part of it. First Raymond's snide comments from behind the bar in the Americana. Then the waiter's feigned surprise at his dining alone. And finally, lying there coaxing sleep, caged in a body that yearned for physical attention but was incapable of giving anything in return except white obesity above a shrunken manhood. He didn't resent Fiona's still wanting the physical pleasures of youth. He resented himself for marrying again, for not being content with the few splendidly happy years with dead Ursula, for trying to reincarnate a lost perfection with someone who was not really of his kind. Fiona had never once openly criticized his taking a second wife, yet she fought frantically to retain her own vanishing youth by subjecting him to public ridicule and abuse. And when he could bear it no longer, he would excuse his own loss of dignity. But it was the simple fact that both knew her cruelty to be only skin deep that held them together. He loved her because she was the dynamo of his lost youth. And she pitied him, and in frequent moments between the bickering, was gentle. He accepted pity as a poor substitute for love, from her, and from strangers who cared to give it. Which was why he continued to wear the white sling, like a red badge of courage.

"Here's someone who will dance with me," she said, flouncing up to Richard.

"Good evening, Lady Pratley," he said, a little hesitantly but nonetheless politely. "I'm afraid I can't."

"Can't? Or won't?"

He had come to the Tudor Room to meet his mother who wanted to be escorted to the cinema. He'd have to wait there until she came in, preferably over at the bar, but her ladyship had no intention of letting him escape. She grabbed his arm and led him to the floor. He wanted to resist, but he was afraid of causing a scene.

"I can't dance for long," he said. "I'm taking my mother to a movie."

"How nice for her." She rested her face on his shoulder. Several respectable middle-aged couples were already beginning to look at them. "I thought I told you not to call me Lady This or Lady That."

"Well, you are a Lady, aren't you?" He wished the floor would open and swallow him up. Ever since Naples he had been trying to avoid her, to make sure that nothing like what happened in Positano could ever happen again. And she had been trying not to avoid him. He was well aware of that, the way she had been watching him at tennis, entering the pool the moment he did, even following him to the library when he went to change a book.

"I don't think you love me any more," she said, deliberately creating a situation from which he could not retreat.

He wanted to tell her that he had never loved her, even for a moment, but said instead, "You've been very kind."

"But you don't want me to go on being kind? Is that it?"

Her cheek had left a patch of powder where she had rested it on his tuxedo. It seemed that everyone in the room was looking at them now. He tried moving his hand so it did not have to touch the warmth of her bare back, and she chose to mistake the gesture for a sign that he wanted her to dance closer to him.

"If we go up to the Observation Deck, you can buy me a drink in the Americana," she said. "And we can see the new moon. You should turn your money—or something—in your pocket. It's lucky."

"I'm sorry. No. I have to wait for Mother."

He could see Sir Gerald looking at them from the bar. Sad, pink, water-filled eyes, almost as though the old boy was cry- ing. It was all too dreadful, dancing with another man's wife in front of him, when you've slept with her, and she more than twice your age. And then, when the orchestra surely couldn't play any longer without an intermission, his mother turned up, pausing in the entrance, looking around the tables, toward the bar, trying to pick him out in the crowd.

"Are you looking for your son?" Sir Gerald asked as she walked toward the bar. "He's there. On the floor. With my wife." He had been drinking and was unable to disguise the bitterness in his voice. "She'll bring him back when she's fin- ished with him. She always does."

"Richard and I are going to see the film together this eve- ning," Mrs. Westcott said. "I'm told it's very funny."

"Never go to the cinema myself. Too big and too noisy. Have a drink, dear lady. If I know Fiona, they'll be quite a time yet. Once she's enjoying herself she never knows when to stop. What's your poison?"

But the dear lady declined the offer. She could tell by the way the Radfords, the Aftons, and the Earls were looking at her that they expected her to be the center of a scene. Richard had seen her and was trying to negotiate Lady Pratley toward the bar, but her ladyship was refusing to be negotiated, cling- ing to him even closer now that she knew she had his mother among her audience.

"Is your arm making a good recovery, Sir Gerald?" Mrs. Westcott asked, trying to be cheerful, desperately fighting back her worst fears.

"Spent the whole of Saturday in Naples having it thoroughly checked, dear lady. Told I haven't a thing to worry about. Pro- viding I keep it well lubricated. Are you sure you won't join me?"

"I understood you were visiting family friends in Positano," she said.

His left eye twitched nervously. "No. I had to have the old arm looked at. Fiona did the visiting."

The orchestra finally decided on an intermission. As Richard came off the floor with Lady Pratley a small crowd gathered round them, pretending not to be there, but nonetheless expecting something to happen and not wanting to miss it when it did.

"Were you waiting for us?" Lady Pratley asked. "Richard is so persuasive. He insisted I had this dance with him. He's too young to realize I have a very jealous husband."

Sir Gerald started to say something but Richard interrupted him. "That's just not true, Mother! I didn't insist on dancing." He turned to Sir Gerald. "You know that, sir. Lady Pratley . . . pressed her attentions on me."

"She's a very pressing woman, young man," Sir Gerald said. "You should be more careful with pressing women in the future, not to take advantage of them. They don't all have silly old coots for husbands."

Her ladyship screwed up her face in disgust and waved him away with her hands. "Oh, go off to the film show with Mummy. I only dance with men!"

Richard took his mother's arm and led her away. "I'm sorry about that,' he said. "She'd been drinking and I couldn't very well say no."

"Saying no is sometimes the most difficult thing in the world," she told him. "But all the same, it has to be said."

When they had gone the little crowd dispersed, sad that the situation had not exploded. Lady Pratley crawled onto the bar stool next to her silly old coot. They sat for several minutes in silence, drinking steadily.

Presently he said, "There was a little girl who had a little curl, right in the middle of her forehead. When she was good she was very very good, but when she was bad . . . she was very very popular. Only Fiona, my dearest, she was a *little* girl."

Lat. 39.06N Long. 9.83W

. . . Compasses compared. Rounds made. Correct time to Engine Room. 22:00 Cape Espichel on bearing 083° (T) × 12 miles. 22:10 Alter course 352° (Gyro) 359° (Std.) 23:45 Berlengas Lt. House on bearing 079° (T) × 10 miles. 23:50 Alter course to 001° (Gyro) 009° (Std.) 23:55 Increase to 90 revs. Estimated current Adv. x 2' Var. 9° W. Wind SE Force 1. Slight swell. Fine visibility.—M.R.

WEDNESDAY May 2, had been a splendid day. The Atlantic had unexpectedly greeted them with a gentle smile, and as they rounded Cape St. Vincent in a midday blaze of heat the pool was crowded with swimmers and the stewards were busy around the edge with frosted glasses of iced drinks. The ship's officers benignly assured passengers that the weather had been ordered for their pleasure, privately thankful that the hell of the passage out was not going to be repeated; but in spite of the pleasant surprise at the clemency of the weather, the passengers shared an after-the-party sense of foreboding which, with the stoicism of the well traveled, they refused to discuss. They would, they agreed, all be pleased to be home again, to be back at the grind, battered by cold winds and sudden showers, resigned to higher taxation, to a lower standard of living than the *Queen Dee* had charmed and soothed their senses with for the past three weeks. No one really wanted to live in Athens, or Naples, or Villefranche. The food would be quite impossible in Rhodes, or Beirut, or Izmir. The people in all those places were so different from those in England: their customs, if not strange, then not very nice. No, to be abroad more than a few days at a time was not to be desired. The sunshine was what mattered. Without the sun, France, or Italy, or Greece, would not be very comforting places to visit at all. There may be a few squalls down the English Channel, but

June was a splendid time of year. Summer in England was never so hot as to be unbearable. There were no smells, no indigestible dishes, no foreign languages, and dear old England had more than its fair share of archaelogical remains. It was good to be going home.

Mrs. Westcott was aware of the mood, but she was unable to share it. Going home evoked for her things less positive, circumstances less precisely defined. There was the new house in Reigate she hardly knew. It was not yet a home; she couldn't be certain where home was any more, except in the grave, next to Arnold. She simply hadn't forgotten him, as she half hoped she might. He was as real to her as yesterday, so much more real than during the first frantic, tenuous years of marriage, when she couldn't be certain they had something that would last. Yet he wasn't real any more: and it hadn't lasted. The taxi driver had seen to that. "I'm sorry, mum. God help me, but I'm sorry." He was not a literate man, but if there was any compassion left in the mechanized whirl of city life, he had expressed it in those few faltering words after the inquest. It was no good blaming anyone that the cruise hadn't worked, least of all Richard, whose love was the one tangible and constant reminder of Arnold. The same eyes, the same full lips. That vulgar woman with a title, throwing herself at Richard the way she had. If only she hadn't been so blind to what was happening. She should have realized what the woman was up to the moment they left Athens. It wasn't good for a boy Richard's age to be without a father, particularly when he'd led such a sheltered life at school. He'd told her very little about what had happened at Positano, and she hadn't pressed him, because the sooner he forgot Lady Pratley and other women like her, the better it would be for him. He had simply said, "I suppose it was all my fault, Mother, because I said yes, and I'm the man." Which showed what a gentleman he was, and how grateful she had to be to Arnold for seeing to it that he'd had such a good education. Poor darling, if only she'd been able to keep him out of that woman's hands; if only his friendship with the nice young French girl had developed the way she hoped it might; if only he still had a father's guiding hand.

"You will come to our little party tonight, won't you, Mrs.

Westcott?" Mrs. Brewer had asked her twice already, and twice she could think of no good reason for saying no. "It's going to be ever so informal, but it won't be a party at all without you and Richard. Kenneth and I feel we know just about everyone in England, having got to know you both like neighbors. The cruise wouldn't have been the same without you."

"Yes, of course I'll be there," she said, trying to hide her lack of enthusiasm. "And I'm sure your John will drag Richard along."

"They're such good friends, aren't they?" Mrs. Brewer said. "I'm so pleased John's been meeting the right kind of people in Europe. When they leave home for the first time it's a dreadful worry. There seem to be so many ways in which young people can do wrong these days."

Mrs. Brewer rattled on, but Mrs. Westcott disengaged herself from the conversation and found a deck chair in a secluded corner from which, alone, she could look out over silvery-green fields of sea and up at the gulls crying at play around the masthead. Oh, to be free and pure as a bird! It was what we all wanted, wasn't it? But we couldn't be, none of us, we had flown too far from the very guts of life, we were lost forever. When she was a little girl she had kept a budgie. One day, in a fit of compassion, she had wanted to set him free. He flew to the magnolia tree at the end of the garden, rested there awhile until he saw the next-door cat, and then flew straight back to his cage. She had been so distressed, having sacrificed her love for his freedom, and he having refused it; but the family only laughed and were amused until she had burst into long convulsive spasms of tears. Poor caged Billie! Poor caged Pammy! She so yearned to grow small, to drift back into the past, to be looked after again, to have a mother's apron always ready to cry in, and never ever to be alone. To be always with darling Richard. To be truly loved, purely loved, by David. To be greeted around the family hearth by beery, bloated, boisterous brother Fred. "If Lady Godiva was alive today and was to ride through Coventry starkers on a white horse, I'd travel a thousand miles to see her. A thousand miles! I haven't seen a white horse for years." Oh, dear God, no! She couldn't go back and face Fred, not Fred. She couldn't go back and face any of them, even sweet Mr. Pulbright. Not after the way she had been carrying on. Not after everything that had happened in the last three weeks. A gull cried, hovered, and slipped backward like a white figurine, pure and free, calling to her to follow, to slip back, back, back into the past, into a gentle mother's arms, into tender oblivion. She stood at the end of the deck, looking down at the foaming wake far below, below, below. And the gull cried to her again and called jump, jump, jump.

"Good afternoon, Mrs. Westcott. Saying good-bye to happy memories?" It was Second Officer Hewson, down from the bridge, making his rounds, like a whiter-than-white Boy Scout in his starch-stiff shorts.

"You caught me daydreaming, Mr. Hewson," she said, startled that by some supernatural power he had heard the gull talking to her.

He stayed a few moments to share the view. "I always prefer it up in the bows myself, Mrs. Westcott. Looking forward. Doesn't do to look back on life too much, I reckon. Will you walk up there with me? I haven't finished my rounds yet."

She let herself be led for'ard, past the crowded pool, past the gymnasium, past the Tudor Room, the Assembly Room, the Orchard Room—all empty except for stewards preparing for evening service—and past the tennis courts to where the pleasure deck ended and dropped to the working deck of hatches and winches and chains and rough-skinned men.

"There," he said, looking ahead toward a completely empty seascape. "As far as the eye can see, and beyond, tomorrow waiting to greet us. I like daydreaming about what it will have to offer me when it does. Don't look back, Mrs. Westcott. There's nothing any of us can do about the past."

He saluted her as he left to return to the wheelhouse. She watched him go, and presently saw him aloft on the wing bridge, binoculars to his eyes, looking steadily ahead. If only she had been seated at *his* table for dinner, he was such a steady, sensible man, with a wife and family, and a skill and an excitement for tomorrow that bounced off his whiter-than-whiteness like religion from the blacker-than-blackness of an evangelist. If only religion was as near to her as it had been to Arnold, it might make things easier. Pammy saying "Gentle Jesus meek and mild . . ." while Billie twittered; but it had stopped there, and church became just a place to get married in, to baptize one's children in, to die in. City life went at such a pace it was impossible to expect God to keep up, or for her to slow down, to relax, to be soothed, to drift away into the oblivion of God-made eternity. We all had to die some time or other, and she couldn't believe in a Devil's hell any more than she could believe in a God's heaven. Just sleep, from which there would be no waking to face again the useless loneliness of a foolish woman. It was so easy, the final act of departure from error and disease, from pity and scorn, from pleasure no longer shared, from pain endured in private comfort, to world without end, for ever and ever, amen. "No, come back! Richard, come back!" She saw him, fair-haired in a breeze, driving his car, the car she had given him, along the seascape horizon, waving her good-bye, speeding from her life into his own, into his own errors, his own diseases, his own pity, his own scorn, his own pain, nothing any more for her to share, to desire, to be desired, to God-is-love. And high aloft, behind binoculars, looking down on her loneliness, the firm slender body of the Chief Officer. Sins of the flesh, world without end, oh David, why couldn't you understand, why couldn't you be gentle with me, help me, help, help, help, caw, caw caw, and the gull higher still, highest in the highest, beckoned her back, back, back, to where Pammy and the world began.

The Chief Officer woke at three-thirty on a cool North Atlantic morning, pleased that the order for the day was a return to regulation blues and they no longer had to masquerade in tropical whites for reasons of passenger psychology. Individual passengers could be amusing, but as a lot they were a deadly crowd. In the past few days he had developed a deep-seated contempt for the company's passenger psychology. Chief Pursers meant a damned sight more to the company than Chief Officers. If he didn't play his cards right with Len Arkwright when he took over, he'd be out almost before he was in. The last few days, confined to quarters, had given him time to think while he ate. Perhaps he'd been pushing both the old man and Pamela Westcott that bit too hard. Maybe he'd be testy when he was sixty-five and facing the scrap heap. And as for Mrs. W.,

it had been so long since he'd met a lady of her kind—in bed
that is—that he'd somewhat underestimated the hypocrisy of
the British middle classes, the "backbone of the nation" as her
beloved Arnold would have called them. They never admitted
publicly to what they were all too eager to enjoy in private.
Mrs. W. had been straining at the leash to play; but she wasn't
ready to publish the banns until the marriage looked right.
What would the neighbors think? Sod the neighbors! Fiona
would. Fiona enjoyed the scandal much more than the cause
of it. She would have relished every moment of being brought
back to the ship by three policemen, would have played the
bouncing-check scene for all it was worth, insisted that it was
duly reported in the ship's newspaper and bought advertising
space to put it there if necessary. But not Mrs. W., who'd even
gone so far as to tell the old man that rather than create a scene
the entire bill could be charged to her account. She was, as
Fiona had said the day they first met in the elevator, a poor
little thing. Metaphorically, of course. Her thousands were still
stacked neatly away in the bank, waiting to be wisely spent. If
she had the sense to take advantage of his wisdom, both of them
could have one hell of a good time for a long, long time
to come. She was a damned sight better to bed than Fiona,
only she didn't seem to realize it. The fact was, she knew how
to be a lady. She didn't bully him, nag him, force him to do
things her way, like Fiona had. Hell, he should have taken her
more easily, not have rushed her so. Maybe he'd have the biggest box of chocolates they had on board sent down to her
cabin as a peace offering. It hadn't been the most tactful thing,
waving Fiona's check under her nose like that. She couldn't
have been more shocked if it had been his joystick he'd flashed
in public. Poor thing. Not to worry. In a few days' time she'd
probably be missing what he had to offer her. That would be
the time to sweeten her again. Chat her up, show her a good
time. He'd take her to a show in the West End when they got
back, and maybe after the next trip, or the one after that, it
would be the real thing. A home of his own. Even if he would
have to settle for a second-hand sissy as a son. She really was a
silly bitch. She didn't seem to realize how much he wanted her.
Just thinking about her had aroused him. He sighed and
turned his thoughts to charts, and echo sounders, and auto-

matic pilots, drank flat coffee from the bedside flask, and presented himself on the bridge at exactly three fifty-five.

"Good morning, Mr. Welch. We're still on a course of one
degree true, running at ninety revs. You should be able to get
a bearing on Finisterre before you hand over to Riggie."

"Thank you, Harry." The Second Officer could go on mis-
tering him as long as he liked and he'd Harry him right back.
Bastard. If Hewson didn't want it to stay a chummy ship, it
would be a decision of his own making. "I'll take over now,
Harry. Sleep well. You'll be getting all the home comforts in a
couple of days."

He calculated that the last dig would really get Hewson
where he lived. He was the kind of man who made a fetish of
fidelity, and in all probability he hadn't so much as cast his
eyes on a second pair of tits in all of twenty years. Not even out
east where they grew like grapes. Pious sod. He had a damned
good suspicion Hewson had been souring the old man against
him ever since Piraeus. Len Arkwright would soon put his nose
out of joint for him. There'd be some smug grins on the other
side of faces this time next week.

"Where's *your* usual cheery morning smile then?" he asked
Third Officer Tyson as he joined him in the chartroom. It was
unusual for Tyson not to be perky. Even if he did hate his guts
like the others, at least he had the good sense not to show it.
There had even been moments when he thought Tyson actually enjoyed his company. Not that the youngster had much
choice. He was in his watch, and that was all there was to it.

"The usual end of cruise parties were a bit much last night,"
Tyson said. "Mathis just told me they had to ask the American
couple, the Brewers, to close it down in their cabin. I got stuck
with the Radfords, the car-dealer fellow. Jesus Christ! the mix-
tures they were pouring down us! The company should be paying danger money."

"Consider yourself privileged," the Chief Officer said wryly.
"Not all of us are allowed to live it up with the paying customers."

Tyson looked at him over the paper streamer of the course
recorder. "I don't think you've lost any sleep over that, have
you, sir?"

"You're damned right I haven't."

He went into the wheelhouse. Climpson was at the helm.
Rogers was on standby. Sinden was on fo'c'sle lookout and had
nothing to report. He made sure the man aft was on the job and
went out onto the wing bridge with his binoculars. It was a
still night, heavy without the moon, crisp with cold currents of
air eddying down from Biscay. He thought it might be possible to pick out some lights on the Portuguese coast with the
glasses, but it wasn't that clear. Somewhere off the starboard
bow was the Duoro estuary, and the lights of Oporto would be
screened by the coastal strip. Nothing but stars, and fresh pure
air, and the splashing of divided water as the old *Queen* cut her
way north for home.

When he returned to the wheelhouse, Third Officer Tyson
was doubled over the auto-pilot in agony. "Gut rot. Pure
bloody gut rot, that's what they gave me," he said.

"You'd better go and fix yourself a dose of salts or something,
lad," the Chief Officer told him. "You can't be of use to anyone in that state."

Tyson had barely been gone from the bridge more than a
minute when the Quartermaster called from the wheel that he
thought he saw a fog patch ahead.

The Chief Officer raised his glasses. "I think you're right,
Climp. Bloody good weather reports they send us down from
the radio room. They should try taking their fingers out."

"It's the time of year, sir," Climpson said tacitly.

The Chief Officer didn't reply. He knew that in late spring
after a warm day, when the night was still and clear and the
sea cold, mist and fog patches were to be expected along this
coast. He looked to the east for a sign of dawn, wondering if
morning was to be greeted with dense clouds of land fog rolling out to sea. The sky appeared to be a shade lighter than it
was a few moments ago, and the visibility eastward no worse.
If the wind would only stop idling at Force 1 and whip up into
a stiff breeze, it would clear the muck ahead. He got through
to the duty Radio Officer for the latest weather forecast, spent
a few moments among the dials and recorders in the chartroom, and decided that the patch ahead was most likely clearing and in all probability was neither dense nor deep.

"Go and find Mr. Tyson and tell him to hurry up with his

bloody bowels," he told the bridge boy the moment he returned to the wheelhouse.

"I would say we'll be coming into it in about four minutes, sir." Climpson was determined to give him the benefit of his years at the helm.

Fifteen knots way on her, one mile in four minutes. Too fast for safety. He telephoned the engine room to reduce to sixty revs and left the telegraph at stand-by. If the bloody muck ahead was more than just a patch, the old man should be called. "We never disturb the Master unless there's any exceptional change." He could hear Hewson's voice breathing down his neck on their second day out. He'd had enough rows with old Corlett as it was, and he didn't choose to have another lousy morning because he'd got out of his bed the wrong side on his account. It was only a small patch of muck. And if it wasn't, then he'd call him.

The *Queen Dee* cut into the fog just as Climpson had predicted, four minutes later. Her bows parted the cloud, then all 33,500 tons seemed airborne. She was drifting ghostlike without visible means of support, silently asleep except for four pairs of watchful eyes, her decks ablaze with light like deserted city streets, the fog blessing her with a saint's halo. And across the void, her siren vibrated the first deep-throated warning.

"What a bloody time for Tyson to be on the bog," the Chief Officer said.

"Yes, sir," Climpson said noncommittally.

He would have liked to take another fix, but it was more important to keep his eyes glued to the radar screen. Hell, he'd forgotten the watertight doors. He turned to the control panel along the rear of the wheelhouse and pressed a row of buttons. Seconds later the code lights winked, indicating that all watertight doors had been automatically closed. He returned to the radar. It was set on a six-mile range. He thought he saw an echo, fading in and out, bearing about thirty-five degrees on the starboard bow. He telephoned to reduce to forty revs. The book, it must be done by the bloody book. ". . . such a rate of speed as will enable a vessel, after discovering another vessel meeting her, to stop and reverse her engines in sufficient time to prevent any collision from taking place." He put the bearing cursor on the echo and watched it for a few moments. It faded out completely. It could be a bloody tanker head-on, reflecting nothing. He went out into the chill damp on the wing bridge and listened, hoping to hear a siren echo through the all-enveloping mist. A minute. Nothing but silence. The *Queen Dee*'s siren vibrated his whole body as she gave another warning blast. Perhaps they were coming out of the fog patch as quickly as they had entered it. The fellow ahead thought there was no need to sound his siren. Still silence. The dampness was soaking through his clothes to his skin. He dare not wait any longer. Damn Tyson's bowels!

Back in the wheelhouse the Chief Officer telephoned both fo'c'sle and aft lookouts. They could hear and see nothing. But the echo was strong again. Less than three miles ahead. It appeared to be narrowing the bearing and crossing from starboard to port.

"Alter course twenty degrees to starboard, Quartermaster," he ordered.

"Twenty degrees to starboard it is, sir."

The Chief Officer scribbled rapidly in the wheelhouse notebook. Then he looked anxiously to see if he had brought the echo ahead. The Master should be on the bridge. If the fog siren hadn't awakened him, he'd have to. Now. The echo seemed to be moving to the port bow. He asked Climpson how the helm was responding at slow speed. "Slowly sir. Very slowly." A moment later he was on the telephone waking Captain Corlett. He had barely put down the instrument when the bridge boy returned, followed by a white-faced Tyson.

"Are we in difficulties, Mr. Welch?" Tyson asked.

"No, but you will be, mister, if you don't get out on the port wing and keep your ears pinned back and your eyes wide open."

The echo seemed to be coming down the screen parallel to their own course. Little more than a mile away. And still not a sight or sound. Seconds later they all heard a fog siren that wasn't their own, higher in pitch, imprecisely ahead. The other vessel began narrowing on the port bow as though she was deliberately trying to tangle with them. The Chief Officer ordered the Quartermaster to starboard his wheel another ten degrees. What seemed like seconds later the high-pitched siren screeched again. On top of them.

"What the devil's afoot?" Captain Corlett came lumbering onto the bridge, eyes bleary with sleep, still hitching his trousers.

"There's an unidentified vessel immediately off the port bow, sir."

"Stop engines!" the Master ordered, trying to grasp a situation of which he had no brief. "Give me a bearing on her. Quickly, man, quickly!"

But quickly was too late. The for'ard masthead light of the other vessel loomed ahead of the *Queen Dee*'s bows and some distance below them.

"Full astern!"

Heart-pounding seconds. The green starboard light came at them at barely a cable's distance off the port bow. They were going to hit her amidships. The siren blasted an incessant warning. Engines thundered in reverse, but seconds, seconds, seconds, and the 33,500-ton floating city still floated ahead.

"Quartermaster! Give her all the wheel you can, man!"

Too late. They hadn't a cat in hell's chance of avoiding collision. The smaller ship took the full impact of the *Queen Dee*'s solid steel stem at right angles, a little aft of her bridge, and with a scream of metal, and battered by a turbulent flood of water, heeled to port as the old *Queen* knifed through plating and decking and bulkheads and tanks finally to come to rest within a few feet of the midship line. And after awful noise, an equally sudden and far more frightening silence.

Lady Pratley was flung from her bed by the impact. When she struggled to her feet and pulled the curtains, she stood petrified by the scene of havoc. The Rose Suite had a full view of the Promenade Deck below. Several seamen were already running forward to the bows, which were a mass of tangled rigging. A broken mast was lying like a vast tree trunk over the anchor cable and winches. And low down, under the towering cliff of the *Queen Dee*'s stem, what looked like a large black whale was spewing its oily guts over the silent water. Even as she watched, both ships drifted in their embrace out of the fog patch. To the east was a golden sliver of light, and the stars

began to fade in the awakening sky. It was going to be another
beautiful day.

"Oh, my God!" said Sir Gerald, standing by the window and
taking her arm in his. "What a dreadful disaster. My heart
bleeds for the Captain. Hurry, Fiona, we must find our life
jackets. In case we have to abandon ship."

Alarm bells were sounding everywhere, waking passengers
and off-duty crew. The plastic corridors padded with scurrying
feet, echoed with the first shouted questions, the first rasped
orders. The younger among the stewards and galley staff were
quick to panic, none of them having previous experience of a
disaster at sea, and many of them undisciplined catering
staff only recently signed on from hotels and restaurants ashore.
Convinced that they were in immediate danger, they began
pushing and hustling sleep-stunned passengers, many of them
still in their night attire, and without waiting for the word of
command made for their emergency boat stations. And their
flight, unabated by the organized calm of a few of the older and
more experienced crewmen or by the shouted orders of the
junior deck officers, filled the hearts of every passenger, first
and tourist, with an awful dread. They, too, wanted to flee,
naked if necessary, and without their luggage: but to where?
Acting on emotional impulse, they filled the corridors, shouting among themselves, demanding of any of the ship's staff they
might see a full account of what had happened and an estimation of the extent of their danger. Then, as they met the
strange barriers of the watertight doors, panic welled in them
even stronger. They ran and trotted in a herd, pushing each
other through staffrooms and service passages to find new ac-
cesses to the higher deck levels and the public assembly rooms.
A fire extinguisher, dislodged and smashed in the scramble,
foaming and hissing near the A Deck elevators, immediately
sent up an unconfirmed cry of "Fire!" The ship's on fire! Save
us! Somebody do something! And from C Deck, where a tea
urn in a night pantry had been sent flying in the upward rush,
trickling its gallons of strong brew under the service doors,
came the cry of "Water!" The ship's sinking! Save us! Somebody do something!

"Oh dear, oh dear!" a hairnetted and nightgowned Miss
Peebles wailed. "I wonder how it's all going to end."

"The butler did it," somebody snapped at the best-selling dinosaur.

The small cabin in which Richard and John were sleeping was in complete darkness. They were awakened not so much by the impact as by the cascade of breaking china in the adjacent pantry. John leaped out of bed and reached for the light switch, but the cabin remained in darkness. Outside, the corridor was in darkness for some fifty yards. The cabins throughout the whole section had been blacked out by the convulsion. A woman in a nightdress, her hair still in curlers, restrained by a puffy-eyed man, was screaming in the doorway of one of the cabins. "We're sinking! We're all going to be drowned!" The man slapped her face and she collapsed, crying, in his arms.

"Get some clothes on," Richard told John. "Anything warm. And go forward to your parents. They may need your help. I must try to get up to the Observation Deck and see what I can do to help Mother."

He spoke with a calm authority that surprised him. He had always been afraid he'd lose his head in an emergency, but here was an emergency, and he was keeping it. He groped for his own clothes and then helped John find his. Then he methodically felt his way about in the darkness like a blind man, until he had located both their life jackets.

"This is your Captain speaking! Attention please, all passengers!" The voice boomed like God in his heaven through the public rooms, down crowded corridors, across confused decks and out over the silent sea. "You are in no immediate danger. I repeat. You are in no immediate danger. All passengers should put on warm clothing. Go with your life jackets to your assembly position. Wait there for any order which may be given you by a ship's officer. Do not hurry. Do not panic. Your assembly position is clearly shown on the notice behind your cabin door, together with full instructions on how to wear your life jacket. If in any doubt whatsoever, ask your cabin steward for advice. Carry out the orders of all ship's officers, promptly and calmly. I repeat. You are in no immediate danger."

Richard found his way blocked by a watertight door. He tried to get to the aft companionway, but other doors were sealing off the section. He returned to the pantry, crunched over broken china, and walked up the service stairs to the pantry above on the Promenade Deck, followed by a squealing mob of blind mice. He reached the main companionway, the vast double staircase molded around the two elevator shafts, but it was impossible to either ascend or descend. Hundreds of night-clad people, some struggling with hastily packed cases or bundled belongings, were fighting either to get up or to go down, trying to find husbands, save wives, comfort children. In the center was the tieless Chief Purser, pleading above the din for order, repeating in vain the Captain's pledge that they were in no immediate danger. No one among that clawing, screeching and disheveled mob looked a particularly first-class passenger.

"I know we're sinking," a fat woman moaned. "I can *feel* myself going down." A second later she had disappeared, still moaning, in the sea of people.

Richard turned back, through the darkened Tudor Room, and out onto the deck. In their panic, no one seemed to have thought about the outside companion ladders. He climbed like a monkey up to the Observation Deck and raced along the port side to the entrance to the cabins. Out of the corner of his eye he saw the sea far below, sullen with oil, glistening in peacock rings of green and purple and blue and violet in the dawn light. Thirty-two. Thirty. Twenty-eight. Twenty-six. He was breathless when he reached his mother's door. He only hoped she'd had the sense to stay there, to wait for him. He turned the handle and pushed. He thought at first it was stuck and heaved his shoulder against it. But it was locked. From the inside.

"Mother! Open up! Please! It's me. Richard."

Only silence. An ominous, heart-pounding silence. He imagined her lying injured, unconscious from a fallen wall fitting, or insensate with fright. He tried using his shoulder, but it wouldn't give. He had to find a passkey. Who would have one? The senior deck steward. But he couldn't see any steward, only half-clad unkempt people asking each other what was happening, and setting flight to new rumors in the asking: It hadn't been the Captain speaking, only a recording of his voice. The ship's staff was already getting away to safety in the boats. The tourist-class accommodation was cut off by the watertight doors and hundreds of people had already perished down below. Richard pushed by them to the pantry at the end of the corridor. No one was there. Trays, prepared for breakfast service, were scattered like a fallen house of cards. There must be a passkey somewhere here. There had to be. He looked in the cupboards. Napkins, bed linen, sauce bottles, packets of detergent. The drawers. Cutlery, order pads, tins of instant coffee. This one behind the door. Locked. Why? Must open it. Knife. Lever. Snap blade. Hell, now how can I do it? Two knives. He forced both blades together between the slit of wood. Please God, let it work. Eyes closed, muscles taut. Splinter and crack. Open. Inside, bottle of arak, packets of Turkish cigarettes, folded Greek shirt, slabs of Italian torrone, no keys. Damn God, damn God, no keys! His searching hands disturbed some papers under the sweeties. Photographs. Negatives. John, Aziz, Hooda, and the Arab sailor. Fear, shame, sex, panic, confusion.

"What the devil are you up to, you sneaking little thief?"

He turned to see the gold flash of a steward's epaulet. Hyslop. Good-natured, salt-of-the-earth, cockney Hyslop. Lips tight. Eyes beady with anger.

"Give me them photographs!"

He knew he should hand them over. Placate the man. Ask him for a key. Find Mother; be with her; help her. But he didn't. A cold, defiant anger such as he had never known before prevented him. He felt himself stuffing the bundle into his jacket pocket and heard himself saying, "No, no, no! You dirty, lousy blackmailer!"

Hyslop made a grab at him to recover the negatives. Richard pushed him away. The man returned the push with a fist blow, and almost before he was aware of what he was doing, Richard was fighting—not in boyish fun, but in vicious, deadly earnest. For John, for John's family, and for something more: for his own conception of what was right and wrong, good and evil, to be accepted or to be rejected. He blindly slammed his fists into the steward's face. The man gasped, came back with even greater fury. Bodies close now. Smell of fetid breath, a single hair sprouting from nostril large as telegraph pole. The man's nails were tearing the delicate skin of his cheeks. Barge him!

He heard Hyslop's body smash hollowly against the far cupboard. He didn't know his own strength. Arms locked, legs trying to trip. Richard saw himself hurtling at jet-speed toward the door post, missed it, light as air into the corridor, sent an elderly lady flying and screaming onto her face, wanted to stop, wanted to apologize, wanted to cry, but Hyslop everywhere, on top of him, under him, around him, punching, kicking, scratching, tearing. For Christ's sake, watch your tackles! Arms around waist, full weight of body, and both on the ground. He dragged the man to his feet, not wanting to hit him again while he was down. He looked so old after the first flush of violence. There was blood freshly smeared over his white jacket. Whose? Richard brought his knee up almost by accident, just as Hyslop hurled himself forward in another attack. A scream of pain. Pale, terrified faces all around. The steward falling backward. Head ripping off chrome door handle. Body limp, motionless, crumpled, on blue plastic floor.

"Young man, you are a disgrace to everything that's British," an elderly gentleman told him sternly. "I insist that you obey the orders given us by the ship's staff. Or none of us will get out of this dreadful situation alive."

Mother. The passkey. The man must have a key on him. He bent over the silent figure, rummaging through the pockets, while the elderly gentleman tried angrily to pull him off and appealed to other disheveled passengers to help restrain the young ruffian. One. Two. Three keys. He pushed the feebly restraining hands from him and raced down the corridor to his mother's cabin. Oh, hurry, please hurry! First key no good. Second key fitted, turned, and the door opened inward.

The soft light of dawn filtered through the cabin curtains. As he closed the door behind him, he shut out all sound from the wailing lost world of the *Queen Dee*. The carpet was soft and comforting under his feet. His face and chest stung with the bruises of battle. And his heart trembled a little as he looked around the cabin, like a child entering fairyland. The beautiful princess, his mother, was lying in the bed nearest the window, her long auburn hair mussed in the pillows, her face waxy-cream in the suffusion.

"Mother? Are you all right? Are you sleeping?"

For timeless minutes he stood by the bed, unable to make

himself believe the truth. She was sleeping the final sleep from which she would never wake. He was aware only that he should be expressing some sort of emotion: but he was expressing nothing, just standing there, motionless, senseless. He wanted to be the handsome prince who would kiss her back to life. He wanted to wind up the clockwork that made her move. He wanted to wake, to find that he was dreaming, that he wasn't in a cabin on the *Queen Dee* with his dead mother at all. Nothing practical, nothing sensible came into his head. It was the first dead body he had ever seen, except a dog killed by a passing motorist outside the school gate. And when at last he began to reason, he was ashamed that his first concern was that her body might start to smell.

"A doctor! I want a doctor! There's been a terrible accident!"

He rattled the phone frantically, but there was no reply. He had to shout at himself to make himself realize that the accident outside the cabin was more terrible than the one within. He took the mirror from the dressing table and held it close to her face, to be certain she wasn't still breathing. Just a little, please Mother, just a little! He felt her wrist. It was cold, and moist, and loveless, and repelled him with its snakelike renitency. It was only then that he asked himself, how? And why? On the bedside table were two empty bottles. One had contained aspirin. The other, handwritten direction scrawled over the plain label, had contained the barbiturates the doctor had prescribed for her after Father had died. She had steeled herself against using them. Said it was better for wounds to heal naturally. Said, said, said—she would say nothing again, to him, to her beloved Arnold, to anyone. Under the empty bottles was an envelope, addressed simply, "To Richard." His hands were shaking so much that it was several minutes before he could unseal it and remove the single sheet of paper. It flittered in his hand as though it had a life of its own.

"Darling Richard. You tried so hard to make me forget but I'm afraid I've let you down. I've made an awful fool of myself, trying to find something that doesn't exist any more, for me, or for anyone. We can but fall in love once in our lives, and some may never love at all. When there is no more love there is no more life. I am better wherever your father is, or nowhere at all. When you are older you may understand and not feel too bitterly of me. At least I do this knowing you are well provided for. If there is a God, may He bless you, my darling son. Your (the word "affectionate" had been crossed out) loving mother."

He read it three times. And then his emotions took control. He collapsed by the bedside crying like a child, cradling the cold, delicate hand, to give it warmth. Sleep Comfort. Sleep Comfort. Sleep Comfort.

When he had come staggering onto the bridge, still hitching his trousers, Captain Corlett looked all of his sixty-five years. But within minutes of taking command, his eyes were sharp as a falcon's, his mind grasping a developing situation as he barked orders to his officers with awe-inspiring precision. Those mirror-moist eyes reflected the shock of the moment; but behind them, deep inside the man, was a tingling contentment. He had complete control in an emergency, just as he had always had. For fleeting moments he was young again. And desperately needed.

"Mr. Rigg. Lower all lifeboats to embarkation position. Mr. Langdon. Send out a general distress call. We'll advise later. Mr. Mathis. Sound the bilges. Let me have your estimation if we're shipping water. Mr. Welch and Mr. Hewson. Take a rescue party for'ard and do whatever needs to be done." And while he barked, his eyes took in the whole of the *Queen Dee*'s electronic brain, watching for any automatic warning of fire or flood.

The collision, as the Chief Officer had anticipated, was with a heavy-laden tanker, a ghost to the radar scan head-on, a helpless floundering mess of steel and oil and men when savaged broadside-on by a vessel four times her size. Before any of the *Queen Dee*'s crew had time to muster for'ard, the tanker's Master was giving the order to abandon ship. The Second Officer and bos'un were scrambling precariously up a collapsed derrick, the tip of which was resting over the edge of the old *Queen*'s guard rails. In the dawn quietness the wood was heard to creak, to splinter, to shift, as the two men panted for safety as nimble as rats. The bos'un tried to get through a fairlead but forgot he was wearing a life jacket and was wedged, blocking the officer's passage. The macabre dance of entangled steel shifted the derrick: it gave, scraped down the white paint on the port bow, and hurled the officer, screaming, seventy feet into the oily filth below, leaving the bos'un still wedged by his life jacket with no other means of support. Two of *Queen Dee*'s deck hands reached him first, secured a rope to his legs and swung him out from the fairlead, dangling unceremoniously head down over the ship's side as he was hauled to safety.

"Rope ladders. Scramble nets. Quickly! If we part company she won't stay afloat more than five minutes."

The Chief Officer looked down from the *Queen Dee*'s bows, trying to assess the extent of the damage in the turbidity of dawn. From the broken thing below that was once a ship he heard confused, gasping Spanish voices. Saw men scrambling up companionways onto decks tilted sixty degrees to port, dangerously awash with sea water and oil. The diffused light began to play optical tricks. He thought he saw men standing in the galley, the steel stem of the *Queen Dee* rammed within inches of the bulkhead, drinking their morning coffee; but seconds later they could be seen to be fighting for breath in an atmosphere heavy with oil fumes, squeezing their sodden bodies between bulkhead and stem in a life-or-death struggle toward the web of rope ladders and scramble nets.

"We're parting, Mr. Welch. Starboard bow's catching the tidal stream." Hewson's face was taut with alarm. There were twenty, perhaps thirty, maybe even forty men still aboard the floundering vessel.

"Advise the Master. Suggest slow ahead with plenty of starboard wheel. Bos'un! Lower Number One and Number Three boats and have the crews standing by a couple of cables on the port quarter prepared to take on survivors."

Seconds later the old *Queen* came slowly to life again, nuzzling into the wound, trying to prevent the inevitable for as long as possible. As she did so, the first of the men came up the scramble nets, unshaven, eyes white behind tanned and blackened faces, some bleeding through the engulfing slime, all muttering foreign prayers for deliverance. Minute by minute they came aboard: and the smiles of a suffering shared was the only welcome their rescuers could offer them. Fleeting moments when language, politics, religion knew no barrier, when all men were equal in distress.

"She's breaking up, sir! Stop engines!"

Even as Hewson shouted, they all heard the wounded ship's final cry of despair, a tearing of metal that vibrated over the still waters, the vast drowning gurgles as millions of gallons of water raced, whirl-whipped and spuming, into her guts. She heeled some more. Only two men remained on board. Her Master and her Chief Engineer. They were flung, as from a catapult, by the rising scuppers, their kapok-packed life jackets spreading their limbs like discarded dolls and skidding them across the oil-plumed water twenty, thirty yards away. And as decks and superstructure yelled and bubbled their way into a seventy-fathom oblivion, the old *Queen* imperceptibly dipped her bows in salute. Three minutes later, all that remained was a widening patch of oil, dotted with splintered wood and empty life rafts. The two lifeboats were easing their way through the debris to pick up last survivors, as the sun rose fiery-red over the silent *Queen*'s bows, festooned with nets and ladders and humbled by her adversary's fallen mast.

The passengers realized that they were—just as the Master had pledged—in no danger the moment they saw the shivering, stinking survivors dripping their way into the Promenade Deck assembly room. Their panic at once gave way to a misdirected wave of sympathy. While Dr. Hammond supervised emergency treatment for the injured, helped by two doctors and three trained nurses from among the passengers, wellwishers found spare garments for the men to wear, pressed on them packets of English cigarettes like magic elixir, and stood herded together, muttering sympathies, until they could no longer bear the sight of men spitting blood like animals, mixed with the foul tissue-searing oil that had choked them nearly to extinction, and crying silently with pain from lacerations salted and caked with working denims. One by one the wellwishers drifted away, back to their cabins to compose themselves, to bathe, to shave, to pamper themselves back to the land of the living. To become first-class human beings again, to ring bells, give orders, demand with feigned innocence to be told why breakfast service was a little late that day.

The full impact of the past few hours began to take their toll on Captain Corlett the moment he saw the two helicopters circling overhead. The final reckoning would come at the formal investigation in seven or eight months' time. Facts would be established, decisions made in the heat of the moment disputed, circumstances weighed. And one thing would be indisputable. He had not been on the bridge, had not been in command of his ship to take avoiding action, simply because that damned whoremaster Welch had chosen not to advise him of potential danger until it was too late, too late, too late. He jerked his mind from the engulfing gloom of recriminations and concentrated on what had to be done, now. Check the watertight security of his ship. Establish that Herrington had no failures in the machinery spaces. Advise the Marine Superintendent of the circumstances of the disaster. Notify other shipping standing by to come to their aid that their services were no longer required. Proceed at caution to the nearest port for an underwater survey. Meet the Master of the Spanish tanker and listen to his account of events leading up to the collision. That was the moment he dreaded most. To meet the man who'd lost his ship under the old *Queen*'s bows. He feared not so much what he would say, but what he wouldn't say: the polite restraint extended to another of his kind, the gentle acceptance of a fate that might strike any seaman, any time, any place, with dignity.

The Chief Officer left it to Hewson to discuss the revised course with the old man, and stayed for some time on deck supervising the clearing-up operations. Then he went back to the chartroom to make a fair record of the log entry. This time he was damned if he was going to take the blame. The bloody tanker had obviously been at fault, cutting from port across their bows, taking not a sodding bit of notice of international regulations for the prevention of collision at sea. The book, it must be done by the bloody book. "When two power-driven vessels are crossing, so as to involve risk of collision, the vessel which has the other on her starboard side shall keep out of the way of the other." Every nit knew that. This time he was not going to let them get him on the hook, make him the scapegoat for some other bastard's error. He'd done everything a man could do. He was simply not to blame, not to blame, not to blame.

The Master was finishing a late breakfast when the Chief Officer came into his day cabin to report. "I want to hear in your own words, Mister, an account of everything that took place on the bridge from the moment you took over the watch until the moment you summoned me," he said, pushing the tray to one side and staring ahead with a gray impassive face. "Just the facts. You can save your excuses for the hearing."

He gave the old fool the facts, just as he knew them, one by one, minute by minute, but he might as well have been talking to a brick wall. Nothing was being received, nothing was being understood behind those cold blue eyes. He didn't want to understand. The bastard wanted to pin it on him. If it was the last stinking thing he did before he was made to swallow the anchor, it would be to shop him for this lot, careerwise to see him washed up for good. Pompous, self-satisfied old sod. Someone would be doing the world a favor if they stuck a marlinespike in his guts one dark night.

"It does not seem to register with you," the Master said, "that you came perilously near to jeopardizing the lives of twelve hundred men and women aboard this ship, apart from the safety of the ship herself. In all my years at sea, I have never encountered a man with so much knowledge stuffed into his head yet with so little responsibility in the application of it."

"I did everything that it was reasonable and possible to do," the Chief Officer protested. "There is absolutely no evidence to the contrary. Had you been called to the bridge earlier the situation would have remained exactly the same. She cut right across our bows. Wrongfully. And dangerously."

"And you didn't see her coming! Visibility was nil, and you still kept steaming ahead!"

"Jesus Christ, you make it sound as though the whole pack of them were drowned!"

"Like the *Torrance?*"

"Yes, like the bloody *Torrance*! You can't wait to needle me with that at the formal investigation, can you?"

The Master's voice hardened, clenched fists restraining his anger with bony knuckles. "I am not bickering with you, mister. I just want the facts. And when we have established them, we will stick to them."

"The facts are there's not a single life lost. We got them aboard with nothing more than a good shaking and a few cuts and bruises. Bloody Spanish seamen. Stooging around coastal waters in an old rust-bucket like that. I don't mind betting the Master was half drunk. The experience will do them good. Make them use their heads a bit more in future."

"I wouldn't be so anxious to start washing the blood off my hands if I were you." The Master dropped his eyes, unable to look the younger man in the face any longer. "Mrs. Westcott died this morning. By her own hand. I almost feel sorry for you, Mister. You might have found a way to forget the men who died on the *Torrance*. I don't think you'll find it so easy to forget someone you've slept with. Or will you? Maybe that's the kind of man you are."

Lat. 43.45N Long. 9.14W

. . . 07:45 Both port and starboard lifebuoy release gear tested and found to be in good order. 08:00 Correct time given to Engine Room. 09:00 Master Officiated at burial of Mrs. Pamela Grace Westcott. 09:30 Cape Finisterre abeam bearing 126° (T) × 13 miles 09:35 Altered course 028° (Gyro) 037° (Std.) 11:00 Vessel searched for contraband. Compasses compared. Rounds made and all's well. Vessel rolling easily. Speed 10 knots. Wind SE Force 2. Overcast. Good visibility.—M.R.

THE *Queen Dee* had limped into Oporto on Thursday afternoon and lay at anchor in the roadstead. And while her passengers resumed a leisurely life, sunning themselves and sipping afternoon tea, the Master had been engaged in a marathon of mentally and physically exhausting organization. A constant exchange of messages with London. A constant arrival and departure of marine insurance representatives, police, immigration and port health authority officials. A constant flow of papers and documents to be checked and signed and dispatched. It would have knocked the stuffing out of a younger man: and by the time he retired at a quarter to midnight, Captain Corlett for the first time in his life felt the full impact of his sixty-five years. He came face to face with the fact that, like it or not, he was an old man. And as he pulled the freshly laundered sheet over himself and settled down in the hope of getting some sleep, he muttered to his Maker, "Please God, I will be seen to have done my duty."

By Friday morning he knew that the end was to come quicker than he expected. The underwriters had flown a couple of experienced salvage divers to Lisbon, thence up to Oporto. With them was Captain Leonard Arkwright, bearing a letter of authority from the Marine Superintendent. The letter was couched in delicate terms. The *Queen Dee* had been delayed. Captain Arkwright would need time to familiarize himself with details of her command before he took over. His presence on the voyage back to Southampton would be a good opportunity for him to do this. He would also take the opportunity of preparing a detailed report on the circumstances of the disaster which Sir Edgar was anxious to receive without delay. Put in blunt terms, as was Captain Corlett's wont, he was no longer regarded as a good risk to get the old *Queen* home without further damage. In a parcel of fancy words, authority had been stripped from him. And Captain Arkwright's words about understanding the full impact of such a human tragedy, not wanting to make himself a burden to anyone during the next few days, willing to give of his service and experience as and when required, was sheer bilge. He commandeered the Fourth Officer's cabin, had a desk placed for his use in the officers' smoking room, and within the hour was advising the Master what orders to give, when, and to whom.

The divers were down for a little more than four hours. Their survey satisfied the underwriters' agent that the old *Queen* was still seaworthy, at least until she could make her home port and the probability of an ignominious month in drydock. There were a number of loose plates, and she'd sprung a leak beneath one of the forward port ballast tanks. The bilge pumps would be more than adequate to expel the flow. All the same, she waited four more hours while the gash was packed with concrete. Then, after two days of anguish, just as the sun was beginning to set, she weighed anchor and sailed northward into the night at a cautionary maximum of ten knots.

"We brought nothing into this world, and it is certain we can carry nothing out. The Lord gave, and the Lord hath taken away; blessed be the name of the Lord."

Captain Corlett was standing with bowed head near the corpse of Pamela Grace Westcott, boxed, and weighted, and draped with a Union Jack, resting on a couple of planks by the open port on the starboard side of the main entrance foyer on B Deck. Beyond, a leaden sea, an overcast morning sky, and in the far distance the southern face of Cape Finisterre.

Richard was standing next to the Master, eyes reddened by tears, staring fixedly at the distant promontory. Behind him was the Chief Purser and several other ship's officers, and behind them, a dozen or more passengers who wanted to be present to offer sympathy, to be in at a new experience, or who were there simply for want of anything better to do.

". . . Now this I say, brethren, that flesh and blood cannot inherit the kingdom of God; neither doth corruption inherit incorruption. Behold, I shew you a mystery . . ."

Richard's first impulse had been that she should be buried next to his father in the great wasteland of the dead in North London. He had no idea of her wishes. He wasn't even sure that she had made a will, and if she had, where it was to be found. But he knew instinctively that somehow he had to get her back to her beloved Arnold, his father. At first the Chief Purser had been most understanding, but very soon he began saying no—in the nicest, gentlest, most purserly manner. Step by step Mr. Craddock presented a score of reasons why interment in England was neither practical nor, from the company's point of view, desirable. There was, as a result of the accident, some doubt as to how long the *Queen Dee* would take to reach Southampton. Her Captain was legally bound not to let the body become a "nuisance" to others on board, whether passengers or crew. The company, of course, regretted its inability to store bodies. Had they been staying longer at Oporto it might have been possible to have the body embalmed, put in a lead casket, packed in an ordinary freight case, and stowed in the hold. At a price. And the price would have been very high. The whole mechanics of death frightened Richard. Dying was no longer fashionable. Grown-ups seemed quite incapable of coping with it, yet it was more natural, more inevitable than abortions, insanity or divorce—all of which they took in their stride, indeed, almost relished. But death was the one subject polite society was too damned polite even to discuss. They all pretended that death was something that happened only to other people. He wondered when he would die. Perhaps he would not die at all: perhaps science would by then have found a way to keep people alive forever. Millions of people forever getting on each others' nerves. What a dreadful thought! He'd prefer to die. In his own bed? In agony in a hospital, because an irresponsible nurse had forgotten to give him his morphine? Alone? Laughing at a joke? Fighting someone a politician had branded an enemy of his country? Or under the wheels of a taxi? His mind jerked back to this last act he had to do for Mother. He was quite certain she would not want to be buried at sea. He had asked to get off at Oporto and see her decently put to rest there. But Mr. Craddock had subtly described the complications of importing a corpse into a foreign country, even hinting that a Catholic community such as Portugal might not take kindly to being asked to bury someone who had died by her own hand. Why was suicide worse than dying of cancer? Some people would not even accept equality in death. There was something so final about burial at sea. It made the break so complete. No place for a headstone, not even the ashes as a physical reminder of a broken bond. Only love remained. And when love had gone, no evidence that the warm gentle creature that was his mother had ever lived to give him birth.

"We therefore commit her body to the deep, to be turned into corruption, looking for the resurrection of the body, when the sea shall give up her dead, and the life of the world to come, through our Lord Jesus Christ; who at His coming shall change our vile body, that it may be like His glorious body, according to the mighty working, whereby He is able to subdue all things to Himself."

It was not the way Richard wanted to say good-bye. The words so inadequately described his mother and how he felt about her. They were so much claptrap. Old Captain Corlett knew it. So did the others standing there, musing with solemn faces on their own departure. And he knew it. Love is God. That delicate emotion nurtured by an umbilical cord broken instantly by selfishness and hate. Love is God. His mother wanting to give him his freedom, lovingly watching him become a man. Love is God. John knew that, and refused to accept society's *mélange* of sex and sentiment. "As soon as you really love someone you want to be gentle with them, careful not to hurt their feelings or their bodies." Love is God. Simone knew that, putting first her duty to her ailing aunt, wanting his friendship and understanding only on those terms. Love is God. Lady Pratley knew that, although she would never admit

it, searching instead in dark corners for new gods, new loves,
but always returning to the all-embracing compassion of her
silly old coot. He felt a gentle grip on his right arm. It was
Captain Corlett, father to all under his command. Love is
God. The Union Jack quivered with a life of its own, as two
seamen raised one end. It collapsed, dead, on the empty boards.
For a thousandth part of a second he saw his mother's weighted
body disappear from underneath it and heard it splash into
where time began.

As he turned to leave, Chief Officer David Welch came up to
him. "I'm sorry, son," he said. "Perhaps there is something I
can do to help when we're back in England."

"Yes," Richard said, "you can. Stay out of my way. I never
want to see you again. Ever."

The Chief Officer watched the youngster disappear into the
nearest elevator, surrounded by Miss Peebles, the Aftons, the
Earls, all offering their condolences. Lucky young bastard.
Some people always seemed to fall on their feet. What he
wouldn't give to be eighteen again, with a bank balance that
said he'd never have to sweat his guts out for a living if
he didn't want to. Bloody little twit. He hoped every stinking
pound would make him as miserable as hell.

He was about to return to his cabin to catch up on some sleep
when Captain Arkwright called him into the smoking-room
office. "Make yourself comfortable, David. I won't keep you
long."

"Of course, Leonard. I'm completely at your disposal. You'll
find she's not much different from the *Ardmore,* given an extra thousand tons or so. Stabilizers are due for a major overhaul. If you ask me, they're obsolete. Design wasn't up to snuff
in the first place."

"Look, old man. I'm sorry about this. Devilishly sorry. I've
got one or two things to tell you which, frankly, I wish I hadn't.
I'd been looking forward to having you as my Chief. Same
club. Shared interests. Better than being surrounded by total
strangers—"

"But?" The Chief Officer bit his lower lip nervously.

"Until the findings of the court of inquiry are known, the
Marine Superintendent wants you ashore."

"God Almighty! And you support him? I'm to be assumed

guilty before I'm proved innocent. Is that British justice for you, Leonard? I ask you, is that justice?"

Captain Arkwright said quietly, "It's what the company wants. And I suspect it's what the underwriters want, too. Don't get so worked up about it, old man. Find yourself a good lawyer. And you're laughing."

The Chief Officer was trying desperately to contain his temper. "Look Leonard, you've got to do something. I'm not going to have the whole shooting match pinned on me. I'm not going to be the company's scapegoat or anyone else's! If I'm put on indefinite leave when we berth at Southampton, I'm as good as washed up for good. You realize that, don't you? I'm through! No good for anything except pushing a pen across some supply-office desk."

"There's nothing I can do, old man." Captain Arkwright betrayed the faintest hint of sarcasm. "Why don't you see what your fairy godmother can do? I'm told the company's more or less permanently indebted to Sir Gerald. On account of injuries received in the line of duty."

"I'll get even with you for that, Leonard. My God, but I'll remind you of that crack one day." The Chief Officer left the cabin, slamming the door behind him. Len Arkwright's betrayal had been the unkindest cut of all, because there had been no need for it. It was sheer bloody malice.

Richard and John ate lunch in silence. John had already expressed his sympathy and was ashamed that words alone were so inadequate to describe how he really felt about someone he liked, someone younger than himself, someone left without a family to go back to whenever he needed to go back. He wanted to intrude on Richard's private thoughts, to tell him he guessed he'd be following his own mother and father back to the States by the fall, that he was grateful he had a mother and father to follow back; but expressed in words the emotion would sound maudlin, and anyhow, when he got back to Paris there would be big black Seth and he'd forget Richard and he'd have his own life to lead and he'd probably send his folks some European goodies for Thanksgiving if he decided not to go back after all. By the fall the world might not be here any more.

"I'm sorry. I'm not very sociable," Richard said.

"You don't have to be," he said, and they lapsed again into silence until the meal was over.

After lunch Richard went to the Americana and stood at the bar sipping brandy and trying to steel himself to do what he knew had to be done. Death left so many problems for those who remained, not the least having to make decisions over clothes and jewels and furniture and treasured little things of no intrinsic value which shaped and molded born-equal flesh so that even death did not utterly destroy. Something of his mother would always remain. As something of Arnold had always remained with her.

When he reached the cabin he found Simone there, his mother's clothes lying neatly folded in piles on the bed. "This is a woman's job," Simone said simply. "I thought you'd like me to do it. I asked the steward's permission."

"It's very kind of you. But your aunt—"

"She suggested it." Simone's small smooth hands neatly pressed lingerie into a silk-lined case. "My aunt says that if you wish you may dine with us this evening."

Outside the cabin he heard Hyslop's cockney voice chatting away to someone. "Now take the expression 'by and large,' madam. That comes from the old sailing terms 'by the wind,' meaning close-hauled, and 'sailing large,' meaning running or sailing free. By and large, under all conditions, see?" Blackmailing bastard. He wondered who he'd try getting his tabs on next voyage.

"Richard," Simone was saying hopefully, "you do *want* to have dinner with us, don't you?"

"Yes," he said, "I'd like that very much."

"Good; then that's settled."

She said it so easily. He wished it was possible to settle everything so easily. Just to say, "Then that's settled" and it was. Tomorrow and the days after tomorrow he had so many things to settle. Whether to stay at Uncle Fred's or Uncle Bruce's or with sweet Mr. Pulbright: or to insist now, instead of later, on being allowed to start his own life, whatever that life would be. He hoped there wasn't going to be any family bickering over the will. Or over him. If there was, he'd prefer not to have a penny of Mother's money. He'd have her love to remember.

That was enough. Then he'd get a job. And try to forget. But what job? Think, think, think. Richard, oh Richard, please think. There must be something in life you want to do, want to be.

"Tinker, tailor, soldier, sailor, rich man, poor man . . ." He was absent-mindedly pulling the petals from a flower in a vase on the dressing-table.

"Richard? Are you all right?" Simone asked anxiously.

"Yes," he said. "Yes, I'm all right."

He watched her close the last case. Suddenly he didn't want to leave the cabin, as though if he did he would be leaving something he could never regain. But Simone stood in the doorway and offered him her hand. He took it and let her lead him away. As she did so, he turned to look at the bed. "Goodbye, Dearest," he whispered.

It was Sunday afternoon, May 6, when the farthermost tip of France disappeared to starboard and the chalky cliffs of England loomed through the drizzle ahead. Captain Corlett stood on the port wing bridge, wearing an oilskin cape, his gray head bare to the steady downpour. They were nearing Fawley when the pilot launch came alongside. In it was Dick Firth. With him were half a dozen reporters and cameramen.

"The press wants to interview you, Ted," the pilot said as he came on to the bridge. "Permission for them to come aboard?"

"I suppose so." The Master heaved a sigh of resignation and turned to the Third Officer. "Welcome the gentlemen aboard, Mr. Tyson. I'll be with them presently."

Dick Firth shifted his gaze awkwardly. "Pity it had to happen on your last run, Ted. Pity." It was all he said.

A helicopter circled overhead like a vulture. Behind the perspex the Master saw the gleaming eye of a film camera. It wasn't a lifetime's good seamanship that was making news, but one damned act of irresponsibility that he had seen coming and had failed to check in time. And for that he was as much to blame as his Chief Officer. The court of inquiry would probably let him off lightly, taking into account his good record, his seniority, his retirement from the company's service. They might even decide that the Spanish fellow was more to blame.

But that wasn't the point. It could have been avoided. And it should have been.

"Hands to stations!"

It was 17:57. Dean's Elbow was off the port bow. South-ampton Waters was busy with ships leaving on the full tide. And leaving was something he would never do again. Not in the old *Queen*. Or any other ship.

"Tugs fast fore and aft, sir."

Deep down in her guts the engines slowly died, and he died a little with them. Inch by inch she was gently pulled and pushed into her berth. Beyond the customs shed a thousand friends and relatives waited like ants, their happy hearts thundering a welcome home.

"Line ashore for'ard."

Winches turned. Husky voices shouted orders on the decks. Ropes creaked and thwacked taut. The tugs blew cheeky whistles and were away.

"Vessel well fast fore and aft, sir."

"Thank you, Mr. Tyson. Ring finished with engines."

The first gangway was in position. The Master walked from the bridge for the last time. The *Queen Dee*'s spring cruise was over.